CW00324486

Al

Jamaican-born **Li**
food, and avid café
since she was a v
certain amount of
to write her own love stories. Contact Lindsay at LindsayEvansWrites.com

AlTonya Washington's first contemporary novel, *Remember Love*, was nominated by Romantic Times as Best 1st Multicultural Romance. Her novel *Finding Love Again* won the Romantic Times Reviewer's Choice Award for Best Multicultural Romance 2004. Her fourth novel *Love Scheme* was nominated as Favourite Steamy Novel for the prestigious EMMA Award of Romance Slam Jam. She presently resides in North Carolina.

Cathy Williams is a great believer in the power of perseverance as she had never written anything before her writing career, and from the starting point of zero has now fulfilled her ambition to pursue this most enjoyable of careers. She would encourage any would-be writer to have faith and go for it! She derives inspiration from the tropical island of Trinidad and from the peaceful countryside of middle England. Cathy lives in Warwickshire her family.

Passion in Paradise

June 2022
Stolen Moments

July 2022
Second Chances

August 2022
Stranded and Seduced

September 2022
Sunset Proposals

October 2022
Holiday Fling

November 2022
Caribbean Escapes

Passion in Paradise:
Holiday Fling

LINDSAY EVANS

ALTONYA WASHINGTON

CATHY WILLIAMS

MILLS & BOON

All rights reserved including the right of reproduction in whole or in part in any form. This edition is published by arrangement with Harlequin Enterprises ULC.

This is a work of fiction. Names, characters, places, locations and incidents are purely fictional and bear no relationship to any real life individuals, living or dead, or to any actual places, business establishments, locations, events or incidents. Any resemblance is entirely coincidental.

This book is sold subject to the condition that it shall not, by way of trade or otherwise, be lent, resold, hired out or otherwise circulated without the prior consent of the publisher in any form of binding or cover other than that in which it is published and without a similar condition including this condition being imposed on the subsequent purchaser.

® and TM are trademarks owned and used by the trademark owner and/or its licensee. Trademarks marked with ® are registered with the United Kingdom Patent Office and/or the Office for Harmonisation in the Internal Market and in other countries.

First Published in Great Britain 2022
By Mills & Boon, an imprint of HarperCollins*Publishers*, Ltd
1 London Bridge Street, London, SE1 9GF

www.harpercollins.co.uk

HarperCollins*Publishers*
1st Floor, Watermarque Building,
Ringsend Road, Dublin 4, Ireland

PASSION IN PARADISE: HOLIDAY FLING © 2022 Harlequin Enterprises ULC.

The Pleasure of His Company © 2017 Lindsay Evans
Trust In Us © 2014 AlTonya Washington
The Argentinian's Demand © 2014 Cathy Williams

ISBN: 978-0-263-31785-5

MIX
Paper | Supporting responsible forestry
FSC™ C007454
FSC www.fsc.org

This book is produced from independently certified FSC™ paper to ensure responsible forest management.

For more information visit: www.harpercollins.co.uk/green

Printed and Bound in Spain using 100% Renewable electricity at CPI Black Print, Barcelona

THE PLEASURE OF HIS COMPANY

LINDSAY EVANS

To my readers: without you, none of this would be possible. Thank you!

Chapter 1

A beautiful man flying above the sea and into the sky wasn't something Adah saw every day. From the beach, she drew a breath and felt her whole body flush as the man sailed across the bright blue water and even closer to her. Thin board shorts and a T-shirt clung to his hard body, the wet material of both outlining every ridge of muscle and plane of skin. He was absolutely gorgeous, and she wasn't the only one looking.

"Damn, he is fine!" A woman down the beach said the words loudly enough to get chuckles of agreement from others nearby, pointing her camera up. Adah resisted the urge to reach for her phone to take a photo; instead she raised her hand above her eyes to shield her face from the Aruban sun burning brightly, even through her sunglasses.

They called it kite surfing. She knew that much from the signs on the event stage she'd seen on her walk from the hotel. And if the reaction of the audience was anything to go by, this gentleman was very good at it. Earlier she'd walked up in time to see him getting ready on the beach. He'd grabbed the edges of some sort of parachute, slipped his bare feet into slots on top of the board and then skated across the water, the bright-blue-and-white material of his parachute snapping in the breeze.

Fine was right.

Adah took off her sunglasses and watched him float across the water and just under the sky, turning somersaults while the audience cheered and called out what she assumed was his name. The announcer of the Hi-Winds Tournament shouted his praise as the man turned yet another flip and landed firmly on both feet on the deep blue sea. Then he was off, flying away from the shore and giving another kiter a turn in front of the rapt audience.

"Did you see that butt?" One of the bikini-clad girls near Adah said to her friend while they both giggled over their bottles of beer.

Her words made Adah blush and turn away from the water. She wasn't much better than this girl, ogling the man just because she was looking for a source of distraction from her own problems. But that awareness didn't stop her from sending one last lingering look across the water to where the man was making a loop in the sky and flying back toward the edge of the beach.

Although watching him made her feel vaguely uncomfortable in her own body, tingly and aware of long-ignored wants, it also felt good to be distracted from thoughts of the phone call she'd had with her mother earlier that morning.

"You have to make up your mind about this marriage, Adah," her mother had said. "You've already said yes to this. Just make it official so we can start making concrete plans for the wedding. Let's at least agree on a date."

A date to join her life with another person's to help save the family business.

Her mother made it sound so simple. Confirm the day for the arranged marriage she'd agreed to when she was a junior in college, depressed from a recent breakup and fixated on the idea that she'd never find a man to love her the way her father loved her mother. Back then she'd been convinced they didn't make men like her father anymore—honest, romantic, ride or die. To her, males of the species were all *boys* and would mature only enough to treat a woman like another notch on their bedposts.

And now, at twenty-six, she was still single but less sure she was willing to give up any chance at passion and love to rescue the family business. That was what she *should* be willing to do. That was what her twin sister, Zoe, would probably have done. But what-ifs didn't matter. Zoe was dead. It was Adah's responsibility to step up.

Seawater rushed over her sandaled toes, and she hissed at the coolness of it. Without realizing it, she'd walked to the edge of the sand and into the waves. Adah skittered back, annoyed with herself for getting water on the expensive leather sandals that had been a gift from her best friend. She should have just worn her plastic Old Navy flip-flops.

Farther up the beach, the tournament continued. Adah was out of the way of the kiters assembling on the beach as their competitors helped them get into their complicated-looking gear. It was a beautiful display of cooperation and partnership.

"You going to walk into the water with your clothes on?"

She jerked her attention from the beach only to find herself immersed in seductive brown eyes. It was the man who had danced in the air above the waves. Up close he was a gorgeous thing. Tall and sun-browned, white teeth blazing in his handsome face, radiating as much heat as the sun overhead. He still wore his loose T-shirt and board shorts, both wet from his time in the water. Mirrored sunglasses hung from the neck of his shirt.

"Things aren't that bad for me yet," she managed past a tight throat. Why was he talking to her? Men this good-looking never went out of their way to engage her in conversation.

"That's looking on the positive side." He grinned again, then came close. "I'm Kingsley."

His mouth was a firm curve, the top lip slightly smaller than the lower, both glistening with some sort of sunscreen or lip balm. Adah licked her own lips, which tasted like cherry Carmex, and imagined his tasted the same.

"Pleased to meet you." She almost slapped herself on the forehead at the inanity of her reply. But she felt completely undone. Her heart beat quickly in her chest, and her tongue felt too heavy for her to speak.

"A mystery woman, then?"

She shook her head but didn't correct him. Better he thought she was being mysterious and coy than an idiot who lost all her cool points just because a hot guy smiled at her. He shoved his hands in his pockets, seemingly unbothered.

"I saw you earlier," he said, eyes moving quickly over her body in a way that was both appraising and appreciative. "I had to come by and say hello."

"You saw me when you were in the air? You must have really good eyesight."

"That's not the only thing good about me," he said. Then he laughed at his own bad joke. "I'm sorry," he said as the last of his laughter faded. "I'm really not that corny."

"Somehow I have my doubts." But he still managed to charm her anyway. Adah felt herself responding to more than just his physical appeal. His eyes were warm with humor and his above-average height made her feel secure instead of intimidated. She could easily imagine cuddling into his big body after sex, her body humming with contentment as he stroked the length of her back in a soothing rhythm.

But there was something destructive in that. Something that made Adah's stomach clench in warning. This wasn't what she'd come to Aruba for.

As if he'd read her mind, Kingsley's look became downright seductive. Heavy-lashed eyes and an intimate smile like the door opening to a softly lit bedroom.

"Would you like to have a drink with me sometime?" he asked.

Adah automatically shook her head although she desperately wanted to say yes.

I'm in a situation. The words from the old Erykah Badu song rang ridiculously in her ear. That was one way to put it. And that was even assuming he felt even a little of what was thrumming over her skin. Pure and undiluted attraction. Lust and the urge to smile back at him just to see those compelling brown eyes narrow even more from his grin, the corners crinkling in the simple pleasure of sharing space with someone attractive. She couldn't remember the last time someone's mere presence had made her want to stay in his company and enjoy the ease of his smile, the comfort of his body. Because it was undoubtedly desire. It coursed through her veins just from looking at him. His undivided attention felt like hands running over her bare skin.

"I can't," she finally said. Not *I don't want to.*

And he seemed absolutely aware of the difference, judging from the way he looked at her, hungry and with the knowledge that the thing he wanted was within reach.

"I…uh… I have to go. Hope you win…whatever it is you're going after." She gestured to the kites still in the air, the stage and the people watching the action from the beach.

"And still no gift of your beautiful name?"

She shook her head again, this time not hiding her smile. "My name doesn't matter."

"I disagree." He paused, his gaze amused and thoughtful. "I have to call you something in my dreams."

Adah rolled her eyes. *Cute and corny.* "Call me whatever you like."

"I think I'll call you Doe Eyes." Then he grinned at her, apparently pleased with himself.

She shook her head a third time. "It was nice to meet you."

"It'll be even nicer to see you again," Kingsley said. Before she could tell him the island wasn't small enough for them to run into each other without agreeing to a time and place, his smile flashed again. "This won't be the last time," he said. The sand pulled at her sandals, and she stumbled, blushing as she righted herself under his amused regard. "Be careful until I see you again," he said with another quick scan up and down her body.

When he turned and walked away, she shamelessly watched him, the loose fit of the drying shirt over his muscled back and the shift of his butt in the long shorts. She bit her lip. There was joy in Kingsley. She thought about what sex would be like with him—undeniably hot, uninhibited—and knew there would be a spontaneous delight about the encounter, a pleasure at living and breathing and being able to gulp deeply from the cup of life. He was a man worth knowing. And touching.

"I know you're looking," he called over his shoulder without turning around. Laughter threaded through his voice. The sound of it should have made Adah blush and look away like a thief caught with her hands in the cookie jar, but she only grinned and kept looking until she could no longer make out the finer details of his physique.

She was still smiling when she walked across the sand and through the beachfront entrance of her hotel. The lavish hotel, though stretching the limits of her budget, was one she was glad to have found. Her room overlooked the water, the entire reason for her visit to an island in the Caribbean.

"Welcome back, Ms. Palmer-Mitchell." The woman at the front desk spared a smile for Adah as she looked up from her computer screen.

"Thank you."

"There's a visitor here for you. She's already in her own room, which she requested next to yours."

Adah stopped. "A visitor?" A bad feeling made

her footsteps stutter. The leftover warmth from the encounter with Kingsley leached from her. She shivered.

"Yes. She arrived about thirty minutes ago."

Adah had been walking the island for nearly two hours, trying to clear her mind and find a solution to the unsettled feeling that had yanked her out of her sleep nearly every night for the past six months. She was desperate for a good night's sleep.

Adah pressed her lips closed and sucked them between her teeth. "All right, thank you so much for letting me know."

After wishing the woman a good morning, she crossed the tiled lobby, each step feeling heavier than the last as she imagined who was waiting for her upstairs. She knew only one person with the means and motive to come to Aruba and turn her peace upside down. When the elevator doors slid open on her floor, there was someone waiting to get on it. The woman, elegant in white linen with her iron-gray hair on top of her head in a simple French twist, smiled at her in equal parts relief and triumph. Adah released a quiet breath.

"Hello, Mother."

Chapter 2

"Surprise, darling!" Thandie Palmer-Mitchell rebounded beautifully from the surprise of seeing Adah in the elevator.

Adah wished she could say the same for herself. Her suspicion had turned into grim certainty when the elevator doors opened on her floor. She felt scattered to the four winds at the sight of her mother, gorgeously styled and smiling in the last place Adah wanted her to be.

"Are you heading down?"

"Not anymore, now that you're here," her mother said.

Of course not. What she hoped was a smile spasmed across Adah's face. "Okay. My room or yours?"

"Yours, of course. You must want to shower and get cleaned up after being out there in the heat." Her mother fanned her face with her slender clutch purse as she stepped back to let Adah off the elevator. "After ten minutes out there, it felt like my skin was covered with sand and sweat."

She fell in step with Adah down the wide and well-lit hallway toward the small room Adah had booked. Adah cringed, suddenly remembering her mess. Although she'd been in Aruba for only a day, most of the contents of her suitcase were already spread all over the room, a tendency toward untidiness she carried over from how she treated her space at home. The common areas were orderly and almost obsessively neat, but her bedroom and bathroom were booby-trapped with piles of clothes, books and makeup in danger of falling over.

She wasn't dirty, Adah often reassured herself, just disorganized. Her habit of just stuffing her rolled travel clothes into her suitcase in no discernible pattern meant she often had to dig to the bottom of her luggage to find the exact thing she needed. Then after all that searching, who wanted to repack everything? There was just no point.

Her mother was the complete opposite. She used packing cubes, elegant and expensive, that she carefully arranged before each trip. Underwear in one cube, dresses in another and so on. Then she just slipped the prepacked cubes into the drawers of whatever hotel she checked into. Adah envied her mother's ability to easily and neatly transition from place to place. But Adah had never made any effort to take on those qualities for herself.

Biting the proverbial bullet, she slid the keycard in and opened her door. "Come on in."

Inside was the same disorder she'd left. Clothes all over the bed and the chair near the window. Her suitcase gaped open on the dresser with her other bathing suit and underwear spilling out. She grabbed clothes from the chair and tossed them on top of the suitcase.

"Sit." She scrubbed a hand self-consciously over her windblown hair. "I'm going to have a quick shower—just make yourself comfortable."

"Don't be silly. It's okay, darling."

But Adah hadn't forgotten her mother's earlier comment about her getting cleaned up. "It won't take me long. Sit and play some music on your iPad or something."

Then she seized the nearest item of clothing on the suitcase and rushed to the bathroom. Barely fifteen minutes later, she walked out, running a brush over her hair, her body freshly lotioned and wearing the fitted floral sundress her best friend had insisted she bring to Aruba.

"Inject some sexy in your life, Adah," Selene had told her as she pressed a large department store bag full of dresses and underwear she'd gotten nearly free in her job as a fashion buyer.

Adah felt like a fraud in the garment, effortlessly

pretty in a way she couldn't pull off in her everyday life. It felt like she was playing dress up, or at least trying to be like her mother. But she swept those thoughts away. Refreshed from her rushed shower, she twisted her straightened hair into a quick topknot.

"What brings you here, Mother?"

"My only daughter, of course." Her mother had truly made herself comfortable, streaming a Luther Vandross song from the small iPad on her lap. She shut it down by closing the cover and set it aside. "I didn't want you to feel all alone in this strange new place by yourself," she continued.

"I'm not alone, Mother. There are thousands of tourists on the island this time of year, not to mention all the people who live here."

"You know what I mean. You're always going someplace by yourself. I think you'd be tired of that sort of solitary existence by now."

Her mother had grown up in a boisterous home as one of six children and often voiced regrets she hadn't had another child after Zoe died.

"With Zoe gone, I'm an only child, Mother. I'm used to being alone. Most times I prefer it." *Like now.*

"Nonsense." Her mother made a dismissive motion. "Nobody really likes being alone. But I can only be with you for a little while. There's some business back home in Atlanta I need to tend to." The business that had shaped the course of all their lives since it started. "I came to treat you to something nice for your birthday. I know your father and I were so busy last month we didn't get a chance to celebrate with you properly."

Weeks before they'd done the annual dinner at Adah's favorite restaurant but hadn't had time for the separate weekend trip to Saint Simons Island that was also part of the birthday tradition.

"It's okay. I know with the company being in trouble, you and Daddy don't have as much time as usual."

"That's no excuse, darling. And that's the reason why I'm here!" Her mother looked excited about whatever she was about to reveal. "I moved you to one of the rooms on the top floor and reserved a half day's pampering session in the most *beautiful* spa. The masseuses there are award winning—although I didn't know massage was something you could get awards for." Her mother frowned like she was giving serious thought to her last remark.

"Mother, you really didn't have to." Adah had come to Aruba by herself to think. The key part of that being *by herself*.

"I know. But I want to." Her mother leaned forward with an even bigger smile. "Our appointments are tomorrow morning. They'll pick us up from here at ten. And while we're gone, they'll move your things up to the new room."

And that was that.

Adah immediately knew her mother's ploy for what it was. And she was half surprised at its transparency. A bribe to get the wedding show on the road and pull the family business out of the fire in which it had found itself despite her parents' brilliance and the relative success of its line of natural hair care products. Still, she allowed it all to happen, the ever-present guilt pricking her into saying yes to whatever it was her mother wanted.

Her twin, Zoe, had died when they were just eleven years old. A car accident on the way home from a young entrepreneurs' summer camp. It was beyond awful that her sister, her best friend, had died. Adah had forced Zoe to sit on the passenger side of the car's back seat just because she'd wanted to sit behind the driver for a reason she couldn't even remember now. The guilt about that still tore her apart. Even at eleven years old, Zoe had been the one eager to take over the family business and make it even better. All Adah had wanted was a job where she could be surrounded by children and hear their laughter all day.

In the end, as co-owner of an exclusive day care complex in North Atlanta catering to some of the city's wealthiest residents, Adah had gotten the job she'd wanted. Zoe had gotten nothing but death.

The next morning, after a restless night spent with her mother on the other side of the wall in an adjoining room, Adah woke and pulled on the same sundress from the afternoon before and the leather sandals. The car that came to get them smelled of the spa, something vaguely citrusy and clean, making her feel as if she were already resting on a masseuse's table and waiting to be transported to boneless relaxation. But she knew peace wouldn't come. Her mother had something to say, and she would state it when she thought Adah was most vulnerable—while she was getting her massage.

She did try to relax during the car ride through the bright and tourist-rich streets of Oranjestad, the car's engine purring through roundabouts and past casinos that burped out victims of the previous night's gambling excesses. Her mother sat across from her, looking content and refreshed, like she'd had the good night's sleep Adah had been denied, her hair perfectly put together in a gray ponytail resting over her shoulder, an ocean-green dress complementing the slender lines of her body.

"You don't really have to do any of this," Adah said.

"I know, darling. But I want to do this for you. It'll mellow you. Besides, after this, your father and I will feel better about not doing enough for your birthday."

Her mother plucked a slice of pineapple from the silver dish sitting between them. Juice exploded from the fruit and dripped down the side of her mouth. On another person, it would have looked clumsy, but her mother's delighted laughter and the delicate way she wiped the juice from her mouth with one of the cloth napkins made her seem charming and young.

Not for the first time, Adah wished she had been the child her mother deserved, a truer reflection of her instead of this awkward and too-soft girl-woman who barely knew how to style herself.

Adah drank from a bottle of water, not wanting to chance any fruit on her dress. With her luck, one of the dark red strawberries would squirt out of her mouth and down her front, making it looked like she'd just suffered a massive nosebleed. Or a mugging.

In the spa, beautiful women in white whisked Adah and her mother away to a serene room that smelled even more like tranquility, this time with low, strings-heavy music and dim lighting. The women gave them fluffy white robes to change into and plied them with cucumber-infused water. An old Deep Forest album, humming with the sounds of chirping birds overlaid by timid violins, played in the background.

Once she was lying on a massage table, with her mother in an identical position a few feet away, Adah actually tried to relax. A silent masseuse began to work on her face, smoothing eucalyptus-scented circles over her forehead and cheeks, while her mother shared stories about what Adah had missed in Atlanta the single day she'd been gone.

"And Petra doesn't seem like the type to fall for someone that shallow, or scary," her mother said, continuing her portion of a conversation Adah was barely paying attention to.

She was talking about a bank manager friend of theirs who'd hooked up with the cold but slightly scandalous anchor of a national news network based in Atlanta. On the outside, Petra seemed boring, and everyone she knew was stuck wondering how she'd managed to snag a man like Gabriel Saint.

"Every woman has something about them that only appeals to a select few people," Adah said. Petra kept things pretty low-key and had a wicked sense of humor she often kept hidden. "Petra is a badass," Adah said. "She just doesn't show that side of herself very often."

"Well, one person must have seen it, and I mean Gabriel Saint, because everyone is mystified about them being together."

"Including you?"

"Including me."

Adah smiled as much as the hands moving on her face would allow. "You only see what you want to see."

Her mother laughed, not admitting to the truth they both knew. And it was so comfortable talking with her about the old familiar things that Adah *did* actually relax.

But then her mother said, "Have you been giving much thought to the wedding, darling?"

Adah released a slow breath through her nose. "No, I haven't." The masseuse paused with her hands on the suddenly tense muscles of Adah's thigh. After a quick glance at Adah's face, she continued the massage.

"You know Errol and Stephanie are excited to officially welcome you into their family." Errol and Stephanie Randal were onetime rivals and now potential in-laws of Adah's, owners of Leilani's Pearls, a successful bath-and-beauty business that was on the verge of the same kind of stagnation pulling down Palmer-Mitchell Naturals. Separately the two companies would flounder, but by joining together they stood a greater chance of succeeding in the increasingly competitive marketplace.

Just about every beauty company had some kind of natural-hair product line now, even companies who'd created their success from selling perms to black women. Despite being in business for over thirty years, Palmer-Mitchell Naturals was a relatively new company and not well-known enough to succeed on its own.

Palmer-Mitchell Naturals needed Leilani's Pearls much more than the other way around. And the agreement to merge companies, and do it in a way that kept the businesses in the family, hinged on Adah's agreement to marry the Randal's son, Bennett. The idea for Adah to become the sacrificial wife had come from her mother during a time of romantic disappointment and on the anniversary of her sister's death. Marinating in pain from all sides, Adah could think only that the less useful sister had survived.

"I know the Randals are anxious, Mother. I know you and Daddy are, too." Her stomach clenched with unease, and she wished she could just say yes and agree to the date without putting her parents through all this worry. Any relaxation she'd gained from the massage had fled. Her muscles felt tight and unwieldy.

"I want you to be certain about your decision, Adah. When I first suggested this idea, you were a young woman in college, practically still a child. I know you're a different person now."

But the situation Palmer-Mitchell Naturals found itself in was the same. Adah pressed her lips together while the anxiety rolled through her, steady and unrelenting. The masseuse's fingers dug harder into her back.

"But—" her mother's tone changed "—think about how amazing this would be for you, too. You could have the financial freedom to realize your dreams. And have a handsome husband to call your own."

As if all Adah had ever wanted from this thing was a man.

She twitched under a particularly firm press of the masseuse's fingers. "I know I agreed to all this before, but I just need a little time right now."

Her mother sighed. "I know, darling. I know."

Then she noticeably withdrew into herself, leaving the room silent except for the sounds of the women's hands on their skin, oil rubbing into flesh and quiet breathing. Embarrassment at airing their dirty laundry in such a relatively public place heated

Adah's face. Although it hadn't been a full-fledged fight, she felt battered and in the wrong. Her mother had always come away from their arguments as the clear victor while Adah was left limping and bleeding in her separate corner. This time was no different. She sighed into the deafening silence.

Later, Adah tried to recapture some of the lighthearted conversation they'd been having before. But her heart wasn't in it, and it was obvious. Soon enough, their spa day was finished. Adah's body was limp from the massage, but her mind was wound too tightly to rest.

After the car dropped them off at the hotel, Adah and her mother picked up the keys to their new rooms and took the elevator up. The penthouse room was beautiful. But Adah gave it no more than a passing glance before she grabbed her jogging clothes and quickly changed.

"I'm going out," she called out through the open door between their rooms, then left before her mother could reply.

Adah took the stairs. Her sneakered feet pounded on the elegant steps, taking her down five flights, away from her mother and the snaking guilt that wouldn't let her say no outright to the gift of an upgrade. For so much of her twenty-six years, Adah felt she'd been stealing her life. A charmed existence taken away from her sister, who'd died before she'd even fully known what she had. Parents who loved her. Parents who could afford to send her to private school. Who had the strength and brilliance to start a small business that became a national company within Adah's lifetime. Her parents wanted more. Adah wanted more. But she knew the things they wanted were no longer compatible with her own wants, if they ever were.

At the bottom floor, she panted rough and ragged, sweat covering her body, heat flowing through her like she wished some new strength would. She was tired of this weakness of hers in the face of her parents' wishes. Marriage was a serious thing. If she couldn't find a man of her own, she'd rather be alone than with someone she wasn't in love with.

The messed-up thing was that she actually liked Bennett Randal. They'd known each other for years and were like brother and sister. But he wasn't someone she wanted to marry. At first, she thought she would be able to do it, but the idea of being with him in *that* way had unsettled her more and more as the years passed. Bennett, she knew, didn't have the qualms she did.

He expected the marriage to happen. While the details were being finalized, he was enjoying being a bachelor, gobbling up all the available sex he could, usually via the hottest reality stars in Atlanta and the world, before he was tied to Adah forever.

Forever.

Just the thought of it made her breath stutter. And

it wasn't just because she was running full speed out of the hotel and onto the beach. Her feet pushed into the soft sand, and she forced herself to take even breaths, trying to put as much distance from her troubles as possible while not getting one step ahead of them.

Adah squeezed her eyes tightly for a moment but kept pace along the beach, which was nearly empty; most of the beachgoers had gone inside for showers and dinner and sex. The moon was fat and gorgeous in the Aruban sky. A paradise. Or it would be if her mother and Adah's own troubles hadn't followed her here.

She ran on. Her breath huffing. The sound of her feet thumping against the sand and the waves rushing up toward her but never touching. A writhing shape in the water pulled her attention from her breath's steady rhythm. The moon glided over whatever it was, showing hints of curves. A couple, she thought, making love in the water and under the stars. She changed her path and ran in an arc away from the water, giving whoever it was their privacy.

But as she moved away, the splashing grew more intense and moved closer to the beach; then a lone body climbed from the water. Adah's footsteps slowed as details of the swimmer emerged under the moonlight. A masculine body firm with muscles apparent even in the dark, bare shoulders, torso and hips. She stared, her footsteps slowing. Was this man naked?

"Doe Eyes?"

She stumbled at the familiar voice and nickname, then without fully realizing it, began walking toward the water's edge and the gorgeous creature emerging from the water, getting barer as the moonlight slid silver fingers over every hard inch of him.

"Ah," Kingsley said, his breath coming quickly after his swim. "I figured I would see you again."

Adah clenched her jaw to stop her tongue from hanging out of her mouth. Kingsley wasn't naked, but he might as well have been. The moonlight outlined him from the top of his proud head to his feet striding out of the water and across the sand to meet her. Pale swim trunks clung to his hips, to the insistent shape between his legs, and the tops of his muscled thighs that were wide and hard enough to make the tips of her fingers ache to sink into them.

He just said something. It's my turn to talk now. She swallowed again.

"I'm just going for a jog to escape my troubles," Adah finally said with her wryest smile. She looked down the beach and saw the illuminated outline of her hotel much farther away than she'd realized.

Damn. How far had she come?

"Should we call it destiny then?" Kingsley wiped the seawater from his face, dragging his hand from his chin down to his strong throat and chiseled chest. Even in the soft light and pervasive dark, Adah could see his grin.

"Let's just call it a coincidence and leave it at that," she said, crossing her arms over nipples that had gone embarrassingly tight.

Kingsley stepped even closer, and she resisted the urge to close the last few feet of space between them and see if his body was as hard or smooth as it looked.

She cleared her throat. "Aren't you afraid they'll cart you off for public indecency?"

He looked down at himself and shrugged. "They'd be false charges if they do," he said, grinning. "Do you think I'm being indecent just by swimming at night? I have a suit on."

"What you call a bathing suit some might call underwear." And the fact that it was a pair of tight white trunks only highlighted what a dark bathing suit would hide. Not that he had anything to be ashamed about. Heat scalded her cheeks, and she yanked her gaze up from his crotch.

"I'm more covered than most people on the beach today," Kingsley said.

He was right. On her walk, she'd seen dozens of European tourists spread across the beach, all body types and speaking so many languages that she'd lost track of how many she heard. But the one thing most had in common was that nearly all the men wore brief swim shorts that clung to their butts and crotches, being just as aggressively sexy as the women in their bikinis. Adah was all for equal opportunity swimwear and enjoyed her walks mostly because of the view. Not all the men were beautiful, but the ones who were gave her quite the eyeful.

She'd been impressed and amused until she saw the more modestly covered Kingsley on the kite and just about lost her mind. Not that she was doing that great of a job of managing herself now. And if his smug grin was anything to go by, he saw through her clearly enough.

Adah could only laugh at herself. "Anyway, it was great to see you, *all* of you." She couldn't resist. "But I've got to get going."

"Nope." Kingsley shook his head. "You can't leave yet."

"Excuse me?"

"I want to see you again, and I don't want fate to determine the time and place."

She should say no. Adah shook her head and pressed her lips together, just on the edge of the confession. "You know I can't…" But she didn't know how to finish that sentence.

"This is nothing more than an invitation to go snorkeling," Kingsley said with a look that was far from innocent. "Aruba has some of the most beautiful waters in the Caribbean. You should experience it with locals who know what they're doing."

"And you're one of these locals?"

"Not at all, but my friends are and they will be there. I'm only local to Miami." He said his home city with an echo of pride in his voice.

Miami was so very far from Atlanta. *Good.* That meant nothing could come of this…whatever it was. No matter how much Adah's eyes drifted low on his body and her heart sped up at the thought of him touching her. But it wasn't all because he was the most perfect male specimen she'd ever seen. He was just so open with his desire for her, so deliriously transparent in a way she'd never experienced before that it was intoxicating. And she also felt like the very air around him smelled of freedom. Escape. A higher plane of living, where pleasure was easy and everything else was inconsequential.

"What exactly do you have in mind?" she asked.

His beautiful teeth flashed in the moonlight again, and her breathing sped up. This was beyond ridiculous.

"We have a snorkeling trip planned for tomorrow night."

She gestured to the high moon and the inky evening around them. "Snorkeling at night? Doesn't that defeat the purpose?"

"Not at all. The sea looks completely different at night, just beautiful. You won't regret it."

Adah started to argue with herself about the safety of going off someplace with a man she didn't know. But all her life she'd been safe.

"Okay." She took a deep breath once she'd committed herself. "Where should I meet you?"

"Do you know where the lighthouse is?"

"Yes." It rose high and majestic, a historic piece

of island history where tourists gathered from morning until night to take pictures, gawk at the scenery and buy food and drinks from the vendors who set up shop at its base.

"Meet me there just before sunset," Kingsley said.

She raised an eyebrow at him. The snorkeling trip now sounded suspiciously like a date. It lay at the back of her tongue to change her mind and tell him there was something else she'd committed to after all. But she bit back the almost-confession.

"Okay," Adah said. "I'll meet you there. Near sunset."

"Perfect."

Adah didn't know about that. She was quite possibly doing the most *imperfect* thing for her situation right now. She didn't need another man in the mix to cloud her already-murky judgment where the potential wedding was concerned. But as she turned away to jog back down the beach toward her hotel and her mother, her mind's eye wouldn't let go of the memory of Kingsley, rising from the water like some Adonis thirst trap, making her heart beat fast and her tongue feel heavy in her mouth, thick with the desire to taste the path where every drop of water had run.

Yeah. Her decision making was cloudy. Absolutely the cloudiest it had been in a long time. But that didn't stop her from smiling the whole way back to the hotel.

Seconds after walking into her room, she heard a knock on the other side of the door joining her room to her mother's, then a muffled voice. Instead of answering what was undoubtedly the question of where she'd just come from, she quickly fled to the bathroom, stripped and turned on the shower. Her mother's questions would have to wait another day.

Chapter 3

Kingsley watched Doe Eyes run down the beach and away from him. He still didn't know her name, and that stirred something illicit in him he never knew existed. She wasn't beautiful in the way he'd grown used to seeing in Miami. She was all klutzy librarian charm with her subtle curves and hidden smiles. And she was *interested.* He'd have to be blind and deaf not to notice the way she responded to him, feminine and helpless, stirring both his lust and the urge to protect her.

Even from across the sand, he had heard her breath catch when she saw him. And he'd felt every second of her long stare at his body, her eyes drifting across his shoulders, his chest and lower while they talked. It was a change from how things were at home when he was Kingsley Diallo, CEO of Diallo Corporation and dressed in his bespoke suits, backed by his family's billions of dollars.

Damn, Doe Eyes was gorgeous.

The way she wanted him made him desire her even more. She watched him with a hunger he felt to the very tip of his toes. His sex had twitched with more than a little interest the longer she stared with the lust so naked on her face. It had been a true miracle he hadn't popped out of his swim trunks and announced to her in no uncertain terms just how very interested he was.

Kingsley drew a deep breath and walked the rest of the way up the beach.

"Should I give you a second to get yourself together?" A voice came from behind the red glow of a cigarette.

His friend Gage sat high up on the sand, almost invisible except for his cigarette and the faint trails of smoke that the wind blew behind him. When the clouds parted, he got a brief view of Gage's curly hair pulled to the top of his head in a man bun, his bare chest and the tattered jean shorts that sagged around his narrow hips.

"Don't be an ass." But Kingsley *did* need a moment to get his head back in the game. Doe Eyes drew him like the sweetest honey, but she was also hiding something. A secret she didn't want him to know. He saw it in the shift of her dark eyes.

He dropped down onto the blanket beside Gage and watched the path Doe Eyes had taken away from him.

"I invited her to the snorkeling trip tomorrow night."

"I heard." Gage ashed his cigarette in the sand beside him. "Do you think that's wise?"

"It's not like I invited her to an orgy or something equally inappropriate."

"Is there such a thing as an orgy of one?" The glowing end of the cigarette made a figure eight in the air as Gage gestured.

"Even I'm not that good." Kingsley grunted.

"After you're done with her, that girl will probably disagree." His friend laughed, a flash of white teeth in the dark. "I've heard the rumors." Kingsley wasn't exactly celibate, not in Miami or here in Aruba.

"Why do you always think I'm out to get some?"

"Aren't you? It's dark as hell out here, but I can still see that woman is stunning and that she's smitten with you. Good odds are you'll have her in your bed in zero minutes flat. Just be prepared for the consequences."

But that was the thing about being away from his responsibilities for the summer. He didn't worry about potential problems. He didn't pay attention to projections and outlooks. He smelled the roses, plucked them if he felt like it, then left them scattered in his wake in mutually satisfying, casual encounters. Enjoyment was something he very much believed in during the normal course of his life. While in Aruba for the summer, it was the very air he breathed.

He almost reached for Gage's clove cigarette to take a drag, both because it smelled so good and to illustrate a point in that one carefree motion. All this was casual. There would be no issues. Doe Eyes was a woman with secrets and a woman, whether or not she was aware of it, in search of passion. He would enjoy plucking the secret from between her lips, from between her thighs. But more than that, he would enjoy bringing and sharing pleasure with her, sweet and deep as the sea around Aruba. Free of commitment and full of all the joy two people could know together.

"Consequences don't belong in a place like this," he settled for saying.

Gage laughed again, the hand holding his cigarette balanced on one upraised knee. The sound of his mirth was loud on the nearly deserted beach.

Kingsley did reach for the cigarette then, plucked it from his friend's hand, and took a deep and slow drag. Sweet smoke filled his throat with a delicious burn before he blew it out into the night. He squinted against the smoke, and the wind carried the gray tendrils toward the steadily disappearing shape of Doe Eyes jogging away from him and toward wherever it was that she'd come from.

"I'm just having a little fun," he said.

Gage took his cigarette back and waved it toward

the woman Kingsley couldn't get out of his mind. "Be careful that fun doesn't come back to bite you in the ass, and not in a good way."

When Kingsley got back to his house—bought nearly six years ago now—from hanging out with Gage, a message about work was waiting for him. Never mind that it was nearly three o'clock in the morning.

"I think we should diversify," his mother said on his voice mail.

This was something she'd been saying for a while. Diallo Corporation had built one of the strongest names in beauty and skin care, but his mother—and chief operations officer—thought that they, like Facebook, had to constantly innovate in order to stay relevant and profitable. He'd just about fallen out of his chair when she'd mentioned Facebook, but he kept an open mind. She wanted them to take on something else, maybe hair care, she wasn't quite sure, but something that would keep Diallo Corporation profitable, visible and on the list of the Fortune 500.

His mother wanted this, but it was up to Kingsley to find out what that next thing was. He already had an idea but wanted to discuss it with her when he was back at home and behind his imported mahogany desk, not when he was about to be naked in his small house more than a thousand miles away from the nearest Diallo.

He sent her a quick email in response.

I agree. Will talk more about this when I get back in two weeks. In the meantime, relay all communications regarding this matter to Carter.

His brother, Carter, didn't have an official title at the company, but he was jokingly called the Magic Man. Along with Kingsley, he knew how to transform nearly any idea related to Diallo Corporation into something viable.

After sending the email, Kingsley groaned and rolled the beginnings of tension out of his neck. He'd only been on the island a day and a half, barely a fourth of the time he usually spent away from his family responsibilities. He wasn't going to let business get in the way of his time off. He pulled off his swim trunks and tossed them in the laundry basket on his way to the shower.

A long time ago, he'd learned to be strict with his vacation time. If he wasn't, no one else would be. His family could talk to him at any time about personal matters, but he was strict about company affairs. Not now. Never here.

Kingsley allowed the steaming water to wash away the remnants of his irritation about his mother's voice mail. He soaped his body from head to toe with body wash, easing the seawater from his skin, then used the washcloth to scrub himself until his skin stung and all he could smell was the mandarin orange scent. He rubbed himself down to pure sensation, the water on his skin, the heat sinking into his muscles, the anticipation of how good Doe Eyes would feel under him.

Truly, he had no intention of seducing her on the snorkeling trip. But his body didn't believe what his mind was saying. He hardened at the thought of her, an inexorable arousal that left him winded.

He pressed his palm against the tile while steam rose around him, water running down the muscles of his back, his butt and his thighs. No, he had no intention of making a move on her. But he wanted. Oh, he *wanted.* And it was with that want sizzling through his veins that he allowed the greed for her to move his hand low and squeeze the breath from his lungs until he was painting the tiles with the hot spurt of his satisfaction. Breathless from the water that still ran over him, the release only made him want the real thing even more.

Kingsley hissed as he touched his sensitive flesh and imagined her mouth. Her body. Her everything.

He groaned and dropped his forehead against the tile, not even the least bit satisfied by his self-delivered orgasm.

Tomorrow, the devil at the back of his mind said. *Tomorrow you can have her.* Kingsley groaned again, and the sound echoed back to him, torture and pleasure, in the enclosed room.

The next evening, he wasn't sure she would come. Yes, he had invited her. Yes, she wanted him.

But there was no certainty. So when he got to the lighthouse, the other three people set to go on the snorkeling trip already waiting down by the beach and having their own pre-sunset party, he only half-expected to see Doe Eyes.

But she was there, wearing a one-piece swimsuit, jean shorts and a short-sleeved shirt partially unbuttoned over it all. His breath stopped at the sight of her, then started again. She stood at the base of the lighthouse, talking to one of the vendors selling coconut water and smoothies. The straps of a backpack hung from one of her shoulders.

She was early by nearly half an hour, the sun barely beginning to fall toward the horizon. The bright sunlight haloed her with the bowl of the green coconut in her hand, as she took occasional sips from the straw sticking up from the coconut. The vendor, old enough to be her father and missing several teeth, laughed when she said something, and she made a face before joining in his laughter.

Damn. She was so gorgeous. Body sleek and compelling in the shorts that barely contained the splendor of her behind. It was hot, much warmer than even the previous days, and the winds weren't nearly as strong. Sweat lined her forehead, the soft skin of her throat. From where he stood, Kingsley could even make out the swell of her breasts under the loose, short-sleeved shirt and bathing suit.

Okay, now he was being creepy.

He cleared his throat and took a single step toward

her, still keeping a respectful distance. He couldn't remember the last time he was so ridiculously horny over a woman, a near stranger at that. He shoved his hands in his pockets, as much to appear casual as to hide the beginnings of interest his body already showed.

"Doe Eyes."

She looked over her shoulder at him, still laughing, then turned back to the man to say her goodbyes before sauntering over to Kingsley with the coconut in her hand.

"Don't you think it's a little ridiculous to keep calling me that?" But she didn't look offended in the least. Instead she looked amused, smiling again in a way that teased, not open and friendly but with a corner of her mouth pressed between her teeth as if she was keeping part of her amusement to herself.

"Until I know your name, I think that suits you just fine."

She shook her head and opened her mouth like she was about to say something, maybe even her name, but something over his shoulder must have caught her eye because she gasped. Kingsley turned. All he could see was the restaurant, the view of the water and the sky turning to a fiery amber.

"This place is beautiful..." she said with breathless wonder.

Her face glowed with the excitement of what she saw, her eyes widening and the curve of her mouth unfurling to shape a real and complete smile for the first time since he'd met her.

"It is very nice."

"I…I guess I just haven't been paying attention." Her eyes were still focused on the lowering sun and the colors streaming across the sky. "I've had a lot on my mind," she said in a low and faraway voice.

By the look on her face, all those things that had occupied her thoughts just got burned away by the flaming splendor of the sky. She was gorgeous. And watching her, Kingsley wondered if at any point during his many trips to Aruba whether he'd ever taken the time to appreciate the beauty of the island like this. But the setting sun was nothing compared to the woman with her wide doe eyes, drinking up all the colors flaring overhead.

The others going on the trip—Carlos, Steven and Annika—were down on the beach, sipping their beers and talking around a small fire they'd made in the sand. Their boat was anchored in the small cove nearby and sheltered from the rocks. They were waiting for Kingsley to return with the woman he'd told them about. But he could afford to let Doe Eyes appreciate the sunset for a few more minutes.

"We can go closer," he said.

She murmured something that might have been her assent, and he guided her carefully toward the overlook with a plaque detailing the history of the lighthouse and the ship that had smashed itself to pieces on the rocks more than a hundred years before on its way somewhere else.

Doe Eyes leaned against the railing, watching the sky and occasionally blindly seeking the straw in the coconut with her mouth. For the first time since he'd seen her watching him, she was completely unguarded. It suited her.

He smiled at the way she seemed to unconsciously lean into his shoulder with her eyes trained on the horizon, watching the slow fall of the sun into the sea. The flash of light grew increasingly dim until the sun fell completely in the water and the sky glowed with the remnants of its flame.

"I could see this every day," she breathed.

"We have similar sunsets in Miami," he said although he didn't know where that came from.

"Similar but not the same."

"Similar but not the same," he agreed.

Miami was unquestionably striking to him. Just the way that Jamaica, the island where his grandparents were born and where his immediate family returned year after year, was the most beautiful place in the world to him. And he'd been around the world enough to see most of the competition.

"You should see Jamaica if you haven't already," he told her, pressing his shoulder into hers. "The sunsets there will make you cry."

She laughed and turned briefly to him, the sunset's colors brushing her face in shades of amber. "Have they made you cry?"

"Not yet, but I'm a hard sell."

She laughed again; this time he could see the distance in the smile that lingered, that her attention was no longer on the sky and the joy it made her feel.

"You ready to get going?" he asked.

She bit the corner of her lip. "Yes."

He waited for her to finish the coconut; then took her down to the beach where the others waited. She walked just ahead of him, watching his three friends sitting around the fire with a mixture of wariness and relief, obviously having suspected that it would just be the two of them after all.

"We didn't think you'd make it back," Carlos said in Spanish. With his cropped hair, thick beard and full-sleeve tattoos, he looked like a typical hipster.

"I can see why," Annika said in Dutch, smiling widely at Doe Eyes. "She's pretty. How did you manage to find such a hot woman to play with after being on the island only a few days?"

Steven, serious and slender in his designer T-shirt and matching shorts, watched all the action like someone at a tennis match, gaze moving back and forth between the players.

Kingsley shook his head. "English, guys." Then he laughingly introduced her as Doe Eyes, enduring his friends' inevitable teasing that the woman he wanted hadn't even told him her name.

"I speak a decent amount of Spanish," Doe Eyes said. "If it makes you feel more comfortable speaking your own languages, it's okay with me."

Annika laughed. "We love her!" she crowed in English, then jumped up from her cross-legged seat near the fire to hug Doe Eyes, who grinned widely and hugged Annika tightly in return.

"Hi!"

"I might just love her, too," Carlos said, this time in Dutch, as he watched the two women, dark and light, as they hugged.

"Pervert," Kingsley muttered.

"Not at all, just a lover of women."

Steven greeted her in his subdued way, squeezing her hand before sinking back down into a graceful lotus on the sand. He wrestled a beer from the depths of the cooler and gave it to Doe Eyes.

"Thanks for being okay with me coming out with you all," she said, looking at each face around the fire. "I've never gone snorkeling at night, but Kingsley says it's safe." The lilt in her voice plainly asked them to confirm the safety of what she was about to do.

"It *is* safe," Steven confirmed. "I've done it more times than I can count."

Annika nodded. "It'll be fun. Even though I've lived in Aruba for nearly two years, I haven't done it before. But Kingsley said it's something I absolutely have to try."

"He's very convincing," Carlos said. "I swear if he said I had to eat fire to be a real Aruban, I would do it even though he doesn't know a damn thing about being from here."

"Or about fire," Kingsley said with a laugh.

"It burns," Doe Eyes murmured, looking at him.

Kingsley locked eyes with her. "It certainly does."

Annika laughed, her pale blue eyes brimming with mirth. It was embarrassingly obvious she knew what Kingsley was up to. Yes, if he got the chance he would absolutely sleep with Doe Eyes. Well, not exactly sleep. He wanted to make long and deep love with her, press her into any available surface and show her just how much he knew about making a woman feel good. Kingsley cleared his throat and sat on the side of the fire opposite her, hiding the sudden tightness at his crotch with his beer.

They finished their drinks while the lights in the sky faded into gray, leaving trails of dark against the paleness of the moon. Dusk amplified the light from the crackling fire, a signal for them to get ready.

Steven was the first one to stand up. "Ready whenever you guys are."

Although Steven had been the one to organize the trip, he'd asked Kingsley to give the prep talk to the group about the particulars of night snorkeling and partnering up. He also passed out the waterproof flashlights. Annika snickered when Kingsley announced he was partnering with Doe Eyes even after he told her the obvious reason, which was that Doe Eyes hadn't done a night dive before and would need all the help she could get.

"But what about me?" Annika asked with a mischievous grin, determined to torture him. "I'm a newbie, too."

At a look from Kingsley, Steven grabbed her by the waist and pulled her off toward the boat anchored nearby.

With everyone else sitting in the small motorboat, Kingsley pushed it into the water. Once it was far enough, he released the anchor and climbed in. Steven started the engine and it growled, propelling them toward the place where the sun had disappeared nearly half an hour before. The engine's noise took away the silence, and the five of them were lost in their own thoughts and in the beauty of the night as they raced toward the reefs.

Kingsley sat across from Doe Eyes, watching the beach and their banked fire get smaller and smaller. Nervousness vibrated from her, and he wanted very much to slide closer to her and convince her nothing would happen tonight she didn't want to. The sea was a vast and frightening place. But that didn't mean he would allow her to disappear beneath it.

"Here we are," Steven said. He cut the engine.

In the sudden silence, the boat bobbed in the dark water, the sound of the sea slapping gently against the hull.

"Here" was far away from shore and nowhere in sight of their fire at all. There was nothing but the dark and writhing water around them.

"It's a little creepy out here," Annika muttered, most of her bravado gone.

"Yeah, but it's nice," Carlos said. "The quiet is very soothing."

Doe Eyes sat with her hands curled around the edge of the boat, the fear slowly clearing from her face the longer they sat in the quiet with the sound of the water lapping at the boat.

Kingsley leaned close to her. "You okay?"

She jumped, looking away from the dark and rippling water. "Yeah. I'm fine. This is just…it's all new to me. Amazing. Scary."

He lifted his gaze from her to take in their surroundings, trying to pretend the others weren't watching every move they made. "Facing the things that scare you is a great way to grow."

Doe Eyes snorted. "And to get eaten by a shark, too, I'm sure."

"No shark bites here." Kingsley pulled off his shirt to show his unscarred belly in the moonlight. Annika snickered, having apparently gotten over her own nervousness. He thought he saw a smile from Doe Eyes. When her hands loosened from the edge of the boat, he considered his mission of distraction a success. He shoved his shirt in his waterproof pack while Annika laughed at him outright.

"Gear up, everyone," Steven said, unsuccessfully hiding his own laughter.

Although there had been a quick tutorial on the beach, Kingsley stayed close to Doe Eyes to make sure she put on her gear properly. Despite her obvious nervousness, she put on her snorkel and fins with easy and practiced movements, checking the fit and the security and brightness of the flashlight secured to her wrists, while everyone else did the same. After a quick verbal check all around, the group slipped into the water. Kingsley and Doe Eyes were the last.

"Ready?"

"Absolutely." She looked like she was trying to convince herself, and he wondered why. But he mentally shrugged and slipped into the water first, keeping his head above the surface and his body close to the anchored boat. He flicked on his flashlight. In his board shorts and otherwise bare skin, he felt the pressure of the water, the night's brisk breeze on his face and neck. A shiver of reaction climbed up his spine.

She sat in the belly of the boat for a moment, watching him, then walked to the very edge, took a quick breath and splashed down beside him. The splatter of water made her blink her eyes behind the mask, and he floated away from the boat slowly, signaling for her to follow him.

His flashlight illuminated a long line of water around them, pushing aside the shadows and, he hoped, any potential fear for her. She brushed against him briefly, and he felt her tremble. Then she adjusted her mask, gave him the thumbs-up, turned her face into the water and began to explore. After a moment Kingsley began to do the same.

The reef was close to the surface. Only a few feet separated the tips of Kingsley's fins from the coral alive with color and darting fish whose scales shimmered under the light from their torches. Sea urchins, spiny and dangerous, poked out from holes in the coral. Kingsley tapped her shoulder and pointed to make sure she saw them.

This wasn't Kingsley's first time snorkeling at night. He'd even done some night diving, traveling down to the ocean floor to watch octopi, their bodies dotted with phosphorescence, slide along the coral. He'd swum through massive schools of brilliantly colored fish not present during the day. All of it had been breathtaking.

But there was nothing like the wonder on this woman's face, her eyes widening, hands clutching fiercely at his when she saw something new: the powerful and steadily moving sea through the beams of their torches, large schools of bright blue parrot fish swimming lazily in the night waters. He wanted to show her more. He wanted her to see everything.

This feeling wasn't a new one, wanting to preen and introduce a woman to the best of what he knew. What was new to him was the lack of urgency. Kingsley enjoyed the brush of her arm against his, rising up to the surface to take a breath and catch sight of the twin globes of her bottom resting on top of the water. It was a deep and pure pleasure he could bask in for hours. But despite the vague possibility of this unnamed and beautiful woman disappearing from his life at any moment, he wasn't frantic in his desire for her.

He knew he would have her.

Still, his ache to touch her was almost a painful thing, a desire that clung to the backs of his teeth and burned steadily. It was slow. It was hot. And it easily melted away the memory of any other woman he'd ever wanted.

In just his mask and fins, he swam farther down, holding his breath and lighting up the darkness for her. Deeper into the water, he saw a school of spotted turquoise fish, their scales bright even in the small grotto where they hid. Kingsley propelled himself up to the surface, taking a deep breath when he hit fresh air. She took out her snorkel.

"You okay?"

He nodded yes. "There's something you should see, lower."

Her eyes widened. "This is snorkeling, not diving," she said.

"You can handle it."

She gave him a curious look, then put her mask back on, refitted her snorkel and nodded at him in acceptance of his challenge. Kingsley grinned, took her hand and dove deep with her fingers wrapped tightly around his.

Nearly an hour later, they surfaced for the last time to the sound of MC Solaar playing from the speaker Carlos had brought. It was a miracle they'd gotten any reception on the battered, old thing. Kingsley could hear Annika "singing" along to the old-school French rap and laughing at herself when she tripped over the words. A look at his watch told Kingsley they'd already been out there for nearly three hours and at almost ten o'clock at night, the others were ready to wash off the salt, get someplace dry and drink something a little harder than beer to close out the night.

A sleek head appeared from beneath the surface barely a foot away, and Kingsley smiled at her automatically, having quickly grown used to the brightness of her eyes behind the mask and the way she grinned around the snorkel in excitement at the things they'd found together. He pulled off his mask, and, after a glance around them, she did the same. She wiped water from her face.

"Time to go in, huh?"

"Yup. They've probably been waiting for us a little while."

Doe Eyes didn't hide her disappointed look, but she nodded, cast one look at the glare of his flashlight that illuminated their bodies just under the water. "Let's go then."

Kingsley gestured for her to go first. Once she'd swum a fair distance in front of him, he followed at a leisurely pace, enjoying the last of their privacy.

"I thought you two were going to stay out there until sunrise," Carlos said, blowing a stream of cigarette smoke over his shoulder.

"I'd prune up too much by then," Doe Eyes said. "I value the softness of my skin too much."

"Even at the risk of denying yourself the company of this hunka burnin' love?" Annika tossed a look at Kingsley as he clambered into the boat.

He ignored her and turned up his nose at Carlos.

"The only thing burning up out here is our nose hairs from that cigarette. You couldn't wait until we got back to land to light up, Carlos?" His friend smoked the cheapest and most offensive cigarettes known to humankind, having exchanged his addiction to hard drugs for one to nicotine.

"You know I have a vice, man." Carlos blew another stream of smoke, this time through his clenched teeth.

"Those things will kill you just like the other crap you gave up," Kingsley said. He sensed Doe Eyes watching him with curiosity.

"Not this again." Steven groaned over the long-standing source of disagreement. "Everybody ready?"

After he got the appropriate number of grunts and yeses, he started the boat's engine and propelled them back toward land.

At the beach, Steven anchored the boat and cut the engine. The others moved slowly to get their few belongings, sealed in watertight bags, and climbed from the boat to the beach, where the battery-operated lantern they'd left stuck in the sand still blazed but the fire had long since died. Kingsley felt pleasantly exhausted but didn't want to go back to his place yet. Although his body was tired from the swim, he felt mentally energized by the snorkeling, and by the presence of the woman he couldn't get off his mind.

"I'm tired, but I'm not tired," Carlos said as he zipped up his backpack with the last of his stuff and hefted it onto his back. "You get me?"

"Yeah." Steven sighed with his own exhaustion.

"You don't have to go home," Annika said. "I told you to come over to Elina's place. She's having a thing tonight."

"I'm not going to bust into a party I wasn't invited to," Steven said.

"Consider yourself invited then, damn." Annika rolled her eyes. She was sleeping with Elina and Elina's boyfriend, Alexander.

She dragged her own pack to the sand as she helped Kingsley disassemble their camp on the beach, put away the lamp and the rest of their gear in the anchored boat and under a secured tarp.

"That's good enough for me." Carlos grinned.

"Sounds good." Kingsley didn't give it a second thought. It was either that or invite Doe Eyes back to his place in a shameless attempt at getting into her pants. "You should come," he tossed to her over one shoulder.

Doe Eyes already had her dry clothes back on and, with her backpack on one shoulder, looked ready to head back to her hotel.

"I don't think I can stay out any later than this," she said, regret and reluctance coloring her voice.

Kingsley jumped out of the boat and shouldered his pack. "What, do you have a curfew or something?"

Her shoulders went stiff like someone had just poked her with a pointed stick.

"No, I don't have a *curfew*. You ever thought I might have to get up early tomorrow for something?"

"No. You're here on vacation. Unless you're getting up early for a sunrise wedding or one of those boring-ass island tours they sell to tourists."

She winced again, and Kingsley could feel the others watching them even though half had already climbed into Annika's van. Annika was at the wheel and tossing them occasional annoyed glances. She was ready to go.

"The party should be pretty low-key. Nothing at all to challenge your virtue or your tolerance for loud music," Kingsley said. "But if you get bored or scared, I'll take you home."

His house was only a ten-minute walk from Elina's. If Doe Eyes truly wanted to go home, he could easily take her in his truck. "A win-win situation, really," Kingsley finished.

She looked skeptical but interested, her hips inclined toward him even as she plucked at the frayed edge of her shorts, apparently thinking seriously about the offer of a decent party with good booze and people. "Why does it feel like I'm being lured into the lion's den?"

Kingsley gave her a mock roar. Incredibly, she laughed at his weak joke. "Okay. I'll come."

As soon as she got in the van, Annika drove off, barely giving Kingsley time to pull the door shut.

"Whoa, girl!" He fumbled fast for his seat belt.

"I heard Alexander got that magic tongue," Carlos teased from well out of Annika's reach. "After the bedroom looks you and her—" he jerked his chin at Kingsley and Doe Eyes "—have been giving each other all night, she's eager to get in some lovin' of her own."

"Don't be jealous, Carlos." Annika flashed him a dangerous look. "I told you I can share Alexander with you whenever you're ready."

Steven's shout of laughter drowned out Carlos's response.

With their teasing and laughter, the ride toward the south part of the island passed quickly. They talked about Annika's interesting relationship with the couple, Elina and Alexander, that had lasted well over a year now and was, in her words, more satisfying than any she'd ever had before.

"Doesn't anyone get jealous?" Carlos asked, looking voyeuristically fascinated.

"There's nothing to be jealous of," Annika said with a shrug.

They pulled into the drive of the small house. It had the soft, pulsing beat of trance music pouring from beneath the front door. After a quick rap on the red painted door, Annika pushed it open. Once inside the smell of marijuana smoke and the sound of "Glory Box" greeted them, promising a laid-back, if slightly illegal, vibe. Walking behind Annika, Kingsley stayed just behind Doe Eyes as they made their way into the open living room, whose intimate darkness was amplified by multicolored Christmas lights. It reminded Kingsley of an off-campus college party. He suspected there was a keg or two stashed someplace.

Despite his desire for the opposite, he was ready for Doe Eyes to change her mind and tell him she wanted to go home. Her eyes darted to each face in the room as if trying to make the decision about whether or not to stay based on the expressions she found there.

Everybody seemed like they were having a good time. Some swayed in the center of the living room to the beat of the music with bass heavy enough to vibrate in Kingsley's chest. Others sat in chairs or on the floor, talking or laughing or drinking from their red plastic cups. The house was so full that guests overflowed into the backyard.

"I need a shower," Carlos said from behind Kingsley.

"Go have a shower then," Annika said. "The bathroom's through there." She pointed down a darkened hallway past a couple passionately dancing together near a wall, their hips pressed together but their mouths and eyes set in a way that seemed like they were also having some sort of serious discussion. Maybe a discussion about politics.

"Cool." Carlos headed in the direction she pointed.

"Is there another one?" Steven asked, making Kingsley jump since he'd completely forgotten the other man was there. "This sand is squirming into too many places."

"Sure," Annika said without hesitation. "Use the one off the master bedroom." She waved Steven toward the same hallway. "And if you want some clothes, just grab some from the cupboard in the bathroom. The green cupboard, not the black."

"Does that mean we have to wait our turn?" Kingsley asked, trying hard *not* to think about showering with Doe Eyes.

He focused instead on how his thin shorts were drying against his skin, making him feel like an alligator with salt water and sand stuck to him. He had another pair of shorts in his bag to change into. While riding over in the van, he'd vaguely thought of going home to shower and change but knew once he went home, he wouldn't want to leave.

"You can do whatever you want," Annika said in response to his question, turning a speculative gaze toward Doe Eyes. "There's an outdoor shower by the pool if you're desperate."

He turned to Doe Eyes. "Are *you* desperate?"

That must have been the cue to leave because Annika turned her back on Kingsley and walked away.

"What did I say?" When Doe Eyes just shook her head, he dismissed the whole thing with a shrug. "How about a drink?"

Now she actually smiled. "Why are you offering me a drink at someone else's house?" There was a hint of nervousness to her words that made him want to gather her close.

"I've been here enough times," he said, trying to pitch his tone to one of reassurance.

She plucked at the hem of the shorts, not looking any less anxious. "I don't even know why I came here with you." White teeth nibbled at her full lower lip.

"Because you enjoy my company, obviously."

Her lip was getting more bruised and soft-looking the more she bit it, and Kingsley was having a hard time keeping his attention away from her mouth. In desperation, he cast his eyes around them, taking in the DJ and competitors he recognized from Hi-Winds who came to Aruba nearly every year. The house was full, and, although he didn't want a drink, he urgently needed something to do with his hands other than wish they were touching a certain tempting woman.

"Let's go grab that drink," he said. "It'll relax you and help take your mind off the whole needing-a-shower thing. At least until Carlos and Steven get out of the bathroom so we can have a turn." She hissed softly in reaction, and he stared down at her. "Get your mind out of the gutter," he said. "I meant our *separate* turns in the bathroom for a shower. If I wanted to invite you for sex, that wouldn't be the way I'd do it." There were a thousand more elegant ways and more convenient places.

"Fine." But she dipped her head, looking anywhere but at him.

Kingsley grinned. "Well, if you do want me to invite you to have a shower with me..."

She shook her head, raising a hand as if she meant to poke him. But her hand dropped as if she realized they weren't quite at that stage of their relationship yet. His grin widened.

At the makeshift bar, he got them both bottles of local beer, then guided her to a narrow and recently vacated space on the sofa that smelled of cigarettes and spilled beer. The impression of being at a college party only grew worse. Funny, he'd been to parties at the house plenty of times and hadn't gotten that vibe. He shifted next to Doe Eyes and wondered what she thought of all this. The music pulsed, warm and mellow, around them.

"So what was it you were talking about with your friend earlier?" she asked, leaning close enough that her breath whispered over his cheek, his mouth.

"I talked about a lot of things," he said.

"You were talking about cigarettes and addiction."

Ah. His mini-confrontation with Carlos in the boat. He wondered why she was even interested in talking about that. It felt like she was latching on to any conversational straw to avoid acknowledging the attraction between them. But he could play if that was what she wanted.

"That's more Carlos's baggage than mine," Kingsley said, then paused before sharing information about his friend that Carlos himself was pretty free with. "He's been in Narcotics Anonymous for a minute, but he replaced drugs with cigarettes. He clings to them thinking that if he gave up cigarettes, then he'd regress to drugs. He goes through a lot of packs in the day."

"That's just replacing one addiction for another. Doesn't seem healthy."

"For him, it's the safest. Everyone has their own way of coping with lesser demons."

As they talked, they leaned more toward each other, and Kingsley didn't realize the sound of the music was rising, getting louder until they were talking practically with their mouths pressed to each other's ears. He lifted the beer to his lips, nodding as they talked about addiction and Carlos and the inherent danger of swimming in the sea at night.

"We don't always need to see where we're going in order to get there," he said. "Sometimes there's a path already charted for us. We just have to head toward our destination and trust."

She turned to him, her mouth damp from her beer bottle. "Are you talking about religion now?"

"I'm talking about life." He looked down at her, watching as she licked away the wetness of the beer but only managed to dampen her lips even more. His own mouth tingled with the urge, ever present now, to kiss her.

"Do you believe in anything?" she asked him.

"Of course. Lots of things." Like the ability of lust to blind him to rational thought and action. With any other woman, he'd already have had her name, maybe even her body spread out in his bed.

She didn't ask him to elaborate on his beliefs or lack thereof; instead she tapped her thumb thoughtfully against her bottom lip. "I believe in making the best choices we can to avoid future pain," she said.

With a nod, he acknowledged the neat way she avoided talking about religion but still managed to reveal something of herself to him, as casual as the revelation had been.

"How about making the best choices to encourage present pleasure?" The way he practically shouted the words in her ear was far from seductive, but he felt her move against him, the press of her thigh against his, skin to skin, growing damp together in the room rapidly filling with people whose very presence battled a too-weak air-conditioning unit.

"Pleasure is fleeting." Her mouth briefly brushed his ear as she spoke, and Kingsley didn't even hide the jolt of desire that moved through him. His mouth opened, and his tongue flicked out to taste the air.

"But it is one of those things that makes this life worth living," he murmured. "I work to keep my family in the style to which it's grown accustomed, but also to afford the things that make me happy. My car, my country club membership, first-class plane tickets to Aruba and everything else I can do to get a certain beautiful woman into my…arms."

He felt her laughter before he heard it, her body shaking with mirth, a bubble of merriment that vibrated off her skin before he heard it just beneath the pounding bass of the music.

"You have very eager arms then," she said.

"You have no idea." He lightly closed his lips around her earlobe as he spoke and heard the soft noise she made despite the loud music.

Kingsley was more than ready to take her to bed.

"King, baby..." A woman stumbled into their private bubble, her knees knocking into his. "Come dance with me." She didn't make it an invitation but a demand, reaching down to grab for his hand.

At his side, Doe Eyes glanced up at the woman, then at him, slowly blinking away the arousal that had clouded her eyes just moments before. Kingsley wanted to see that look on her again.

The woman was a few drinks past drunk, so it was easy for him to slip his hand from hers and refuse what she was offering. "Another time, Chris. Find me later on. I'm trying to close an important deal here."

Chris made a show of pouting, then swished her hips from side to side in her tight skirt. But Kingsley was used to more compelling incentives than that. He shook his head again, and she shrugged before wandering off to find a more willing dance partner.

"You're missing out on a sure thing there," Doe Eyes said when she leaned close to him again.

"That's not what I want tonight," he said.

"What do you want?"

"I think you know."

Again he felt how close to each other they were. The press of her skin against his, bare thigh to bare thigh, on the sofa that held at least three other people, all minding their own business.

She bit the side of her lips, gaze falling to the beer bottle clasped in her lap. "We were talking about choices."

"Were we?"

"Yeah…"

The mood was over. So Kingsley spoke with her of other things while attraction hummed just beneath his skin, a steady and thrumming heat that made him perpetually aware of just how close she was to him. The volume of the music rose until they were simply resting their mouths at each other's ears, following the skein of thread in a conversation that was becoming less and less important.

The smell of marijuana that had been subtle in the room before grew stronger. A quick glance to the left confirmed that the man at the far end of the couch had just lit up a blunt and was offering a hit to everyone nearby. Kingsley noticed the wrinkling of the feminine nose next to him.

"You want to relocate?" He jerked his chin toward the sliding patio doors.

She nodded, nose bumping into the sweat-damp line of his neck. He couldn't stop the spike of want that lanced down his belly and directly into his lap. Kingsley took a quick swallow from his bottle and stood up. He put out a hand to help her off the couch, but she was already on her feet and heading past him toward the door.

He watched her butt, a twitching temptation, for long moments with the taste of beer almost sour in his mouth and the lust rising, hot and steady, in his lap. After subtly adjusting himself, he followed after her through the crowd and slid open the patio doors to escape into the fresh air.

It was cooler outside, but only because of the wind. It howled in the small backyard, where a hammock swayed from the weight of three bodies and the lights were just bright enough to illuminate the dozen or so people in various stages of relaxation, some floating lazily in the pool.

The smell of marijuana still clung to Kingsley's clothes, even outside. He slid the patio door closed behind him, following Doe Eyes toward a recently vacated lawn chair with a footstool beside it. She sat on the footstool, her legs stretched out in front of her.

Kingsley hesitated. "You should take the chair," he said.

"No, thank you." She slipped him an odd smile, then looked around the backyard at the scene that was as familiar to him as any boardroom at Diallo Corporation. The carpet of Astroturf laid down instead of grass that would drink up a whole house worth of water. A stone path leading to the small, round pool in the center of the backyard. Quiet conversation and intimate sounds drifted from the couples and small groups sharing the pool.

At one time, Kingsley would have happily indulged himself in one of these scenes, but not now.

Not with Doe Eyes here. He sank into the lawn chair and calmed his nerves with his second beer of the night.

A sigh came from the beautiful woman near him, and she looked around again with envy in her face. “My mother would never expect me to do something like this.”

“Do her expectations matter that much to you?” Kingsley asked.

“I’d like to say no, but I feel like being truthful tonight.”

“Truth is a good thing, even between strangers,” Kingsley said, intentionally poking at whatever secret it was that she held from him.

She made a noncommittal noise, shrugged and lifted her beer to her lips. Also her second. Someone passing by stumbled into her. With a magician’s skill, she held her drink high and away from her body as she tumbled sideways and into Kingsley’s knees. He caught her in his arms, instantly aware of the warm sweetness of her, the salt smell in her hair and clothes from their evening in the sea, the scent of beer on her lips.

“Oops! Sorry.” The man laughed out his apology as someone else helped him upright, then away from Kingsley and Doe Eyes.

The feel of her against him was a delicious and sensuous weight he didn’t want to give up. He could happily hold on to her all night, but she shifted against him, and he helped her sit upright again on her footstool.

"It's a night for missteps," she said.

"Or to loosen the stiffness from your spine." Another sip of beer, another glance across at her.

She licked her lips and turned her bottle around and around between her hands. Kingsley could still feel her against his palms, could still smell the salt and sweat of her skin. He wanted nothing more than to pull her into his lap and taste her, but he didn't reach out. He wanted her to make the first move.

Her eyes, when she raised them to his, were full of conflict. And need. "It's not okay to follow every impulse you have, you know."

"True. But, conversely, not every impulse should be denied."

"How very self-serving of you," she said.

Kingsley smiled in the dark. He'd been called much worse. "And what would be self-serving for you?"

"I'm already here, way past my bedtime. I'm drinking with strangers, and God knows what could happen to me out here."

"The only thing that will happen to you here is what you say you want." He reiterated what he'd told her earlier, meaning every word. His desire for her was a firm and constant thing that ached to be satisfied, but it only demanded satisfaction if she did, too.

When she didn't respond, he put down his beer. "Listen, let me take you home and—"

His words were cut off when she sank into his lap. Her thighs spread over his thighs, feet on the ground, her bottom a round weight in his hands that automatically reached down to cup and bring her close. Her soft arms slid around his neck.

"This is my impulse," she said and kissed him.

Her mouth on his, body settling close, a blanket of heat and passionate goals. But maybe that was him. His intentions rising up to meet whatever it was that she wanted from him.

The kiss was sweet. At least it started off that way. Her breath huffed against his cheek as she turned her head in that age-old choreography of intimacy, her palms sliding up to cup the back of his head. The rake of nails over his scalp, an unexpected sharpness, jerked his hips up, fired pleasure through him and made him abruptly want more. She laughed against his mouth. He licked her lips in answer, gripped her hips and pulled her against him again. Her laughter died as she slid deeper into his lap, the V of her sex flush against his. Her mouth was hot and soft, tongue sliding against his in a way that made him want to take her to bed. *Right damn now.* Kingsley groaned into her mouth.

The sand caught in his clothes rubbed under his shorts and in the vulnerable places under his shirt, making her touch even more potent. He shivered under the smooth caress of her hands down his back, her nails sinking into his shoulders, the press of her bottom in his lap. From just this, kissing, she was going to make him explode.

And he still didn't know her name.

She pressed into him, a ravenous and insistent weight, kissing him like she was devouring something she hadn't had in a very long time. She tasted of beer and sea salt and lust. And Kingsley wanted to drink her all up.

"I like your impulse," he gasped into her mouth as he pushed his hips into hers again.

She hummed and matched him movement for movement, her hips dancing against his in an arousing rhythm, hardening him even more. Her long fingers latched on to his shoulders and her nails dug in deep enough to make him gasp again. She opened up wider for him, and he sucked her tongue, licked every part of her mouth she let him have while his body grew hotter under his clothes. Her fingers dug into his chest through the shirt, then plucked at the buttons, ripping them open. Everything around them disappeared. The people. The music. The right and wrong of what they were doing.

His shirt was open, and her fingers gripped at his skin. The intensity of her desire was merciless, and it brought his want surging up hard and tight. This was no longer some snuggling kitten. She kissed and clawed at him like she wanted to consume him, and he matched the pace of her movements, of her wants, gasping into her mouth as their bodies twisted together.

She yanked her mouth away from his, and Kingsley growled again, this time in disappointment. What he'd done was too much. This wasn't what she wanted from him, and he opened his mouth to apologize. But the apology became a grunt when her lips locked onto the side of his neck, her teeth on his skin, her fingernails raking over his bare nipples and the heated skin of his chest. A firestorm of pleasure exploded in his belly.

Kingsley gripped the hair at the back of her head, pressing her mouth harder into his skin. "Do that again," he groaned into her ear.

She pinched his nipple and bit him again, and Kingsley's hips surged up, once, then twice, mimicking what he wanted to do with her. The lawn chair groaned underneath them. The breeze brushed cool and lush over the wetness left by her mouth as she dipped lower to suck and bite more of his throat. Another long and low grown left Kingsley's throat. He wouldn't be able to last much longer. His heartbeat pounded in his chest. The blood rushed through him fast, and faster. He gasped and held on to her hips grinding rhythmically down on him. He was going to lose it right now, and there was nothing he wanted to do to stop it.

With his fingers tangled in her loose hair, Kingsley opened his mouth to gasp her name, realized he didn't know it and hissed out a curse instead.

"You're killing me!" He moaned when her hand closed over him through his shorts.

"Not yet." Then she bit down on his nipple again, apparently oblivious to his friends, who'd drifted out of the crowd to watch Kingsley damn near explode in her hand.

Chapter 4

"I think I won that bet."

The voice—Carlos's—from too close made Adah jerk her mouth away from Kingsley's chest. She tried to pull completely away, but Kingsley followed with his mouth, panting. She kept him back with a hand pressed against his chest and felt the hard and unsteady beat of his heart, the firmness of his bare muscles. Embarrassment and residual desire flushed her from head to toe.

Carlos emerged from the otherwise anonymous crowd, beer in hand, along with Annika, who was smoking a cigarette.

When Adah had chosen this spot to sit, it had been the most private place on the patio. Everyone else had been situated by the pool or near the wide concrete slab of the patio. But the area had quickly become swarmed with people, and—her cheeks flushed with embarrassment at the thought—she hadn't cared when she'd climbed in Kingsley's lap to kiss him.

She turned back into the conversation happening near her in time to hear Annika say, "You didn't win anything yet. They aren't having sex. That's just kissing."

They were talking about her and Kingsley. She flushed again and felt the firm touch of his hand at the small of her back trying to keep her in his lap.

"Let me up," she said, scrambling away from him.

Adah was almost disappointed at how quickly Kingsley let her go, hands falling away to grip the sides of the chair. His eyes were deep pools of swirling emotion. Want and eagerness, his mouth wet from their kisses, his chest heaving under the press of her hand. She drew her hand back as if burned, not realizing that she'd still been touching him even as she fought to get away.

She didn't know what had gotten into her. Making out in public with a near stranger wasn't something she ever did. She hadn't drunk that many beers; she wasn't that tired. But she remembered the sweet twine of the smoke from the people who had sat near them inside the house. Yes. It had to be that. A contact high making her act in a way she normally wouldn't.

"I need to go," she said.

She could still feel him on her mouth, tingling and warm, the desire pooling her lap, leaving her molten and needy. And frightened. Adah dragged the back of her hand over her damp mouth and thought she saw a flash of hurt in Kingsley's eyes before he lowered them.

She tugged the edges of her unbuttoned shirt closed over obviously hard nipples and stood on shaky legs, trying to control her breathing and the desire rippling through her that even now pulled her back toward him. His taste was still in her mouth. She swallowed it.

"I need to leave here," she said again and started toward the path curving around the side of the house to the front yard, fully intending to walk back to her hotel. The island was small. It couldn't be that far away. She vaguely heard Annika and Carlos talking with Kingsley, then the sound of his sure footfalls behind her,

"I'll take you home," he said when he caught up. "It's not safe for you to walk at night by yourself."

But she kept going. It felt too dangerous to be with *him*. If it hadn't been for the interruption, she didn't know how far she'd have taken it. Kissing him had felt so damn good. She'd been moments away from begging him to slip her panties to the side and slam their bodies together. She nearly groaned at the thought.

"What am I doing?" she muttered out loud.

Kingsley grabbed her, and she whirled around to

face him, ready to tell him to go to hell. But his hand left her arm as quickly as it landed.

"My truck is that way." He pointed toward the left and a sandy strip of a path leading away from the main road where the van had taken them earlier. The road was well lit and a pair of large dogs, one white and the other golden brown, settled themselves under a nearby tree and watched Adah with glowing eyes. She flinched away from the dogs and dropped back until she was walking a little behind Kingsley, prepared to use his body as a shield if they attacked.

"You don't have to be afraid," he said, his voice soft and much too close. "I won't let them bite you."

He sounded confident, but her experience with dogs had taught her how unpredictable they were. A neighborhood dog had bitten her sister when they were toddlers, and she never forgot it. The growling menace of the dog, the blood on Zoe's leg, the trip to the hospital and the shots she'd had to get afterward. Keeping a close eye on the nearby dogs, Adah gripped her arms to stop herself from reaching out and grabbing on to Kingsley like a frightened child.

"It's this one." He led her toward a fenced front yard.

The house behind the low white fence was small and narrow. Smaller than the two-story house they'd just left behind with its sprawling single level, lights on in the drive, and farther back, a high wooden fence closing off the backyard from view. Details of deep green exterior walls, a wooden front door and a nearby garden of tall cacti emerged in the dark.

An older-model truck stood small and silent in the front yard, and a set of keys jangled. "You can get in," Kingsley said. "It's open."

The passenger door opened with a squeak of its hinges, and Adah climbed in, immediately rolling down the windows to release some of the heat trapped inside. Kingsley started the truck after a single glance at her.

"Where am I going?"

She told him the name of the hotel.

"That's a far walk," he said. "You would still be walking come sunrise."

"I'm faster than I look," she said.

His smile flashed. "I don't doubt it."

Moonlight glinted off the curve of his mouth and revealed again the muscled flesh beneath his mostly unbuttoned shirt. Adah took deliberate and deep breaths to stop herself from crawling into his lap again. This was getting ridiculous.

Kingsley started the truck and put it in gear. It rumbled over the rock gravel of the driveway, rolling out into the street with a full-throated growl. Silence swayed between them with each movement of the truck down the paved road.

Although it was mostly dark, Adah could see his hand work the gearshift, a commanding and sexy manipulation of the vehicle that vividly recalled the feeling of his hands on her. She shifted in the seat and looked away from his strong, thick-veined hand. With the shuddering breath she took, Adah could practically smell the arousal wafting up from between her own thighs.

She cleared her throat. "I'm sorry for what happened back there."

He looked at her. "Are you? Why?"

"Because…" *I'm practically engaged.* "Because we just met. It was inappropriate." She winced at how like her mother she sounded. And of all the times to be thinking of her mother…

"There's nothing inappropriate or wrong about what we did. Nobody forced you to sit in my lap, and there sure as hell wasn't a gun to my head when I grabbed your ass like it was mine." He playfully leered at her. "I'm into you. And I'm reasonably sure you like me. It's all perfectly normal."

Adah made a sound of frustration. Of course, it would seem fine to someone like him. He probably had women lined up every place he went. She was just the one weirdo who basically dared herself to go to a party with him, then, while potentially under the influence of a contact marijuana high, practically had sex with him in public. No, this wasn't at all a "normal" thing for her.

"Enjoyment is not all that determines whether or not something is wrong or right," she finally settled on saying.

"It's a good place to start, though," he countered.

This conversation felt far too familiar, like they'd

already discussed pleasure and its larger meaning before. How could she have recurring topics of conversation with a guy she just met? She shook her head at the foolishness of it all.

"This is my hotel," she called out with relief when she saw the familiar archway just outside her hotel's parking lot. But Kingsley was already turning into the palm-tree-lined driveway, obviously familiar with where he was. The lot was full, an indication of how popular the locale was, especially during the summer high season. It was a great combination of luxurious and intimate with its four-star reputation and homey feel. The long and wide front veranda was one of the things that had made her love it at first sight. From now on, though, she was going to adore it a little less. The woman sitting on the veranda watched the truck with an intensity that was obvious even from so far away.

Fighting a blush of embarrassment, Adah sighed under her breath and opened the truck's door, aware of both Kingsley sitting silently beside her and of the woman curled up on one of the chairs on the veranda.

"Mother, what are you doing up so late?"

Her mother, draped in an oversize scarf and bundled up against the late evening breeze, sat on one of the rattan chairs, looking nearly half asleep but prepared to wait there all night.

"I could ask you the same question."

Or you could not. Adah opened her mouth to tell her mother just how much of a grown woman she was, one who could stay out all night if she chose. But her mother looked away from her and toward Kingsley, who climbed out of the truck just then.

She flicked her gaze to the side to look at him and bit her lip. There was nothing she could say in her defense. Kingsley looked like he'd been mauled by a wildcat. Or had been rolling around in bed with one. His shirt was unbuttoned halfway down his chest to show claw marks over his pecs and around his nipples; the board shorts sat low on his narrow hips to emphasize his undeniable maleness.

The breath left her mother in an audible hiss, like air from a deflating tire. "Young man, you should be ashamed of yourself for carrying on with an engaged woman."

"Mother!"

They both stared at her.

"What?" Her mother looked at her with disappointment and a hint of anger around her elegant mouth. "We don't do things like this, Adah. We just don't." Adah noticed Kingsley's twitch at the sound of her name. But she couldn't pay attention to that now.

But I'm not engaged, she wanted to shout. *I haven't agreed to anything yet.*

Kingsley nodded like a puzzle piece had finally fallen into place. "You're engaged," he said. It was a statement, not a question. Like he'd known all along.

"Yes, she is," her mother answered for her. "And

you should leave her alone. This is not very noble of either of you."

Kingsley winced. "Don't worry, ma'am. If I'd known about her engagement, I wouldn't have let things get this far."

Her mother's gaze swung to Adah and over her figure as if she could see the events of the night imprinted on her. "*This far?* What does that mean exactly?"

Adah cursed under her breath. She wanted to touch Kingsley in reassurance, to let him know she hadn't hidden an engagement from him, that this wasn't about blatant infidelity or something equally repulsive. But he was stepping away from her, abandoning the pose of protection he'd taken on once out of the truck. Like he was finished with her. Something in Adah's chest squeezed painfully.

"I'll see you around…Adah." Kingsley spoke her name like a stranger, like the Doe Eyes he'd known and caressed had disappeared completely, leaving an unknown and unappealing woman in her place. After a nod to her mother, he climbed back into the truck. He was gone before Adah could think of what to say to him.

"What were you thinking?" Her mother stood up. What should have been a threat looked like defeat in her. Lines dragged down the corners of her mouth; her eyes looked haunted.

Oh God. Adah pressed the heels of her hands into her eyes. She wanted to just sink through the floor.

Her mother's disappointment was a heavy thing, unwieldy. Something she was tired of bearing.

This time, though, she knew she deserved it. She'd taken Kingsley up on the invitation to go snorkeling understanding that it had the possibility of leading to more, knowing that her blood turned to fire in her veins at just one look from him. Even if nothing had happened between them in the water or during the course of the night, it would only be a matter of time before she gave in to her attraction to him. And, at the back of her mind, she'd thought it would be worth it. A night of exquisite recklessness in exchange for apologizing profusely for her bad behavior. But looking into the face of her mother's disappointment made her doubt the value of the exchange.

"I thought you wanted to marry Bennett," Thandie said. She adjusted the shawl around her shoulders, pulling it tightly. Like Adah's bad decision had chilled her in a way the night's brisk breeze hadn't been able to. "Everything is already set for this marriage," she said, as if she couldn't imagine putting a stop to what had been put into motion for her daughter and for her company. A sacrifice of one and the rescue of the other.

"Mother, I want to help you and Daddy. I really do." Adah wrapped her arms around her own waist, holding tight to stop herself from flying apart. She barely stopped the "but" from leaving her lips. "I'm tired, Mother." Adah sighed and took a step toward the front door.

"Is that all you have to say?" Thandie asked; then her look changed. She stepped closer. "Are you okay? That man didn't do anything to you, did he?"

"No, no. He didn't. He was perfect." She bit her lip, afraid of whatever else she might say about Kingsley and the time they'd spent together. "We can talk tomorrow."

Finally giving in to the urge for escape, Adah walked into the hotel. She didn't remember getting in the elevator or going to her room. She didn't recall taking a shower and getting into bed, but soon she lay huddled under the covers with her hair wet and plastered to the back of her neck and to her cheek. She stared at the chair across from her bed overcrowded with clothes, and she felt the messiness was reflective of her life.

"I need to get it together."

She didn't know if it was tears or water from her wet hair that slipped down her cheeks. But in the end, it didn't really matter. The feeling was the same.

The sound of her ringing phone jolted her out of a dream that was all water, a slippery eel sliding over her arms and belly, stinging her with sweet jolts of electricity that pulled her farther and farther down into the sea. She was happy, her body more alive than it had ever been even as she sank to certain underwater death. The eel tightened its grip around her thighs and her waist, and its tender hold on her throat threatened pleasure more than anything else. She awoke with a gasp, jerking her head up, her body floating out of sleep like she was surfacing from a dive.

"Hello?" She didn't look at the glowing screen of the phone to see who it was.

"Girl, are you okay?"

The remnants of the dream evaporated with the sound of her friend's voice on the other end of the line.

"Selene?" The last she'd seen of her had been at the Atlanta airport, dropping her off and wishing Adah clarity to decide what to do about this marriage she'd agreed to before she'd known any better.

"You said you'd Messenger or WhatsApp me when you got in. I gave you a day to get it together, but now you're just inconsiderate." Her friend's accent was sweet as sugar, but when she was pissed, every word could burn like acid.

Adah muttered a curse. "Sorry! My mind's been..." She didn't even know what else to say about her state of mind.

"You don't have to tell me how your brains are more scrambled than a platter of Waffle House hash browns, but what you do have to do is let me know you weren't killed by some roving maniac on that damn island."

Chastised, Adah sighed and subsided back into the sheets. "I'm sorry. I'm safe."

"The first part I'm sure of, but what about the second? I heard your mama took off after you as soon as she found out you left town." Adah opened her mouth to ask the obvious, but Selene just kept going. "Before you ask foolish questions, I'll just go ahead and say I was *not* the one who told her where you went."

Adah rolled back to the center of the bed and sat up, propping herself up on the overstuffed pillows. "It doesn't really matter anyway. She's here—"

"And making trouble?"

"And making things even harder than before. I already wasn't sure about what I promised, but now she's just pushing me more and more in that direction. And the more she pushes, the more I want to resist." Suddenly Adah felt her throat close up, her eyes burning with tears.

"But there's more, right?" Selene asked. She seemed to know Adah better than she knew herself some days. Their time going to the same schools and living in the same city all their lives only reinforced their bond and sometimes uncanny knowledge of each other.

"I met someone."

"Are you fu—" Selene stopped. "You've been down there for less than two days. How are you gonna meet a man when you're supposed to be working on your own damn issues?"

"I got lucky?" Adah made sure her tone conveyed the very opposite.

"Let me guess, your mama found out about your

island stud and now she thinks you're deliberately setting out to ruin the company and the family name at the same time."

"She didn't do it on purpose, but you know how focused she can be sometimes. It's not malicious."

"Damn, girl."

"I know."

At times Adah felt like a walking symbol of everything her parents had lost when her sister died. Someone smarter, more vibrant and willing to sacrifice herself for the good of the family. Zoe wouldn't have hesitated when it came to marrying Bennett. She would've seen it as her duty and her privilege. But now the responsibility fell to Adah, who felt conflicted by the desire for a life she shouldn't want. Her cowardice and lack of commitment to anything other than her wish not to be tied down made her feel weak.

True, she hadn't taken a lover since committing to the marriage. Instead she'd focused her energies on building the boutique day care service that had become her passion. She'd cultivated her friendships, traveled to more than a dozen countries, enjoyed everything life had to offer that had nothing to do with sex. But all those years of self-denial were catching up with her. Lust for Kingsley had swept her out of her mind and right into his lap. She licked her lips, and although she tasted only sleep, she imagined a hint of him still rested on her tongue.

"Your mama can be scary," Selene said, bringing her back from the memory of Kingsley in her mouth.

Adah laughed, a rough and unhappy sound. "She isn't. Not really."

She could practically hear the shrug on the other end of the line. Selene knew it was fear of disappointing Thandie rather than fear of anything she would do or say that had kept Adah in line for so long. She sighed.

"I just don't know what to do." Adah climbed out of bed, wiping a hand across her face. "I'm just stuck in this strange I-don't-know phase. It's like I'm in high school all over again."

A rustling came through the phone line, Selene probably rummaging through her fancy closet for clothes to wear during her ridiculously early workout. "What do you want to do?"

"I want to run away," Adah whined.

"You already tried that, and your mama and all your worries just followed you down there."

Now Adah wanted to swear and throw things. "You're right." She stumbled to the bathroom to rinse the sleep from her mouth and peer at herself in the mirror. Hair in a bird's nest, face puffy from sleep, a look of hopelessness pulling down the sides of her mouth.

"What should I do, Selene?"

"Honey, you already know what to do. You just don't want to do it."

Adah stuck her tongue out at her reflection in the mirror, pretending it was Selene. "You're not being helpful." She started brushing her teeth.

"Oh, please. I'm just not giving you an easy out." Sounds of more productivity came from the other end of the line. Adah imagined the muffled thump was one of Selene's expensive pots against her tiled countertop. "Speaking of what to do, I hope you don't think Bennett has been as faithful to your premarriage as you've been."

"I don't expect him to be." Adah said the words around her toothbrush and the white foam from the toothpaste building up in her mouth.

Although Bennett was one of the few reliable and much-loved men in Adah's life, he and Selene didn't have much to do with each other. They seemed to orbit Adah's existence in two separate directions, connecting very rarely.

"You should," Selene said about Bennett's apparent infidelity. "He is your soon-to-be fiancé after all." She made a disapproving noise, sounding just like Thandie in a way she wouldn't have liked one bit if Adah pointed it out. "Although no one in town would believe it since he's so very discreet, that man has been petting every peach between here and the Mason-Dixon Line."

Adah laughed and almost choked on her toothbrush. "How do you even know that?"

"What? I didn't understand a word you just said."

Adah spat out her toothpaste and repeated her question.

"I have eyes, honey, and so does Blake." Unlike Adah and Selene, their friend Blake was happily married and had a baby on the way. She wasn't around these days as much as before she got married, but she was still an integral part of their trio. "She saw him at the High Museum with a girl who was hanging all over him. Later that night, she swore up and down that she saw them step into one of the closets for a quickie."

Adah giggled. "Damn, is she stalking him now?" She wasn't surprised by her lack of jealousy at hearing the news of Bennett's very active sex life. Sometimes she wanted to care more about his hypothetical infidelities, but the stories her friends told her about his antics only made her laugh. Yes, she felt vaguely scandalized by those stories but she also wanted to hear more, impressed by the set of brass ones he must have to get away with half the things he did.

"Not stalking. She just cares about you, just like I do," Selene said.

"I know..." Adah stuck the phone between her cheek and shoulder to smooth argon oil and leave-in conditioner in her hair.

Over the years Bennett had become more of a brother to her than a fiancé. Even a *potential* fiancé. They talked every now and then, both over the phone and in person during epic three-hour lunches, sometimes about their intended future together but most times not. He was easygoing and utterly confident as only the sole child and privileged son of relatively well-off Southern parents could be.

He loved women and sailing. After college, he'd borrowed a boat from one of his Exeter classmates and sailed around the world on his own, stopping wherever he felt like and staying however long he desired just because he wanted the solitude and the challenge. Sometimes Adah felt jealous of him being able and willing to do anything he wanted without worrying about his parents' disappointment or disapproval. Maybe he would understand what she was going through.

"So are you going to talk to him?" Selene reached into Adah's mind and plucked the thought right out of it.

"I think I need to."

"And what are you going to say?"

"Why are you asking me questions I don't know the answers to?" She turned and left the bathroom.

Selene laughed at her. "Girl…"

"I know."

After Adah hung up, she felt a lot better. She took her morning shower and went out to the balcony to make the inevitable phone call. Cell phone in hand, she sat on one of the two reclining chairs and looked down on the sand and the stretch of blue water shimmering like diamonds under the sun.

She was second-guessing her decision to call Bennett when the phone rang.

"I hear you're already getting yourself in trouble down there in Aruba." Bennett's voice rumbled through the phone.

She drew in a breath of surprise, and happiness.

Unlike the quiet domesticity of Selene's surroundings, she could hear the chaos of a bar wherever Bennett was. Thudding dance music and the sound of laughter, high and manic, that came at the height of a night's debauch. She looked at the phone in amazement.

"Isn't it eight o'clock in the morning?" she asked.

"It's five o'clock somewhere," he said with laughter in his deep voice. "Besides, I'm not in Atlanta. And don't try to change the subject. What's up with you?"

The music faded away even more. Adah heard the bang of a door closing, then the quiet murmur of voices. She blew out a breath of air. "What do you know?"

"Selene called me. She said you might need to talk."

Adah frowned. She didn't think Selene and Bennett knew each other well enough to have each other's phone numbers. Thinking back to the conversation she'd had earlier with her best friend, she tried to think of anything Selene had said that would hint at some sort of friendship with Bennett.

Through the phone, he made a tut-tut sound.

"Don't get distracted yourself either. I called you on a mission."

Adah choked on a laugh. Sometimes she thought he knew her better than he ought to. Unpredictable but unfailingly kind and generous, Bennett was the kind of man most women dreamed of. She wished she could jump in and commit to him like their parents wanted. There were worse men out there.

But she didn't think those reasons were enough for her to marry him.

"Tell me," he prodded when she was quiet too long.

Adah took a breath. "I'm not sure this marriage thing is for us."

"It worked out fine for our parents," he said. "Don't be so cynical." There was humor in his soft drawl, a warm invitation to tell him everything on her mind.

"What if this is a mistake?" She heard the quiver in her voice, but it was too late to take back the whining uncertainty of her declaration.

"This is only a mistake if you allow it to be. Do you want something else?"

Adah shook her head although an image of Kingsley immediately came into her mind. "I want to be sure."

Bennett didn't hesitate. "Then take your time to be sure. Our parents can wait. This is our lives, not theirs."

Adah swallowed. It would have been much easier to break off the agreement if she didn't like Bennett so much and if he wasn't such a damn nice guy. A good man who would make a great husband someday. *For someone else.* The words crept into her consciousness and wouldn't be silenced.

She dropped her head back and pressed the heel of a hand over her closed eye.

"It's not that simple," she said.

"As usual, you're overthinking, but far be it from me to deprive you of one of your favorite pastimes." His laugh was soft and warm though it was just a breath from being mocking.

"Just relax on your island, Adah. Go swimming. Make love with a handsome stranger—" she nearly choked "—and when you're completely liquid and sitting in the seat of who you are, your mind and heart will know what to do. Stop making a bigger deal of it than it is."

She didn't have to make a big deal out of this. This was *already* a huge issue, even if he was blasé enough to ignore the ramifications of what she was contemplating. But Adah took a cue from him, drew a breath deep into her lungs and slowly released it.

"Okay."

He laughed then. She pictured him standing on top of one of his beloved rooftop bars or clubs in some country she'd never been to, the nighttime city spread out below him, aglow with light.

"That's all you have to say?" he asked. "Just okay?"

"What else is there? You don't have my parents—at least not yet—so you don't know how trying to get away from their expectations is like struggling to crawl out from under an avalanche. It's nearly impossible."

"I believe in you, baby girl."

She shook her head finally, unable to deal with his blind optimism. "I'll talk with you later, Bennett."

"All right. Let me know how it works out."

"You'll be one of the first to know," she said with a twist of her lips.

"Oh yeah. Right." He laughed again, careless and carefree, as if whether or not to choose to go ahead with their marriage wouldn't affect him in the least. "Take it easy, baby girl. We'll talk soon."

Adah wandered back into the room, thinking about what Bennett and Selene had told her. And she thought about Kingsley's face the last time she'd seen him, the flinch in his eyes when her mother told him she was engaged. The beginnings of a headache throbbed above her left eye.

After a shower and properly seeing to her hair, Adah left the hotel, deliberately being quiet so as not to disturb her mother. Although she wouldn't have called it "sneaking out." Not really.

She had a decision to make, but before then she urgently had an apology to give.

Although at the best of times Adah was absent-minded, she actually had an excellent sense of direction. The ride from the party had been distracting, to say the least, with Kingsley a temptation to her senses and her apparently loose sense of morality. But between taking peeks at his body unselfconsciously bared by the open buttons of his shirt, she'd also looked at the landmarks they'd passed, taking note of everything around her. She called a taxi to take her to the entrance of the modest community in the hills where she was 90 percent certain Kingsley lived.

It didn't take her long to find his house, a single-story building with a narrow facade and, as confirmation that she was in the right place, a solitary older-model truck in its front yard. It was early, barely nine o'clock, but she assumed he would be home.

Her feet crunched in the gravel as she approached the house, nibbling on her lip and trying to think of the best way to tell him she was sorry for...everything. Well, maybe not exactly *everything.* She was about to knock on the door when the sound of a warning yip yanked her gaze to the road just in front of the house. It was the two dogs from the evening before. This time they had two more dogs with them, both bigger. Their tongues hung out in the morning heat as they eyed her with uncertain intent.

Adah shrank back on the veranda, looking around. There was no one else on the street, just her and the dogs, who seemed resolved to walk into Kingsley's front yard. Her heart started a panicked beat in her chest. She gripped the railing and backed away from the dogs.

Damn!

They came closer, sniffing vaguely at one another, then at the air in front of their noses while watching Adah, like they were making a game of it and stalking her. Adah didn't think. She jumped over the railing of the veranda and took off toward the nearest escape from the dogs. The gate leading to the backyard. She grabbed the handle and rattled it, cursing when it refused to open, practically feeling the dogs' hot breath on her heels. Panting in fear, she gripped the top of the fence and levered herself over, yelping when one of her sandals fell off.

She landed on the other side of the fence with a gasp. Her knees jerked from the landing, and gravel dug into the bottom of her naked foot. But she was safe. She leaned back against the fence with her eyes closed and her palms flat against the warm board of the fence.

"This is unexpected."

Her eyes flew open at the sound of Kingsley's voice.

She almost squeezed them shut again. Kingsley was lying by the side of his pool, his gorgeous skin spread out and glistening under the sun, absolutely naked. Adah swallowed hard and pressed her fingernails into the wooden fence at her back.

"I promise you I didn't do this on purpose." She tried to look everywhere but at his body, but her eyes drifted down from his face with each passing moment she looked in his direction. Finally Adah settled for staring at the empty space just to the left of his jaw.

"The dogs, right?"

He sounded amused, and although she wasn't looking—she really wasn't—she saw him sit up from the chair and put aside a stack of official-looking papers. "They can be a little scary," he said.

She thought he was going to grab a towel to cover himself, but he only braced his elbows on widespread knees to give her his undivided attention. Adah licked her suddenly dry lips. Since it would be idiotic to tell the man to put on clothes when he was clearly relaxing in his own backyard, where she was trespassing, she settled for standing up straight against the fence and tried to look more at ease, straightening her knees and taking subtle deep breaths, trying not to ogle him. He was making it very, very hard.

Adah cleared her throat. "I came to apologize about last night."

For a moment he said nothing, made no motion. Then he stood and walked toward the pool. She took a breath of relief when he sank beneath the surface of the water, inch by inch, his legs, feet, calves, the narrow hips and… Adah yanked her eyes up to his face but got distracted by the muscled planes of his chest and the faint marks from her fingernails she saw there. She felt him smile before she saw the curving amusement of his mouth.

"What part of last night are you here to apologize for, *Adah*?"

Adah flushed and watched as he swam lazily to the deep end, the water covering him all the way to his chest and splashing at the edges of the pool.

With him safely on the other side of the yard, she came closer, skirting the pool to perch next to the chair he'd just abandoned.

"There is a lot to apologize for," she said, thinking of the kiss she'd initiated without full disclosure of her circumstances. "I'm sorry I put you in that awkward position. It was selfish. And I should've known better. I do know better. I was just…" She trailed off, not knowing how much to reveal of what had been tearing her apart. "I'm sorry."

For a long moment, he looked at her, steady-eyed and handsome, the sun sparkling off the water gilding his face and throat. It didn't seem fair that all she wanted to do was slink closer to him and kiss his face all over, tease his mouth with her tongue and touch him until every anxiety she had simply disappeared, leaving just him and her and the sun and whatever could blossom between them. But Aruba wasn't a place to plant seeds, and this was not what she had come to him for.

"Tell me," he said, as he tread water in the deep end of the pool. "What exactly are you sorry for? Tell me. Explicitly."

He rolled the last word in his mouth in a way that made her want to drop to her knees in front of him, risk drowning in the pool to give in to every temptation he presented. And he knew exactly what he was doing. The way he watched her, eyes unrelenting and hard, said as much.

She had to open her mouth and start speaking twice to finally get the words out. "I made a mess of my life." Adah chewed the corner of her lip until it felt raw. "There's an arrangement that was made a long time ago. I agreed to it. Marriage." The last word felt like it curdled in Adah's mouth. "I shouldn't have kissed you."

"And now you're here for…?"

More. "To throw myself at your abundant mercy?" She tipped her head at him in question, repentant and almost willing to grovel for his forgiveness and whatever else he wanted to give.

Kingsley was too beautiful, floating in the water just out of arm's reach. Despite what Bennett had said, this wasn't easy. There was no decision for her to make. Her course was set, and there was nothing she could do about it except minimize the people she hurt before she acquiesced to the inevitable. She pursed her lips at Kingsley while he floated in the water and seemingly pondered her prostration.

Then finally he said, "My…mercy is nothing if not abundant. Despite what I wanted when we met, we can be friends instead. I'm not a slave to my penis. It's fun to pretend that I am, but—" He grinned, warm and teasing as the frost melted from his gaze. "I control the thing more than it controls me."

She felt an answering smile twitch across her face. With deep relief, she leaned all the way back in the chair, feeling an unspoken permission to look at him now. A mistake. He was waist deep in the pool, water dripping down his face and neck to sparkle in the sprinkling of hair on his chest and the dark trail dragging her eyes down. Adah drew in more air through her nose and felt her thoughts scatter like marbles across a slippery tile floor, a cacophony of color, noise and frustrated intent. Why was she so helpless to his charms?

She liked to think she'd known men more attractive than Kingsley. But she couldn't recall a single one. Bennett was very attractive. When she'd offered to take one for the team by becoming his prefiancée, she thought she was getting a pretty good deal. But that first look at Kingsley on the beach, floating above her head with his bared chest and focused attention, and she'd felt a full burst of lust that took her completely by surprise. She was used to denying herself, though, so it had been nothing to walk away from him. Now it was difficult to follow that routine. Nearly impossible. But, like Kingsley had said, maybe she could keep him in her life as a friend.

She cleared her throat again and dragged her eyes from what they were desperately trying to see below the water line. "Okay. That's good. That was all I wanted. To apologize and make sure you weren't put off by the things my mother said last night."

"Mothers have said worse to me." He winked at her.

Adah shook her head, a smile teased out of her and into the early afternoon despite herself.

"Would you like to stay for breakfast?" he asked, swimming closer. "Friends do that—right? Have breakfast together?"

She tried not to think of the exact circumstances where she'd love to have breakfast with him—but the images came hot and fast—sweat, sex, the groaning pleasure of him on top of her, inside her. Then after, a light breakfast in bed, him feeding her luscious red strawberries, before pulling her down into the sheets to wear her out again. Adah dipped her head to press a burning cheek into the relative coolness of her shoulder.

"I wish I could," she said. "But I have to go." *Before I do something I should regret.* She stood up, brushing off the back of her shorts. "Enjoy your swim. I'm sure I'll see you again."

"I am, too," he said, his tone low and teasing. "If you want to take the initiative, know you're welcome to visit me here anytime you like."

"Um…thanks." She would definitely not be taking him up on that invitation.

"Are you on the island for much longer?" Kingsley asked the question just as she turned away.

More than enough time to get in trouble with you again. "Another five days," she said. "Not much more time."

"Good to know," he said. "I'll see you soon. *Friend.*"

The word was loaded with sensuality. And that both frightened and excited her.

She rolled her eyes at her own idiocy. *Get a grip, girl!*

"See you around, Kingsley."

Chapter 5

He still wanted her.

Kingsley finished the reports his assistant had suckered him into reviewing before leaving for the beach and his freestyle kite-surfing event at Hi-Winds. Adah stayed in his mind the entire time. The way she'd looked jumping over his fence, chest heaving with fear as she glanced over her shoulder toward the no longer visible pack of dogs. And when she'd seen him, it was like she was facing the dogs all over again, her face twisted in shock.

She wasn't for him, this woman who couldn't give him any of what he wanted.

But he still wanted.

On the beach the sun was at the perfect height,

and the morning winds pawed at his skin, warm and friendly. He had loved taking part in the long-distance kiting the day before, a chance to skim across the sea and sky with friends and competitors he hadn't seen in a year or so. But today was his favorite event. He had to beat his friends to take home the money and the trophy. The $5,000 prize money didn't impress him. He had that much in his spending cash for the week. It was the physical challenge of the kite and the water, the pull on his muscles and on his senses, adrenaline sparking through his body like sex, and the view like no other.

Kingsley prepped for his event, stretching and curling his toes in the hot sand as he watched the water, where his closest competitor performed a reverse somersault and landed upright. The crowd cheered, wild and congratulatory. *Yeah.* He needed to get his head in the game and off Adah.

When it was his turn, everything in him focused on controlling the parachute in the air and keeping the board balanced. He was all in. His body responded like it was meant to, breath controlled, the shock of landing on the water reverberating through the kite board and into his knees. His breath rushed out.

Yes.

He harnessed the wind under his parachute again and flew up. One breath in, then *higher.* Muscles tight. The sweat pouring off him, seawater salting his lips and tongue, and then launched into the double flip he'd been practicing all week. Breath out. The shock of the landing. Applause. Kingsley grinned as he sailed across the water, then up into the air as the wind came back for him, maneuvering him neatly above the shimmering water close to the beach, the deeper blue as impenetrable as a certain woman's gaze. And he slipped, looking over the gathered crowd to see if *she* was there.

But no. A beach full of pale bodies. No Adah. His arm twitched, and he felt himself losing control of the kite, his body jerking hard in the air as the wind pushed him farther out and away from any possible sighting of Adah. He had to get his mind off her.

Kingsley drew in a hard breath and got back to business. A flash of pale under the water caught his eye—a shark—and he frowned, tightening his grip on the kite straps and fighting the instinctive surge of panic. Now he had another reason to keep his head in the game. He landed on the surface with a splash, grunted when the kite tugged at his harness. He yanked the brake line, feeling the answering roll in his shoulder muscles, the flexing and undulations of his back as he got the kite closer to the beach.

Max, one of the guys who'd gone up before him, grabbed the leading edge of the kite and guided it to the sand while Kingsley kicked off the board to the renewed applause of people watching.

"That was cool! I didn't know you perfected that triple flip you almost killed yourself over last year." Max offered up a fist bump. "Nice going."

"Thanks!" Although it hadn't been a necessary part of the competition, Kingsley had obsessed about pulling off the triple. He'd damn near fallen on his head a few times while he was practicing it. But out on the water, it had felt effortless, a symphony of his muscles and breath working together to produce one of the best moves he'd ever done. Now that the challenge was met, what was next? A thought of Adah flashed in his mind.

"Good luck out there, Max. The wind is nice, but I spotted a shark. Far out but still there."

Max cursed. "Those things freak me out."

"You're not the only one," Kingsley muttered.

When he'd seen the shark, a cold fear had come over him. It wasn't his first time seeing one while up in a kite, and he didn't want this to be his first time getting bitten by one. He preferred his limbs right where they were, attached to his body.

"You were really great out there."

A trio of women walked up to Kingsley. Max gave him a look before lifting his hand in a wave.

"See you later, man." He seemed to enjoy the bikini-clad backsides of the girls as he walked away, grinning and giving Kingsley the thumbs-up behind their backs.

Kingsley accepted the compliment from the women with gracious thanks and continued rolling up his kite. He felt their eyes on him, all three of them, hungry like the shark he'd managed to avoid in the water.

"We'd love to buy you a drink," one of them said.

They were all pretty, dressed in colorful bikinis that showed off their shapes and newly acquired tans. It didn't seem like one was trying to get him more than the others; instead all three women seemed intent on pursuing him. He hadn't been offered a foursome in a long time. Kingsley thought about Adah and the flash of her eyes, her soft body and the fit of her hand in his while they were snorkeling together.

"Sure," he said. "Where do you have in mind?"

He was a single and completely available man. He didn't have a wife or girlfriend to stop him from taking these women up on whatever it was they were offering.

"There's a bar at the Sundowner." A hotel not too far away. "They have great drinks and big beds." The third one spoke up now, the curviest of her friends, with a tilted mouth that reminded Kingsley a bit of Adah. He clenched his jaw tight. He didn't need to think about her. She was as good as married and off-limits.

"Okay. Why not?"

He exchanged numbers with the women and agreed to meet them at the hotel bar that night. The rest of the tournament was an exercise in frustration. He alternately congratulated and criticized himself for agreeing to meet the women for what was guaranteed to be a confusing foursome. But he couldn't have Adah. Not in the way he wanted. Not in the way *she* obviously wanted. There was no point in torturing himself by letting the hard, pulsing ache he had for her go to waste.

He got to the bar early and sat drinking a beer and chatting with the bartender. The beer was soothing on his tongue, and the conversation was easy on the brain. He ignored the occasional clench in his belly that told him he wasn't so much anticipating as dreading the arrival of the three women.

This was what he wanted. Kingsley tried to tell himself that with every sip of his beer, his gaze slipping past the bartender to the mirror reflecting his own ambivalence back at him. He looked calm enough, but in the mirror, he saw his fingers tap impatiently on the bar, his lips tighten in disgust when he thought of what would happen with the women upstairs in one of the hotel beds. A date like this would be any other man's ultimate fantasy. But…

He blew out a breath.

Kingsley saw the women coming up to him in the mirror before they spoke.

"We're glad you made it," the curvy one said.

They were all similarly dressed again. Tube dresses in different pastel shades, high heels, hair long and loose around their shoulders. From the look of them, he sensed they would be interchangeable in bed, deliberately so even as they tried to outdo one another in pleasing him. He'd been there before. Suddenly he made a decision.

"I actually came to tell you in person that I can't stay."

He internally winced as their faces fell as one. "Something else came up, and I didn't want to be rude," he said.

The one who'd approached him first looked the most disappointed. She came close and dropped a hand on his thigh, blue fingernails sinking into the thin denim of his jeans. "Are you sure? We have plenty to drink, and eat, upstairs."

The one who reminded him of Adah, lush-hipped and a mouth that hid its own smiles, wrapped her arm around her friend's middle and pulled her back. "We're disappointed, but we also understand—right, Katya?"

The third one nodded and looped her arm through the first girl's. "You're missing out," she told Kingsley as she licked her full bottom lip and tipped her shoulders back to emphasize her breasts.

He tried to look regretful. "As tempting as you all are, I can't. There's something else I need to do tonight."

That *something* turned out to be standing in his kitchen and drinking another beer. Hours later, he stood looking out his kitchen window and wondering what Adah was doing at that exact moment. If she burned like he did. He pressed the beer bottle to the center of his bare chest and sighed at the coolness of it, imagined that it was the touch of her lips on his skin. He hissed in reaction when the bottle brushed across his nipple.

No. He wasn't doing this right now.

But his hardness pushed against the front of his jeans, demanding relief. He gripped the beer bottle in his fist instead and rested it on the counter. His sex throbbing, Kingsley stared out into the dark evening and wished he was a less honorable man.

Kingsley stretched out on the beach, a thick blanket separating his skin from the fine-grained sand while sunglasses covered his eyes and the sun warmed him through a glistening layer of sunscreen. He wasn't scheduled to compete today. It was just a day for him to take it all in.

He pillowed his head on his backpack and watched the dozens of windsurfers race across the water, their multicolored sails whipping against the background of the deep blue sky.

Desperately needing the escape, he'd climbed out of his tangled sheets to watch the day's competition. He couldn't stop thinking about Adah. He'd dreamed of her—their limbs entwined, bodies joined, satisfaction exploding between them. Hours later, he still burned.

"Hey, why aren't you up there?" Max wandered down the beach toward him, his board shorts and T-shirt flapping in the breeze. He pointed to a place farther out from the competition arena where kiters were just enjoying the air and showing off for one another.

"Not feeling it today." Even as he said it, Kingsley winced. He *always* felt like kiting; damn near everyone knew that. That was why he was on the island in the first place. But thoughts of Adah were keeping him earthbound.

There was something irresistible about her, even after finding out about her impending marriage. It was a cliché straight out of one of his sister's novels. Kingsley had been into other women before, but never like this. Maybe his obsession was so intense because he'd never gotten her into bed. Maybe.

He sighed. "I'm a little sore from being on the water all day yesterday," Kingsley told Max truthfully enough. "I need a break."

Although Max hadn't known Kingsley long, Kingsley could sense the other man didn't believe him.

"What's her name?" Max laughed. "Is it one of the girls from yesterday?"

Something in Kingsley's face must have told him otherwise because he gave him a knowing look. "Ah, another girl then. Someone from before."

Kingsley didn't bother to lie. Adah was in his blood, throbbing through his veins into the seat of his sex. It wasn't something he could hide.

"It's not going to go anywhere. She's committed to somebody else."

"If she could only see all the girls trying to pull

you on this island," Max said. "She would jump on you in a heartbeat."

"This isn't about scarcity, my man. If she wants me, she can have me. I'm pretty easy, and she knows it. She just doesn't want to take what's right in front of her."

"That's not something anybody here will believe," Max said. "She has to be crazy not to just snatch you up. Even I can say objectively you're not bad-looking for a guy."

"Thanks." Kingsley had to laugh.

"Anytime, buddy." Max slapped Kingsley on the shoulder and stood up, brushing the sand from his knees. "I'll see you later. This breeze is too nice to waste."

"Yeah, later." The breeze really *was* nice, its strong gusts coming from the direction of Venezuela and bringing with it the faint scent of flowers and fresh coconuts.

Any other day and Kingsley would've been in the air even though he wasn't scheduled for any events; he loved the sport that much. But today he was too distracted.

Everything reminded him of Adah.

He watched Max launch into the air and wondered if his friend could see everything happening on the beach, and if he could see Adah.

Damn. Maybe she was somewhere nearby right now but he just couldn't see her, a problem he wouldn't have if he was in his kite. Kingsley sat up and started to grab his stuff. If he left now, he could be in the air in less than half an hour…

A pair of bare legs and a plastic bag carrying a green coconut appeared in his view.

"Hey," Adah said.

His mood switched so quickly from desperation to relief that he almost felt light-headed.

Cool it, man.

He forced himself to relax, to switch back on the casual flirtation they'd both grown used to. Kingsley deliberately trailed his eyes along her legs, taking his slow and good time appreciating the sheen of her skin, the long limbs he'd imagined wrapped around him, the loose fit of her denim shorts hiding the warm heat he longed to bury his face into. He forced his gaze abruptly higher. That tactic wasn't a good one either.

"What brings you out here?" Kingsley asked. "Are you looking for a new guy to cheat on your old man with?" He clenched his teeth. That was completely uncalled for, but dammit, she had him twisted up in so many knots he didn't know if he was coming or going.

Adah winced at his words and looked ready to bolt. He reached out and grabbed her ankle, startled at how delicate and soft her bones felt between his fingers.

"Sorry." He deliberately bit his tongue. "That was a stupid and mean thing to say. Take a load off. I promise not to say any more dumb things to you. At least not for the next few minutes."

Adah hovered above him, obviously undecided, obviously hurt. He brushed his thumb over her ankle.

"I was being an idiot. It's a bad habit I default to sometimes." Without waiting for her to say yes, he moved to make room for her on his blanket. "Sit. Please."

When she sank gracefully down on the blanket next to him he released the breath he'd been holding. She chewed on the corner of her lip, waiting, it seemed, for him to say something else that would hurt.

"When I don't get what I want, I can be an ass," he said.

"No kidding."

She stayed next to him instead of getting up and walking away like any sane person would. She cradled the plastic bag in her lap, her fingers tugging nervously at the handles of the bag. Then she took out a straw and put it in the coconut, which sloshed with sweet water. She began to drink, watching him from beneath her lashes. Suspicious. Curious.

"Do you want to start over?" she asked.

Christ, yes. He chuckled, shaking his head ruefully. "Her Majesty is so very generous to her foolish subject."

"I learn from the best."

She drank, thirsty and purposeful, from the coconut in her hands and watched him in a way that made *him* thirsty and purposeful. He looked away from her mouth around the straw, to the water and the beach. It was already full of spectators and sun worshippers at half past two in the afternoon. Down the beach, he noticed a familiar trio. The girls from the day before.

They wore bikinis again today, solid-colored bottoms in bright shades with halter tops fringed like western wear. He knew that was the current style now, fringes along bikini tops to make women's breasts look bigger. It wasn't an illusion he appreciated.

His gaze landed on them for only a moment. But it was long enough for them to notice his attention and for all three to notice Adah, who sat like a queen on his blanket, mistress of everything near her, especially him. One of the girls winked at him, and Kingsley raised his eyebrow at her before looking away. He still wasn't interested in what they had to offer.

The sun was hot on his nearly naked body, burning through the white Speedo he'd absentmindedly pulled from the dresser drawer, his mind already on what the day would bring. But with Adah so close and doing a terrible job of hiding her interest in seeing him half-naked, he felt himself stir. Kingsley shifted and cleared his throat, amused. He hadn't lacked this much control of his body since he was a kid and waking up sticky from dreams he barely understood.

"Do you want to go for a drink?" It was early

enough in the day that an invitation like that was a little questionable. But he didn't want to go kiting now, and he certainly didn't want to go swimming with her and expose himself as the desperately horny teenage boy he'd suddenly become.

Adah hesitated a moment before she shrugged. "Sure. I could use something more interesting than this coconut water."

From the sounds she was making with the straw, the coconut water was almost finished. Perfect timing. Without looking, Kingsley reached behind him and into his bag for the jean shorts and T-shirt he'd shrugged off earlier.

"I know the perfect place."

As he pulled on his clothes, he thought about the girls from the day before and the offer they'd made him. A drink and sex. A bar and a bed. Kingsley tried to convince himself he wasn't offering Adah the same thing now.

He finished buttoning his shorts. "You ready?"

"Yeah."

He wanted to feel more regret about leaving the tournament and the beautiful kiting day behind. The wind was perfect and could easily take him high above any sharks or temptations lying in wait for him. But Adah was what he wanted now, her warm presence by his side, her skin that smelled like a sweet-and-spicy mix of ginger and sugar and glowing with more color than when he'd met her. She walked, steady and unafraid, by his side. As if even though she didn't know exactly where Kingsley was going, she would confidently go there with him.

"Have you been in the water today?" he asked.

"Not yet. I was hoping for later this afternoon when the heat is less intense. The water feels really good on my skin near the end of the day."

He hummed a response, mentally tripping over the image of her in the water. Bikini and sunlight. Wet skin and vulnerable belly begging for his touch.

"Sounds like a good way to spend the hottest part of the day." He convinced himself he was being generous for a moment before he opened his mouth again. "You can come over and take a dip in my pool if the sea gets too rough for you, or you don't feel like getting sand in your bathing suit."

She grinned at him, genuinely amused it seemed. "You're so kind."

"I am. I'm glad you finally realized that."

They walked down the beach toward the quieter stretches of sand, past million-dollar houses and empty plots of arid land that investors had yet to take advantage of. Kingsley had thought a time or two about investing in more than just the small house he'd bought for his own private use while he was on the island. Maybe a hotel or restaurant, something separate from his family's corporation and financial interests. But something in him was reluctant to make money from a place he found so much pleasure in. Some deeply buried hippie part of him wanted to keep it "pure" in a way the business part of him thought was highly impractical.

He stopped Adah with fingers on her lower back when they got to the modest beach bar owned by an old friend. "This is us."

She looked over the bar fronting the smooth stretch of white sand and calm water, the quaint wooden structure with a thatched roof and handmade wooden stools in front. Reggae music played from behind it. On the sand closer to the beach, a half dozen hammocks swayed under the *palapas*, whose coconut-thatched roofs rustled in the perpetual Aruban wind.

A place like this, affordable and old-fashioned in the best way, would normally be overrun by tourists, Kingsley knew. But Josue kept word of it quiet, inviting only a select few to his bar. He didn't turn away the tourists who found him, but he wasn't exactly welcoming to them either. His scowl and crappy service were usually enough to send them packing—even with his delicious rum punch in their bellies—never to return.

"I like this music," Adah said. She was smiling and walking up ahead of him to approach the nameless bar.

From behind the counter, Josue waved at Kingsley. His tersely offered "Afternoon to you" made Kingsley grin.

Josue's broad body moved with slow skill as he mixed drinks for the people taking up space on four of his eight stools. He was by no means the fastest bartender out there, his nearly three-hundred-pound frame with its massive hands weren't made for speed. But everything he concocted was good in a way that made Kingsley do a double take, wondering if he'd been drinking his mai tais and Long Island iced teas wrong all these years. Josue was also a good man. Slow to anger. Steady in his friendships. A solid foundation to the community Kingsley had found on the island. Josue slid tall glasses of a red-and-white drink in front of two of his patrons.

"It's not a *good* afternoon?" Kingsley asked.

"Too early to tell," Josue said, although it was nearly three. He watched Adah approach, sizing her up not unkindly. "Who is this poor thing unlucky enough to meet up with you?"

Kingsley leaned against the bar to exchange a quick hug with Josue before inviting Adah to sit on a stool. Once she sat, he did the same. He introduced them.

"Pleased to meet you, miss," Josue said. "Although you hanging out with this guy makes me worry for you."

"Hey now. I only have the most honorable intentions here."

Josue wiped down the bar, swiping his rag past Adah's resting hands, close enough to give them a pat of sympathy. "What can I get for you?"

Kingsley asked for the rum punch and encouraged Adah to do the same. Ordering the drinks he did in the lounges in Miami seemed a shame and a waste of Josue's considerable skill, although the bartender could make something as simple as a Cuba Libre taste incredible.

"I think I'm in love," Adah said with a wide smile at the bartender once she'd tasted her drink.

"I'll just add you to my list," Josue said, deadpan.

She laughed. After a few minutes catching up with Kingsley, Josue excused himself to tend to the other patrons. The space between them and where Kingsley and Adah sat was enough to give an illusion of privacy. The sound of the waves was a muffling sort of white noise that amplified the effect.

"I'm glad you came out this afternoon," Kingsley told Adah as he turned on his stool to face her. "Although I'm sorry for taking you away from the tournament. The kiters are fun to watch."

Her bottom lip slid from between her teeth, reddened and plush. "To be honest, I only came by to see you."

Her confession wasn't exactly a surprise. But the blood still thudded through his veins when she actually said the words. "You came by to see what your new *friend* was doing?"

"Yes?" The way she made her response a question made Kingsley smile. "The dogs scattered my mind yesterday," Adah continued. "I didn't tell you everything I came to. I thought if I dropped by today in a clearer state of mind, then I could let you know what was going on and really give you an explanation for what happened the other night."

Kingsley wondered if it was just the presence of the dogs that had scattered her mind. If she'd been feeling anything close to what he'd felt, aroused from their proximity to each other and aware of the bedroom not very far away, he understood why her thoughts hadn't been very coherent. It had taken nearly an hour after she left for him to calm down enough to make any sort of sense of the reports he was looking at.

"You want to tell me now?" He wrapped a hand around the thick glass of rum punch. The condensation and coolness seeped into his palm.

"Will you listen?"

"Of course." *I'll listen to anything you have to say all day and all night long.*

She blinked at him, and for a moment, Kingsley thought she'd read his mind. She took a sip from her drink, then looked down the bar to where Josue talked with someone who looked like a relative, only with long hair around his shoulders and a naked back covered in tribal tattoos.

She shook her head, a dismissive motion he was sure would lead to more avoidance on her part. He wasn't wrong.

"This is the life," she said as if she hadn't just asked him to listen to something important she had to say. "Drinking rum punch and sitting at the bar next to a gorgeous man." Kingsley grinned at that, his ego decisively stroked by her casual compliment. "I could get used to this. But I always overthink things. That's my problem."

"There's absolutely nothing wrong with enjoying a warm body by your side and a delicious drink in your belly. That is some of the best stuff of life."

"But I'm sure that's not all you want to do with your life," she said.

"You either," Kingsley responded. "I am very sure of that."

"How can you be so certain when you just met me a couple of days ago? You don't know."

"Well, I do know. You don't strike me as the lazy type."

"I love kids." Adah brushed her thumb against the rim of her glass, a slow back-and-forth motion that distracted Kingsley more than it should have. "Although I don't think I'll have a lot of them, maybe one, maybe none at all after this mess with my engagement, I'd love to be surrounded by them. They're so sweet and innocent, they are the best of us, distilled into the smallest packages."

Kingsley agreed. Someday he, too, would like to have kids, but only after he found the right woman. His gaze lingered on Adah's face, on the beauty and kindness he found there. Someone like her should have children if she wanted them. It was easy to imagine her surrounded by a nest of pillows and propped up in bed with a baby at her breast. He ignored the part of him that thought it should be *his* baby.

He took a quick drink of the punch to moisten his suddenly dry throat. “What makes you think you might not have any children?”

Kingsley watched her stutter over the beginning of a thought. She fidgeted on the stool and did not meet his eyes, her hand moving toward her glass of rum punch, then away without picking it up. He finished his drink with a deep gulp and signaled Josue for another. After his drink came, Josue nodded at him before wandering away again.

“When I was twenty,” Adah finally said, “I made a decision I regret now.”

An abortion? Kingsley drew a quiet breath of sympathy. He imagined Adah young and studious, a vulnerable girl who’d fallen prey to some slick college senior with pretty words in his mouth to talk her into things she wasn’t ready for. A need rose up in him to protect and shelter her.

“Choices are there to be made,” he said. “We all have had to deal with difficult ones at one time or another.”

Adah glanced down to the other end of the bar again, as if checking to see if anyone was paying any attention to their conversation. But Kingsley knew from experience, as both talker and listener, that people tended to ignore the discussions of foreigners. If Adah had been a local, her business would’ve been all over the island before she could climb off the stool and head back home. Even Kingsley, someone who came to Aruba every year and made connections with people he found interesting, was generally ignored. Just like he ignored the threads of gossip about some islanders.

"It was stupid," Adah finally said. "My parents were in trouble."

Kingsley's head jerked up. *Her parents?*

"Wait. You didn't have an abortion?"

Adah stopped and wrinkled her brow at him. "What would make you think that?"

He shook his head, gave a soft laugh. "Never mind. Nothing. I was just presuming." Would Adah have allowed herself to be taken advantage of by some ignorant college punk? When she kept frowning, he waved his drink at her in dismissal. "No, really. Keep talking. What you have to say is much better than what I thought you were going to say anyway."

"Okay…" She sucked at the corner of her mouth. "You're a weird guy—anyone ever tell you that?"

"Strangely enough, you're the first."

"People have been lying to you all your life then," she said. "Anyway." She paused again. "My parents have a company they started just after they married. They became partners in life just about the same time they became partners in business. Their company did well for a long time. At least well by their standards. A small niche market loved Palmer-Mitchell Naturals, and they were happy with them as customers." A proud smile lit up her face. "They loved their company."

Kingsley's eyebrows twitched up. He was surprised to hear the name of a company that his sister Adisa loved. She'd never had any chemicals in her hair and swore by everything from the Palmer-Mitchell Naturals line, never abandoning them to get on the bandwagon and embrace other, more popular products that had come along to take advantage of the natural hair care movement.

"But they ran into some trouble along the way, nothing immediate, but it was something they had to deal with using a long-term plan." Adah sounded like she was repeating what had been told to her about the company, not what she had discovered for herself. "They had to find a partnering company to help pull them into a new and more profitable era, especially since the competition has grown exponentially over the years with so many companies that had been in the hair-perming business suddenly creating products for natural hair. They had to create a strategy that would keep them in business and maximize their profits without compromising quality." She paused and looked into the middle distance, a wrinkle forming between her brows as she turned over whatever it was that only she could see.

"My parents brought up a hypothetical situation that involved joining two companies. Theirs with another that would make both stronger. But they wanted to keep the business in the family. Daddy insisted on it and Mother thought it only made sense, especially since she knew of two companies that had gone through the same thing. A business marriage had joined and saved them both."

Kingsley could see where this was going from a mile off. His parents probably would've had the same idea, but he doubted they would have compromised the happiness of any of their thirteen children to make it happen.

"I was in college at the time," Adah said. "I had broken up with a boyfriend and was actually a little burned-out on relationships."

"At twenty years old?" Kingsley remembered what he'd known about relationships as a college student. Precisely nothing. He had only been playing at being a grown-up then.

Adah took a sip of her now-watery rum punch. "In hindsight, it was a foolish promise to make. But I did make it. When my mother asked me to, I offered myself up as half of the company to be joined in marriage to a potential business partner. At the time, it made sense since…" She pressed her lips together, suppressing whatever it was she was about to say. "Anyway, it's done."

"And now you're having second thoughts?"

"Now I'm thinking I made a mistake. Bennett is a great guy—" Kingsley frowned at the mention of another man, her fiancé apparently, feeling an unfamiliar kick of jealousy in his belly "—but he's not the man for me."

"Is he forcing you to go through with the marriage?"

"No. He's been nothing but supportive. He says that whatever I want to do is fine with him. But…" She pressed her lips together again. "This isn't just about me. My parents need this. And I'm the only child they have left."

Kingsley wasn't a believer in no-win situations. Adah was an adult. She was a person who could determine her own future—she didn't have to rely on others to sketch out what that future would look like, especially since she wanted children and was willing to compromise that most basic and essential of desires just to make other people's lives more tolerable. As a businessman and as a person who determined the fate of dozens of people and billions of dollars on a weekly basis, he was already turning over the problem in his head and trying to find a solution.

"You don't have to accept that as the final decision, Adah. You deserve to be happy."

"I know," Adah said, but she didn't sound convinced. "It's been more difficult than ever the last few weeks. The closer we come to finalizing the engagement, the more uncertain I get. I just don't want to let my parents down."

But I don't want you to marry another man. "I know what it's like to have the weight of your family's expectations pressing you down," he said. "It's a burden, and it's also a responsibility. Family, blood and chosen, is important in a way that nothing else will ever be. I understand not wanting to disappoint them." He flexed his fingers around his nearly empty glass. "Ultimately, you have to do what feels right for you."

A sad smile curved Adah's mouth. "I just want to run away from it all."

Kingsley would happily provide that escape for her if that was what she wanted.

"So, now you know my story." She took a long and loud breath.

"I do." Her situation was one he understood too well even though he had happily and gratefully taken over the responsibility of being CEO of his family's company. He had the mind for it, the time and the interest. Unlike most of his siblings, who had other interests and would rather build their fortunes and their financial lives separate from the Diallo empire. "Thank you for sharing it with me."

"You're welcome. And now I think I'm done talking about it." She looked pained, and Kingsley felt like an ass for being the reason she had to dive back into that place that brought her so much discomfort.

Talking about her troubles with a virtual stranger, even if it was someone she wanted to take to bed, obviously only made the pain of it all more intense and amplified the weight of the burden she was trying to avoid. But escape was only a temporary solution. Kingsley's own yearly diversion was temporary, as well. He had no desire to completely sever the responsibilities of being a Diallo. Distance was what he craved, that and the ability to just be himself for a few weeks, separate from the face of the Diallo Corporation, and even from Miami.

"All right," Kingsley said. "Let's be done then." He drained the last of his punch, noticed Adah was nearly finished with hers and ordered another round for them both after she nodded in agreement.

Then another round of drinks and another hour of conversation passed. Kingsley was just telling Adah about his best friend, Victor, and his new wife when he noticed they were about to have company.

A trio of men walked toward them from down the beach, their focused gazes making it clear they were heading for the bar. There weren't enough seats to fit them all.

"Let's move to the beach," Kingsley said to Adah once they'd gotten their latest round of fresh drinks from an amused Josue. She tipped her shoulder in agreement and picked up her drink to follow him across the hot sand.

The water was calm, a nice change from the day he'd arrived. A storm had followed him from Miami to cloud the waters, making the swimming unpleasantly rough for at least two days. The day he'd met Adah was actually the first clear day since he'd been on the island. He'd celebrated that beautiful bit of happenstance with a sunset swim. Tranquil water and Adah. A beautiful and unforgettable correlation. He wished still waters for her as well, so she could see her way out of her dilemma. In the meantime, he'd see for himself what options were available to her.

The *palapa* he led her to was one of seven scattered on the beach in front of Josue's bar. Beyond the bar and farther from the beach was a hotel now closed for renovations. This meant the beach was less busy than usual, nearly empty, the hotel's *palapas* left unoccupied and dozens of unused beach chairs piled nearby. With the bar over a dozen yards behind them and slightly uphill, the stretch of beach felt deserted.

Kingsley guided Adah to the *palapa* that had a hammock already strung beneath it.

"Climb in," he said.

She looked at him, blinking and clutching the glass of rum punch to her chest. "Where are you going to sit?"

He confessed to himself in that moment that he might have been a little bit tipsy. Tipsy enough that sharing a hammock with Adah seemed like a good thing, a practical thing even, to do. They would be talking. They could rest their drinks on the small shelves within arm's reach at the corners of the *palapa*. These were thoughts that he may not necessarily have had while completely sober. Or maybe he just wouldn't have acted on them.

"I'll lay at the other end," he said. That sounded feasible enough.

Adah must have thought so, too, because she handed him her drink, kicked off her sandals and climbed into the hammock, swinging up into the dark cloth in a way that was by no means graceful but incredibly cute. He coughed out a laugh.

"Are you laughing at me?" she asked once she was settled into the depths of the swaying hammock.

"Well, I *am* laughing."

She shook her head and subsided into the swaying thing, one leg hanging over the side. Kingsley put both their drinks on the shelf near her head, then got in beside her, tucking their hips side by side, being careful to keep his feet away from her face. As he settled in at the opposite end, instead of avoiding *her* feet, he clasped them between his hands and rested them on his chest.

"There's sand on my feet," she said, trying to pull them out of his hands.

"I'm sure there's already sand all over me from before," he said and kept her feet right where they were. He dropped his head back and sighed, breathing in the salty sea air and allowing relaxation to overtake his body. "This is nice."

She shifted against him. "Yeah."

He heard her hum again in agreement and felt her gaze on him, but he kept his eyes shut and enjoyed the vague fuzziness in his brain, a luxury he didn't often indulge in. Although he wasn't on duty as CEO of Diallo Corporation while on the island, he usually kept his intoxication to a minimum, wanting to be ready at a moment's notice if anyone from home urgently needed him. Even in his freest moments, he caught himself thinking of his family and other responsibilities. They were never far from his mind. His phone in its waterproof case was zipped into the pocket of his shorts and set to vibrate so he would feel it ring.

It was a long time before he felt Adah's feet relax against his chest; a slow loosening of fine muscles, then her toes drooping to point toward opposite sides of the hammock. With his eyes still closed, he patted the lean line of her foot. He felt a tremor ripple through her leg before he heard the sound of her drinking from her cup. He popped an eye open.

"What about me?" He reached out his hand and she rolled her eyes at him before stretching to the shelf near her to get his drink. Her fingers were hot when they brushed against his, scorching compared with the cool condensation on the glass.

"Thank you." Kingsley lifted his head to drink deeply. He finished it in a few long gulps, then passed the empty glass back to her, the hammock rocking with his movement. Adah's body was so beautifully warm against him, pressed hip to hip, thigh to torso. They lay together in the swaying hammock with the wind buffeting their bodies, the light moving slowly across the sky and the beach toward sunset. It was fast becoming one of the best times he'd ever spent at Josue's bar.

"I feel like I should be doing something else," Adah said, her voice low and relaxed, beautiful to hear after the tension that had vibrated through it while they'd talked at the bar.

"What else do you have to do?" Kingsley asked, trailing his fingers over the tops of her feet. "You're on vacation, aren't you?"

"Like you said, I'm escaping from a situation I've put myself in. I should be strategizing, planning. Or at least planning my outfit for the funeral pyre."

He rolled his head to look at her, very much enjoying the outfit she was wearing now. The shorts showed off her slender thighs and hips while the tank top draped loosely in alluring lines over her modest breasts and flat stomach. "Make sure it's something that catches fire quickly and looks good on Instagram."

She giggled. "What do you know about Instagram?"

"I have younger brothers and sisters I need to keep an eye on. I know every way there is for them to get into trouble."

"Damn. Really? You sound like a scary big brother to have."

"I'm the kind of big brother those hoodlums deserve," he said, feeling the smile spread across his face at the thought of his younger siblings. All of them, even the two who were married and living lives beyond the house where they'd all grown up in Miami.

Adah caught the smile and turned away to put her drink on the shelf nearby, something unreadable on her face. When she turned back to him, Kingsley saw envy, admiration.

"Do you have any siblings?" he asked.

The look on her face changed, became one of pain. "No. Not anymore."

Damn. "You don't have to talk about it if you don't want to."

She fumbled for her glass and took a long swallow from it, draining it down to half. "Good, then I won't." She put the drink back and her head lolled in the hammock as she looked at him, then away toward the horizon where the sun was beginning to spread the warm colors of sunset. After a moment's quiet, she looked back at him. "Am I a downer or what? Pretty soon I won't have anything we can talk about without me crying my eyes out."

"I haven't seen any tears today. You must be talking about another Adah." He caressed the tops of her feet again, wishing he could take all her sorrow away. When she allowed herself joy, she lit up like the sky at noon.

A shaky smile claimed her mouth. "You're surprisingly sweet."

"I'd prefer another adjective, but I'll work with that for now." She bit the corner of her lip, obviously still uncomfortable about where their conversation had meandered before. Kingsley brushed his fingertips along the softness of her toes, her ankles, the bottoms of her feet.

"Oh my God, stop!" She jerked against him,

laughter gushing from her mouth as she yanked her feet away from his hands. With her feet safely out of his reach, her laughter trailed away. She blinked at him as if he'd just betrayed her.

"I guess you're ticklish then."

"Don't even think about it."

"I won't. Promise."

Although she watched him with suspicion, she slowly brought her feet back to him, her muscles tense in preparation to pull back again.

"I always keep my promises, Adah." He said the words very seriously.

"Okay." She relaxed against him again, and he only held her feet between his palms, thumbs making soothing circles around her ankle bones.

"Now, tell me," he said once she was no longer on the brink of flying away from him in a flap of limbs like some startled exotic bird. "What things have you done since you've been here? If I'm going to distract you with an escape, I need to know what you like."

Her lashes flickered low over her eyes, sleepy-tipsy; then she began to talk.

Adah talked like she wanted to release everything. Her exhaustion, her commitments, the secret desires she'd held for herself and away from everyone who knew her.

"I thought about going skydiving, but what if I died?" Her lush eyebrows went up. "Maybe if I died, I wouldn't have to worry about marrying Bennett."

Kingsley let that comment go without making one

of his own, let her continue what was essentially a monologue on what she loved or thought she loved or wanted to try. He continued to caress her feet, delicate touches of his fingers that soon had her squirming against him while she talked and he responded with hums of agreement or some input on his own experience with that particular thing. He tried to ignore the minute movements of her body alongside his, the hot press of her thigh against his thigh, her hips rocking in a subtle but rhythmic motion that helped move the hammock in the breeze.

It built a slow arousal in him, the sensation of her skin beneath his fingers, her undulations, the purr of her voice entangled with the sound of the sea. The noise from the bar behind them seemed far away, so far away that he could easily pretend it didn't exist.

"I'm not too interested in De Palm Island, but I did try it once," he said in response to one of her comments.

"What did you think?"

"You should try it for yourself, then tell me what *you* think."

She tilted her head to look at him, her tongue caught between her teeth. Kingsley's fingers gripped tighter than they should have. He felt the catch of her breath in the way her feet moved, not a flinch but a twitch that spoke of something else than an awareness of pain.

A bolt of arousal churned Kingsley's hips in the hammock and her gaze dipped to his lap, and stayed.

"I don't think..."

When she didn't say anything else, he let go of her feet, tucked them together near his shoulder. He didn't mistake her look of disappointment for anything else, and it was that more than anything that made him climb from the hammock, making it sway dangerously. She gripped its edges, simply looking up at him, watching to see what else he would do.

Kingsley had nearly four drinks in him. He should leave this alone and go back to his house and handle things with a few strokes of his hand. Instead he climbed back into the hammock so they were facing the same direction, sighing in gratitude and anticipatory pleasure when she slid back to give him room. His hips in the hammock next to hers, then their legs stretching out together, their bellies touching, his head rising up higher than hers to look down into her waiting eyes and see what she would do, wait for what she would say.

"Kingsley..."

The way she said his name undid him. He cupped the back of her neck, moaning quietly at the arousal that pooled in his belly, heavy and warm. He could smell the rum punch on her breath, the lingering remains of some sort of flavored lip balm.

"There's a ride on the island you should try..." He dipped his mouth toward hers the same time that she moaned out a laugh, but it was perfect. *She* was perfect.

Their lips came together in an openmouthed kiss

that was immediately hungry, wet. Her mouth under his was so pulse-poundingly arousing that he cursed himself for not indulging again long before now. It might have been the place, the rush of the ocean over the sand—like a whisper of *yes, yes, yes*—it might have been the way her legs shifted against his as she turned into the shelter of the hammock, or it might have even been the sunset's burn in the sky above them. Whatever it was made him ache with lust and want and desire and everything in between.

Her hand slid up his chest, over his shirt to the bare skin of his throat. She was a yielding, soft thing to his kiss, but the way her hand drifted to his throat spoke of firmer desires. And he remembered all too well the way she'd raked her nails across his chest and nipples the night of Elina's party. He wanted that ferocity from her again. The ache in his groin demanded it.

She must have read his mind because her tongue slid firmly into his mouth, meeting his stroke for stroke, a wet snaking, powerful and fierce, that negated anything that he had ever thought about her being a tender thing to be seduced. She took her pleasure from the kiss just like he did, meeting the demanding caress of his tongue with one of her own, the wet slide of their mouth, the slow curl of her hips against his in the hammock. Their hips rocked together. Slow. Hard.

A dim part of Kingsley, the sober part, wanted to say something, wanted to stop himself, but their kiss was quickly becoming something beyond his control. He tightened his hand at the back of her neck and heard himself actually growl when she licked his mouth, her tongue hot and sweet, so damn good that he felt it all the way down to his toes and every spot in between.

Kingsley cursed. "I want you," he gasped into her mouth. "I want you so damn bad…"

He gripped Adah's hips to keep her still, the most he could do toward self-control, aware in some part of his mind of Josue's bar behind them somewhere in the darkness, the constant flow of customers moving to the bar, then away, tourists walking along the beach at a polite distance from the *palapas*. But Adah still squirmed against him. She rubbed her hard nipples against his chest through the layers of fabric, groaned her pleasure into his mouth.

He felt her hand slide down his chest, aware of every movement of her palm over the thin material of his shirt, nails scratching him through the cotton. His breath sped up, and he pressed even more into their kiss, gripping her tight to him with the spread of his hand at the back of her neck and the other traitorous hand on her hip, guiding her small movements against him. He ripped his mouth from hers, breathing too fast, trying not to embarrass himself in his shorts. But she wouldn't let him go, and he thanked every deity he could think of when she slid her hot palm under his shirt, over the shifting muscles of his back, then down over the rough denim of his shorts, guiding him in the intimate dance they were doing on the public beach.

"We shouldn't do this." Kingsley thought she was the one who spoke. It had to be her because he was beyond speech.

He felt the puff of her breath against his mouth before her tongue licked his teeth and slid against his again. A damp and ecstatic sound gathered lightning at the base of his spine. She *must* have said it. Or maybe he did. But then hands slipped between them. His or hers. And he felt the rough fabric of her jean shorts, the hard disk of her button, then her zipper. She moaned into his mouth, lips sliding away from his in a pant of hot breath against his ear, his jaw. He yanked down the front of her jeans, fumbled at the edge of the soft fabric of her panties and found—

Adah hissed in his ear, bit down on his shoulder, and that was all the incentive Kingsley needed to continue the creep of his fingers past the edge of her panties, over the coils of her pubic hair to the slickness of her waiting for him.

She sobbed into his throat. Her fingernails scraped down his back and clenched into the muscles of his ass through the rough denim shorts.

It felt so *good.* It felt so good they had to stop.

"Adah…we should—"

But she opened her legs, and he was lost. Heart stuttering in his chest as she flung her thigh over his and sank her nails deeper into his flesh. He claimed her mouth again, licking its hot interior the way he wanted to lick the womanly softness of her. She was wet and hot around his fingers, swollen with desire for him. He stroked her slickness, and she moaned.

His tongue flicked out and mirrored the motion of his fingers inside her panties and he could hear her panting through the scant space between their mouths when they pulled back from each other, gasping for breath, their mutual eagerness feeding the other, his fingers moving in her slickness, then up to the firm button of her pleasure. She jerked against him, a frantic motion that pushed the cradle of her hips against his hardness and made him even harder. The want throbbed so fiercely in his shorts that it *hurt*.

He gripped her hips again, this time to press himself even harder against her, the two of them moving in delicious counterpoint to each other, Kingsley high against her hip and Adah against the finger stroking her eager clitoris.

His head swam in the heady scent of their desire and he drank up the sounds she made, sucking her tongue, licking her lips, her teeth, nibbling at her throat, anything he could reach. He'd never tasted anything more tempting. He wanted more.

With a more deliberate and focused motion, Adah bucked against him as her fingers raked his back.

"I'm—"

"—close."

They bucked against each other in the same moment, her flesh tightening around his fingers. That was all it took to yank him over the threshold with her, a gush of heated wetness in his shorts. Dimly he thought he should be embarrassed, but the feel of his spilled desire only made him want to strip off her panties, her shorts, her little shirt, and lick her entire body until he became hard enough again to slide inside her body and take them both toward pleasure once more. He was nearly mindless with it.

Adah pulled her mouth away from Kingsley's and pressed her forehead into his throat. He held on to her, curving his palm protectively around her sex while small twitches and pulses moved her against him. His heart pounded in his chest; his breath huffed out of control. The sun had dipped completely behind the horizon and left the sky painted in violets and gray, clouds trailing across the deep bruise of it.

Slowly, as his breath came back to him, Kingsley rubbed the small of Adah's back while curses and recriminations slowly began to grow from the postorgasmic hush of his mind. Despite the lack of a real commitment to her man, what they'd just done was wrong. He didn't do this kind of thing. Ever. Kingsley licked his lips to speak.

But she beat him to it. "I shouldn't have done that. I'm sorry."

Although he'd wanted it as much as she had—maybe even more—Kingsley had to agree with her. The orgasm helped burn away the last of his alcohol buzz, and the resulting clarity was brutal.

"It's my fault. I shouldn't have let it get this far."

She was as still as death against him. “Me either.” Adah apologized again, apparently completely sober, too, and began to climb from the hammock. “I should go.”

Although Kingsley thought he was the one who should leave, the filthy state of his shorts stopped him from declaring his own intention. He swayed in the hammock after she climbed from it, feeling cold where her body had pressed so warmly against his before. Even in the dark, he felt the brush of her eyes over his crotch, the hem of his shirt dragged up to his bare chest and the new marks she’d made there.

He cursed again. “I’m sorry.” Because he’d been the one to climb into the hammock with her, to kiss her like the right belonged to him.

“I know,” she said.

Then she was gone.

Chapter 6

Adah made it back to her hotel on shaking legs. The cab ride there had given her enough time to replay every delicious yet horrible moment of her loss of control with Kingsley. She'd only had three drinks, only three, so it wasn't much of an excuse. Just like the last time she and Kingsley had ended up together. She was weak for him. Inexcusably weak. Well, maybe it had been four drinks.

"Adah, is that you?" Her mother's voice came through the slightly open door between their rooms.

Who else would it be in my hotel room? She thought the words but did not say them out loud. There was no reason to take out the result of her bad judgment on her mother.

"Yes, Mother." She sounded like a kid again, vulnerable and guilty, but she didn't have it in her to disguise her tone.

"Do you want to have dinner soon?" Her mother appeared in the doorway looking like she was on the way to a bridge game with the girls in a pale blue sheath dress and her hair braided in a high Cleopatra crown.

What Adah wanted to do was shower, then crawl into bed and stay there for the rest of her stay in Aruba. But she wasn't going to be a coward.

"That sounds great. Let me just take care of a few things first."

From the doorway, Thandie frowned, her eyes picking apart Adah's expression. "Are you okay, honey?" She started to come closer, bringing with her the powdery scent of her perfume.

But Adah quickly backed away. She wasn't sure she wouldn't collapse under the weight of her mother's concern and simply confess everything. "I'm fine. I just need a couple of minutes." She grabbed her phone off the bedside table and escaped into the bathroom.

With the door firmly closed and at her back, she dialed Bennett's number.

"Hey," she said when he answered. "Can you talk?"

Adah heard a busy hum in the background, the usual chaos whenever she called him. He never seemed to be alone or unoccupied.

"Not right now. But how about in an hour?"

"Okay. That sounds good."

"Cool."

Adah disconnected the call and put the phone on the edge of the sink. She pressed her lips together and stared at her reflection in the mirror. Trembling fingers lifted to touch her bruised-looking lips, the flush she could still feel in her cheeks.

She looked like she'd just climbed from a lover's bed. Hair messy and wild despite the braid she'd pulled it into only hours before. A bruise forming just under her jaw from the press of Kingsley's teeth.

Between her legs was slippery and hot, and without closing her eyes she could still feel Kingsley's touch, firm and insistent, between her thighs. A shivery pleasure undid her. She felt both loose and tight, like he'd sunk into the very being of her, leaving all of her sore and bruised and aching for more. Shame and regret coursed through her. Not because of what she'd done with Kingsley, or at least not completely, but because she wasn't being honest with herself. Not about what she wanted, not about what she would do.

Damn, she was spending a lot of time staring in the mirror after making a series of bad decisions where Kingsley was concerned.

But was it a bad decision?

The question came out of nowhere and caught her off guard.

You wanted to be with him. He's a man you're at-

tracted to and who's attracted to you. You enjoy him touching you in a way you haven't been in years.

Adah squirmed at the truth of it. She planned to call Bennett and confess, ask his forgiveness for something that really had nothing to do with him and everything to do with her. He probably wouldn't care much about what she did with another man before they officially bound their lives together. Bennett was practical. And he was no hypocrite.

Adah bit her lip, then turned away from the mirror. Time to wash the mistakes from her skin and get ready for Bennett's phone call. In the shower, she scrubbed her body under the near-scalding water, carefully washing between her legs while she tried not to think about Kingsley. She was mostly successful.

After her shower, she was sitting on the bed and about to slip into her sandals when her mother stepped through the door after a quick knock.

"Are you ready, darling?"

"Sure." Adah sighed, knowing that this wasn't just going to be dinner. It would be another interrogation. And it would be another disappointment. She couldn't give her mother the answer she needed, not yet. Not until she confessed what she'd done to Bennett and got her conscience clear so she could start their new life together in a way that made her feel okay about it all. And there was something that had been gnawing at her.

"Mother… Mama…" Adah pressed her lips together as words she wasn't sure she was ready for built up in her throat. Thinking about this pending marriage to Bennett over the past few months had brought so many things rushing to the front of her consciousness. Things that she'd gone through years of therapy for but still not managed to release.

"What is it, love?" Thandie stepped closer, concern in her face. Her hands fluttered up to gently press into Adah's cheeks. They both knew it wasn't every day Adah called her "Mama."

There was nothing for her to do but say it. "Do you wish it was me instead of Zoe who died?"

"What are you saying?" Her mother flinched back and her hands dropped away from Adah's face. "Why would I wish something like that?" She drew a trembling breath and took Adah's hands in hers. Her fingers were ice cold. "What's wrong, honey?"

"This marriage and the family business. It just seems like it would all be easier if Zoe was the one dealing with them instead of me. She would've been so much better at all of this."

"No, no! We almost lost both of you. You were in the hospital for so long after the accident…" Sudden tears washed down her mother's cheeks, and Adah felt instantly guilty. More guilt on top of the old. She'd nearly forgotten about her long hospital stay, the weeks she'd missed school. "Your father and I loved Zoe, and we love you, too," her mother said.

"We'd never trade you for her! Never. Don't say that again, please." Her voice broke. "Please."

Once Adah started, though, she couldn't stop. "I feel so guilty sometimes that I was the one who survived and not Zoe—"

"There's nothing for you to feel guilty about! You weren't driving the car that took Zoe away from us. You didn't do anything wrong."

"I can't help what I feel. You want this marriage so badly and I—"

"You don't want to go through with it?" Thandie shook her head quickly, not waiting for Adah to finish. "You don't have to do this if you don't want to. *Any* of it." She squeezed Adah's hands so hard it hurt. "Your father and I have been proud of you all these years. We love you. If you don't want this, all you have to do is say so."

Adah didn't believe for a moment it was that simple. Palmer-Mitchell Naturals needed rescue. Perhaps not at this moment, but definitely sometime in the very near future. If the merger with Leilani's Pearls didn't go through because of Adah, not only would her parents be disappointed; the business they'd nurtured for years would be left in ruins.

"Mama, I don't—"

A knock on her door cut off the rest of her words. She frowned and exchanged a look with her mother, who squeezed her hands once more before releasing them.

"Are you expecting company?" Her tone was soft, but something in Thandie's face said who she thought it might be.

"No." Even though she hadn't known him long, she was sure Kingsley would never show up at her door unannounced. That was her habit of bad behavior, not his. She went to answer the knock, feeling her mother's eyes on her with every step. Frowning, she opened the door.

"Has it been an hour yet?"

Adah stared at Bennett. "Hi!"

"I figure a visit is better than a call. What do you say?"

Bennett Randal stood in the doorway, larger than life and smiling with mischief in his cinnamon-brown eyes. He wore blue suede shoes, slim-fitting jeans and a pale blue dress shirt rolled up at the elbows.

Adah blinked at Bennett, unable to get over her shock at seeing him. He didn't wait for her welcome, or lack thereof. He stepped into the room and greeted Adah's mother.

"It's good to see you, Mrs. Palmer-Mitchell," he said, dropping a kiss on the older woman's jaw and making the mouthful of a last name sound both elegant and easy.

"What a pleasant surprise." Her mother welcomed him with a warm hug. "Adah and I were just about to go out for dinner. Would you care to join us?" A smile as wide as all of Aruba lit up her face.

Bennett glanced over his shoulder at Adah, who could do nothing but stare at him. "Well, if you don't mind, I'd actually like to have some time alone with Adah. It's been a while since she and I saw each other, and I believe we have a lot to discuss."

"Of course, of course." Her mother looked more and more pleased with each passing moment. "I can have room service brought up for myself, or head out to join some new friends who're dining in town tonight." She made a shooing motion, like she was passing Adah off to Bennett.

"Thank you." He kissed her cheek again before making his way to Adah. "Are you ready?"

"Um…yes. Sure. Let me…let me just grab my bag." She still didn't know what to expect from Bennett's surprise visit. The ground was shifting too quickly under her feet.

"Good," Bennett said with his trademark dimpled smile.

After she grabbed her purse, clutching the small leather strap like a lifeline, she fell in step with Bennett, who waited in the middle of the room, completely at ease in his designer jeans and platinum watch, looking curiously around the room. If it had been anyone but Bennett, Adah would've cringed at the untidiness. But Bennett was familiar enough with how she kept her living space, had visited her in college enough times to see the piles of clothes and books stacked on various surfaces, her laundry basket full with weeks' worth of laundry.

If it had been Kingsley, on the other hand... She yanked her mind away from Kingsley. There was only one direction things would go from there, and she wasn't ready to think those thoughts with her mother or Bennett standing right there.

"Let's go," she said to Bennett. "I'm ready."

"Excellent. A buddy of mine told me about this place that's supposed to have real Aruban food. We'll head there and see what the rest of the night holds."

They said good-night to Adah's ecstatic mother and stepped out into the hallway. Away from her mother's probing gaze, Adah drew a steadying breath. "What are you doing here? I thought you were in Monaco or Dubai someplace."

"I was, but I figure I was needed more urgently here. Plus the partying over there gets a little stale after a while."

"I'll take your word for it," Adah said with a reluctant smile.

"Please do."

Despite her feelings on what happened between her and Kingsley, just Bennett's very presence brought her close enough to a good mood. He loved and lived life with such joie de vivre and passion that being around him was like getting a shot of energy.

She didn't know where he found the stamina to be all over the world, all over Atlanta, party until dawn, then perform his duties as chief strategy officer for his family's company. His job was luckily one he could perform remotely, and he did it well if current profitability statistics that her parents routinely shared were anything to go by.

Naturally, Bennett had rented a car when he got to the island. He guided Adah to a white compact car in the hotel's parking lot and opened the door for her, waited until she was properly settled in the passenger seat before firmly closing the door. He sank into the driver's seat and started the engine.

"So how are things going with my wayward fiancée?" He skillfully guided the car out of the nearly full parking lot and onto the road like he knew where he was going. Maybe he did; maybe he was as familiar with the island as Kingsley was.

Adah ducked her head, wincing at the thought of the man she apparently couldn't get out of her mind for five damn seconds. "Don't even joke about that."

"That bad, huh?"

She sighed and fiddled with her seat belt, ready to tell him everything, or at least the edited version of what had happened between her and Kingsley on the beach. "I can't go through with the wedding." She blinked. That was *not* what she'd planned to say.

"Okay," Bennett said.

She felt his eyes on her, a comforting sensation

despite her own dawning horror of what just came out of her mouth. "That's all you're going to tell me?"

"Do you want me to say more?" Bennett tilted a playful brow her way. "No one is going to force you to marry me, Adah. I've seen you struggle with this decision practically since the day you made it. The only person dragging you kicking and screaming to the altar is you."

"Don't say that!"

He chuckled. It wasn't a mean sound, but it did make her feel a little foolish. "Having our families joined by this damn agreement would be great for the company and for the idea that our parents had, and the key word here is *had*. But we adapt and change to circumstances, my girl. And this, you falling for some surfer in the middle of nowhere—"

"He's not a surfer!" She sputtered despite herself.

"Definitely qualifies as a change in circumstances," Bennett finished.

Adah pressed her palms against her face and shook her head. She was still wrestling with the words that had jumped out of her mouth without permission. Was she willing to commit to them and call off the wedding based on nothing but a couple of heavy petting sessions and eleventh-hour jitters?

"I just can't do this," she said again. "I…he and I hung out today and things went further than I planned."

Bennett took his gaze from the road to glance at her in surprise. "You finally got some?"

Her face flushed. “Oh my God, stop! You’re just as bad as Selene.”

Another smile, something warmer, almost indulgent, flickered across his mouth. “There are worse comparisons you could make.”

He was right about that. Selene was one of the best women, the best *people*, she knew in the world. Adah remembered telling her friend about the plan to marry Bennett and save Palmer-Mitchell Naturals. Selene had asked her if she was sure, talked her through the cons of her decision and later comforted her when the doubts struck.

Selene never thought the decision was the right one, but when Adah, in a fit of annoyance, had snapped at her to drop the subject, Selene let it go and never brought up her reservations again. And even as the years went by and Adah began to voice her own doubts, not once had Selene said “I told you so.” Adah didn’t think that, in the reversed position, she would have been that noble. She sighed.

“So what’s up with you and this guy anyway?” Bennett asked. “Are you two trying to elope or something?” He skillfully guided the car through the narrow streets, one hand on the wheel while he changed gears with the other, occasionally glancing away from the road to rest his gaze on her face. “I hope you’re not basing a life decision on the ability of one guy to rock your world.”

"Please! I'm not that impulsive." *Almost, but not quite.*

"Just making sure, love. You know I have no problem with you changing your mind about this marriage thing. Our parents will get over it and make other plans, but I don't want you to get hurt. Not even by your own decisions."

Adah tucked her tongue between her lips, thinking very carefully before she spoke. "It's not about him—I mean, yes, I met him and he…affected me in ways I never expected, but I've been indecisive for a while now. You know that."

"I do. I do." He pulled the car into the parking lot of a one-story colonial building, the gravel crunching under the tires. "As long as you do, too. Men are interesting creatures." He looked at her as he turned off the engine. "And by interesting, I mean we think with our dicks most times. And we assume women think with their hearts and make decisions based on their lust for marriage, or whatever. If he knows the whole story, he might think you're breaking this thing off just for him. That might scare him off."

Adah shook her head. "I don't think that'll happen. I've been pretty clear that, I'm…" What exactly was she doing anyway?

"Just having fun in Aruba and he could've been any guy as far as your sweet little libido is concerned?"

She laughed, even while heat flooded her cheeks. Bennett had always been able to make her blush and laugh easily. "Not exactly. But it's been really physical between us, and I want to explore that without feeling guilty about hurting you." Although they both knew Bennett wouldn't be hurt by anything she did. She wondered if he even had a jealous bone in his body. He applied his own "live and let live" attitude to everybody around him.

He gave her a look that said exactly that. "Watch out for your own tender bits, little one."

Adah shook her head, smiling so widely that her cheeks hurt. How could she have thought marriage would work between her and someone who called her these ridiculous names? *Little one.* She loved him for that and for his overall tenderness, and for never pretending the feelings between them were something different from what they were.

"I love you, Bennett."

He helped her out of the car with a grin. "Don't let your mother hear you say that. She'll get the wrong idea."

At the mention of her mother, Adah rolled her eyes and dared to make a joke. "It's not her fault you're perfect son-in-law material."

They walked into the restaurant together, a homey space with paintings of different landmarks around Aruba hung on the walls, glass display cases containing small pieces of handmade local jewelry for sale, and tables spread out at a comfortable distance from one another.

The host immediately greeted and seated them

and had barely turned to go back to his post when a waiter came with water and an offer to get them something stronger. The waiter took their orders and quickly left, the height of efficiency and good customer service.

"Mama's going to kill me when she finds out I called off our engagement," Adah said once they were alone again.

Bennett laughed at her. "You'll survive this, and so will she."

"And the family business?"

"It'll be fine, too."

Since the marriage agreement had been made, Leilani's Pearls, thanks to Bennett's hard work and business sense, had recovered to the point where they didn't really need Adah's parents anymore. Any decision Adah made now would affect her family more so than Bennett's.

Adah cursed. "I feel so selfish right now."

"It's not selfish to want to be happy, doll."

"Of course you'd say that."

"It doesn't make it any less true." He tapped the back of her hand with two fingers, his version of reassurance. "Life is too damn short to make sacrifices this big."

Across the table from her, he looked relaxed and happy, a man without a care in the world. Would he be sacrificing anything if their marriage went on as planned?

"What about you, Bennett? Isn't there anyone who makes you reconsider any of this?"

He drew his hand back and braced his forearms against the table. The handsome planes of his face went blank as he seemed to think about his answer. "There's someone I would give this all up for if she was interested in me the way I'm interested in her," he finally said. "But she isn't, so my feelings don't matter."

Adah drew back, surprise blowing into her chest like a sonic boom. She'd asked the question almost as a hypothetical, believing that someone like Bennett simply lived and loved because he wanted to, not in reaction to the fact that a woman didn't want him the way he wanted her. "I'm so sorry," she said softly.

"Don't feel sorry for me, doll face. I got over that a long time ago."

She didn't believe him. "Okay…"

The waiter came then to bring their drinks and took orders for their meals. Bennett took a slow sip of his wine and gave Adah a pained look. "I didn't come here to talk about me," he said.

"And I didn't come to Aruba to fall into bed with a well-hung stranger either."

Bennett cringed the same time Adah did. "That was *way* too much information."

"I know, right?" She pressed fingers to her lips, embarrassed and shocked at herself. "I don't even know—" But she cut herself off before anything else could come out of her mouth. Bennett was already looking at her in disbelief.

"So you haven't even slept with this stud yet?"

"Sort of. I mean, we..." She blushed as she said the words, unable to continue.

"Again, even though I just asked, let's just keep it to broad strokes, shall we?"

A giggle bubbled up from Adah's throat. "So to speak."

"An unfortunate choice of words." He grimaced like he'd just found out where babies actually came from, and she nearly doubled over in laughter, reaching for his hand across the table and holding fast, so grateful for him and the way he was able to help her forget about her problems.

"I'm so glad you came tonight."

He smiled back and squeezed her hand. "Good. I figured face-to-face was the best way to have this conversation. That way you couldn't bullshit your way out of what you needed to say."

"I was going to call you and confess all my sins, then agree to set the wedding date."

"My little martyr."

The sound of laughter near the entrance of the restaurant drew Adah's gaze. A blonde head appeared—Annika from the nighttime snorkeling trip. She had her hands in the pockets of a stylish jumpsuit that skimmed her model-lean figure. Still laughing, she turned her head to look at someone walking up behind her. A blond man Adah didn't recognize. Then

Kingsley walked in, gorgeous in a white, open-necked shirt and dark jeans. Adah lost her breath.

Although he seemed completely engaged in the conversation with Annika, he looked around the restaurant as he walked in and immediately saw Adah. His eyes narrowed, and the animated look on his face become more subdued.

She snatched her hand from Bennett's. With a complete lack of tact, he turned to look toward the source of the noise and took in what was going on with a quick sweep of his gaze.

"That's your new friend?" But it was more of a statement than a question. "We should go say hello." His dimples flashed with mischief.

Adah frantically shook her head.

"No. We shouldn't." But telling Bennett what to do was like telling lightning not to strike. He gave Kingsley an appraising look, watched him and his party get seated on the opposite side of the small restaurant. Just as Bennett was about to get up and make a nuisance of himself, their food arrived. Adah breathed a soft sigh of relief.

But she had no sooner picked up her fork to eat when a quiet presence moving across the restaurant and toward their table drew her attention. She looked up with the fork clenched in her hand.

"Adah." Kingsley approached the table with the confident and predatory rock of his hips that made

Adah's mouth water. "I didn't expect to see you again today."

Again. Both she and Bennett would have had to be deaf not to hear the significance of that word.

She cleared her throat. "It's good to see you." She deliberately avoided the word *again*, then swallowed, put her fork down. "I didn't think I'd leave the hotel for the rest of the night, but Bennett paid a surprise visit." She gestured to him sitting across the table from her, and he stood up, holding out his hand to shake.

"I've heard a lot about you," he said to Kingsley, and Adah wanted to kick him.

Kingsley offered his own hand and his first name. "I may have heard a thing or two about you."

Was it her imagination or did he grip Bennett's hand a little too hard?

"Will you be in town long?" Kingsley asked after he released Bennett's hand. He stuffed his hands in the pockets of his slacks, the equivalent, Adah thought, of wiping off his hands.

"Not very." Bennett stayed standing. "I'm making a quick stop over to see this lovely young woman before I head back to the States."

"Well, I hope you enjoy everything the island has to offer while you're here. It's a beautiful place, and not only because Adah is here." He dipped his head once to indicate Adah and to catch her eye.

"I'll keep that in mind," Bennett said, his eyes flashing merciless amusement at Adah's expense.

A hiccup of awkward silence made Adah want to say something, but she held her tongue before something stupid could trip off of it. More seconds of stilted silence ticked by while the two men loomed over her, looking at each other.

"I'll let you get back to your meal," Kingsley finally said. "It was good to meet you—Brandon, was it?"

Bennett corrected him with a cheerful flash of teeth. "Same here." He sank down into his chair before Kingsley could step away, apparently bored of the game now. "I'm sure I'll see you again."

"I'm not so confident of that. But we'll see what the future holds." He looked at Adah again. "Take care."

She swallowed the hard lump in her throat and could only nod at him before he turned away and headed back to his friends. Adah could hear their voices speaking in Dutch and laughing easily. She didn't watch him walk away. She couldn't.

"Well. He certainly wants a repeat performance."

Adah ducked her head, still unable to speak. Her stomach was twisted up in knots and the food that seemed so appetizing before now made her turn away in revulsion.

"You okay, little one?" Bennett asked, taking her hand.

"Not really."

"Do you want to leave?"

She shook her head, and her entire body trembled

with the violence of the motion. "No. Let's stay. I know you're hungry. I'll get over this."

But it was unbearable. Kingsley's presence had destroyed any sense of equilibrium she'd found after her conversation with Bennett. Nearly an hour later, with her plate mostly full and her stomach still too twisted to do any of the formerly delicious-looking food justice, Adah wished she was anywhere but in the restaurant where she could still hear the sound of Kingsley and his friends' conversation, the rumbling bass of his voice, their laughter that continued uninterrupted.

Bennett put down cash for the meal, his dessert finished.

"Let's go. Any more of this and I feel like I'm torturing you." He didn't wait for her to get up, just pushed his seat back at the same time she gave him a grateful look, her chest still tight with discomfort while her belly churned, a twisted roller coaster. He helped her from her chair and guided her out of the restaurant, apparently trying to be subtle with the placement of his body between her and where Kingsley was sitting.

In the car, he started the engine without comment. When they were back on the road, coasting toward Adah's hotel, she felt his eyes on her again.

"Is there any place you want me to drop you?"

It was such a pointed question that she caught her breath. He wasn't suggesting…? "Wouldn't that be a little presumptuous of me? He might not even go back home after the restaurant."

"He might not. You're right." Bennett tapped his fingers on the steering wheel in thought. "Come out for a drink with me—then I can drop you off at his place later tonight."

Adah wanted to say no. She shouldn't go to Kingsley's and disrupt his life any more than she already had. But the desire to see him was a sudden and demanding ache. Once Bennett suggested it, there was nothing else she wanted more.

"No," she said. "I won't drink tonight, but I will have some ice cream with you." She nearly looked away in embarrassment at Bennett's knowing grin.

"That's my girl." Bennett flashed her a smile and squeezed her shoulder. "Where should I take the fair princess?"

They ended up near Palm Beach and the high-rise hotels. The gelato place Adah chose was the best she'd found on the island so far with enough flavors to satisfy her taste for variety. She insisted on treating Bennett to a second dessert, and they walked through the small shopping area that was alive with browsing tourists and the slow meandering of cars on the small side street.

"Thank you again for this," she said.

Finally, her intense reaction to Kingsley's presence at the restaurant was beginning to subside. The awareness of him was still there, a faint pulse beat under her skin, but it was no longer a fight-or-flight impulse that would only lead to recklessness.

"I couldn't do any less for one of my best girls."

Adah laughed. "I'm not sure what I should say to that."

"How about 'thank you'?"

"Thank you, Bennett." She looped her arm through his, and they walked on.

He kept up an amusing patter of conversation, distracting her with the unusual things he'd done since they'd seen each other last, the people who'd asked him about her in Atlanta, his plans for his family's business and the timeline for implementing them. He was so driven, so skilled that she half regretted his loss from her family. He was the perfect son that her parents had never had.

They meandered back the way they had come, passing the same restaurants again, their gelatos long finished. Despite the street lamps, the darkness felt heavy, rich with possibility. And the significance of that, and the fact that it had nothing to do with Bennett, made her fingers twitch where they rested around her purse strap. Bennett was nothing if not observant.

"You ready to get dropped off?" He showed her the glittering face of his watch. Nearly two hours had passed since they'd left the restaurant.

Adah's fingers tightened on her purse strap. "Sure. Yes." The word wavered in the air, sounding uncertain. Adah tried again. "Yes, I'm ready." This time her voice was stronger. But that still didn't hide how nervous she was.

"We don't have to go right now if you don't want to. There's nothing pressing I need to do either tonight or tomorrow."

God, she loved this man. "Let's walk for a little longer. I can pick up a souvenir for Selene."

"Okay. Let's do it."

But the little time she bought herself getting the aloe skin care set for Selene passed all too quickly. Barely an hour later, she stood on the front step of Kingsley's house while the taillights of Bennett's car retreated into the distance.

She thought of what she would say to Kingsley, how she would explain herself. The memory of another time she'd tried to do the same thing, and how it had failed, came back to haunt her. But there were no dogs chasing her tonight.

Adah rapped her knuckles against the wooden door.

After two rounds of knocking, though, any confidence she had evaporated when Kingsley didn't come to the door. She glanced at his truck parked in the drive, walked back to feel the still-warm hood under the tentative touch of her hand. Adah knocked on the door again, then again. No answer.

Was he spending the night with Annika?

Adah breathed deeply to push away the disappointment and dismay crowding into her throat. She took a step back, ready to call for a cab back to her hotel. Her hand fell to the door handle, and she reflexively gripped it. A click and the door eased back on quiet hinges.

Startled, Adah stared at the triangle of darkness just inside the door, then walked in without allowing herself to fully think about what she was doing. Timid footsteps drew her into the shadowed living room, its dimensions gradually becoming clear through the moonlight cascading past open blinds, showing her the sparse furniture, the hallway leading to more private rooms.

Softly, she called out Kingsley's name, but there was no reply. Her hands clenched at her sides. She took a step back. Then a step forward, then another until the shadows of the hallway brushed her shoulders, her face. All the doors off the hallway were open.

The first room showed the silent silhouette of a powder room, the other a furnished but otherwise empty bedroom, and the last... Adah drew in a deep and steadying breath.

Kingsley slept naked. His screened windows were open and allowed in the coolness of the night breeze. There were no curtains over them to flap, no blinds to tap distractingly to the rhythm of the fierce wind, no papers to flutter madly about the room. Just Kingsley lying heavily in the bed on top of white sheets, his legs splayed wide, arms above his head, his face turned away from the bedroom door.

Adah truly felt like an intruder. She bit her lip and

took a step back. But the figure in the bed shifted, legs, hips, chest, arms. A full-body movement that dragged her gaze all over him until at last she was looking at his face and his eyes staring at her. Those eyes widened slightly, but other than that, Kingsley gave no sign of being surprised.

"Another unexpected visit, Doe Eyes?" His voice was sleep roughened and dragged along her sensitive nerves, hot and urgent.

She licked her lips. "I wanted to explain about what you saw at the restaurant."

"You don't owe me any sort of explanation." Kingsley scrubbed a hand over his face, grabbed for his cell phone on the bedside table and glanced at its clock before he put it back and gave her his full attention. "You were having a lovely meal with your fiancé. Nothing any woman should have to explain. Especially not to a man she barely knows."

She wanted to tell him not to dismiss his importance to her so easily. She wanted to tell him so many things.

"He's not my fiancé," she settled on saying.

"Fiancé-to-be, then."

"Not even that."

Kingsley sat up in the bed and put his back to the headboard. He drew a deep breath. "What are you saying?" The question sounded weighted, expectant. Or maybe that was just Adah's foolish hope.

"He and I agreed to call off our potential engagement. It wouldn't have worked between us. Bennett is a very good friend. Nothing more."

"From what I've seen, good marriages have been based on less," he said.

Adah didn't want to talk about marriages. She licked her lips, nervous and on the brink of flight. "Do you want me to leave?"

Kingsley's gaze moved down her body, then up, a slow drag full of intent and desire. Then he shifted in the bed again, raising the knee closer to her to shield his lap in a way he hadn't seemed worried about doing before. Instead of replying, he held out his hand.

Adah swallowed. Was this what she wanted? The question seemed foolish enough with the desire pooling like liquid fire in her belly. She was walking across the room to him before she could think anything else. She slid off her sandals and knelt on the bed. His hand closed around hers, warm and firm. He pulled her the rest of the distance across the sheets and against him. With her heart fluttering madly in her chest, she was hyperaware of his nakedness, the press of her clothed body against him, the hot slide of his palm against hers, then his hands along the backs of her hands, up her arms, then higher to clasp just above her elbows.

"I've already told you what I want, Doe Eyes. Now it's your turn."

She shivered at the intensity in his voice, rough

and soft at once, as it rubbed over her sensitive nerves and laid her bare to her own desires.

"I want you," she said. "I've always wanted you."

He didn't seem surprised by her confession. If anything, her words seemed to only confirm what he already knew about the flood of desire that took her over whenever she saw him and thought of him.

"Good," he said. "Now we're finally on the same page."

"And in the same bed."

In the moonlight falling into the room, she saw the corners of his mouth curve up, beautiful and unashamed. No amusement this time, just a predatory certainty.

"Yes," he said. "Finally."

His eyes captured and held hers; then his hand crept to the back of her dress and pulled the zipper down. His fingers traced the line of skin the zipper revealed, a light caress until he reached the end of the zipper at her tailbone and Adah was trembling with need.

"Show me what you want," he said, voice growling, hand on her hip.

She flushed under her open dress while her mind conjured it perfectly. Having him just like this, under her and inside her. Adah crawled over Kingsley, straddled him and pushed him until he lay flat on his back, watching her with his night-dark eyes. He was already hard for her.

Under her flattened palms, his chest rose and fell

with steady, even breaths. She raked her fingers over his muscled pecs, through his chest hair. Even in the dark of night, he was unmistakably gorgeous. A hard and virile man willing to please her.

She slid her parted thighs over his, their flesh brushing with the sound of whispers. "This is what I want," she said.

The long nights in her lonely bed when she did nothing but think of him despite other things looming on her horizon had prepared her for this moment, his skin under hers, the wetness sticking her underwear to her body, him groaning when she settled her bottom on the hard jut of his desire.

"Then take it," he said.

The breath shivered out of her. "Do you…do you have anything?"

Without taking his eyes from her, Kingsley reached back for the drawer of his bedside table, hand fumbling inside until it emerged with a six-pack strip of condoms. He pulled one off and dropped the others on top of the table.

"Just in case," he breathed.

Adah smiled and took the condom from him. "Yeah…?"

He drew in a deep breath when she touched him, his abs tightening, fingers clenching on their tight hold on her hips. He was silk-covered steel in her hand, beautiful and ready for her. With his hardness grasped in her fist, she hovered over him, tugged aside her panties, then slowly lowered herself. Inch by delicious inch.

"Adah..."

She hissed at the stretch of him inside her but didn't stop until she was fully seated on top of him, their pubic hair a delicious and damp tangle. Her dress hung off one shoulder, just a breath away from falling down and showing Kingsley the eager hardness of her nipples.

"If you don't... God...if you don't move soon, you're going to kill me," he groaned out, his fingers flexing and curving around her waist, biting into her skin through the dress. His hips bucked up. Once. Kingsley muttered an apology, his face strained with self-control.

"Okay." She breathed out the word, matched his motion. "Oh!"

The pleasure made her vision go white, and she dug her nails into his chest. He gasped but didn't move. From the way he lay there, watching her while desire made him wet his lips and caused his breath to come faster, he planned on letting her do exactly what she wanted. Adah moved again, pressing down on him in a slow grind that stroked her deeply and sent fire racing through her. She moved faster. Tangled her fingers in his chest hair.

"God. Damn..." Kingsley bucked up into her and grasped her breasts through her dress, his thumb unerringly finding her nipples poking at the thin cloth.

A bolt of pleasure sizzled between Adah's nipples and the hot place between her thighs. She arched into his touch, snaked on top of him in search of more of the sweetness pouring through her body. She rode him faster, building the feeling, pushing the harsh sounds of her breath and his into the darkened room. The dress fell completely from her shoulders, and he gripped her exposed breasts, squeezed her nipples to pull her arousal higher and higher. It had been so long. So damn long.

The peak of her pleasure slammed into her, a sudden avalanche of feeling that dropped her down into him, crying out and gasping for breath. Her sweat-slick chest against his. Her heart galloped madly. Kingsley caught her, grabbed the back of her neck and brought her open mouth to his in a desperate and sloppy kiss. Then she was on her back, and he was rising over her, pushing her thighs even wider to expose where they were still joined. He pushed her dress up to her waist.

"My turn!" he breathed into her mouth.

He slammed into her, and she gasped at the sensation of him moving against her still-sensitive flesh, plunging into her again and again while she just held on, gripping his back, her neck arched. Adah cried out Kingsley's name. The sound of their sex was a liquid syncopation in the room as he took her again and again. And her desire rose again, swimming up to meet his.

"You feel so good," he groaned into her throat, his thrusts getting more erratic until he froze, buried at the deepest point inside her, spilling himself into the condom. She clenched her thighs against him, rubbing against him, wanting more.

He lifted his head, his eyes glittering and lips parted from his gasping breaths. "More?"

Mindless with want, she reached between them to touch herself. "Yes!"

Kingsley shoved her hand away and replaced it with his own, pulled out of her even though he was still hard. Her eyes rolled back in her head when he stroked her clitoris, slid what felt like three fingers into her clenching wetness.

"I have more," he growled.

Through the night, he gave and she took, then he took and she gave, an unending ouroboros of sex. When one was exhausted, the other took the reins and yoked pleasure around them again. The sheets dampened. The strip of condoms grew smaller. Every inch of Adah became almost too sensitive to touch, but she didn't want to stop. It was nearly dawn when Adah fell into an exhausted sleep on top of Kingsley, the two of them tangled together, the pillows tossed on the floor and room heady with the smell of their hard-won satisfaction.

Adah ached in the most wonderful way. She stretched in the soft sheets and felt the pull of muscles she hadn't used in years, the throb of bruises on her bare hips and her wrists where he'd held her down as he filled her over and over again with hard proof of his desire.

She rolled over in the bed, smiling around a moan of pleasure that slid past her lips. Faint sunlight from the bare window poured over her, warm and delicious, its tendrils sinking into her body with the sensation of a caress. Adah felt absolutely *amazing*. This intense physical satisfaction was something she could get used to, no matter how long it lasted. She opened her eyes to share the feeling with Kingsley. But she was alone in the bedroom.

Surprised, she sat up, and the sheets fell away to her waist, leaving her even more exposed to the blossoming sunrise. With her eyes fully open, she saw that her dress had been carefully folded and placed in the chair near the window, her purse on top of them, and her shoes tucked side by side on the floor.

She called Kingsley's name, once, then twice, but all she received in return was silence. No note rested on the bedside table. No smells of breakfast being made floated in from the kitchen. She frowned. The warmth she'd felt from their night of sensational sex began to fade. Quickly, she left the bed and got dressed.

After a quick exploration of the small house, she found the rest of it empty. No note. No idea of where he'd gone. Her first thought was to find him at the Hi-Winds Tournament. From what she remembered of the schedule, there was a men's kite-boarding race taking place that day, but it was in the afternoon. With the corner of her lip tucked between her teeth, she replayed the night before. The touches, the things they'd said to each other, what she may have said to him to scare him out of his own house.

All she remembered, though, was a passion-filled night and the hope for more before she went back home. No promises given or asked for. Just really, really good sex.

But on their after-dinner walk, Bennett had said something that haunted Adah now. *Men pay for sex with commitment and love, he'd told her. Women pay for love and commitment with sex. If he's like most guys in his situation, he probably thinks you want some sort of commitment from him to replace the one you're giving up with me.*

Adah had disagreed with him. Kingsley wasn't stupid enough to think something like that. She blinked and looked around the room, wondering. The longer she stood in the cold silence of the house, the more the words reverberated in her head. Did Kingsley really think she wanted that much more from him? The silence didn't give her another reason for his absence.

Okay then...

She fought the sharp stab of disappointment that he was the kind of coward to run away instead of telling her he didn't want more than a vacation screw. After washing her face and brushing her teeth with his toothpaste and her finger, she called a taxi and left his house the way she'd found it.

The taxi came quickly. The ride was unfortunately just long enough for her to replay everything that happened between her and Kingsley. The sex had been nothing short of amazing. The way he touched her, like he thought she was worthy of both lust and tenderness. He met her bite for bite, kiss for kiss, the fires of desire between them rising and falling through the night, only fully extinguishing when they both passed out from exhaustion.

Adah would have gladly loved to repeat the experience. But not if he was too much of a coward to tell her the limits of what he wanted and what he was willing to give.

She asked the driver to drop her off just short of the hotel. She walked the rest of the way and took a detour along the beach. The sun was rising still, and the island was faintly cool from the night's embrace. She shivered in her sundress and brushed her palms up her arms in a search for warmth.

Farther up the beach and just past her hotel, a group of people gathered in fluttering, semiformal clothes. A wedding. Or at least the end of one. Purple cloth, fine as gossamer, roped off an aisle leading to an arched arbor near the very edge of the beach and a few feet from the rush and retreat of the sea.

Nearly a dozen people gathered around a couple taking photographs while the purple cloth wavered in the early morning breeze. The wedding attendees all wore shades of yellow, and the bride and groom both wore white. The guests lifted full champagne flutes in the air and, after a toast that Adah couldn't hear, drank from their glasses before raining applause down on the newlyweds. Everyone looked happy.

Chapter 7

"Was it that good, or that bad?" Gage ashed his cigarette in the small saucer by his side.

Kingsley didn't say anything. He slumped down into the sand beside his friend and almost wished for a cigarette to clench between his teeth. What he really wanted to do was slip back into bed with Adah. It had been hell to leave her in the sheets that smelled like the two of them and were still warm from her body.

"Ah." Gage's teeth flashed in the low morning light. "You ran out on her like a little b—"

"No." Kingsley sighed. "Well, yes." He wasn't a strong believer in self-delusion.

He didn't know what he'd been thinking. Or

maybe that was it. He *hadn't* been thinking when he'd crawled out of bed and, after grabbing his clothes, out of the house. A walk through his neighborhood hadn't answered any of his questions, so it wasn't too long before he found himself on the comfortable stretch of beach where he and Gage occasionally swam, hosted parties, even slept on particularly debauched nights. And it hadn't been a surprise to see his friend awake and wandering the beach, smoking his habitual clove cigarette, hands shoved into the pockets of his cutoff shorts, his unbuttoned shirt blowing in the breeze.

Kingsley had wordlessly joined him, and they walked together toward the very edge of the beach, where the water flirted with their toes.

"So what's up with you and this chick, then? I thought you liked her."

Although Gage didn't hang around with Annika, Carlos and the rest, he knew just as much about what Kingsley got up to while on the island. They were good friends, not as tight as he was with his best friend, Victor, but nearly so.

"I *do* like her," Kingsley said. "That's the problem."

"Oh come on, dude." Gage blew out a stream of scented smoke. "Don't tell me you're one of those types who backs off as soon as the girl they're chasing shows some reciprocal interest."

"No, it's not that."

"Then what is it?"

It was a question Kingsley didn't want to answer. He liked Adah. He liked her to the point of distraction. She was beautiful, and sexy, and vulnerable even with her sharp edges. The problem was that after less than a week he liked her and enjoyed her company more than any other woman's. He wanted more of her. More time. More sex. More of everything. He was nervous about the sharp urgency of it all. But he was also nervous about something else.

"She was supposed to get engaged."

"I heard *was* in that sentence," Gage said.

"Yeah. She broke it off."

"Good. No problem. You can screw her guilt-free. I know you're one of those moral guys, all twisted about stuff like that."

Kingsley laughed. "Yeah. I typically think about right and wrong."

Although it *had* been a close thing with her warm and tempting in the hammock the night before when he knew all about the potential fiancé and still put his hand in her pants.

"She dumped him, and now she's probably looking to find a replacement. I'm not ready for that."

Gage drew on his cigarette, and the tip glowed hot in the low morning light. He blew the smoke toward the sky. "Did you ask her that mess, or just assume?"

"What else am I supposed to assume? She's at the age when most women get married. She just got rid of a fiancé out of necessity, and now she needs a replacement."

"You're assuming she's looking at this, at marriage, like a business arrangement. She's not the CEO of a billion-dollar business. From what you told me, she's not much of a businesswoman." He sucked on his cigarette again. "No shade, though."

Kingsley leaned forward to balance his elbows on his knees. His back twinged and his thighs burned, reminding him sharply of the night before, as if he even needed a reminder. Down on the beach, a couple in matching shorts and tank tops jogged past. He wondered vaguely if Adah was into things like that. Couples jogging. Matching outfits.

"Her parents need an investor to save their company. I looked into their business. It needs the help." Then he told his friend the whole story.

Gage narrowed his eyes, took his time sucking the last from the cigarette and ground down the butt into the white saucer between them.

"So, you're saying to me that you just had sex with a woman you've been calling all kinds of saint and gorgeous and everything else the last couple of days." Gage pinned him with a piercing stare. "You're talking about how she may be the one you've been looking for, and now that you got her into bed, now that she tossed aside this guy she's never even had sex with but promised herself to out of some crazy sense of family duty, now that she's done all that, you're saying she's some sort of a corporate gold digger using her body to get you to do what…?"

When Gage put it that way… "I'm not sure," Kingsley said. But his summary was accurate enough. He rubbed the back of his neck and cursed under his breath.

"You, my friend, are something else." Gage picked up the ashtray and stood up, the wind blowing his long curls away from his face. "Stay as long as you want. I gotta get ready for work." He walked away from Kingsley, taking the nearly hidden path toward his house far up on the beach.

With Gage gone, the sound of the wind seemed to pick up, rattling in Kingsley's ears like an accusation, taking up the slack where his friend left off.

Was he really that kind of guy? Kingsley stared at the peaking sun with the denials rising up in his mind. Of course, that's not what his actions meant. He wasn't looking for an excuse not to be with Adah now that she was free and could be with him as little or as much as he wanted. And he didn't want anything permanent. She was beautiful, and he was single. He just wanted some fun.

But maybe that was what she wanted, too? Gage's words rang in his ears again.

Kingsley let the sun rise over him, heating his body and bringing the sweat to the surface of his skin, warming to the point where he could smell himself, and smell Adah, too. He drew in a deep breath and took in all of it. His feelings, the sun, the lingering traces of her that clung to him like perfume.

He wanted to see her again. He wanted to touch her again. And as much as he was afraid of what *she* wanted, he was terrified of his own need that rose up in him every time he was around her.

Most nights, as he lay in bed and thought about her, it felt too intense to be real. A throbbing awareness that was more than sexual desire. More than simply enjoying the company of a beautiful woman. More intense than anything he'd ever experienced before.

With the sun free of the horizon and burning brightly in the sky like the realizations tumbling through his mind, he finally stood up and brushed off the bottom of his shorts. He drew a steadying breath and began to make his way home.

But when he got into the house, she wasn't there. Not that he could blame her. With no lover and no note, he could hardly expect her to just sit around and wait for him. Standing in the doorway of the bedroom that still smelled like their sex, he wanted nothing more than to have her back there again. In his arms. In his bed.

He needed to speak with her. He needed to see her.

After a quick shower and a change into presentable clothes—he didn't want to look like a complete bum if he ran into Adah's mother again—he drove to Adah's hotel. As he walked up to the front desk, he cursed under his breath, realizing he didn't know her last name.

As he walked up to the desk, he realized the woman there was vaguely familiar. Maybe she knew him enough to give him the information he wanted without him downright begging for it. He put on his most charming smile.

"Good morning, miss."

The woman looked up, smiling, from the stack of papers she'd been making notations on, a pen clasped between her fingers. Her smile disappeared when she saw Kingsley's face.

"Good morning, sir. May I help you?"

This was not his lucky day. The woman who looked back at him with a near scowl on her pretty face was one of the women who'd offered him the foursome days before. He'd assumed they were all tourists, but this was one of the girls who hadn't talked much. And even then, her Dutch accent had simply marked her as another visitor from the Netherlands enjoying the warmth of Aruba before going back to her European tundra. Faint malice stirred in her eyes.

Kingsley could see it was a lost cause, but he tried anyway. "I'd like to have one of your guests called, please."

Her eyes glinted. He could tell she wanted to say something about meeting him on the beach, maybe even about him leaving them high and dry at the hotel, but she pressed her lips together instead and shook her head. "Do you know this person's name or room number?"

"Her name is Adah." He looked her straight in the eyes. At least he knew her by more than just Doe Eyes now. Not that he'd get anywhere asking this particular woman for any information.

"And her last name?"

He clenched his teeth. "I don't know it." He might as well have just confessed to a one-night stand with a stranger. Someone he'd chosen over this woman and her two friends.

"Then I'm afraid I won't be able to help you." Her smile from earlier came back, pleased and sharp. "Sir."

He purposely kept his hands loose on top of the counter while he mentally searched for any clues to Adah's full name or how to get this woman to give up the room number, or at least call Adah and let her know he was down there waiting to see her. His eyes flicked up to the woman's hair, and its fall down her back despite the island heat. *Hair products.* Her family's business. An image of the jar his sister used on her hair nearly every day flashed in his mind.

"Mitchell," he said. "Adah Mitchell."

The smile fell away from the woman's face. With obvious reluctance, she typed something into the computer. When she finished whatever search she made, her sharp smile was back.

"I'm afraid we don't have an Adah Mitchell here," she said.

"Are you sure?" He resisted the urge to grab the

computer and yank it toward him so he could see for himself. "How about Adah Palmer?"

Just then another employee, this time a man, wearing a burgundy bow tie neatly tucked under the collar of his starched white shirt, appeared behind the desk.

"Excuse me, sir," Kingsley said. "Can you verify something for me?"

"Of course, I'll be more than happy to." After a puzzled look at his coworker, he sat in front of another computer station and tapped the mouse. "What can I do for you?"

The woman looked ready to throw something at him, but Kingsley was unbothered. He asked the young man about Adah.

"We don't have an Adah Mitchell or Palmer registered but we do have an Adah Palmer-Mitchell who checked out early this morning."

"Checked out? This morning?" It was barely eight o'clock.

"Yes, sir. She is no longer a guest with us."

Kingsley cursed under his breath. "All right. Thank you very much for your help." He turned to the woman, who still watched him with poison in her eyes. "And you, too."

He left the hotel and went back home, ignoring the alarm on his phone he'd set to remind him of his tournament later that morning. Online, he found out more about Adah Palmer-Mitchell than he'd known before. She lived in Atlanta and was the co-owner a fancy day care. Seeing photos of her on the computer only reinforced how far he was away from her, and what an idiot he'd been. Kingsley shut his laptop down and called his secretary.

Chapter 8

Kingsley glanced down at his phone when it vibrated for the third time in as many minutes.

Did you find the place OK?

Then:

Are you having trouble getting her? We put you on the list.

Then finally:

Let us know when you have her, OK?

He restrained himself from rolling his eyes, but just barely. His brother Wolfe had asked him to pick up his daughter from her Atlanta day care since he and his wife were stuck in a meeting that ran later than expected. It was only pure luck that Kingsley was even in town. Three weeks after leaving Aruba, he was still desperately searching for Adah. Every one of his online or phone leads had stopped at a dead end. Like she was being deliberately protected by someone or something. He stopped himself from outright hiring a private investigator. That would be creepy and strange. Instead, he'd taken a few days out of the office and flown to Atlanta himself, determined to find her the old-fashioned way.

So far he hadn't had any luck. But he was at least able to spend a day or so with his brother and sister-in-law, who were working an unexpectedly long-term business project in Atlanta. They'd been in the city for months and had their young daughter, Yasmine, with them.

And today, Wolfe had volunteered Kingsley to pick Yasmine up from day care.

Kingsley stuck his phone in the inside pocket of his blazer and climbed out of his rental SUV, opening the back door to check for the fifth or sixth time the stability of the car seat. He'd thought about using the day care's parking lot, but since he had to make a couple of phone calls before he got out, he didn't want to seem like a creep lurking in a place with children, especially a place where they didn't know him from Adam.

Kingsley shut and locked the car door with a chirp of the remote, then crossed the quiet street littered with pink summer blossoms from the trees swaying overhead. The music of children's voices rang up and down the tree-lined block.

The building in front of him was an attractive, two-story brick Georgian straight out of a fairy tale with kudzu clambering up its walls, and a small attic room framed in white perched on top of the roof. A low iron fence separated the wide front yard from the street, and a brick walkway led from the gate up to the short flight of steps and the wide porch.

He pressed the buzzer to the building, making sure to look straight into the camera he immediately noticed above the door.

"Good afternoon, sir." A warm voice greeted him after an electronic pulse. "How can I help you?"

"Good afternoon. I'm here to pick up Yasmine Diallo. I'm her uncle, Kingsley Diallo. Her parents should have my information on the appropriate list."

"One moment, sir."

The voice disappeared, then after about half a minute came back, welcoming him into the building.

The inside of Rosebud Academy was just as impressive as the outside, both professional and warm, with the person belonging to the voice on the other side of the intercom just a few feet from the door. A slim young man sat behind the desk, a laptop open in front of him that clearly showed a picture of Kingsley and a scanned copy of documents Kingsley couldn't make out from where he stood.

"Welcome to Rosebud Academy, sir."

"Thanks." He felt like he was about to pick up a stash of gold bricks. "What do I need to do now?"

"Yasmine is in her play session. It's almost over, so you can go there and pick her up." He gestured to a woman nearby Kingsley hadn't noticed before. "Mariah will escort you there."

In her low heels, black slacks and military-looking blouse, Mariah seemed official, welcoming *and* perfectly capable of kicking his ass if he so much as looked sideways at one of the kids. If he ever thought about enrolling any of his currently nonexistent kids into a day care of any kind, this was the type of place he'd want. He felt eyes on him at every step of the way, the setup of the school making it clear the welfare and safety of the children were top priorities.

Mariah walked beside Kingsley and made pleasant if forgettable conversation, guiding him down a brightly lit hallway with framed art on the walls. The air smelled faintly of lemons.

"Here we are." She stopped at a door leading outside, scanned a card attached to a lanyard around her neck and opened the door.

The backyard was another fairy tale. A high brick fence was decorated with colorful, wooden butterflies, snails and other creatures in large enough sizes for the kids to appreciate. The grass was lush and freshly cut, while swing sets and jungle gyms in miniature sat on one side of the large backyard next to a clearly marked area for hopscotch and jacks. Ten children who looked no older than three sat, ran and played on the spotless Astroturf in the center of the otherwise grassy yard. Everything was in perfect geometric order but still managed to convey a sense of warmth that the children seemed happy enough in.

Mariah pointed to Yasmine, but he'd already seen her. Tiny and coily-haired, she sat opposite another girl on the Astroturf, rolling an ambulance toward the girl's fire truck. They sat together, smiling and chatting in whatever common language they'd found while three women carefully watched the children, walking between them, sometimes stopping to ask questions or even playing with them.

A pair of legs stepped between Kingsley and his view of Yasmine and he tilted his head to glance around them and catch his niece's eye. But then something made him look up, heart suddenly beating triple time as he traced those bare feminine legs up to a close-fitting gray skirt and a pink blouse comfortable enough to wear in the summer heat, its collar loose around a slender throat. Adah's throat.

Unlike the version of her in Aruba, who had her hair in a ponytail or in thick waves down to her shoulders, this Adah wore her hair twisted to the crown of her head in a wispy bun with delicate tendrils floating around her face. She looked both professional and breathtakingly gorgeous.

Kingsley stared. The woman was in profile to him but it was unmistakably her. Smiling down at a boy who moments before had seemed on the verge of throwing a tantrum because neither of the girls nearby wanted to play with him. Kneeling down so she was at eye level, Adah soothed the boy with a touch and soon he was smiling back at her and showing her the toy train he'd discovered nearby.

Even though he'd been searching for Adah for nearly three weeks, all Kingsley could do was stare at her. It was like all his prayers had been answered in one heady rush. Kneeling only a few feet from Kingsley, she nodded and looked interested in everything the boy had to say, obviously encouraging him to show her how the toy train worked and distracting him from the tantrum he'd been working up to. Her face was gentle and smiling. She looked better than fine, even better than the last time Kingsley had seen her. In his bed.

The memory of her sleeping in his sheets shook him from his paralysis. He strode toward her, but his niece chose that moment to look up and, despite the fact that the woman he'd chased almost two thousand miles was kneeling temptingly close, he changed direction and headed toward Yasmine instead.

"Uncle King!" she gurgled softly and laughed, yanking at her playmate's sweater to point at Kingsley. "Uncle," she said again.

Adah stood up then, her eyes wide, a hand going to her waist. At first she stared at Kingsley like she didn't recognize him. Then he remembered he was wearing a suit, a bespoke Tom Ford that was just one of many in his closet and part of his CEO uniform. It was a *very* different outfit from the one he'd worn the last time they'd seen each other. Granted, he'd been naked at the time.

Before he reached Yasmine, Adah rushed over to him, careful of the children scattered like so many flower petals around her feet. She gripped his arm, and he felt her touch through every layer of cloth, smelled the unforgettable sweetness of her.

"What are you doing here?"

Before Kingsley could answer, Adah was dragging him away from Yasmine and toward the door he'd stepped through with Mariah moments before. Mariah, though she frowned in confusion, immediately stepped out onto the yard to take up watch where Adah had been. Kingsley took a moment to admire how efficient the place was run before he allowed himself to be propelled through the door, down the hallway with a click of Adah's heels and into an office.

"What are you doing here?" she asked again. "You can't be here."

Away from the children, her mask of control dropped away. She dropped his arm and stepped all the way across the room and behind her desk as soon as they were behind the closed door together.

About to explain about his niece and the reason

he was at the day care, Kingsley frowned. "Why can't I be here?"

"The children..." she stuttered. "This is my life. I left you behind in Aruba." She stood up even straighter, her palms pressed against her belly while light from the wall of windows behind her haloed her rigid figure. "Just like you left me that morning."

Kingsley locked his muscles to hold off the tremors, a reaction to her words, he could feel gathering. This wasn't going to be an easy discussion. Not about him leaving her in bed that last morning, and definitely not about the reason he was in Atlanta searching for her. And though he'd put so much energy into finding her and trying to explain, now he was simply tongue-tied and didn't know what to say to make her listen to him.

"I'm sorry." That was a decent start.

But she didn't seem impressed. "That's what you came here for? That could have been an email. That could have been something you said to your priest and kept it moving."

He winced. It wasn't like he didn't deserve her scorn, though. "I was an idiot," he said. "I made some assumptions and acted on them without even talking with you." He was too embarrassed to say what those assumptions were. But her face said he didn't have to. His cowardly behavior that morning said plainly what he'd been afraid of.

"I wasn't ready to be anyone's fiancé." He said the words out loud anyway, just to get his stupidity out there. "That's what I thought that morning. That's why I ran."

Just like Kingsley thought, he wasn't telling her anything she hadn't thought of herself. "And now you're here, do you still think that?" Adah shifted, arms crossing over her chest, her feet planted wide.

Before he could answer, a knock sounded on the door. Adah looked toward it and raised her voice.

"Yes?"

"It's getting late, Adah. Perhaps Mr. Diallo needs to make an appointment to speak with you at another time when it's not so close to dismissal." It was Mariah on the other side of the door, as levelheaded as Kingsley expected her to be, brief though their acquaintance had been.

"We'll only be a few more moments, Mariah. I promise not to let him kidnap any of the children on his way out."

The dead silence from the other side of the door gave Kingsley an idea just how funny Mariah thought that comment was.

"I only came to take one child with me," he said raising his voice so the woman on the other side of the door could hear him. "I don't want Mariah to gut me based on your bad jokes."

"I'll tell Yasmine you'll be out here shortly," Mariah called back to him the same moment Adah drew a sharp breath and slapped her palms down on the desk as if to brace herself against a blow. The fading sound of Mariah's practical shoes against the floor dominated the brief silence.

"You have a child here?" Adah asked softly, her tone making it clear that she'd not only felt betrayed by him in Aruba, but expected the same treatment from him here, as well.

"My niece is here," he rushed to explain. "Yasmine Diallo."

"Oh." Her face softened just the tiniest bit. The hydraulic chair behind the desk hissed softly as she sat down. "She's beautiful."

"Yes, she is. Beautiful babies do tend to run in our family."

"Not to boast or anything?" Adah raised her brows in question and leaned back in the chair. She looked, suddenly, exhausted. Outside when he'd first seen her, she'd looked even better than the last time they were together. Now that they were away from the chaos of the children and the distractions of other people, he saw the signs of skillfully applied makeup, a slight puffiness around her eyes. She looked stressed.

"How is your mother?" he asked. "Did she let you out of the agreement without any trouble?"

"She did, actually." A faint smile touched her face. "It was all so much easier than I thought. It hasn't taken her long to come to terms with my decision. She's almost happier now."

"Good."

Silence, broken only by the faint hum of the air

conditioner, closed in on them. The wall of windows behind her looked out onto the backyard with the children, but the glass was visibly tinted, allowing light in, but not unwelcome eyes.

Kingsley felt awkward looming above Adah in her own office. He sat in the chair across from her desk and shifted to be as comfortable as he could in an uncomfortable situation. "Do you regret it?" he asked her.

"Regret what?"

"Any of it."

Adah sighed again and dipped her head to stare thoughtfully at the neatly arranged surface of her desk while Kingsley watched her every move. His belly clenched tight, he prepared himself for her to say she regretted meeting him and hated the night they spent together.

She lifted her head and met his gaze. "No. I don't."

If Kingsley had any doubts he was doing the right thing by chasing Adah to the other side of her world, they all vanished with that one look. He'd pursued her, seduced her from her promises to another man, then run off like a coward and a fool once she ended up in his bed. Still, she didn't hate him.

Here, in her everyday life, she was as lovely as she'd been under the Aruban moonlight. Seductively sweet with her plush mouth and angular cheeks. Compelling from him the desire to make her smile, make her respond to him, make her stay. This wasn't just about vacation sex. On the island, it had actually scared him how much he felt for her. He wasn't scared anymore.

"Will you have dinner with me tonight?"

The mask of indifference fell back over her face, and she stiffened. "Why?"

"Because I've missed you." It felt freeing to say the words.

"How can you miss someone you never had?" she asked.

"I never had you, but I shared your company, and I thought we enjoyed each other."

She shook her head, the mask slipping when she bit the corner of her mouth.

Something terrible suddenly occurred to him, and he sat up in the chair. "Are you seeing someone?"

"No!" She looked like he'd just accused her of murder. "You came into this place by complete happenstance. You didn't know I work here. I just… I don't want you to ask me out because you think it's what I want. I'm not going to force you to pretend you want to still fool around with me just because the world is a small place." Adah drew a breath, looking everywhere but at Kingsley's face. "We slept together, and it's really no big deal."

"It is a big deal to *me*," he said, very carefully weighing his next words. "Sure, I stumbled into you here by pure dumb luck, but I've been searching all over the place. Online, off-line, everything. I searched so much that it felt like you were trying to hide from me."

"I..." Her eyes flickered wide in surprise as she seemed to take in what he just said. "I'm not into the social media thing and the business is listed as an LLC."

"That explains it. I guess I'll have to get to know you properly the old-fashioned way."

"The 'old-fashioned way'?" she asked softly. "That's a little too late for us—don't you think?"

The memory of their night together flared abruptly to life in Kingsley and he had to clench every muscle in his body before his reaction became too obvious. He cleared his throat.

"Nothing is too late for us," he said. "Have dinner with me and we can start over, do things the right way." He paused, wanting desperately for her to say yes. But he didn't want to look too eager either. "So...is that a yes?"

She breathed a gentle laugh. "Okay."

"Tonight?"

Adah laughed again. "Tonight."

"Seven o'clock?"

"Let's do eight instead," she said. "I have a few things to take care of first."

She gave him her home address, and he tried to play it cool as he typed it into his phone. But he was pretty sure she saw his hands trembling. After he'd gathered Yasmine in the car seat and taken her to Wolfe and Nichelle's rented condo, amused and fed her until they showed up nearly two hours later, he realized he didn't want to wait until dinnertime to see Adah again. It was at least another two hours away. He'd searched for her for nearly three weeks. Another two hours was too long for him to wait.

So as soon as Wolfe and Nichelle were settled in with their daughter, he left and went back to the day care. When he got there, only two cars waited in the parking lot. He pressed the buzzer on the porch's intercom system and waited. And waited. He was about to turn away and head back to his car when the intercom crackled to life. Her voice sounded through the electronic box and he smiled in relief.

"You know we're closed." But there was warmth in her words.

"Yes, but I figured you'd make an exception for me."

"You're very cocky," she said as the door released with a soft electronic chime.

"You would know," he said the last under his breath, and he slipped through the door, making sure it closed and locked firmly behind him.

Without bothering to ask where she was, he followed his memory to her office where he found her seated behind her desk and watching the door expectantly.

"I wasn't going to cancel on you tonight," she said.

"I know." He closed her door and leaned back against it, shoving his hands in his pockets. "I didn't want to wait," he said.

Adah looked at her watch. "Dinner is less than two hours from now. Are you that impatient?" But there was a flare of something in her eyes, something that matched the answering fire low in his belly.

"Yes, I am." He finally gave up his nonchalant pose by the door and crossed to her desk while she watched him with a fraction of the hunger he felt building inside him.

"I really did look for you everywhere," he said. "I bribed people to tell me where you lived. I think I even called in a favor from an old girlfriend who works at the DMV. Nobody would tell me anything about you."

He leaned on her desk, his palms flat on its surface in a mirror of the pose she had taken when facing him earlier that day. The desk felt cool under his hands, his own body well on its way toward overheating.

"Whatever you want to know, all you have to do is ask me." She leaned back in her chair and smiled serenely up at him.

"Will you marry me?" The words tumbled up out of his hot throat.

"What?" Her serenity disappeared. She shoved back from the desk with the explosion of sound, looking at him like he was crazy. Maybe he *was* crazy.

Kingsley swallowed convulsively, shocked at himself. He wasn't an impulsive man. Not by any means, but this… He opened his mouth to take the words back but immediately realized he didn't want to.

It wasn't his fear of Adah asking too much that

had made him run; it was because he wanted her so immediately and completely in his life that it frightened him. His own desires, raw and unfamiliar, for one woman and one woman alone had made him question everything. From fear of the unrelenting firing squad of those questions, he'd simply pulled on his running shoes and fled like his very life depended on it.

He didn't need to run anymore.

"Will you marry me, Adah Palmer-Mitchell? I want you in my life. I want to snorkel with you and make love with you all night, then breakfast in the morning. I want to share *everything* with you. Will you have me?"

"I…I don't know. This is a little soon, isn't it?" She stared at him, her eyelashes fluttering in agitation.

Was it too soon to know whether or not you wanted to spend the rest of your life with someone who made your pulse race, your heart soar and your moods light? Kingsley knew at some point, it could be too *late*, and he didn't want that.

He knew he was acting impulsively, but he also knew he was doing the right thing. With her wide eyes firmly on him, Adah stood up from behind the desk, a slow rising to her feet that revealed to him again the sweetly slender form, her hips clad in the gray skirt still somehow managing to be alluring despite its conservative shade. She watched him as if she expected him to flinch back and run like a startled animal.

"Ask me again." She rounded the desk, her footsteps soundless on the thin carpet.

He asked without hesitation.

"Okay." She reached his side of the desk, her scent of ginger and sugar undoing him breath by breath. "If you're still in Atlanta in the morning, I'll give you a proper answer."

Kingsley moved even closer to her, breathing her in after an absence that had nearly torn him apart. Her answer wasn't exactly the one he wanted, but he could work with it. For now, her breath and her presence were enough.

"Can I still see you tonight?" he asked, every breath he took spiced by her sweet scent.

Adah pressed her lips together, her eyes darting down his body, then away. She sighed, the look on her face one he recognized as the one she wore when she was accusing herself of doing or saying something stupid.

"I… Yes." With a delicate twist of her body that brought Kingsley's eyes skimming her waist and hips, she turned away to grab a notepad from her desk and scribble something on it. "This is my phone number. Call if you're going to be late."

He took the note like it was a lifeline. "I won't be late."

"Good. See you then."

Chapter 9

At 6:53 p.m., Adah clutched her cell phone and told her mother that no, she didn't need to come over. But Thandie Palmer-Mitchell could ignore her child like a pro, and within thirty minutes, she appeared at Adah's front door with a bottle of red wine and a bowl of sliced fruit.

"I have some deconstructed sangria." She held up the bottle and fruit as she walked past Adah and into the apartment. "You can tell me what's wrong while we put this thing together." She dropped her purse and scarf on the couch, then looked searchingly at Adah. "I heard something strange in your voice earlier so don't waste your breath telling me nothing is wrong."

Ever since Aruba and the broken pre-engagement, her mother had been even more attentive than usual. Adah was consumed with panic and fear about disappointing her parents, and was sure her mother sensed those emotions.

"Mother… Mama, everything is fine. I just had a little surprise today—that's all. Nothing to worry about," Adah said.

But Kingsley showing up at her workplace in his designer suit had been more than a *little* surprise. He looked like a completely different person away from the sea and the tropical sun, his unforgettable body clothed in a tailored suit. But the look in his eyes had been the same. Alternate hunger and amusement. Like he wanted to both devour her and laugh with her. Maybe both at the same time.

Adah shivered at the thought, then glanced at her watch. How long did her mother plan on being here?

After the first *and* last time her mother and Kingsley met, Adah wasn't eager for the two of them to see each other again. At least not until she was certain where she and Kingsley stood. He said he was done running. But lip service was something Adah was very familiar with. After all, she'd been giving her mother plenty of it over the years when it came to her proposed marriage with Bennett. Adah sighed and reluctantly followed her mother into the kitchen.

"Mama, I promise you I'm okay." She stopped herself from looking at her watch, knowing damn well she only had about twenty minutes until Kingsley showed up. If he was the punctual type.

"I don't believe you, darling." Her mother was pouring the wine over the fruit in a punch bowl. "I don't want you to feel alone in whatever you're going through. I made you a promise, and I intend to keep it."

Adah smiled, warmed by her mother's words. It meant everything that they'd come out on the other end of the marriage disaster with their relationship stronger than before. But she also didn't want it all to implode when Kingsley showed up at her doorstep.

Her mother had taken the broken potential engagement better than Adah thought she would. It also helped that less than a week later, a billion-dollar beauty corporation even Adah had heard of made her parents an offer of partnership with Palmer-Mitchell Naturals that had the family celebrating for days.

"Now we just need to let this soak for about an hour or so while we talk." Her mother looked so pleased with herself that Adah didn't have the heart to throw her out.

She nibbled on her bottom lip despite the lipstick she'd freshened up a few minutes before. "In that case, there's something I need to—" The doorbell rang, cutting her off.

Her mother frowned. "Are you expecting someone else, darling?"

I wasn't expecting you, Adah thought. But she bit her tongue and threw a glance toward the front door, then back to her mother. "I invited a friend over," she said, making her way toward the door.

"A *friend*?" Her mother braced her palms on top of the kitchen counter, frown firmly in place. There was no way she'd misinterpreted what kind of friend Adah had invited to her apartment. "So soon?"

Adah blushed and turned away, alternately wanting to placate her mother and needing to invite Kingsley in so he wouldn't disappear again. "He's actually someone I knew from before."

Her mother followed her from the kitchen, her high heels tapping against the hardwood floors like the sound of a telltale heart, which only made Adah's actual heart beat faster in nervousness and dread. She drew a breath and pulled open the door.

Of course it was Kingsley. And he looked…

Her heartbeat raced in her chest, but this time the reason for it was completely different. Even with her mother behind her, Adah couldn't stop her body from responding to him. He'd changed into another three-piece suit. This one was a dark gray with a tie and pocket square the same gold as his skin. The vest accentuated his flat belly, and she dropped her eyes immediately to where it parted in an inverted V just above his crotch. Adah licked her lips and swallowed.

"I'm a little early," he said, his voice a deep bass settling hard in her belly.

If her mother hadn't been in the room, Adah would have dragged him into her apartment and jumped him. Maybe it was a good thing her mother was there after all. In lieu of doing what she really wanted, she devoured his gorgeous body with her eyes.

"Adah, aren't you going to introduce us?"

Kingsley looked over her shoulder at her mother's words, and Adah forced her mind to focus.

"Um…come in." She stepped back to invite him inside. To Thandie she said, "You've met him before. At the hotel in Aruba."

Her mother drew in a shocked breath. She started to speak the same time Kingsley said, "If this is a bad time, I can come back."

"No!" Adah practically shouted. She ignored her mother's surprise, and half hoped she would allow him the same courtesy she'd shown Bennett when he showed up at her door in Aruba. But no such luck. Instead her mother stepped forward with her hand extended.

"I'm Thandie Palmer-Mitchell," she said. "And you are?"

Adah squeezed her eyes shut in embarrassment. "Mother…"

But Kingsley was already stepping forward to shake her mother's hand. "Kingsley Diallo, ma'am. I'm interested in marrying your daughter."

The resulting silence didn't last long.

"Why only *interested*?" Her mother glanced up at Kingsley with her arms crossed. From the look on her face, she might as well have been looking down at him. Kingsley didn't seem the least bit intimidated.

Instead, he stood respectfully quiet, nodding once at the loaded question.

"Because your daughter hasn't told me yes."

Her mother made a show of examining Kingsley from head to toe. The frown she'd been wearing deepened even more. "I know you," she said.

"Mama, I already told you. You met him at the hotel in Aruba. He just has more clothes on." Adah bit her tongue after she said the last part, wondering what the hell was wrong with her.

"No, there's something else…" Her mother's eyes widened, and a hand went to her throat. If she'd been wearing pearls, Adah swore she would have clutched them. "Are you one of the Miami Diallos?"

"I am, ma'am." Kingsley said it calmly while Adah was the one to frown now. What did where he lived have to do with anything?

"Oh." Her mother looked shell-shocked.

"Mama? Are you okay?" Adah stared at her mother, then at Kingsley, confused.

"Yes, love," her mother said, but she still looked like she'd just received the surprise of her life. "I'm going to leave you to your…whatever it is you and Mr. Diallo have planned for tonight. You can have the sangria anytime you like." Then she was gathering her purse and scarf from where she'd dropped them on the couch. "We'll talk later." She nodded at Kingsley. "Let me know how your proposal goes."

He smiled. "I will, ma'am."

Once her mother pulled the front door shut behind her, Adah turned to Kingsley. "What was that about?"

"A business proposition my company presented to her last week. Nothing you have to worry about."

But Adah couldn't let it go so easily. "Wait a minute. You're from the Diallo Corporation?"

He nodded. "Is that going to be a problem for you?"

"But…but…" She couldn't even think of a proper objection. He'd basically saved her parents' business, no, her *family's* business. Because of his connection with her.

"It was business," he said with a shrug, walking toward her with a compelling and graceful movement of hips that made her mouth water. "It makes sense to us. You brought Palmer-Mitchell Naturals to my attention, but after talking it over with the board, they agree the partnership makes good business sense."

"Oh." Adah felt like she was losing the basic ability to speak.

"Now, about you and me…" A lopsided smile tugged at his sinful mouth and took whatever else was left of Adah's reasoning abilities.

She stayed right where she was while he stalked toward her. "What about you and me?" The words didn't leave her mouth above a whisper.

Earlier when he'd asked her that ridiculous question, she'd been shocked. This from the man who ran from the passionate bed they'd shared as if it were on fire. It didn't make any sense. She'd just left one engagement behind, for God's sake.

But between the moment he'd left her at the day care and when he appeared at her front door, she'd relived what it had been like without him over the last few weeks. Not just the sex she'd ached for, even though it had been unforgettably good. But the way he'd brought his own light into her life. His fearlessness, his humor, his strength. It didn't matter he was suddenly a millionaire or billionaire able to be the savior to Palmer-Mitchell Naturals her parents wanted. He was what *she* wanted.

"Be with me." His breath whispered against her lips. "However you want to do this, just be with me."

His words rang through her, resonating with every desire she'd ever had. "Yes," Adah said while the feeling rose up inside her like the sun-washed tides of an unforgettable Aruban sea. "Always, yes."

She met his lips halfway and allowed his desire, and hers, to sweep her completely away.

* * * * *

TRUST IN US

ALTONYA WASHINGTON

To my mom and dad, Alphonso and Carolyn Washington. Thanks for being the leaders of the best support team any author could ask for!

Chapter 1

"It'd be real nice of you to have this all wrapped up by the time I get back."

"Now, you know I'm good, boss. But even I won't boast that I could make that happen in a couple of days."

Gage Vincent kept his eyes fixed on the open folder, which had been hoarding his attention for the past ten minutes. The response from his assistant commanded a smile that accentuated his words with imminent laughter when he finally spoke.

"Jay wants ten days, I'm giving him ten days," Gage told the young man who occupied the paper-littered sofa on the other side of the office suite.

Webb Reese's chuckle was a touch muffled behind the papers he held close to his attractive, heavily bearded face. "*You* taking a ten-day break? That'll be a first."

Gage's face held a stony yet sly expression.

In a show of defense, Webb raised his hands, sending the papers sprinkling down onto the black suede of the sofa. "Just sayin'," he sang.

Gage returned his focus to the folder, shut it and gave it a wave in Webb's direction. "Time to start earning that insane salary I'm paying you."

Webb's nod was brief. His earlier playfulness had now adopted a more solemn element. "You're really leaving it all up to me?"

Gage's lone dimple made a quick appearance when he smiled that time. "You've earned it." He watched Webb come forward to claim the file.

"This is a big deal, boss." Webb emphasized the reminder by giving the folder a deliberate shake.

"Sure is." A thick glossy brow rose with challenging intent and Gage studied his assistant of five years with a look of mock suspicion. "Have you learned nothing from your vast experience in my presence?"

Webb attempted to laugh over the tease but seemed too nervous to do so.

Taking pity, Gage pushed aside the other files that required his attention. He reared back in his desk chair while leveling a deep chocolaty-brown stare at Webb.

"I'm leaving this to you because I trust you to handle it right." Gage inclined his head slightly when he noticed Webb's eyes widen. "I have a building full of people who'd be happy to chime in with their two cents, argue against your points of view and suggest I fire you upon my return."

Webb laughed then.

The "building full of people" Gage had referred to—more specifically, the senior executive staff—were all employed by Vincent Industries and Development, or VID, as it was more affectionately known locally—in and around Charlotte, NC—nationally and internationally.

"I need someone to have my back on this, Webb." Gage was serious, which was made evident by the intermittent flash of the lighter hues in his rich gaze. "You're the only one who knows my tastes. You know what offers I think have merit and which ones I think are bullshit. In short, you won't just accept a bid based on the amount of zeroes it brings with it. You'll look at the people the bid is attached to, their backgrounds, the people attached to them and *their* backgrounds."

Webb's emerging toothy smile hinted at his appreciation of Gage's words.

"Are you saying you don't think your top circle of people will care about those things?" he asked.

"My *top circle* cares about the money they make me." Gage reared back again in the desk chair, which coordinated with the sofa and other office furnishings. "That's one reason they belong to my *top circle*—because *I* care about the money they make me.

"But I also care about the pockets that money comes from before it comes to mine," Gage shared once the round of low laughter between him and Webb subsided. "That care involves certain hands-on work that I won't be able to be a part of, as I'll be off somewhere wasting my time."

Webb's laughter then sounded abrupt. "Dang, sir, you make it sound like a hassle."

"A hassle." Gage focused on a point across his expansive office and appeared to be turning the word over in his mind as he reflected upon the observation. "It's not exactly a hassle. I just don't see the positive in bringing together the bridal party before the wedding." He shrugged, sending a ripple through the crisp fabric of the olive-green shirt he wore.

"You've known me and my gang long enough, Webb. My boys and I can find drama where none should ever exist. Mix in the bride and her gang… Well…you get the picture I'm trying to create here…."

"It could still make for less drama," Webb said, evidently adopting the role of devil's advocate. "Think of it as a chance to meet and get to know each other on a less stressful level before all the real pre-wedding festivities get under way."

"Less stressful." Sighing, Gage massaged his eyes while considering the upcoming bachelor-and-bachelorette getaway that had been suggested by the bride-to-be.

"It's also a time to get to know the bride better," Webb added while moving to collect the papers that had been strewn around the office during the course of the morning's meeting.

Resting his head back on the chair, Gage bridged his fingers and factored that element into his thinking. His oldest friend, Jayson Muns, had recently stunned his close group of friends with news of his engagement to Orchid Benjamin. The woman's background boasted old money. Old as in antebellum old, rare for an African-American family of the South, but it was what it was.

Unfortunately, Jay's black society princess had a reputation that had been earned on the wilder side. It was a reputation that Jayson seemed totally oblivious to.

"Ten days in the Caribbean…" Webb reminded him. "And I'm betting it won't be any hardship on the eyes at all to be around Ms. Benjamin and her crew. You can learn a lot about people by the friends they keep."

Webb continued his tidying—and missed Gage smiling miserably in agreement.

Myrna Fisher used her free hand to pile her shoulder-length bobbed hair into a loose dark ball atop her head. With that done, she reinserted the outfit just below her chin. She'd folded down the hanger to improve her observation in the full-length mirror.

"If I didn't know you better, I'd swear your ambition was the only thing motivating you to take this trip." Myrna barely turned her head to throw her voice across her shoulder.

Alythia Duffy snuggled deeper into the tousle of thick pillows along the head of the high-canopied bed. Her bright eyes never left the snow globe as she shifted it upside down, right-side up and back again.

"I *don't* know any better," Alythia conceded, the bulk of her attention on the rush of white confetti drifting down around a miniature replica of the Charlotte skyline.

In playful retaliation, Myrna tossed the outfit she'd been debating over. The garment landed across Aly's bare feet, which were only partially visible given all the other articles of clothing Myrna had tossed there during her rushed packing job.

"In spite of my cluelessness, ambition isn't my only reason for going." Alythia defended herself in a tone harboring a fair share of mock indignance.

"But it *is* a reason?" Myrna challenged. Silence met her query and she did an about-face toward the canopy, shooting a glare in Alythia's direction. "This *should be* the one time we all put business and all of those other obligations aside, you know?"

Undaunted, Alythia propped herself higher against the pillows. "This coming from the woman who missed her own nephew's high school graduation for a bikini fitting?"

"Oh, please, Aly…how long are y'all gonna give me grief over that?" Myrna began to rifle through the outfits that would make the cut to be packed for the upcoming trip. "The designer was only in town *that* night and I'd already been paid five *large* figures for that shoot."

"Right…" Alythia took care not to mask any of the sarcasm she was aiming for. "A little business won't hurt anything," she reasoned.

Myrna's mouth fell open and for an instant Alythia thought the woman had gone into shock.

"Are you serious right now, Alythia? One of our group is about to take the vows." Myrna curved a hand between two perky D-cups and put in place her most sincere expression. "*Vows,* Aly. Do you get how *huge* this is?"

Oh, I get it, Alythia thought. She got it all too well. No one, from the local media to the woman's closest friends, had been more surprised when bad girl around town Orchid Benjamin had announced not only an engagement but also an actual wedding date with her on-again, off-again flame, Jayson Muns. Yes, it was *huge.*

Melancholy took root inside Alythia, souring her interest in the snow globe perched in her lap. "I'm gonna be there with bells on for her, Mur," she said, returning the bauble to the white marble night table near the bed. She caught the quick look her friend sliced at her through the mirror.

"I'll be sure to give Orchid all the attention she needs." Aly debated slipping back into the rose-blush canvas shoes that matched the drop-tail hem top she wore with denim capris. Myrna didn't appear impressed or trusting of the promise.

Still, the woman shrugged. "At least you'll be there in body if not entirely in spirit."

Thankful for the reprieve, Aly resituated her head on the pillows and studied her anxious friend with greater interest. There was a noticeable weariness to Myrna, given her usual and almost annoying state of cheerfulness. After more than a few seconds of observation, she pushed herself up to half sit among the litter of clothes and pillows.

"What is it?" Alythia's demand was present in her amethyst eyes. The orbs contrasted beautifully against the dewy caramel of her skin.

"Don't pay me no mind, girl." She gave an airy wave. "This bridey stuff is already taking its zany effect on my mood."

"I don't buy it." Alythia raised her hand when Myrna opened her mouth to argue. "I already saw the expression, so spill it."

"I'm just being stupid."

"Okay…" Alythia's drawling reply noted that she wasn't about to argue her friend's insight.

Myrna's smile was more genuine despite the slight strain she couldn't quite shadow. She tossed a blouse at Alythia's face.

"Aly?"

"Yeah?"

Myrna moved the clothes to be packed, clearing a spot to sit on the armchair. "What do you think about

Orchid's engagement?" she queried in a tiny voice, as though someone might overhear them even though they were completely alone in the monster penthouse apartment Myrna kept in downtown Charlotte.

"Why?" Again, Aly pushed herself up a smidge higher on the bed. When Myrna just watched her, she shrugged. "I mean, I'm happy. . . ." She shook her head, certain that there was more to the question.

"I'm happy, too." Myrna scooted to the edge of the chair. "But don't you think it's all a little too-too soon?"

"*You're* asking this?" Alythia's words were half matter-of-fact and half playful.

Myrna Fisher was one of the most sought-after lingerie models in the country. The fact that she was black made the accomplishment even more noteworthy. Still, for all Myrna's savvy allure, her weakness was for relationships. It was well known that the lovely model didn't go long without a man on her arm. The woman so adored relationships that she had a tendency to become suffocating—a thing most men didn't handle well, regardless of the woman's beauty.

Moreover, it did Myrna's reputation no favors to end things with one adoring suitor only to have another one before the close of the following week.

Appearing somewhat offended by Alythia's response, Myrna pushed off the chair and returned to holding outfit possibilities before herself in the mirror. "Unlike our friend, at least *I* don't pick up random guys to take home."

Alythia kept her eyes downcast, allowing wavy jaw-length tresses to shield her expression from Myrna's sight. Myrna's usual defense was one of many. To her, partners were significant others. No one seemed to have the heart to tell Myrna those "others" were significant only in *her* mind.

"People can change, Mur."

"Sure they can, but do people change *that* much in the span of two weeks?"

"What do you know?" Alythia tilted her head in an attempt to spy Myrna's actual face rather than its reflection in the mirror.

Myrna was cagey, pretending to be involved in her outfits. "There's nothing that I can prove." She suddenly whirled around to point a finger in Alythia's direction. "And I'm *not* jealous."

Aly didn't think it was wise just then to challenge the vehement declaration as a lie in spite of what she saw lurking in Myrna's brown eyes.

Alythia Duffy and her close circle of acquaintances had been friends since middle school. They'd been through tense times but always stuck up for each other and defended each other whether or not that defense was warranted.

Though with age came a certain clarity, Alythia thought to herself. There were times when one had to see another for what he or she really was. By all accounts, Orchid Benjamin's reputation had been tarnished by one sexual disgrace after another since high school.

"I just don't know if getting married is the best idea for her, that's all," Myrna continued.

Alythia, who was now seated in the middle of the bed with her legs folded beneath her, tuned back into Myrna's diatribe. "Are you suggesting that we say something to change her mind about going through with the wedding?"

The question tugged Myrna's rapt attention off the mirror and the gossamer lounge dress she was debating over. Again she looked to Alythia and gave a smug gaze. "I'll reserve judgment till I get a bead on the happy couple during our fun-filled getaway."

Gage Vincent was well respected; his reputation was well earned from his fellow industrial entrepreneurs. That respect turned into merited admiration with a hint of envy when the discussion fixed on his stunning success with the opposite sex. It was regarded with an abundance of love when his close circle of friends was in the vicinity.

Gage had known his riotous crew since the days of their rough-and-tumble boyhoods. College and grad school had split the foursome for several years but the bonds hadn't been broken. The four often traded war stories over drinks, dinner, games of cards or games of a more athletic variety.

While not linked by business, Jayson Muns, Zeke Shepard and Dane Spears were quite appreciative of the fact that Gage's business saved them the expense of having to purchase their own modes of air travel.

Orchid Benjamin wasn't overly impressed. The private aircraft had bold silver streaks trekking both sides of the fuselage to meet at the fin to form the letters *VID*. Not that the plane wasn't dumbfoundingly impressive and then some, Orchid thought. What gnawed at her was that her fiancé hadn't had the good taste and judgment to purchase one of his own.

"I mean, what are we gonna do on future trips?" Orchid asked the woman who had exited the limo behind her. "I know he doesn't expect me to fly commercial." She shivered as though the idea were too awful to dwell upon.

"He probably didn't see the need, Ork." Myrna pulled sunglasses from her head and perched them across the bridge of her nose. "What for? When his best friend has three of them?"

The rationale apparently pacified Orchid enough. She ran across the tarmac to greet her intended with a throaty—and, in Myrna's opinion, theatrical—kiss.

Two men stood a few feet away from the affectionate couple. Myrna immediately cast them as friends of the groom. As the other men in her line of sight were in some variation of uniforms, it was a logical guess. From the way they stood back on long legs, hand over mouths, heads inclined toward each other, it also wasn't hard to guess the topic of their private chatter.

Myrna had been part of enough staged photo settings to have a fairly passable grasp on reading body language. Yep, she thought, Ork's rep had surely preceded her on the trip. The surge of an approaching engine caught her ear and Myrna let go of a bit more of her apprehension. She released a purely girlish shriek and hurried over to greet the fourth member of their circle.

"How'd you guys manage to swing leaving town without the entire local media descending?" Jeena Stewart placed a hand across her brow while observing the jet in the distance.

"They say Gage Vincent can swing anything." Myrna dropped a kiss on Jeena's cheek when they pulled out of their embrace. "Guess that includes leaving town without the whole world knowing about it."

Jeena nodded, sudden weariness drawing her face

into a tight honey-toned mask. "I wish returning my phone calls were one of those things that he could swing."

Myrna masked her smile, knowing Jeena would take it as an insult. Word was—and speculation ran high toward that *word* being fact—that Jeena Stewart owed her fortune to the world's oldest profession. There was nothing anyone could prove, however. Part of the reason for unsubstantiation lay in the fact that Jeena could claim clients for her so-called dating service at local and national government levels, or so it was rumored. Additionally, the woman ran her business like a...well...like a business, with salary and benefits for employees—female *and* male.

Myrna thought it was all absurd, hence her suppressed, knowing smile. "Guess we're about ready to take off." She noted the limo driver passing off her luggage to a member of the baggage staff. "Of course, we're still one short." She spared another glance across the tarmac.

Jeena rolled her eyes. "Why am I not surprised?"

"Ah...dammit," Alythia said in disgust.

She had hoped taking her car, as opposed to hiring a driver, might play into her excuse of bad traffic, which would have resulted in her missing out on the luxurious flight.

But to her dismay, she arrived at the airstrip to find the plane still waiting. A chorus of birds were chirping somewhere amid the late-morning air as if they meant to welcome her to fun and excitement. Alythia appreciated the welcome but all the while considered circling back to the interstate in hopes of getting caught up in a traffic jam—a tad unlikely at that time of day, but who knew? It all could work in her favor and she might get—

"Can I help you with those?"

Alythia turned, her jaw dropping while her eyes zoned out in a show of surprise.

"Lucky." She breathed the completion of her thought aloud.

She wasn't sure if the man who stood within touching distance had sparked such a reaction because of his height. She stood just shy of five-ten in her bare feet, but this guy had to be six-two at least. Sure, it could've been the height or the muscular build—more lean than massive. Alythia was more inclined to wager on the man's remaining attributes.

Whoever he was, he had the most remarkable shade of skin, an unblemished tone of black coffee. The richness was offset by a long, steady brown gaze enhanced by overt gold flecks. His hair was straight textured and close-cropped. Thanks to the morning's powerful sunrays, Alythia could tell that his hair was of the same deep brown as his eyes.

He was smiling and the curve of a beckoning sculpted mouth was made more attractive by the singular dimple accompanying it. Still, that stare of his was impossible to ignore and difficult to perceive as anything other than intensely observant. His gaze also lent a well-blended mixture of heat and cool to his smile.

"Are you okay?"

She heard him speaking to her, his smile carrying more heat when he leaned close to ask how she was. He extended a hand as if he meant to cup her elbow but barely let his thumb graze the bend of her arm.

Alythia ordered—no, begged—the sudden and completely uncharacteristic desire to moan to cease and desist with the pressure it applied to her larynx.

"I, um— I'm good," she managed, and then followed up the lie with a laugh. "I *was* good before I got here and saw that my ride was kind enough not to leave without me."

He roared into laughter, the sound causing Alythia to jump at the full honesty of it. Despite the contagious effect of the reaction, she winced when he looked her way.

"Sorry, I know I sound ungrateful," she said.

Curiosity intermingled with his amusement. "Why do you think you're ungrateful?"

"Most people dream of visiting the Caribbean." She looked toward the jet once more. "Of those who have actually had those dreams come true, few get there on a private plane."

"Um, could I take that stuff for you?" he inquired of her bags again before the dumbfounded amusement on his face started to make her feel uneasy.

"Sorry. Um..." Aly began to relinquish her bags. "Thanks for your help— Oh, wait."

Easing the strap of a tan duffel over his shoulder, he watched her fumble through a plump midsize purse.

"Dammit...I knew I had a five or ten in here...."

"Hey." He cupped her elbow that time. "There's no need to tip me."

Alythia blinked toward the plane. "I'm pretty sure you guys are way behind schedule because of me."

"We'll get there." He voiced the soft reassurance while applying a light massage to the elbow he cupped. "They aren't gonna leave without you." He winced a little against the sun in his eyes when he glanced at the plane. "This is a vacation. No clocks. Say it. 'No clocks.'"

"No clocks." Alythia nodded in a hypnotic manner while repeating the phrase that sounded like heaven. "No clocks." She gave in to a smile that demanded to be seen.

Clarity surged in the liquid chocolate of Gage Vincent's stare and he realized that the woman standing before him had no idea that the plane was his or who he was for that matter.

He dipped his head to peer into Alythia's eyes and observed her that way for several seconds. He nodded, evidently satisfied that her outlook was improving and more than a little captivated by the stunning shade of her gaze. He then took four of her five bags, effortlessly hoisting the straps across his shoulders and angling one at his neck.

Alythia held on to an overnight case—the smallest of the five. Her smile brightened in approval of the button-down shirt he wore. The short sleeves revealed the flex and ripple of well-toned muscle accentuated by the flawless café noir of his skin.

"Shall we?" He motioned her ahead with the hand secured about the handle of a boxy brown-and-beige case.

"Do you think your boss will be a jerk about me holding up the party?" Alythia asked once they were crossing the tarmac toward the waiting plane.

"You're good." He paused. "The man's a sucker for women. Especially women who look like you."

"Thank you." Her words were delivered coolly enough even though his remark had threatened to halt her stride. "Um…will you be on the flight or…?"

"You'll see me around." He halted at the foot of the mobile stairway.

"Thank you." Aly made no secret of the fact that she was attempting to memorize his face before she headed on up the steps leading into the plane.

Gage's smile went from friendly to smoldering within seconds of Alythia's exit. He thought her legs seemed to go on forever beneath the airy white skirt that flared above her knees. She wore an emerald racer-back tank that matched strappy sandals that added emphasis on trim ankles and shapely calves. Not until one of the actual baggage handlers interrupted his survey to ask for the cases did Gage look away.

Chapter 2

Gage inclined his head a fraction as though he were attempting to obtain a better view of what he was observing. Absently, he moved the back of one hand across the sleek whiskers that had just started to shadow the strong curve of his jawline. He'd probably have a full beard by the end of the trip, he mused, still staring fixedly at the screen of his MacBook Air.

The golden flecks lurking in the liquid brown of his gaze seemed to sparkle more vividly. He was putting forth a more diligent effort to view the small square footage of space in the same light as the man he videoconferenced with did.

"Sorry, Clive...it's just not working for me," he said, at last accepting defeat.

"That's because you're not seeing it through a tourist's eyes." Clive's voice rippled out through the laptop's speakers.

"I resent that." Gage put up an obviously phony show of being insulted. "I'm as much of a tourist as the next man."

"Woman," Clive corrected. "You also need to see this place through the eyes of a woman."

Clive's robust and genuine laughter rumbling then, Gage raised his hands defensively. He reclined in the swivel chair behind an efficient but more than adequate desk in the office aboard the aircraft.

"You've finally lost me…completely. I'm afraid this requires an expertise that I'm not in any way sorry to say I don't have."

"Are you for real?" Clive was incredulous when the screen split and he appeared on the monitor. Soon, though, he relented with a decisive shake of his head. "Look, G, I don't need you to actually *see* my plans here." He referred to the space along the quaint side street within the resort he owned. "I only need you to tell me that you believe the venture has moneymaking potential."

Gage replayed the clip that had provided a 360-degree tour of the space in question. The area was practically shielded from view due to the overgrown foliage. The camera turned away from the space to offer a brief presentation of the cobblestone street that boasted a twenty-four-hour breakfast bar, nail, wax and massage spa, as well as a bookshop, among its other sole proprietorships.

"Definitely has diversity going for it," Gage murmured, while more avidly assessing the locale.

Via split screen, Clive could be seen rubbing his hands palm to palm. He even seemed to be performing a little excited dance in his chair, the back of which could be seen moving to and fro through the screen.

"Well?" Clive's baby-blue eyes were wide with expectancy.

Smirking with evident devilry driving the gesture, Gage let his old friend sweat out the wait for a few more seconds. "I want to take a look at the site when we land, but based on what's before me now…I can see it."

Clive bowed his head and Gage's smirk turned into a grin when he heard the man's delighted grunt drift through the laptop's speaker. While Gage hadn't truly been able to visualize Clive's business plan for the space at his resort property, Gage saw money. And when Gage Vincent saw money, money was made.

A chuckle accompanied Gage's grin as Clive's excitement infected him to an extent. "When'd you get so interested in fashion?"

"Well, hell, Gage, we can't all be *GQ* superstars, now, can we?" From the screen, Clive waved a hand toward Gage, who looked worthy of a spread in the famed magazine even in the simple button-down shirt, its cream color accentuating the flawless pitch of his skin.

"I still know what I like, though," Clive finished indignantly.

Gage's chuckling rounded out on a quick laugh. He traded stroking his jaw for massaging it and more closely regarded his friend. "Is it the fashion you like or the woman who gave you this idea?"

It was Clive's turn to raise his hands in defense. "I swear it's the money the fashion can make me." The quirky smile that always betrayed his attempts to be at his most serious betrayed Clive then. "The woman only helped me to see it through her eyes."

Gage's infectious, hearty laughter erupted. "Is she a blonde or brunette?" he queried through his laughter.

Clive buffed his nails against the crimson polo shirt he wore. "Neither," he replied.

"Mmm…redhead, then." Gage was confident with his guess until Clive sent him a look of mock smugness through the screen.

"Not…" Gage observed the easy arrogance in Clive's resulting smile and fell into another roll of laughter. "Try and save a few of the sistas for the rest of us, will you?" he asked when he'd come up for air. The teasing pleas held a fair amount of seriousness. Gage knew that his old college roommate fully earned his ladies'-man status.

"You and your counterparts are safe." Clive leaned back in his desk chair. Behind him a view of swaying palms and unending turquoise water rippled in the distance. "Besides, this lady is only interested in me for my building."

"Good for her. Smart in business and too smart to fall for your foolish lines."

"Hey! My lines are gold." Clive shook his head in spite of himself and appeared a touch serious. "You're right, though—she's a smart one. Ambitious, too. *That* combined with your assurance that there is more money in my future is enough for the time being. Besides—" the playful light returned to Clive's expression "—it's going to take a lot of time to get the place in shape. That's more than enough time for me to put my wooing skills to work."

Smiling broadly, Gage shook his head, as well.

"Be sure to let me know how that works out for you." He wiped at a laugh tear in the corner of his eye and straightened in his chair when he took notice of his open doorway.

The woman from the tarmac waved a hand but began to back out of the office. Gage motioned her forward. Satisfied that she was obliging his request, he interrupted Clive midsentence.

"C? Listen I need to go, but we'll catch up as soon as we land, all right?"

"Sounds good. See you then." Clive signed off with a mock salute just before his side of the split screen went black.

"I'm sorry, I didn't realize you were on a call." She bit the side of her lip, watching as he closed down the laptop.

"Come on in." Gage was done with the computer and rounded the desk while giving her another beckoning wave.

She hadn't taken more than a few steps into the office. There she remained. "I only came to apologize."

"Apologize?" His playful frown prefaced a smile. "Now you *have* to come in."

His hand folded down over her elbow, drawing her into the small, albeit state-of-the-art, work space. Despite her reluctance to move forward, she let herself be led into the smartly done office.

"Wow..." She blinked several times in rapid succession, turning to assess every element of the room.

Gage allowed himself to marvel, as well. Sure, he'd marveled over her looks—what man wouldn't? She was tall and possessed more than her fair share of soft curves, as well as a fragile allure that belied a certain strength. The radiant, creamy caramel of her skin, the stunning amethyst tinge of her stare and the wavy tousle of blue-black bobbing about that lovely face had captured a great deal of his interest. Still, her heart-stopping physical assets didn't explain the extent of his attention.

What was it exactly? It annoyed him that he couldn't put a finger on it and yet it beckoned him just the same. Gage believed that once he managed to pinpoint the "it," he wouldn't be nearly as infatuated with her as he surely felt he was becoming.

"Alythia Duffy."

He realized she was giving her name and offering her hand once he'd eased out of the deep well of his thoughts. Taking the hand she extended, he didn't shake it, only squeezed and held. His grip hinted of possession and gave no promise of freedom.

Alythia cleared her throat.

"You weren't out there when the introductions went around earlier and I—" She cast a quick look toward the doorway. "I, um… I missed the first 'getting to know you' session because I was running sort of late."

"Right…" Gage allowed unfairly long lashes to settle over his warm gaze as though he were just recalling that fact. "Right…*happily* late till you discovered your ride *hadn't* left without you."

Alythia hung her head when her eyes closed. Gage could feel her hand going limp inside his and he gave it a few reassuring pumps in an attempt to pull her gaze back to his. It worked.

"Gage Vincent."

"I know." Alythia then placed her free hand over the one he'd clasped about hers.

She'd bowed her head again and moved a smidge closer and he took the opportunity to inhale deeply of the light fragrance she wore.

"I'm so sorry about before." Alythia raised her head suddenly.

"You've already apologized to me twice at least and we haven't even known each other a full day."

"Oh, I'm—" Alythia appeared to be piping up to extend more apologies. Again she bowed her head. "I didn't mean to mistake you for working here."

"Why?" Gage faked confusion, although he knew very well what had her so distressed. "I employ a great group of folks." He shrugged. "It's nice to be thought of as one of them."

"But I shouldn't have assumed—"

"Why not? I offered to take your bags, didn't I?"

"Yes, but—"

"You weren't rude to me, were you?"

"I—" Alythia paused. "I guess not," she said finally.

Imprisoning her hand in both of his then, Gage squeezed again, using the gesture to tug her closer. "You weren't. Trust me, I know what rude is." Briefly, his liquid stare shifted left as though he were about to look across his shoulder.

Alythia piped up once more, this time in order to champion her friends. "The trip hit us out of nowhere. I'm afraid we're all sort of…um…discombobulated." She pressed her lips together.

Gage's eyes locked on her plump bronze-glossed mouth. Silently, he commanded his focus to reside on her words, for the time being, at least.

"Orchid's your typical nervous bride. I guess we're

all nervous." Alythia sounded as though she was speaking the last bit to herself.

Gage narrowed his gaze, cocking his head inquisitively in hopes that she'd elaborate on the last. Instead, she fixed him with a dazzling smile that he admitted pleased him just as much as any clarification she might have given.

"I just don't want us to get off on the wrong foot. It's important for Orchid that the trip goes well and I can't afford to be the one that shoots it all to hell."

Gage felt the wicked flex of muscle along his jaw. "And why should all of that rest on you?"

Alythia responded with a laugh that was clearly tension filled. "There are many 'whys,' Mr. Vincent. Among them my inability to be on time when there's fun to be had." She rolled her eyes. "I don't mean to ramble. Like I said, we're all a little nervous."

Nodding, Gage used the hand he still held captive to pull her arm through the crook of his. "Well, the least an aircraft employee can do is to find a way to settle a passenger's nerves."

With that, he escorted Alythia from the office.

Two delicious mojitos later, Aly was feeling less nervous and far more amused. The dynamics emerging among the newly collected group kept a genuine smile on her face. Whether it was the group or the mojitos that deserved such credit, she couldn't wager a guess.

Gage had escorted her out to the main cabin and had gotten her settled into a seat somewhat removed from where the rest of the group had gathered. He'd then personally seen to filling the order for her drink.

Alythia kept her gaze trained outside the windows

on purpose. She knew Gage's innocent act of kindness was already being rehashed by her friends.

"How are those nerves doin'?"

Smiling at the question, Alythia looked up at Gage while raising her third mojito, which she was only halfway through. "The nerves are much better."

Gage claimed a spot on one of the milk-chocolate suede swivels across from where Alythia relaxed. "And how's the view?"

"The view can't at all be complained about."

"Hmph."

The response drew her stare and she studied him with a knowing intensity. "Guess this is all pretty old hat to you, huh?"

"How often do you travel, Alythia?" he asked, angling an index finger alongside his temple while he watched her.

She turned her attention back outside the window. "Quite a bit, but first class has nothing on this."

"Well, it doesn't get old for me," Gage shared, swiveling his chair a bit. "Every time I take a flight, take time to pull my face out of a report and take a look at the view, I'm reminded of how blessed I am."

"Must've been a hard road to get here."

Gage grinned. "*Hard* would've been nice. My road was about ten times beyond hard."

"Ha! I can relate!" Alythia laughed.

"How so?"

Alythia wasn't of a mind to elaborate. "We're talking about *your* hard road, not mine."

"I'd trade my hard-luck story for yours any day."

"I'd hate to sour your mood for the rest of the trip, and *my* story would surely do that." She sipped at a bit more of the mojito, loving the rejuvenating effects of the crisp drink.

"What if I told you my story could have the same effect on you?"

"All right, then." Alythia faced him fully, her elbows propped along the arms of the chair. "Suffice it to say that my hard-luck story makes me very appreciative of every good thing that comes my way." For effect she raised her mojito in a mock toast.

There was a burst of feminine laughter, followed by the roar of male chortling and additional feminine giggling. The sounds drew quick smiles from both Gage and Alythia.

"Sounds like your friends share your point of view."

Bewilderment sent the elegant lines of Alythia's brows closer, though she didn't remain stumped for long. "We've all weathered storms and learned from them."

"Is that right?" He pretended to be stunned.

Alythia rolled her eyes playfully. "Even rich girls have storms to weather, Mr. Vincent." She aimed a soft smile in Orchid's direction.

"Hey, Gage?" Myrna called from across the cabin. "Are we gonna fly above the clouds for the whole flight? I want to see the water."

"Appreciative of every good thing, huh?" Gage spoke the words for Alythia's ears only and then pushed out of his chair. "Finish your drink." He squeezed her shoulder on his way to join the group.

"So?"

"Gage was popping the cap on his Samuel Adams when Dane Spears's question reached his ear.

"So." Gage took a swig of the beer.

"Don't even try it." Dane's soft admonishment accompanied a playful frown. "What's the story?" he persisted.

"What story?" Gage leaned against the Blackwood counter space inside the bar area where his friend had cornered him.

"Come off it, G. You obviously already picked yours."

Gage eased a measuring look toward his beer bottle. "I think I already had too much to drink." He shook his head at Dane. "What the hell are you talkin' about?"

"Don't take offense, G. Hell, she's—she's beautiful." Dane voiced the compliment as though he was in disbelief of an absolute truth. "If she hadn't been so late to the party, I'd have probably already staked my claim."

Grinning as realization hit home, Gage gave another shake of his head. "This isn't a date." He downed another swig of the tasty brew.

"Who said anything about a date? I'm talkin' about a sure thing." Dane helped himself to one of the assortment of beers chilling in a tub of ice next to the bar. He used the bottle he'd selected to motion toward the women across the room.

"Fine as hell and sure things, every one of 'em."

Gage narrowed a look toward his friend. "Every one?"

"Well…except the bride, of course."

"Of course." Gage enjoyed a few more swallows of beer and enjoyed the view across the room. The view of Alythia Duffy was one that he especially enjoyed. Whether or not he realized it, or would have admitted it if he had.

"Have you met them before?"

Dane settled back against the bar. His arms folded across the snug workout top meant to emphasize an already broad chest as he affixed a keener interest upon the group. "Haven't formally *met* any of them, but anybody who's watched TV or read a paper knows 'em in one form or another. Except for your girl," he said, referencing Alythia. "Keeps to herself. She's a beauty but seems kinda standoffish now that I've met her."

Gage smiled, recognizing the last remark as Dane-speak for "She turned me down." He enjoyed another gulp of the beer, silently admitting that he was as glad of that fact as he was of the appearance of Dane's sulking.

Alythia being relatively unknown pleased him greatly. What pleased him even more was the fact that she didn't claim the kind of status her friends seemed to relish.

"Quiet ones are usually the biggest freaks," Dane chimed in as if reading Gage's thoughts. He shrugged. "I'm just saying that it doesn't look like we'll have to put much work into getting a little somethin' somethin' above- or belowground, is all."

Gage poised his bottle for another swig and changed his mind. "Don't believe everything you read," he cautioned.

"Oh, trust me, my friend. Everything I know about that trio, I didn't have to read."

Instead of drinking from the bottle, Gage pressed it to his forehead, needing the cool to breach his skin. "Don't do this," he sighed. "It's not the time for conspiracies."

"That much I know." Dane seemed to sober. "Already gave it my best shot and Jay's still over the moon for this one."

Gage finally pinned his friend with an expression that harbored no trace of amusement. "What'd you do?"

"Felt Jay had a right to know the word on the street about her." Dane shrugged, downed a bit of the Budweiser he'd selected. "That fool tends to dwell in his own world, you know?"

"Yeah, minding his own business, finding a woman he wants to spend the rest of his life with… Lotta men would love living in that world."

"Don't even try it, G." Dane used his bottle to point in Gage's direction. "Hookin' up with the wrong chick can turn a beautiful life into hell on earth."

"Where's all this comin' from, man?"

"Coming from one friend to another."

"Jay might not see it that way." Gage went back to girl watching and nursing his beer.

"We usually don't see it *that way* when being told something for our own good."

"Right." Gage left Dane's counter-remark unchallenged and pushed away from the bar. "Guys, we can take this stairway down to find our lunch!" he called out to the rest of the group.

Gage waited for Alythia, offering her his arm when she broke away from her friends.

"Thanks." She leaned into him a little. "Those mojitos were no joke."

"There's more where they came from."

Alythia tilted back her head. "That's good to know. Being around my girls for ten days will definitely put me in the mood for more."

Gage slanted a look toward Dane, who responded with a mock toast of his beer bottle. "I know what you mean," he said.

Chapter 3

It went without saying that the lower deck of the jet made quite an impression on Gage Vincent's guests. Myrna and Orchid were very vocal in their appreciation of the sumptuous layout of the combination dining room and sitting room. Myrna oohed and aahed while breaking into a light sprint down the wide aisle. She trailed her fingers across the silk-covered beige sofas and chairs with embroidered finishes. Even Orchid, who had seen her fair share of private jets, seemed impressed by the understated decor of the grand space. She didn't let too much of it show, preferring instead to use the opportunity to school her fiancé. Simply put, if Jayson was confused about what to look for when he bought his jet, use *this* for an example.

Jeena was equally as impressed. She was busy trying to get Gage to agree to a time when they might chat.

"I know neither of us are in the mood to discuss business, but you're so busy every time I call," Jeena rambled while tapping furiously at her mobile as she scrolled through the calendar there. "I'm pretty sure your assistant is sick and tired of talking to me while we try to work on a good time to meet. But I'm flexible with whatever we can..."

While Jeena talked, Gage only half listened. It was of no consequence. If need be, he could have recited her spiel verbatim. A good thing, too, because taking a more avid interest in the woman's rambling wasn't a top priority just then.

Gage kept his gait to a leisurely stroll.

So much the better for Jeena. She hoped she might be on the verge of nailing down a meeting with the elusive entrepreneur. Aside from her, the one thing Jeena's... clients all had in common was Gage Vincent. They were either *in* business with the man or they wanted to be. Jeena hoped to be on the *in* business with Gage Vincent side of things. Having him on her side to smooth the way regarding certain ventures would be a coup indeed. But Jeena didn't realize that she was pretty much carrying the conversation alone, with only Gage's intermittent "mmm-hmms" to punctuate the discussion.

"I'll have my assistant get in touch with you," he managed just as they rounded the corner into the dining area. He didn't spare Jeena a glance. His stirring gaze was set on Alythia as he and Jeena walked into the room, among the last to arrive.

Gage saw the smile enhancing Alythia's profile when she angled her head to look up at the recessed lighting that added a golden glow to the cream, beige and cocoa color scheme. The space was devoid of windows, and woodgrain-based lamps had been added to provide warm illumination. Gage dipped his head, hoping to shield the smile that emerged as he studied her reaction.

"And here I thought the bottom of a plane was only for storing luggage," Aly teased. Turning just as Gage looked up, she favored him with a smile across her shoulder.

Alythia's comment closed off whatever attention Gage had been paying to Jeena.

"So when should I expect your assistant's…call?" Jeena finished disapprovingly when she saw Gage walk on ahead to catch up with her friend.

Jeena's cool, unreadable smile mimicked the one Zeke Shepard wore when he rounded out the group arriving in the dining space. He'd taken a deep interest in the sight of his old friend leaving one beauty to catch up with another.

"My friend has a one-track mind sometimes," Zeke noted to the petite woman Gage had left behind.

Jeena ceased working at her phone. "One-track?" she queried of the slender dark man next to her.

"One reason Gage agreed to this trip is because all of Orchid's friends are dimes." Zeke grinned.

"That's cold," Jeena chided, though lightly. She pulled a stylus pen from her bag and blandly regarded the man in question. "I'd like to think he really wanted to do something special for his friend."

"Well…that, too." Zeke gave a little shrug. "But being surrounded by four beautiful women won't be a hardship."

"Hmph." Jeena tapped a finger to her cheek and slowed her pace a bit. "Are you saying that he plans to sleep with all of us?"

"Nah." Zeke's response was softer, reassuring then. "My man's already made his selection."

Jeena stroked the soft hair tapered into a V at her nape while studying Gage and Alythia. The two stood discussing an oil canvas that was on display inside a cozy alcove a ways down from the dining room. She gave a sideways glance up at Zeke.

"And what about you? Have you made your selection, as well?"

"Not much point in making a selection if your choice is otherwise occupied, is there?" He gave a pointed look toward Jeena's phone.

"Oh, this?" Shrugging, Jeena dipped into a sultrier mode. "It'll do until something better comes along." She used one hand to tuck the phone into the back pocket of her coral linen capris; the other she linked through the crook of Zeke's arm.

"You live very well," Alythia told Gage once he had finished the story of how he'd acquired the piece adorning the alcove wall.

"Thanks." He gave her a gracious nod. "It's not without a lot of hard work."

"Just don't work too hard," Alythia advised with a playful gleam in her light eyes.

"Don't work too hard without having anything interesting to show for it." Gage edited the advice and then smiled encouragingly. "Would you agree?"

Aly regarded the vibrant hues that seemed to shimmer within the canvas and draw the observer's eye to the brilliant meshing of colors. "I'd definitely agree." She sighed as though imagining herself in the seascape depicted in the painting. "I might get around to living that truth if I ever get past the 'working hard' phase."

Gage turned his attention back toward the canvas. "This trip's a good place to start."

"It was supposed to be." Alythia couldn't resist sending an uncertain glance across her shoulder.

"What's that look for?"

It wasn't in her nature to confide so easily, but the man possessed the most coaxing voice. Aly wondered if he knew that and how often the attribute worked to his advantage. Her guess was *quite* often.

"The only reason I agreed to come along on this getaway was because there's a chance for me to get some real business handled."

"Real business, huh? In the Caribbean?" Gage's rich, dark brows rose.

The soothing depths of the man's voice notwithstanding, Alythia had been bursting to share her news. Silently, she reasoned that she could at least count on Gage not to blab to her girls if she told him.

"I happened upon a business opportunity while I was trying to find a little more info on where we were heading for this trip. I hope to own a chain of boutiques one day." She shrugged. "Right now there's only two, but I'm looking to expand. Turns out our resort owner has a shopping village that he's hoping to cultivate. I've convinced him to at least consider giving my shop a chance."

Gage put in a fantastic effort to school his expression.

"We should go check out the place when we land, all right?"

Alythia was already shaking her head no to Gage's suggestion. "It's not necessary and I don't want to mention it to my friends. They're still getting over the shock that I agreed to come along." She folded her arms across the emerald tank that hugged her breasts adoringly.

"It'd crush Ork to know that my priority is once again business and not taking time out with my girls."

Gage's grimace over the outlook triggered the lone dimple in his cheek. "Time out with friends takes money."

"Agreed," she said with a smirk, "but my friends think the way I earn my money takes up too much time." She cast a withering look toward the painting then. "Unfortunately, I don't come from money—" she looked to Orchid "—I'm not model material—" she took note of Myrna "—and I don't have the nerve to earn my money the way *they say* Jeena earns hers."

"That's good to hear." He leaned in close and gave her waist a pat. "And you're wrong. You're definitely model material and then some."

Alythia felt her lips part, but she really didn't expect to handle the task of filling her mouth with words. Thankfully, speaking became a moot point when Gage turned once again, offering her his arm and then escorting her toward the dining room area, where everyone else had already gathered.

Dining room seating consisted of blocky chairs with heavily cushioned seats and backs. A booth seat ran the length of a polished dark oak table and was upholstered in the same embroidered beige silk as the dining chairs and other furnishings.

The space could seat six comfortably, which mattered little to the betrothed couple. They opted to enjoy the late lunch on the sofa that held position opposite the dining table and ran the length of the entire space.

There, Orchid and Jayson lounged in a loving tangle of arms and legs. Every now and then, Orchid would burst into wild laughter over something that her fiancé whispered in her ear.

Across from the happy couple, other companion selections appeared to have been made. Dane and Myrna had laid claim to the booth seat while Zeke and Jeena engaged in their own private conversation from the cushiony chairs that put them side by side. Across from them, holding court at the other end of the table, were Alythia and Gage.

"Do you think our travel companions care what's on the menu?" Gage asked, reclining in the chair he occupied, elbow relaxed along the arm with his hand at his mouth as he spoke.

The question gave Alythia the chance to observe her friends, something she'd been trying *not* to do since the game of "choose your lunch partner" had gotten under way several minutes prior.

"I don't think it matters," she managed. Inwardly, Alythia was cringing. Jayson and Orchid's…demonstrativeness was understandable. The rest was, in Alythia's opinion, not a good idea. Not that she was in any way against enjoying all the delights a Caribbean getaway was supposed to offer. Only…if someone got the wrong idea and became disappointed, things would not bode well for the feelings of good cheer desired between the bride's and the groom's friends. From the looks of things, Aly noted, it didn't appear that anyone would be disappointed anytime soon.

From her periphery she could see Gage looking her way. She felt no pressure to make conversation. He was only…looking. She realized that he had a way of doing so that soothed instead of stirred her. Not that his gold-flecked browns didn't have the power to stir. There was just something about him, some element to his demeanor, that was intensely calming. It was a good thing, too, Aly thought. She was sure to require every calming agent she could summon before the end of the trip. She decided to give that train of thought as little brain time as possible and turned to face Gage fully.

"Forget them," she said. "*I'm* very interested in what's on the menu."

Chuckling softly, Gage pulled away the fist that supported his cheek. "I think you'd rather see it for yourself instead of listening to me trying to describe it."

Everyone, in fact, tuned in to the wait staff, who had arrived balancing trays of covered dishes and baskets of golden bread.

The late lunch was sort of a preamble to the kinds of delicacies the group was sure to enjoy during their ten-day Caribbean stay. The travelers dined on catfish, flown in fresh from the Outer Banks of North Carolina that morning, in a succulent white-wine-and-scallion sauce; chilled shrimp with a tangy tomato, orange and lemon glaze drizzle; steamed squash; and zucchini. There was fresh apple butter for the yeast bread and a decadent apple-cinnamon cobbler for dessert.

Once again private conversations and laughter resumed. The soft talking mingled with the infrequent clinking of silver- and other dinnerware.

"Tell me about your business." Gage took advantage of their measure of privacy to ease some of his curiosity about the woman dining to his right.

Alythia gave a one-shoulder shrug, keeping her light eyes downcast toward the zesty fish. “It’s just a store.”

His smile was equal parts desire and disappointment. “Why do you do that?” He clenched a fist to resist trailing his fingers along the caramel-toned length of her bare arm.

Again she shrugged. “I’m guessing that selling clothes would sound pretty silly compared to what you do all day.” Faintly, she acknowledged that she really had no idea *what* he did all day.

“I don’t think selling clothes is silly.” Gage allowed mock bewilderment to cross his dark, attractive face. “I can think of at least three people in this room who I have *no* desire to see without their clothes.”

Alythia tried to quiet her laughter when Gage fixed pointed looks upon each of his three best friends.

“Does your laughing mean you’re in the mood to tell me how you got into the clothing business?” he asked.

Alythia took a moment to observe him then. He’d propped his fist to his cheek again and she wondered whether it was a habitual stance. Whatever the case, it kept her settled in a comfortable frame of mind conducive to talking.

Everyone appeared relaxed and truly involved in their conversations. The food—which was quickly disappearing—smelled wonderful and tasted even more wonderful. The room where they dined was as much like a work of art as the exquisite pieces that adorned the wall spaces of the aircraft.

Aly thought that the lamp lighting was soothing, very much like the sound of Gage’s voice when he called her name to tug her from her thoughts.

“It’s not such a surprise that I’d go into the clothing

business." She saw his probing stare narrow dangerously and raised her hands in a show of playful defense. "I swear I'm not trying to make light of it."

Gage had dissolved into laughter. Once done, he relaxed back into the chair and waved his hand in a mock show of permissiveness, urging her to continue with her story.

At ease, Alythia forked up another plump glazed shrimp. "I've always dreamed of being surrounded by beautiful clothes." She popped the morsel of meat into her mouth and took a moment to relish the taste. "Mostly because I never had any growing up. None of us did." Her expression saddened somewhat when she looked toward Myrna and Jeena. "Then we met Orchid." She beamed.

"How'd *that* friendship happen?" Gage glanced over to Orchid and Jayson. "I thought, with her family's money, she'd have been in some private school."

Aly levered a weighty look toward her friend. "Yeah, she was, but there were…problems with following a few choice rules and Mr. Benjamin said if she wanted to rule-break, he wasn't gonna pay an arm and a leg for her to do it. So he sent her to public school."

"Damn. I heard he was a tough man." Gage studied Orchid for a moment or two and then shook his head. "Hard to believe she got into so much trouble with a parent like that."

"Well, Ork's always done her own thing…but Luther Benjamin was a really great man." Alythia set down her fork and leaned back into the chair, reminiscence filling her striking stare. "He never treated his daughter's new public school girlfriends with anything other than acceptance and respect. He was the kind of dad we all wanted." A sigh followed the admission.

"Wanted but...didn't have?" Gage carefully probed.

"Myrna's mom and dad separated when she was little." Alythia hugged herself a bit, raking her square French tips over suddenly chilled arms. "Jeena never knew her dad, and mine..." She resisted the urge to allow resentment to close her eyes. "Mine was in and out, in and out of my mother's pocketbook when he'd drank or gambled off his own. If he didn't steal it, she'd give it to him, no questions, no matter if she had to pay rent, buy food or..."

"Clothes."

His voice was quiet with understanding that made Aly smile while she nodded slowly.

"My mom died of a broken heart. She tried to be everything my father wanted. When that didn't work, she tried to buy his love and when that didn't work, she killed herself."

The stunning revelation was interrupted when a belt of laughter rang out from Zeke and Jeena's direction. Gage paid no mind to the outburst on the other side of the room. He appeared stricken and remorseful.

"Hell..." He groaned, having taken her elbow and drawn her so near to him that she was practically seated on the line between the cushions of his chair and her own. "God, I'm sorry for making you remember that."

"No, Gage." She smoothed her hand across the one that clutched her arm. "It wasn't like that. She—" Aly inhaled around the sudden emotion swelling her chest. "She passed slowly over time. There was nothing... physically wrong. She just didn't want to live—lost the will..."

"I'm sorry anyway." He squeezed her arm and gave it a little tug.

"Thanks." Her smile harbored none of its earlier somberness. "I'll never own up to the idea that I have any 'daddy issues.' My sister and I are too busy living our lives for that."

"I like the sound of that." Gage applied a soft thumb stroke to the bend of her arm.

"It's true. We live our lives in tribute to our mom."

Suspiciously amused, he smiled. "How?"

The high back of the chair provided the perfect headrest and Alythia indulged. "My sister is married to a pretty awesome guy who I'm not ashamed to say I'm just a little in love with."

Gage's whistle ushered in quick, hearty laughter. "Does your sister know this?"

"She does." Aly joined in when Gage laughed again. "Doesn't matter, though. The man only has eyes for her. He's been known to actually stop talking midsentence when she walks into a room. And that's just a *little piece* of what makes him so incredible." She sighed, but the sound held a dreamy vibe. "Men like him are in short supply."

Gage focused on where his thumb brushed Alythia's skin. "So while your sister is taking great men *off* the market, you're putting great clothes *on* it?"

Alythia's expressive gaze widened. "That's a fantastic way to look at it. Hmph, do you mind if I use that?"

Again he performed the permissive wave. "Not at all."

"Your attention, please."

The mixed conversations were interrupted then by

the sound of the captain's voice merging in among the warm drone of voices, clinking glasses and laughter.

"We are within thirty-five minutes of our arrival time and ask that you please begin your return to the main deck..."

"We'll have dessert and coffee upstairs, guys," Gage called out while the captain continued his message.

"Can we talk more later?" he asked Alythia while the others were pushing out of their seats.

Her smile brightened and she accepted when he offered her his hand.

"I'd like that," she told him, barely noticing the looks passing between the other couples at her and Gage's expense.

Chapter 4

As the captain's instructions hadn't demanded an *immediate* return to the main level, some decided to indulge in a few additional moments of getting acquainted. Alythia and Gage had the main cabin all to themselves for over fifteen minutes following the group's departure from the dining area. The bride and groom were the first to rejoin them.

Alythia didn't frown on Orchid's missing earring or too-tousled hair. A little lovemaking among the clouds would be the first of many happy memories for the soon-to-be-married couple, Alythia hoped.

Her contented thoughts about lovemaking at plus or minus forty thousand feet began to ebb when the last two "couples" arrived. Myrna was smoothing down flyaway tendrils of her straight shoulder-length bob. The gesture may not have seemed so out of place were it not for Dane. He strolled in behind Myrna and made no secret of drawing her back to him for a throaty kiss before he situated himself inside his jeans and tugged the zipper in place.

Zeke and Jeena proved to be a bit more discreet. They were not quite beyond the cabin's viewing range when Zeke plied Jeena's cheek with a parting kiss. He took it upon himself to secure the remaining few buttons on Jeena's blouse before they rounded the corner to join the others.

Alythia lost her taste for the drink she'd been watching Gage prepare. She reclaimed her spot along the window and far away from the main seating area. She'd been seated less than five minutes when a heavenly smell drifted beneath her nose. She found Gage setting two plates of the fragrant apple cobbler on the table between them. He retrieved their drinks from the bar and then took his place across from Alythia's seat and handed her one of the Baileys on the rocks.

When Aly looked his way, an understanding smile was tugging at the appealing curve of his mouth.

"It helps when you just ignore it," he said.

Aly didn't pretend to misunderstand. "And at what point does that become impossible?" she countered.

Gage sipped at his Baileys. "Been asking myself that for years," he muttered.

Aly raised her glass, set it down on the table and crumbled into uninhibited laughter. Gage joined her moments later.

Anegada, British Virgin Islands

Sitting farthest north of the British Virgin Islands was Anegada, a low, flat island known for its miles and miles of white-sand beaches and its commercial fishing success. While tourism served as the primary business on the island, the area was sparsely populated throughout much of the year. Alythia felt her well-being improve the moment she'd inhaled a few gulps of the floral air and absorbed the dazzling hues of blue and green that composed the environment.

Curiosity instigated a frown when she focused in on the local who had greeted them and was then shaking hands with Gage and his friends. By the time the man had made his way around to *her* friends, Aly knew exactly who he was.

"Clive Weeks?" she said before Gage could make the introductions. "Alythia Duffy," she supplied, watching the man's expression go from welcoming to surprised to stunned to pleased.

"Incredible!" he greeted, taking both of her hands in his and shaking them energetically.

"How?" Alythia looked to Gage, her meaning clear.

"College roommates," Gage and Clive explained in unison.

Alythia nodded but she didn't feel quite as at ease as she would've liked to at the moment.

"Absolutely incredible." Clive was pleased enough for them both.

The fact settled Alythia's suspicions somewhat. She was, however, very aware of her friends, whom she wasn't quite ready to share her business plans with. Thankfully, all the new lovers were still wholly absorbed with one another.

"C, why don't you let the woman get some rest before you load her down with business?" Gage suggested as though he'd sensed Alythia's reluctance to get too chatty with Clive around her friends.

"Right, right." Clive's baby blues registered apology and he gave Alythia's hands a final shake. "What was I thinking?"

"It's fine." Aly's smile was genuine. Clive's enthusiasm was very contagious.

"We'll talk tomorrow. Tonight is for fun." Clive left Alythia with a decisive nod before he turned to regain everyone else's attention. "Folks, the shuttle will be ready to carry us back to the resort in just a second!"

Jeena and Myrna had been conducting a silent inventory of the pier. For the time being, their minds seemed to be off the new men in their lives and on their surroundings.

"Clive? Will it be like this the entire time?"

Clive's accommodating smile never wavered. "What do you mean?" he asked Myrna.

"She means dead," Orchid said.

Alythia closed her eyes out of equal parts dread and mortification.

"You're about to be amazed," Clive promised, apparently taking no offense to the insult to his home.

From a brief conversation amid the group, Alythia learned that one year Clive had visited Anegada during the off-season. He'd taken an extended vacation from his once-thriving law practice in Greensboro, North Carolina, but he'd never gone back. He'd been in love with Anegada for ten years and mentioned that the love affair showed no signs of growing old.

"You guys are arriving, luckily, on the tail end of the storm season. It's also after our tourist season, as well," Clive continued. "That accounts for the lack of bodies, but I can assure you that my resort, which is just outside Keel Point, is definitely not *dead.*"

This news drew hearty laughter from everyone—including Alythia, who had mixed a healthy dose of relief into hers.

Clive stepped aside to speak with his shuttle driver. In minutes he announced they were ready to set out. Alythia celebrated the fact that Gage and his friends were speaking with Clive and missing the conversation while she and her girls boarded the shuttle. Just then, Jeena was agreeing with Orchid that they would've expected for Gage to have a car waiting for them.

Anegada Weeks Resort was a play on Clive's surname and a tribute to the love he had for the place he called home. The multilevel main villa was a grand structure that provided a spectacular view of any area of the property.

Wide floor-to-ceiling windows were accentuated by billowing drapes, filling the expansive, comfortably elegant rooms with refreshing breezes that mingled with the scents from vast floral arrangements that decorated every room, corridor and window.

Aside from the staff and grounds, only the guests rivaled the resort for beauty. As Clive had promised, the place was certainly not dead. While there wasn't an overflow of bodies, the surroundings were more than alive with the sounds of music, life and laughter. The Weeks Resort boasted live music twenty-four hours a day, seven days a week. The grooves were piped in to all areas of the vibrant establishment, with the exception of the suites.

The amount and variation of the excitement must

have appeased Orchid, Jeena and Myrna, for they were quick to abandon their male love interests. Their plan was to follow the baggage carriers to their suites for a quick change of attire and then return to the array of bars, hot-tub lounges and poolside cafés for an afternoon of socializing.

As pleased by her friends' contentment as a mom leaving her squealing child with a sitter, Alythia envisioned an afternoon of sleep. She hoped her friends would find much to do and not miss her company for at least a couple of hours.

Aly could have kissed Clive Weeks when she discovered she and her girls had been spread out in suites along different wings of the resort. Satisfaction settled like a warm blanket the moment the door closed behind the polite porter. The middle-aged Haitian man must have sensed Alythia's exhaustion, for he bid her pleasant dreams before making his departure. Happiness manifested then in the form of a sigh when Aly marveled at the king bed with its four tall posters. The engraved mahogany supported gauzy curtains that puffed out in an elegant display thanks to the tropical breezes that circulated through the open windows. The broad frames were bumped infrequently by the heavy leaves of gigantic palm trees that danced wildly amid the wind.

Alythia approached the windows, wishing to be showered by the strong gusts of air. She discovered that there were fine screens behind the panes that admitted the sensational breeze and not much else.

The lullaby performed by the palm-tree leaves gradually returned Aly's thoughts to her desire for sleep. She'd kicked off her sandals and managed to exchange her travel clothes for a new pink-and-black sleep ensemble when the sound of jolly chimes mingled with the palm tree's song. Her mobile. She'd almost forgotten having taken it off airplane mode after they left the jet. Myrna and Jeena had suffered no bouts of amnesia. They'd made quick work of reminding everyone to rejoin the land of the living when they dug out their phones.

Tired as she was, Aly didn't resent answering the call when she saw the name on the faceplate.

"Well, hello!" she greeted her business manager.

"You sound awfully chipper." Marianne Young's husky voice would've sounded much deeper were it not for the underlying amusement that often colored her words.

"So how goes it?" Mari queried. "Any new scandals brewing?"

"Mari, shame on you," Alythia halfheartedly scolded while she placed her sandals in the elm-wood wardrobe across the bedroom. "Why would you think such a thing?"

"Oh, Lord…is it that bad?"

"Not yet. Suffice it to say that bed partners have already been selected and…tested."

Marianne whistled. "Wait a minute. How are you talking about this? Where is everyone else?"

"Separate suites, on separate wings of a huge resort."

Another whistle sang through the phone line. "Did you arrange that?" Marianne asked.

"Hmph." Aly wiggled her freed toes. "Not me. The fates did." She smiled when Marianne laughed.

"So? Any word?" she asked once the woman's chuckles softened.

"No decision has been made yet." Marianne needed

no clarity on what her client was referring to. Alythia had been in an almost-constant state of anxiety over the past few months. "Our proposal is sound, Aly. Try not to worry over this while you're there."

"Do you think there's anything more we can do to better our chances?" Aly persisted, perching on the arm of a deep chair near the open windows. "Maybe we could amp up our radio and TV advertisements. Do you think that might help?"

Marianne's laughter had returned. "Girl, you're too keyed up. You know that, right?"

"I know. . . ." Alythia went boneless as she eased down into the chair, her long legs dangling over the arm. "I've been really edgy with the girls, too, and they don't deserve it. They're here to have fun, like I should be doing."

"Exactly." Marianne's strong voice was successful at driving home her encouragement. "We've done everything we can for the time being. Trust me, I've checked to see if we've left any stones unturned and I'll continue to check, all right?"

"All right."

"All we can do is wait."

"All we can do is wait." Alythia came down from her anxious high while repeating Marianne's precaution.

"Good. Now, you enjoy what I'm sure is gonna be an exquisite getaway."

"It *is* that." Aly closed her eyes as a strong breeze hit her face. "It's definitely that, but all I want to do right now is go to sleep."

"Well, there you go! I'm hanging up now. Sweet dreams…" Marianne's connection ended a second later.

"Sweet dreams indeed." Alythia sent a dreamy look in the bed's direction. She left the chair with the intention of placing her mobile on the stately elm-wood-and-bamboo nightstand. Rethinking that decision, she returned it to her overnight case. There was enough business to keep her occupied in Anegada without calling home for more.

Aly was on her way to bed when there was a knock. She stopped just short of the door to offer up a fast prayer that it be none of her friends. Not yet—she really needed just a couple of hours of downtime. Heck, she'd settle for *one* hour at this point.

Fortified by the prayer, she pulled open the door and let Gage witness her relief when she saw him in the hallway.

As relieved as Alythia was, though, Gage appeared anything but. A mixture of uncertainty had illuminated his dark, handsome face. "Is this a bad time?" He put obvious effort into asking the question.

"Going to bed." Aly rested her head on the side of the door. Her tone was lazy, eyelids heavy in anticipation of sleep.

"That part's obvious." A peculiar smile curved his fascinating mouth.

Alythia hadn't noticed him blatantly raking his beckoning stare along her body before. When he lowered his gaze in a more direct manner that time, she took heed and received her second round of mortification for the day.

She'd been so focused on praying for it not to be her BFFs on the other side of the door that she had completely dismissed what she was wearing when she opened it.

Gage briefly set his hand across his mouth to shield a broadening smile as she bolted from the door to go in search of a robe.

He shut the room door and followed her deeper into the suite. In the bedroom he leaned back against the door and indulged in the long, unconscious glimpses she offered of surprisingly shapely limbs and other plump assets that were emphasized by the skimpy top and panties she was about to wear to bed.

A scrap of peach-colored material caught his eye and Gage braced off the door to investigate. He discovered the robe she was so obviously searching for. A light fragrance drifted from the satiny garment when he pulled it from beneath a bag on the armchair nearest the closet. He stole a moment to savor the feel of the material between his fingers. He let himself imagine how the item must feel with her filling it.

"Is this what you want?"

Alythia straightened, turning into his deep, close voice. She resisted the urge to let her lashes flutter out of embarrassment as she took what he offered.

"Thanks." Her tone was hushed as she slipped on the robe. "I probably shouldn't tell you I'm sorry about this, huh?"

His laughter was short but humor filled. "I can't think of one thing you have to be sorry for right now."

"Most men don't like to be teased." She reached for the ties at her waist.

Gage moved in, locating the other end of the belt. "Is that what you believed I'd think?" He secured the belt for her.

"I...shouldn't have said that."

Gage bumped her chin with his fist and then propped it there and waited for her eyes to meet his. "Will you answer me?"

"How could you *not* think that when all your friends have had their worlds rocked by all of mine?"

As impressed as he was that she had come right out and said it, Gage was still taken aback that she had. Her voice sounded strong, but he could sense that she was very exhausted. "Maybe it's a little early for this discussion?" he noted.

Exhaustion had indeed claimed the energetic lilt of her laughter. "*Never* is too early to have this discussion," she mused.

"If that's the case, I'm afraid we'll have to find something else to talk about over dinner."

"Another meal with the gang? Yaay." She gave a lazy twirl of an index finger. "What time do we need to be there?"

"*You and I* should be there around seven."

She blinked. "Just us? Just…you and me?"

"That's right." Gage realized he'd been rubbing the underside of her wrist where she had been holding her arms folded near where he still held on to the robe's belt.

"Seven?" he queried, smiling in a manner that proved he sensed both her reluctance and her willingness.

"Seven." She gave in to what she wanted. "What should I wear?"

Gage had a fine idea that his expression was probably all the response she needed. "I don't really think you'd benefit from my suggestion. It'd be a pretty self-serving one anyway."

The words made Alythia laugh until he gave the belt a sharp tug, which caused her to balance herself by bracing her hands against his unyielding chest when she jostled him. She dug in her fingers just enough to determine whether he felt as unbelievable as he appeared.

He dropped a kiss to the corner of her mouth. "Rest up," he murmured while his lips still grazed her skin.

Alythia stood fixed to her spot when Gage moved away. She watched him make his way out of the room. She maintained her position until a minute after the main door closed behind him.

What the hell was going on? The words blasted around inside her head, which must've had a stimulating effect, because she stripped off the robe. She let it lie where it fell and then eased beneath the inviting turned-down bedcovers.

She hadn't come here for this. She'd come for work and, if time permitted, a little lazing near the pool, a few drinks… She hadn't come here to fall in—

"Stop it." She punched the closest pillow as though it had somehow been to blame for such thoughts filling her mind. She barely had time for her friends. She surely had *no* time for a high-maintenance relationship.

Something told her that an involvement with Gage Vincent would be high maintenance. Not in a bad way, of course. She could, however, take one look at the man and be pretty much reassured that he'd keep her…busier than business ever could.

"Stop it…" She moaned the word as if begging herself for mercy.

Sex—or the lack of it—was the very last thing she needed at the forefront of her mind. The idea gave her pause and she ceased her fidgeting beneath the sheets. Giving in might not be such a bad thing after all. Well…

no, it wouldn't be a *bad* thing at all. Would it really matter what he thought of her later?

Chances were high that they wouldn't even see each other after the wedding. It'd just be a Caribbean fling. Who didn't deserve to have at least one of those? she thought, renewed drowsiness beginning to settle in as the perfect mattress and pillows cushioned her entire body, beckoning it into relaxation.

"No…a Caribbean fling wouldn't be a bad thing. He already wants you, Aly…" she murmured, the breeze and palm leaves lulling her as surely as the bed and its trimmings.

"And he'd really be a pleasure to…have…. Mmm…" She snuggled down almost into the center of the bed, thinking of those stunning eyes of his, the flawless coffee skin taut across that amazing chest.

A Caribbean fling wouldn't be a bad thing at all….

Chapter 5

Alythia's late-afternoon nap had worked wonders. The exhaustion that had threatened to buckle her knees when the plane had landed in San Juan had been effectively vanquished by the three-hour snooze. She awoke refreshed—and starving. The delicious and filling onboard lunch had worn off hours ago.

Thankfully, the hunger hadn't affected her appearance. She looked rested and stunning. She'd showered, dressed and then critiqued her image in the full-length mirror. Unless she was going out on the town, she rarely wore foundation. Her usual enhancement was a light dousing of eye shadow and lipstick. She'd packed a nice supply of all things makeup related but decided in that moment that they would remain packed. A healthy dose of sleep, rustling palm-tree leaves and a heavenly bed were the real secrets to radiance!

There was a knock and she felt a twinge of self-consciousness then. “Let’s hope my date thinks so.” She checked the gold-filigree clock on the dresser across the bedroom. She spared a minute for one last twirl in the mirror, loving the way the long hem of the lavender halter dress whirled around the flat sandals that highlighted her fresh pedicure. With one last quick toss of her blue-black waves, she headed for the door.

Had she had any concerns about whether Gage would disapprove of her joining him barefaced, she did away with them the instant she noticed the brilliant smile that set his gaze sparkling.

“You already answered my first question—did you sleep okay?” he asked with a striking grin. “Hungry?”

Alythia threw back her head as though she were depleted. “Starved, but sleep had to come first for me.”

“Surprised that you got three uninterrupted hours of it.” He leaned on the doorframe while voicing the observation.

“I still can’t believe that, either.” She blinked as if the remark gave her pause. “Did I miss anything…best left unmentioned?”

Gage bowed his head, studying his thumb as it traced the links of the silver timepiece he sported. “I think it’s safe to say that everybody had a pretty quiet day.” He pushed off the frame then, invading Alythia’s space to course his hands over her bare arms.

“Got a wrap or anything?”

Gage’s question went unanswered, his touch having rendered Alythia speechless and immovable for a weighty second. “I, um…” She motioned to the sofa, where a mosaic-print garment lay carelessly on a cushion. "Just there," she directed, thinking that he'd intended to collect it for her.

"Gage?" she called, tilting her head curiously when he only stood there smoothing his hands across her arms. "Hey?" She gave a tug to the cuff of the black shirt he wore outside cream-colored trousers.

"Right." He blinked and seemed to snap out of his reverie.

Alythia returned to the bedroom to grab her purse while Gage went to claim the wrap. She couldn't resist making another stop before the mirror to tousle her naturally windswept hair.

Gage was in possession of the wrap and had come to the bedroom door to watch her fussing in the mirror. Where the devil had she come from? He posed the question in silence but could still hear the bewilderment holding the words.

How was it he had never heard of her? He posed the second silent query and then caught himself. Heard of her? Exactly how up-to-date was he on any movers and shakers in the boutique business? Besides, Charlotte wasn't exactly a town where one saw his or her neighbors at the corner market on the regular. Still… what were the odds of meeting such a woman on a trip like this?

Such a woman? He considered that wording. Exactly what type of woman did he mean? He had a fine idea what type of women her friends were. He didn't hold that against them, but that wasn't Alythia.

She was very protective of her girls and he admired her for that. But was that all? Her looks and sexual appeal had captured him, there was no doubting that, but there was more. He believed that solving the mystery of her would simply ensnare him, happily entrap him far more than he already was.

Alythia offered up a sheepish smile when she turned from the mirror and found Gage staring. "Ready," she gushed, not reading the true intensity lurking in the liquid chocolate of his stare.

She reached for the wrap, but Gage held it out of her grasp, choosing to place it across her shoulders.

"You think I'll need this inside?" she asked.

"Doubt it." His response was canyon deep and absent.

Alythia didn't ask why he was draping it over her shoulders, then.

A good thing, too, because Gage wasn't sure she'd appreciate knowing that his reason was only that he wanted to touch her. The flat sandals were chic, sexy in a totally subtle way. She would most likely have been closer to his eye level were she wearing anything with a more substantial heel. Her lithe, fragile build beautifully enhanced the full B-cups and nicely rounded bottom that Gage was more than a little curious to discover the feel of cradled in his palms.

"Second thoughts?" she was asking, seeming curious about his fixed expression. She gave another light tug to his shirt cuff and smiled a bit brighter when he dipped his head to veil a suddenly bashful expression.

"Let's go." He cocked his head just slightly toward the door.

Quietly, they headed out.

Alythia was surprised to feel faint pinpricks of apprehension take hold. She knew what had stirred them but had no plan as to how to approach the subject.

"So where are we eating?" she asked instead.

"The resort's got a pretty good Italian restaurant. Um, loads of other stuff, too, if Italian's not…not your thing."

Uneasiness aside, Alythia couldn't help but smile over how concerned he seemed about making her aware that the choice was hers.

"You seem to know a lot about this place." She eased into the next phase of quelling her curiosity and satisfying those annoying pinpricks. "Must be nice to have a friend in the hospitality business."

They had arrived at the elevator bay. Gage had already pulled Alythia's arm into its usual place across the crook of his elbow. They walked the corridor, golden lit at night by the electric candles lining the walls. By day, rich sunlight was powerful enough to filter through the picture windows at either end of the space. Softly evocative tunes from the band on schedule for that evening piped in to enhance their stroll along the otherwise silent hall.

"Having a friend in the business is very nice but Dane, Zeke and Jay benefit more than I do." He depressed the elevator's down button and then hid his hand in a front trouser pocket. "My visits down here aren't usually about vacationing."

"Hmm…" Alythia tapped her fingers along the powerful cords of his forearm. "Sounds like *your* friends and *my* friends both have *workaholic* friends in common." She joined in for only a moment when Gage laughed to concede her point.

"Is that all the enjoyment you get from Clive's brainchild?" She ventured more steadily into the topic she had wanted to open since they left her suite.

"Clive doesn't complain." Gage shrugged. "Especially when my trips down here result in free business advice for him."

The elevator car arrived with a melodic and subtle ring.

"Does Clive only make moves you give the green light on?" Alythia asked once the doors closed and they began their descent.

Gage leaned against the rich oak-paneled car and regarded her with a fresh awareness. "Alythia?" He waited for her eyes to rest on his. "Clive isn't about to back out on this deal because of anything *I* say."

"I didn't mean—"

"Yes, you did." His words held no accusation, only soft amusement.

Sighing disappointedly, Aly lowered her eyes to the short carpeting beneath their feet. "Orchid's always warning me about being so anally involved in my business."

The close confines filled with the hearty rumble of Gage's laughter. "Do I even want to know what that is?" The question tumbled out on a chuckle.

The doors opened into the exotic music-filled lobby. Gage offered his arm, which Alythia accepted without thought.

"The explanation was forced on me," she said in a resigned fashion. "No reason why I can't share it with you."

Gage's ready laughter resumed as he led them deeper into the lively lobby.

"So I guess you finishing off our appetizers means you approve of the restaurant?" Gage drained the last of his beer and signaled the waiter for another.

Shameless, Aly scraped the last of the guacamole from a porcelain bowl. "It takes talent to make great guacamole and these folks have talent to spare."

"I'll have to make sure Clive keeps his cook staff, then."

There was a moment of quiet and then a flood of laughter between the couple as memories of their earlier conversation filtered in.

"So…anally involved in business?" Gage recalled the other path of their conversation before it had veered off into Alythia's ravings over Anegada Weeks' West Wing Restaurant Row.

The resort boasted over thirty eating establishments all along various wings inside the resort's main building. Each eatery carried a different theme and was staffed by Caribbean, Latin and Italian natives.

Alythia helped herself to more of the crisp sangria she'd ordered. Settling back, she studied the colorful liquid through the tall cooler she held.

"I prefer to think of it as being detail oriented. Orchid thinks I make a big deal of things when no big deal is required. It's a flaw I'm trying to work on." She shrugged and then drank deeply of the sangria.

Gage frowned. "I wouldn't say it's anything you need to stress over."

Aly held her glass poised in the air. "Excuse me? Are you the same man I just interrogated on the way down here?"

"I wouldn't have called it an interrogation."

"No…you're too polite to do that."

The assessment made him laugh again. Alythia didn't begrudge the attention he drew. Women turned in appreciation of the man and the sound of his amusement and Aly couldn't deny its ability to soothe.

"You don't know me very well." He sobered a bit. "Being detailed or *anally* involved is often a necessity in business. Those who aren't do so at the expense of their own interests."

"I see your point, but I think I could really stand to be a little less curious."

Gage tapped the base of the beer bottle while relaxing in his chair. "Questions aren't bad things, Alythia."

"Tell my friends that."

To himself Gage agreed that questions could prove pesky for anyone who lived as footloose as her girls—or *his* boys. "How often do you find yourself on the receiving end of their disapproval?" he asked.

Aly appeared stumped by the question but didn't have to locate an answer straightaway. The server had arrived with a fresh chilled beer for Gage and to take their entrée orders.

"You should try the sangria." Aly sang her words of encouragement.

"I'm good." Gage was pouring the brew into a tall frosted mug.

Aly was insistent. "If you try the sangria, I could order a pitcher instead of this inappropriate cooler."

"Order the pitcher, Alythia."

"And drink it by myself? Thanks for making *me* look like the lush."

"It's the Caribbean," he chuckled.

"It is, isn't it?" She reciprocated the waiter's smile. "A pitcher of sangria and bring *two* coolers, please. In case Mr. Vincent changes his mind."

"You know, I promise not to give you a hard time if you want to chug the damn thing right from the pitcher."

Aly threw back her head and laughed vibrantly. Gage propped his chin on his fist and simply enjoyed the sound of it. Each time he caught a glimpse of her eyes, he was struck by their amethyst shade and the enchanting way the light filtered through the almond-shaped orbs.

He thought she may have spied the intent way he watched her, because her laughter quieted a bit too abruptly. She seemed to withdraw a bit into herself. He didn't want to push, but he didn't care overmuch for the haunted look that had suddenly crept into her eyes.

"Alythia?"

"I love my friends, but they make me nervous." She blinked then, as though sharing the confession had all at once drawn her up and out of her thoughts.

"I can't believe I said that." She slapped her hands to her cheeks and watched Gage as if she was in awe. "You're a little *too* easy to talk to."

Gage leaned close to pull one hand down from her face. "I promise it goes no further than our table."

"I still shouldn't have said it."

"Don't you have a right to your opinion?" He gave a flip wave and reached for his chilled Samuel Adams. "My friends make me nervous all the time—I never know when I'll need to have bail money ready." He smirked. "But I guess they feel the same way about me. It's to be expected when it comes to friends, especially the wild and crazy ones." The smirk became a lopsided grin that was intended to make her smile.

Aly put forth a real effort, but clearly her heart wasn't in it. "It's not the same," she said.

"Because you're women?" he guessed.

The sangria arrived blessedly fast and Aly watched the rich red drink being poured as though she were a woman dying of thirst.

"Sir? Will you be joining your lady?" the server asked.

Alythia stopped the glass midway to her mouth. Her eyes clashed with Gage's and she looked away, desperate for something to focus on across the dining room.

Gage didn't appear at all displeased by the waiter's unintentional slip. "I'd very much like to join my lady."

"Yes…it's different because we're women." Aly waited to voice her agreement until after they'd taken a few sips of the sangria.

"Alythia—"

She waved off the apology he was about to utter. "Blame it on my stupid curiosity, but I really want to know what's going through your mind right now about my friends."

Gage set aside his cooler, losing his taste for the fruity drink. "Honey, I don't know 'em well enough to voice an opinion like that."

"Not even the bride? That's strange considering she's about to marry one of your best friends."

"Jay tends to live in his own world and has always had a problem with ridicule. Besides, he's kind of kept us all in the dark about this."

"Ah…so he'd expect some kind of ridicule if he'd shared things with you guys about Orchid?"

Gage made another stab at finishing his sangria. Silently, he complimented Alythia's sharp mind while simultaneously condemning his loose tongue.

"I promise that nothing you say here will go further than our table. . . ." She smiled.

"What do you want to know?" He set the cooler down.

"I'd like to know what you think of my friends."

"And what's that got to do with why they make you nervous?"

"I'll make it easy for you," Aly countered, expertly sidestepping his question. "What do you think of them based on your impressions during the flight?"

Gage rested an elbow on the table. Tapping fingers against his brow, he let her glimpse his weariness. He couldn't see their conversation going anywhere but down. "I didn't bring you out for this," he said finally.

Aly shook the fruit at the bottom of her glass and shrugged. "I'm sure you didn't."

"That's not fair, Alythia."

"I'm not accusing you." She fixed him with a non-judgmental look. "You'd be well within rights to expect I'd follow in my friends' footsteps. I just think it's best to get it out of the way and tell you you're wasting your time with me if you expect that. I'm not made that way."

"Your dining requests are coming through just now."

The attentive server returned with the food update. Gage pushed back his chair and stood, drawing the waiter aside, where they conducted a brief and quiet chat.

Alythia watched Gage push a few bills into the man's shirt pocket, and then he was helping her from her chair and escorting her from the dining room.

Nerves mixed in with a considerable amount of regret, but Aly kept up with Gage's long strides out of the restaurant. She could almost feel the waves of fury he radiated. He surely had every right to be pissed, she thought, recalling Orchid's consistent accusations about her anal involvement in business. That was an inaccurate summation. She was anally involved in friendship drama, which always found a way to weave itself in and make her a complete basket case.

Alythia decided not to waste time in trying to explain herself to him. She'd just accept the silent treatment on the way back to her suite. At least he wasn't too angry to walk her back. Then they could forget their poor attempt at following their friends' dance steps to the bedroom and get on with enjoying the rest of their vacations separately.

It was then that Alythia discovered they weren't headed back to the suites but out of the resort's main hall entirely. Aly shivered as much from the chill of the evening air kissing her bare skin through the wrap as she did from the anticipation of what was to follow their sudden departure from the dining room. Curiosity had her close to bursting, but she pressed her lips together to silence any questions that might have tried to slip past.

"Questions aren't bad, but there are occasions when the timing is," he said from where he stood behind her once they were on a deserted strip of the beach.

Regardless of what was in store for the remainder of the evening, a portion of Alythia's unease did begin to fade when the ocean's quiet roar reached her ears. Awed, she moved as if tugged by some unseen force toward the sound of the water. The surf was just visible via the strong moonlight and a powerful glow radiated along the rear expanse of the resort to douse the beach with a mellow illumination.

Once again the sea air that had calmed her upon arrival so many hours earlier had the same effect as she inhaled it then. Even the rush of the waves bumping the shore induced a great degree of solace. She smiled when the cool water sluiced between her toes, gliding between the soles of her feet and her sandals.

Gage stood off to Aly's side several feet away and just outside the range of the seeking water. Head bowed, his hands were propped lightly at his lean hips.

"My friends make me nervous because they do things that other people expect me to do when I'm with them." She at last gave him the answer he wanted. "So much of me wants to be that way, free and without a care for the consequences, but I—I can never trust it and relax enough to… Part of me wonders if I just care too damn much about what people think of me or…maybe I just…" *Care too damn much about who I'm free with.* She could only share the last with herself.

"Jeena thinks I'm a Goody Two-Shoes." She laughed and then turned to Gage, who stared fixedly while she confided. "I know you hate apologies, but I really am sorry for ruining your night."

He regarded her for a few moments more, tracking his golden-chocolate gaze up and down her body. Slowly, he covered the distance between them. Smoothing his hands over her arms, he massaged her through the silken material of the wrap.

"You didn't ruin my night." The massage he applied to her arms served to draw her closer even as it pampered her.

"I wanted to have dinner, laugh and talk…not about this…." He joined in when she laughed. "My night was about as far from ruined as it could get."

His head dipped and he plied her with what was intended to be a peck. That peck turned into something worthy of residing in the realm of full-blown lust. In the back of her mind, Aly remembered what she'd said about not being able to relax enough. That was a myth that Gage Vincent was effectively demolishing as his tongue enticed hers into a lazy duel.

The act progressed, slowly at first, as though Gage was more intent on exploring than taking. He stroked the roof of her mouth, crested his tongue along the ridge of her teeth before returning to play with her tongue. He evaded when she would have engaged and chuckled when she whimpered her impatience at his tactics.

Aly wouldn't, couldn't, stop to consider what type of mixed signal she might have been giving him. After all, she'd just claimed that she could never relax enough to be free, only to turn around and kiss him senseless. She didn't care what he thought in that moment, only that he kept doing what he was doing.

Alythia hadn't given thought to how hungry she was for affection until it was being oh so incredibly given to her. She reciprocated the suckling intensity he treated her to when he had her tongue entangled with his. She planned to give and take for as long as she could.

Or until the sound of glasses, dinnerware and cutlery filtered through her erotically charged thoughts. Alythia sighed her disappointment when Gage patted her hip, easing her out of the kiss as he did so.

Opening her eyes, Aly immediately searched for the source of the sounds that had interrupted her romantic moment beneath tropical stars. Blinking owlishly, she frowned at the sight a few yards from where she and

Gage stood. There was a table set for a candlelight meal for two. She looked to him.

Gage slanted her a wink. "Dinner is served."

Chapter 6

Dinner looked amazing and she was in fact starving. Alythia was, however, willing to let her stomach take a backseat to her… She wouldn't finish the thought. Not even silently. Instead, she tried putting on a gracious look, yet felt her facial muscles failing her miserably.

"Clive sure does pull out all the stops for his friends," she noted as they neared the beautifully set table. "At least *you've* got friends who offer less stress than they give."

"You didn't know him in college." Gage grinned, then sobered a bit. "Clive's a good guy." He rounded the table after pushing in her chair and looked to be debating his next words. "He's ethical, too. You can believe me when I say that he'd never accept or back out of a deal because of anything I or anyone else might say."

Alythia shook her head, hitting her cheeks with a

few wavy locks. "I shouldn't have said that, assumed that he was—"

"What? Like most of the men you've done business with?"

"Ha! No…no, actually, I've been fortunate enough to deal with mostly women in my business so far."

"Glad to hear it."

Alythia was wincing. "That didn't sound quite so cold in my head."

"I'm still glad to hear it. If your effect on Clive is any example, you'd probably have more men than him falling in love with you."

"In love?" she said with a laugh, and then reached down to unfasten and remove her sandals. "He sure is easy to please. We haven't even had a real conversation in person yet."

"The man's been known to fall in love during a phone call, so…" Gage provided a noncommittal shrug.

The couple indulged in a round of laughter at Clive's expense. Gage was the first to sober and had more fun watching Alythia succumb to another bout of mirth. His laughter had curbed into a smile as he shifted, reclining comfortably in his seat, and watched her. He'd wanted to kiss her since he saw her, wanted to know if her mouth was as soft as it looked and if her tongue felt as sweet as the words it formed sounded.

He shifted again, realizing that his *wants* were starting to affect parts of his body best left settled.

"Bless you," Alythia was saying as the servers set dinner in place. She had ordered a petite sirloin with scallops and au gratin potatoes.

Chef salad and rolls served as the table's centerpiece.

Gage indulged in a heartier New York strip, his side portions just a tad larger than Alythia's. They dined in companionable silence, which was marked only by the sound of waves and the faint vibration of music. The grooves bumped from either the resort's main building or the beachfront bar a ways down the shore—it was hard to tell which. Nevertheless, the sounds were a perfect accompaniment to a delicious meal.

The sounds *were* a perfect accompaniment to a delicious meal until they were marred by the unmistakable undercurrents of argument. Gage caught the voices before Alythia did. She heard him curse and looked up and back over her shoulder, closing her eyes at the sight of Jeena and Zeke.

The couple stormed down the beach, their bodies turning slightly inward as they spoke what appeared to be increasingly heated words the closer they came to where Gage and Alythia dined.

Zeke and Jeena had yet to notice their friends eating a few yards away, but their voices were well within range. Alythia bowed her head, feeling the sting of the words Zeke directed at her friend as though they were being aimed at her.

"Such a joke," he spat. "Do you know how stupid you sound talking about healthcare plans for a bunch of hookers?"

Jeena was tough to the bone. Alythia knew she'd refuse to cower or cry regardless of how deep the words cut.

"At least it's something *I* built! I don't have to sponge money off of a more successful friend to scratch out a little *piece* of something like that pitiful brokerage firm of yours! How many gasps of air has it taken this week?"

The lovers' spat went back and forth. Aly, though reluctant to do so, finally sent a look over to Gage. He appeared as beleaguered as she felt.

Gage shook his head. *I'm sorry,* he mouthed.

Aly's smile almost turned into a grin. It seemed that the phrase had become a staple of their brief acquaintance. Jeena's and Zeke's voices raised another octave then.

"I was so wrong about you!"

"Then we're a perfect mixed match!" Zeke threw up his hands. "'Cause I was exactly *right* about you! Guess a person really is what they do for a living. Least I didn't have to pay for it!"

Whatever toughness Jeena claimed dissolved. Then she was running, stumbling along the stretch of beach away from Zeke, Gage and Alythia.

"Jeena!" Aly scrambled from the table to call out to her friend. It was no good. She looked to Gage.

"I should go see about her." She sent a regretful look toward her half-finished meal.

"Go." Gage waved a hand.

Aly hesitated another few seconds, then backed away from the table and turned to race down the shore, kicking up tufts of sand as she went after Jeena. She'd bypassed Zeke, who was extending his hands as though he was about to plead his case.

Zeke let his hands fall to his sides in an "oh well" gesture. He turned, giving a start as though he'd just realized Gage was there.

"G!" Easy and lighthearted at once, Zeke gave an

approving smile at the table. He took a seat in the chair Aly had just vacated.

"Looks good!" he raved. Sniffing at a glass, he realized it was water and tossed the liquid to the sand in order to refill the glass with the wine left chilling in the bucket near the table.

Defeated, Gage resumed his seat and rested his forehead in his palm.

"Thanks for letting me ramble on so late or so early in the morning. What time is it there?"

Marianne yawned through the phone line. "Too early to try and get my eyes to focus in on a clock."

Aly smiled. "Thanks anyway."

"What you pay me for, hon."

"Not exactly." Aly rubbed at her temple. "I don't pay you to listen to stupid tales of drama featuring me and my friends."

"Well...if it affects your well-being, it *is* my business, so it's all good."

"Get some rest, Mari. You've earned it. We'll talk later."

"*Much* later. Can you at least try and take *one* day for yourself?"

"I'll try." Aly hoped that wouldn't turn out to be a lie and ended the call. She set aside the phone and returned her attention to the view from where she sat in one of the cushioned bamboo chairs along the balcony.

The suite was dark. She hadn't bothered with the lights after returning from Jeena's room. It hadn't been easy, but she'd finally gotten her friend settled enough to get some sleep. Too wired to sleep herself, Aly had decided to call Marianne, to whom she had been venting for the past forty-five minutes.

Aly checked her mobile for the time and figured she'd best *try* to get a little sleep herself if she hoped to appear halfway among the land of the living when she met with Clive Weeks later that day.

On perfect cue the doorbell rang. *No more.* Alythia dropped her face in her palms to muffle the sound.

The bell was followed by knocking and Aly heard her name on Gage's voice. After a second's hesitation she left the chair and padded through the living area. Her forced smile was an appropriate match to his concerned one when she opened the door.

"You okay?" he asked.

She could only nod, a gesture that ceased when Gage moved closer to rest against the doorframe.

"Did you eat?" His gaze seemed to intensify tenfold as he peered down at her.

Aly laughed abruptly, looking bewildered, as though she couldn't imagine where she found strength to fuel the reaction.

"I managed to convince Jeena to have some soup. I took some for myself but it was a far cry from the dinner I didn't get to finish."

"How's Jeena?"

Aly could only shake her head.

Gage provided a weak smile. "I could always apologize."

She backed away from the door as though he'd told her he had a plague. "Could we please find another phrase to put in place of 'I apologize' or 'I'm sorry'?"

Gage lifted his thumb to the corner of his mouth and appeared to be debating. "How about 'That's too bad'?"

"Sold!" She was surprised by the honest ripple of laughter she gave.

"I think my suggestion should come with a peace offering."

Aly saw the straps of her sandals dangling from his index and middle fingers. "Hmph, good thing I didn't get more comfortable."

"Mmm-hmm." Whatever interest Gage had in talking seemed to have vanished, for he suddenly pushed off the doorframe and advanced.

Alythia had opened her mouth to thank him for returning her shoes but he never gave her the chance. For the second time that day, her body reacted to the delicious sensation of his mouth on hers. Again he began with a tentative exploration that quickly blossomed into a sensuous entwining of their tongues.

Gage withdrew from the kiss to outline the curve of her cheek, brush the sensitive skin behind her ear and trail his nose along her neck.

"Gage?"

"Mmm…"

"Do you kiss all women you know so soon after you meet them?"

He nipped at her earlobe. "Would you believe that I've forgotten every other woman I've ever met?"

"No," she gasped, still enraptured by his touch and feeling the vibration of laughter through his body.

"You really know how to hurt a man."

"It's not out of habit." Aly felt her sandals bumping her bottom when he switched them to his other hand while he held her. "So what do I have to do to get my shoes back?" she murmured against his jaw, wanting his mouth on hers.

Something in Alythia's question, however, cooled Gage's ardor, for he rested his forehead on her shoulder as if he was suddenly drained. He straightened.

"You don't have to do one thing." He glanced around the living area, grimacing slightly, as though he was displeased with himself.

"I'll…um…I'll let you get some rest." He retreated to the door.

"Okay…." Her agreement was at odds with the questions and confusion clouding her mind. Had she said—done—something wrong?

Gage offered the sandals and she hoped her efforts to mask disappointment were good enough. Aly took special care not to let her fingers touch his hands when she took the shoes.

"Thanks." She didn't bother to show him to the door and he left without a look back.

"Is this only day *two* of our *fantastic* Caribbean getaway?" Jeena moaned, holding her head in her hands while she and Alythia took in the beach view from Jeena's balcony later that morning.

They had ordered breakfast for Orchid and Myrna, who were on the way to join them. Aly enjoyed the breeze and shade while relaxing in one of the lounge chairs surrounding the squat glass table that carried their breakfast fixings—fruit, biscuits, cheeses, turkey bacon and sausage, and a bowl of breakfast potatoes. Matching tea- and coffeepots were the table's centerpieces.

"You should eat," Alythia ordered from beneath the wide brim of a floppy straw hat. She risked taking a peek at Jeena, smiling when the woman pouted for a moment longer, then delved into the filling meal.

Aly took on greeting responsibilities when she heard the faint chime of the doorbell. She found the last two members of her crew on the other side.

"Long time no see," Myrna drawled, tugging Aly into a hug.

Orchid had no time for such pleasantries. She'd already pushed her way past Aly and Myrna and was headed to the balcony.

"What the hell did you say to Zeke?" she demanded of Jeena.

"Dammit." Alythia rolled her eyes toward Myrna. "I just got Jeen to calm down. This is the last thing they need to be talking about."

"You can forget that," Myrna countered while they speed-walked to the balcony. "Zeke was bitchin' to Jay about it pretty much all night. Ork's not in much of a 'benefit of the doubt' frame of mind."

Aly stumbled to a halt. "How do you know that?"

"Oh, Dane and I stopped by their room before we went back to ours."

Alythia delivered a quick prayer that the falling-out sure to occur when Dane relieved Myrna of the notion that they were a couple would wait until after things settled with Zeke and Jeena.

Or *Orchid* and Jeena, as it were. Aly arrived out on the balcony to find her oldest friends squared off in the middle of a shouting match.

"How can you take that jackass's side over mine!"

"Because I've heard it all before! You always get upset when somebody tells you the truth about what you do for a living!"

"Orchid—"

"Passing yourself off like some kind of business-woman." Orchid ignored Alythia's attempt to interrupt. "All you are is a pimp."

Myrna gasped.

"Bitch," Jeena spat. "I'd rather be a pimp than a slut. At least a hooker gets paid."

Orchid winced as though the words were a physical blow. "What are you tryin' to say?"

"You never were very bright, were you?" Jeena sneered, folding her arms over the red robe she'd thrown on over matching pjs. "Then again, you never had to be, with Aly in your corner."

"Don't even try it! Y'all are *not* drawin' me into this!"

The women didn't seem to notice Aly bolting from the balcony.

"Aly to make you seem smarter than you are, your family's money to make you seem more respectable that you could ever hope to be and a parade of idiots in your bed to solidify your slut status!" Jeena wailed. The wind whipped her short hair about her face and added to the wild aura she cast.

Impossibly, the voice volume continued to heighten. In the living room, Aly could only hope the women wouldn't come to blows. As she was on her way out, Myrna would indeed ruin her manicure trying to break them apart.

"You're crazy, Alythia Marie Duffy, if you think you're leavin' *me* here with them fools," Myrna hissed when she raced out into the living room behind Aly.

"It's okay, Mur, I already called Jay to come get his fiancée." Alythia patted a side pocket on her rust-colored shirtdress to ensure her room key was inside. "You only have to keep the peace for a few more minutes. If you get nervous, call Dane."

"And where are *you* going?" Myrna propped her hands, fingers-down, on her hips.

"I have a meeting." Alythia sighed in relief, not seeing the need to hide her motives any longer.

Myrna straightened, her cool, lovely gaze narrowing with discovery. "That's why you came on the trip, isn't it?"

"And it's a good thing, too. At least I'll get something out of it besides catfights."

Myrna glanced in the general direction of the balcony. "Don't you even care enough to help me calm them down?"

"Please, Mur, Jeena will see what an idiot she was to have sex with that horse's ass thirty minutes after she met him."

Myrna blinked. "Is that what you think about me and Dane?"

"Sweetie, you and Dane are *not* a couple." Aly's tone was full of sympathy but she wouldn't apologize for her honesty.

"You're wrong. We've been talking and we plan to keep on seeing each other when we get back."

"I'm sure you will. He's not ready to close off a new sex pipeline so fast."

"You take that back!"

"Ah, Myrna, do you hear how childish you sound?" Aly clasped her hands in a pleading gesture against the front of her dress. "Y'all have been ridiculous with these guys."

"Well, Aly, maybe me and Jeen want to find what Orchid has! Unlike *you,* maybe *we* don't want to wind up lonely with only a bank account to show for a long life."

"Mur." Alythia's expression was one of sudden suspicion. "You don't think Dane's gonna marry you?" She could see in Myrna's eyes that she held on to just that hope. "Sweetie, you and Jeen are just something they wanted to play with for a while."

Myrna was shaking her head. "Do you ever get sick of being so upstanding? So high, mighty and right all the damn time?"

"I'm sorry you think that, Mur. I don't mean to hurt you. It's just so clear what's happening. I'm just sorry you guys can't see it."

"Go to your meeting, Aly." Myrna smirked. "Business is the only thing you'll probably ever get off on anyway."

Alythia watched Myrna head back into the argument on the balcony. Her fingers ached with the need to pull the woman back, hug her and try to work it out. She resisted, for the first time feeling that a permanent line was being marked between her and her dearest friends.

Chapter 7

The Weeks' Resort Outlet Lane had all the quaint charm of a Mediterranean village. The cobblestone streets and stone structures seemed right at home amid the tropical loveliness of Anegada. Partially hidden by the lush palm tree leaves, the area gave its visitors the revitalizing feel of stepping into a world long past.

Alythia judged from the number of resort guests she saw inside and along the streets of the shopping village that such an effect was most probably quite successful in opening wallets and purses.

"I could see it," she announced to no one in particular, and heard soft chuckling afterward. Turning, she saw that Clive Weeks was the culprit.

"May I take your reaction to mean that we'll be doing business?" she asked.

"Only if your business manager agrees."

"She's fired if she doesn't."

They shared a laugh.

"She'll agree based on the location alone." Aly sobered a little and took closer inventory of her surroundings. "That way she can delude herself into believing her workaholic client is at least a *little* distracted from business."

Clive pretended to be crestfallen. "So the place would only distract you a *little?*"

"Well, I wouldn't want her to think I was *completely* falling down on the job." Her shrug was as playful as her smile.

"Well, you already know what *my* business manager thinks." Clive folded his arms over the pale blue shirt he wore and relaxed against the framing along the glass doors at the back of the proposed retail space for the boutique.

Alythia continued to walk in slow circles, assessing the area and conjuring promotional ideas. "And what about you? Do you really believe a clothing store would fare well here?"

"Are you kidding? I'm surprised I didn't have the idea sooner."

"Well, maybe the right idea hadn't come along yet."

"Yeah..." Clive's playfully crestfallen look returned. "Now I've got the right idea—and a woman after my own heart, if only my friend hadn't met you first."

Alythia took no offense to the teasing gibe, though a curious element crept over her expression. "Your interest in the boutique now wouldn't all be part of a favor you're doing for that friend, would it?"

Clive moved from the doorframe, a wave of seriousness having claimed him, as well. "The idea appealed to me so much I wasn't sure whether to trust it, so I asked Gage for his opinion." His guileless grin returned. "I'm happy he agreed, otherwise I'd have had to go against one of the best minds in business."

"You won't be sorry about this, Clive."

"I know." He rubbed his hands together and looked around the snug, sunny space. "I think I'll give you time alone to get acclimated to the place."

"Sounds good." She took both his hands and shook them as enthusiastically as he did hers. "Thanks, Clive."

He left her with a wink and a nod. Alythia waited for him to disappear down an overgrown side road and, after making sure there were no other prying eyes, broke into a carefree dance around the space. She stopped short then, recalling her talk with Myrna earlier that morning. Business wasn't all she could *get off* on, but it would have to do for a while longer.

Though smaller than her other two locations, the Anegada space boasted large picture windows to the front and rear of the main floor. There would be perfect natural lighting during the day and a lovely view of twinkling lights from the resort at night. Alythia made a note to return one evening to see the effect for herself.

Beyond the double glass doors, the rear exit opened out into a small courtyard and offered a striking view of the beach. Dropping down to one of the lounges, Alythia envisioned daily fashion shows in the space to entice patrons inside for a closer look.

Aly pressed her head back into the navy-and-gray lounge cushions and commanded her brain to take a break. Her business was pretty much concluded, then, and it was time for a retreat from all things dramatic and confusing.

Gage Vincent came to mind then. Confusing? No, he was pretty much laying it all on the line about what he wanted. Wasn't he? She thought about his behavior when he'd come to check on her after Jeena's battle with Zeke. Maybe he'd decided to call it quits before anything really got started between the two of them. She certainly couldn't blame him in light of the drama he had been witness to courtesy of her friends.

But that wasn't quite fair, was it? What about *his* friends and their behavior? Couldn't she just as easily back away from him in light of what *she'd* been witness to?

"Mmm… Aly, it's too early in the day for all this heavy thinking." Besides, she'd done enough of that with Clive. Satisfied, she rested with her eyes closed while she inhaled the floral air and treated her ears to the sounds of rushing water, wind and birdsong.

"Looks like Clive made a sale…."

Smiling, Alythia added the sound of Gage's voice to her list of soothing elements. "You bet he did. I'm gonna hire people to run the shop and just spend my days out here."

Gage took a seat on one of the accompanying lounges. "Sounds like the workaholic's getting tired of working so hard?"

"Can you blame me?" Aly took a long, indulgent stretch. "Honestly? Who could think of working with a view like this?"

Tell me about it. Gage knew the view he had in mind had nothing to do with the sand and waves. He could have watched her all day but the watching would definitely lead to a desire to touch and that was what was causing all the…issues that were presently revealing themselves. Wouldn't she expect him to fall in line with his friends and make a play for her? Hadn't he done that already? They'd kissed more than once and she'd seemed to enjoy it as much as he had. Was there any more to it? he wondered.

The only thing he was sure of was that he didn't want to stop seeing her after the trip. Problem was, she might not be so interested if *his* friends and *her* friends kept butting heads. If he took her to his bed only to have things go awry… A voice chimed that at least he'd have had the pleasure of her in his bed. He lost himself in a study of the length and shapeliness of her legs bared beneath the knee-length hem of her dress. He finally tuned in that she was calling out to him and he saw her watching him inquisitively.

"Will you come dancing with me tonight?" He roamed the length of her legs again. "I planned for us to do that last night but, well…"

"We didn't even get through the eating part of our date," Aly laughed. "Do you really want to test fate again?"

"I'm willing." Gage leaned forward, resting his elbows on the khaki shorts covering his thighs. "I promise you'll have a good time if you let me show you one."

"I could use one." Alythia pushed a hand through her hair, held it there. "I could use a lot of things—another nap, breakfast…"

"You didn't have anything?"

Her smile was sad. "Breakfast with the girls got a little out of hand."

"Yeah…" Gage slumped back against his lounge, tossing a leg on either side and planting feet adorned in Crocs in the sand. “Jay came down on Orchid pretty hard last night.”

“He did?” She pushed herself up to prop on an elbow and watch him expectantly. “Maybe that’s why she came down so hard on Jeen this morning. Myrna must’ve missed Jay getting on her case about it last night when she and Dane stopped by. She said Ork didn’t have much sympathy for our friend.”

“That part’s true.” Gage tented his fingers above his abdomen, intermittently bumping them. “How much do you know about their relationship—Jay and Orchid’s?”

“Not much.” Aly rested back on the lounge. “Just what I told you before. It was all very sudden. What, um…what do you know?” she asked hesitantly.

“The wedding’s for show, Alythia.” He closed his eyes for a moment or two. “To secure some deal between Jay’s family and hers.”

“That’s insane! Orchid wouldn’t even go for something like that. Do families still even do that?”

“You’d be surprised how well a company’s stock can do by a good run in the press. Everyone loves a wedding.” He gave Aly a resigned smile. “It’s all for show. According to Jay, Orchid’s father threatened to cut her off if she balks.”

“My God…” Aly was sitting up straight in the middle of the lounge, hand over her mouth.

“It’s probably a good idea to keep this to yourself. Jay only told me after Orchid went to bed and Zeke left with Dane and Myrna.”

“That explains all the overwhelming affection….” Aly shook her head, still incredulous. “And why she’s so hell-bent on everybody getting along.”

Gage watched Alythia cradle her head in her hands,

the wind whipping her hair into disarray. The last thing he'd wanted was to upset her.

"Let's get you some breakfast," he suggested.

"My appetite is suddenly gone."

"Then let's find it." He stood, offering a hand, and pulled her from the lounge when she accepted.

"I could just get room service." She slapped her hands to her sides. "Turn in after I eat."

"I don't trust you to do that." He reciprocated her gesture. "I do trust that I'll get you to eat and then put you to bed myself."

She rested a hand against the white tee he wore beneath an unbuttoned denim shirt. "Are you trying to save me, Gage Vincent?"

"No." He pulled her arm through his. "But I do like taking care of you."

Together they left the courtyard.

The Glow was located along the wing that housed the resort's bars and dance halls. Gage and Alythia had planned to meet there instead of him picking her up at the suite.

Aly didn't see her date right away and took a trip to the bar for a drink—*one* drink. While more would be enjoyable, it wasn't advisable. Besides, the early nap following lunch in the breakfast café located in the shopping villa had really hit the spot.

Aly had barely taken a sip of her piña colada when a man who had taken the seat next to her at the bar offered her another round.

"You should move on, sir. The lady isn't alone," the barkeep advised. He waited for the suitor to relinquish his seat and then acknowledged Alythia's curious stare.

"Mr. V's on his way, miss." He nodded.

Rather dazed, Aly turned on the barstool to see that Gage was in fact making his way through a moderately heavy crowd. His expression was unreadable even though he pulled many hungry looks from single and attached patrons.

His handsome face brightened when he saw her waiting. "Thanks for not standing me up," he teased.

"No problem." She shrugged. "My other options weren't very appealing."

"That's good to hear." He grinned, fingering one of the silver tassels dangling from the capped sleeves of her flare-legged powder-blue jumpsuit.

"Mr. V." The barkeep provided Gage with a drink.

"Wow, that's some gift. You didn't even tell him what you wanted." Aly propped her chin on her palm and watched Gage take a swig of a Samuel Adams brew. "Or is it that you've been here so often that everyone knows your favorite drinks?"

"Li'l bit of both," he said, throwing her a wink.

"Bartenders looking out for your drinks, your date… Nice. He practically kicked out this poor guy who tried to buy me a drink…." She trailed off, having captured a glimpse of a muscle flexing wickedly along Gage's jaw.

"Boyd was just looking out for *you,* actually." He cast a disapproving look around the bar. "Some places in Clive's resort can be…a challenge for a woman on her own."

"In what way?" Aly smiled when another barkeep provided her with a fresh drink.

"Usual." He shrugged. "Same as with any other club—drinks spiked with more than extra alcohol, for instance."

Aly gave her glass a cautious nudge. "Does that happen a lot?"

"Enough so that it's a concern for Clive." Gage turned to lean back against the bar and observe the establishment more fully. "The staff's on high alert when they see a gorgeous woman on her own at the bar."

"I see." Aly sipped her drink and then smiled. "And what if the gorgeous woman is the one doing the spiking?"

Her question roused Gage's laughter and Alythia soon joined in.

"That *would* be interesting," he said. "I honestly have no comeback for that."

"I'll bet." Aly laughed into her glass.

Gage extended his hand. "Maybe I'll think of something while we dance."

Playful skepticism brightened her expression. "Do you really think I can be trusted?"

His warm stare made a quick heated dip to the subtle V-cut bodice of her suit when he invaded her space a little more. "I'll trust you if you trust me. How's that?"

"I don't know.... I still think you're dangerous." Her playfulness curbed when she noted the change in his eyes.

"I believe I've been a very good boy." Again he toyed with the tassels at her sleeves. "Compared to some," he added.

"That's what makes you so dangerous." She tilted her head, lashes fluttering slightly against his whisper-soft touch. "You've got uncanny control over your restraint."

Gage nodded as though her point hadn't surprised him. "You know, that's what I used to think."

They were close then. Alythia was without word or

the ability to even produce one. She felt him squeezing her upper arm, patting her hip as he did so.

"How 'bout that dance?"

"That's what we're here for." She eased down off the barstool.

Gage acknowledged the truth in his words moments into the dance. Yes, the restraint he'd once prided himself on having was in fact gone, but the realization of that forced another question. How much restraint had he ever *truly* had?

His methods were—at least, he *hoped* they were—more refined than his friends'. Nonetheless, when it came to women, those methods were all meant to achieve the same goal: a new woman in his bed. Alythia Duffy was a beauty, no doubt, but beauty was what he tended to surround himself with. While her looks were what had first and shallowly beckoned him, they weren't his primary thoughts when she came to mind.

So what was it, then? Her concern for her friends? Dedication to her job? Or was his attraction more selfish—more about what she made him feel when he was in her presence?

What Aly felt then was calm, a stillness that had rooted itself someplace deep and was not budging. The music, while lovely and soothing, barely registered. She didn't care if her stance, pliant and clingy, unnerved him. She planned to enjoy the moment, indulge in every bit of what he was making her feel.

And how far was she willing to go in her desire to indulge? She inhaled from where her face rested in the side of his neck. Subtly, she arched, binding herself into his impressively athletic frame. She craved just a bit more of the incredible pleasure that his closeness provided.

Gage released her hand, which he'd curved into his chest. Then he was smoothing his palms across her back and shoulders. He massaged them down again, cupping her hips and enfolding them to bring her closer and seal her in the circle of his arms.

Somewhere the faint sound of shattering glass cluttered the air but the effect had no sway over the oasis sheltering them.

"Alythia…"

"Mmm…"

He brushed a kiss to her earlobe, gave it a dry suckle before applying the same attention to the sensitive skin beneath. "Will you think less of me if I ask you to come to bed with me?"

"Hmph." Her response was more of a sigh. "Will you think less of me if I accept?"

He straightened his stance then, curving a hand around the base of her throat. He kissed her hungrily, and she responded with equal fire, thrusting her tongue against his, rotating and stroking as if she was desperate for the friction.

Alythia heard a gasp, understandable. Kissing the man was a definite treat with the power to send tingles to every nerve ending she owned. The only problem was that the gasp hadn't come from her and had sounded more outraged than…sensual.

Sounds of a commotion had followed the shattering glass, at last encroaching upon the sweet oasis Gage and Alythia had enjoyed.

"They've got to be doing this stuff on purpose," he

murmured when he and Aly emerged from passion's sweet spell to discover that their mutual friends were at the center of a lovers' spat.

"No…" Aly groaned. She felt Gage take her chin and squeeze.

"Come with me," he encouraged when her bright eyes met his warm chocolate ones. "We really don't need to be here, do we?"

His question was answered by Myrna Fisher.

"Flaky backstabber!"

Dane Spears wasn't offended. "You should be happy to get rid of me. This place has lots more fools to screw and pretend they're your man."

Myrna responded by throwing a sticky mixed drink in his face and shoving his chest before she stormed out.

"We don't need to be here, but we probably should be," Aly said.

Gage kept her near when she attempted to move from his side. "One day I hope to have a friend as good as you."

Alythia closed her eyes and smiled. "Me, too."

Then she was gone. Gage's soft expression vanished the moment she moved through the chaotic crowd to reach Myrna.

A storm brewed in Gage's striking stare as he went to seek out his friend.

Alythia caught up to her girlfriend just as she approached the elevator corridor. Thankfully, the area was deserted. Myrna was so upset that Alythia didn't have to probe her for details. Myrna shared it all in a stream of anger and pain. She told her that the man of her dreams had slept with someone else.

"The masseuse, of all people! I'm such an idiot." Myrna punched the up arrow on the elevator's panel. "I thought it'd be fun to have a couple's massage. Dane decided to spend half his time in the sauna. He didn't spend it there alone."

Alythia reached out. "I'm sorry."

Myrna shrugged off Aly's hand when it touched her shoulder. "Go on and tell me you told me so. I just want to get the hell out of here." She punched the up arrow again. "Forget this getaway, get-to-know-you—whatever the devil it is."

"Mur." Aly stifled her instinct to move closer. "You can't do that. Orchid's really counting on us right now. It's really important to her." She pressed her lips together, annoyed that she couldn't explain the particulars of *why* it was so important to their friend.

Myrna slowly turned from the elevator to fix Aly with a scathing look. "Do you ever get sick of being such a hypocrite?"

"Mur—"

"So it's okay for *you* to traipse off to handle business when our friends need us, but I can't leave even after I've just been humiliated?"

"Honey, I didn't mean it that way." Aly rubbed at her temples.

Myrna snorted. "Yeah, right." She turned back to the elevator.

Losing whatever patience she'd thought she had, Aly flinched and then drew her hands from her face and gave a resounding clap. "You know what? Do whatever the hell you want—you will anyway. Do you really think Dane Spears came here to find a soul mate?" She laughed the words. "He didn't care a bit more about that than any of the other dozens of guys you've taken to bed hoping they'd put a ring on your finger the next morning. Open your eyes, Mur. You're better than this."

Myrna had turned from the elevator again and still regarded Alythia coolly. "Since we're giving advice, Aly, I should tell you to keep your eyes open, too." She moved closer, ignoring the elevator car that arrived just then. "If you think that Gage Vincent is such a golden boy because he hasn't taken you to bed just yet, you can think again. From what I hear, that one loses interest very fast once he's gotten the panties and the fact that he hasn't taken yours yet isn't a token of how good he is." Myrna gave her a sulky once-over. "He's just trying to make it last. We *are* gonna be here for nine more days, you know?"

"Let me guess." Aly brought her hands to her hips. "Your soul mate told you this?"

Myrna stiffened but she didn't cower. "Just because you've got your face stuck in spreadsheets and faxes all day doesn't mean the rest of us don't have a clue about what's going on. Charlotte is still a small place. People talk—even about men as powerful and discreet as the great Gage Vincent." She left Alythia with another quick once-over and then turned. "You have a good night, Aly," she threw over her shoulder, and then disappeared inside an elevator that opened at the end of the bay.

Chapter 8

"An entire day, boss? Nice. I was up yesterday at six a.m. waiting for your call."

Gage forced a smile at Webb's tease. "Sorry I disappointed you."

"Pleased by your progress, sir," Webb Reese raved, and then cleared his throat noisily. "I hope you're in the mood for discussion, 'cause I'd love to know which way you'd lean on this bid thing."

"Nice try." Gage celebrated his urge to chuckle. "I only called to see if you were in any state of mind to answer your phone. Things must be going pretty well if you're able to manage that."

The sound Webb returned then was a cross between weariness and amusement. "Deciding this stuff is murder. Folks act like they'd either kill or sign over their firstborn to win out."

"It's not a game for the fainthearted." Gage shifted in the chair he occupied on the patio. "But if it helps, I always find it a good practice to carefully view all the information at hand and then just go with your gut."

Webb forced out another weary chuckle. "Going with my gut could be dangerous. Especially when the rest of my body's weighing in on it."

"Being propositioned already, huh?" Gage sipped OJ to muffle his laughter. "Webb, I'm impressed."

"Hmph. Thanks, sir, but it's nothing like that. Unfortunately."

Gage continued to chuckle.

"Some of the women are real go-getters, though," Webb mused. "I've yet to be so unforgettably propositioned, but I'm sure there are some who might not be against the idea."

"Welcome to the world of big business. Just remember that your head—the one on your shoulders—and your gut are the only body parts you need to consult with to get the job done."

Laughter then flooded both ends of the phone line.

Alythia had planned to spend the day on her own before she remembered that Orchid had arranged for the group to have breakfast together that morning. She'd spent half the night debating on doing exactly what she'd told Myrna she *couldn't* do. Hypocrite indeed, she acknowledged.

Still, accepting that the trip had been a bad idea and booking a ticket on the first flight out of paradise seemed like a fine decision. As bad as things had already gotten in the two days they'd been there, Aly couldn't help but believe they were going to get even worse and she couldn't put a finger on exactly how. She could only hope that the next uproar wouldn't be between her and Gage. They certainly hadn't spent much time together. Perhaps that would work in their favor and keep them away from each other's throats.

Yet that was just where she remembered being the night before, her face cuddled into his neck as they danced. He had asked her to come to bed with him.

Alythia stopped just short of the patio reserved for the group's breakfast. Gage had been the first to arrive and she watched him chuckling into the phone at his ear. He'd asked her to come to bed with him…and she'd accepted. She'd so wanted to go with him. Still did.

That one loses interest very fast once he's gotten the panties.

So what? she reasoned. They had only nine more days counting that one and she certainly wasn't looking for the soul mate Myrna had hoped to find.

Gage was done with the call and dropped his mobile to the rectangular table covered in white silk and set for eight. His eyes settled on Alythia and he stood.

"How'd it go last night?" He slipped a hand into the back pocket of his denim shorts and looked as though he was trying to predict her reply.

Aly didn't make him guess. "Not well." She trailed her fingers along the table's edge. "How's Dane?" He didn't respond and she didn't need him to. Judging from his sour look, it was clear to see that Dane Spears hadn't received a reassuring hug.

"Wonder if anyone else will even bother to show up to this thing?" She hissed an inaudible curse. "Why did Orchid have to get us all tangled up in this mess?"

"I'm kinda glad she did." His tone was soft, matter-of-fact. "We both work too hard to have met any other way."

Aly strolled the patio, seeking to draw calm from the blue sky above that was dotted with puffs of white. "I'm pretty sure the *fun* you and your boys are having on this trip is a far cry from what you're used to."

"You don't want to know what we're used to, Alythia."

"Why so glum?" She mimicked his stance, shoving a hand into a back pocket on her black denim shorts. "Sounds like you've all got successful love lives."

"Sex lives, Alythia. Major difference."

"You're right. A lot less headache."

"Don't be so sure."

"There's no reward in anything more."

"You're wrong. There's the truest reward."

"What do you want from me, Gage?"

Jayson and Orchid arrived before more words could be exchanged. Orchid appeared in high spirits, rushing over to Alythia and tugging her into a fierce hug.

"We need to get out and *do* something, Aly," Orchid was saying as she led her friend away from the men. "Maybe sightseeing or shopping, stopping off for a drink…"

"Orchid?" Aly dragged her feet. "Didn't you hear about last night? With Myrna and Dane?"

"That airhead." Orchid waved her hand. "Just what she asked for…."

"Orchid! That's a little harsh, isn't it?"

"It is what it is."

"So why is it so important for us to stick around when we aren't getting along?" she asked, hoping the woman would confide in her.

Orchid's smile possessed coyness. "Oh, we got along pretty well to start." She gave Aly a look. "Most of us, anyway." She shrugged, unmindful of her sundress straps easing down her arms. "Jay and I are very close to our friends. We need you guys here—marriage is a serious thing." She rubbed her arms then, briskly, and eased the sundress straps back in place.

"We need our friends around us, Aly, and if everyone's getting along, even better."

"And if we can't get along?"

"Well..." Orchid reached out to tug the hem of Aly's striped Henley tee. "As long as my most levelheaded friend isn't makin' an ass of herself, it's all good."

"Thanks."

Orchid reciprocated Alythia's playful smirk and turned to observe the men talking across the patio. "What I want to know is what's taking you so long to seal the deal with Gage? I want to know if he's as damn good as he looks."

Aly gasped and then dissolved into a wave of laughter. Not long after Alythia burst into a fit of giggles, Orchid followed suit.

"How do you know I haven't 'sealed the deal'?" Aly asked once they had calmed somewhat.

"Sex changes things." Orchid looked across her shoulder again. "He still looks at you like he wants to devour you. He's so intense. The intense ones are usually the freakiest." She turned in time to witness Alythia's reaction and laughed.

Equally amused, Aly took her by the arm and led her to the buffet spread on the patio. "Lack of food has you light-headed. Let's eat."

* * *

Breakfast was a hearty affair and the food disappeared much too quickly, especially once Dane and Zeke arrived. Jeena and Myrna had not graced the group with their presence. Still, Alythia and Orchid used the occasion to make plans for the rest of the trip—time with just the girls. The guys were rolling with laughter over something at their end of the table when one of the two missing guests made an appearance.

"Jeena!" Alythia stood to welcome the woman to the table.

Despite her plans to hop the resort's clubs with her friends, Orchid offered the barest hint of a smile when Jeena approached. Jeena continued her trek toward the end of the table where the men sat talking and laughing over the remains of their breakfast.

Alythia read Jeena's intentions a split second or more before they were put into action. Later she would wonder if she'd withheld her warning out of surprise or spite.

"What the—" Dane's outburst collided with the thunk Jeena's fist made when she landed her blow to the center of Zeke's nape.

The punch sent Zeke face-first into an unfinished bowl of oatmeal. The cereal enhanced by cinnamon and honey had grown cool and had adopted a gummy texture. What remained of the oatmeal was either forced from the sides of the bowl to make way for Zeke's face or it clung to the man's skin, as was evident when he regained control of his faculties and sat upright.

Fearless, Jeena bent to speak directly into one of Zeke's oat-spattered ears. "Think about this the next time you insult somebody, you jackass." She slapped the back of Zeke's head, grinning while she turned away.

Pandemonium erupted before Jeena had even taken a few steps. Orchid, who hadn't given her girlfriend a second's interest, was the first to jump in front of her.

"Dammit, Jeen, what the hell!" Orchid raged, sending Jeena back a few steps with the quick tap she applied to her shoulder. "If you got such a problem with people telling the truth about what you do for a living, then maybe you should stop doing it!"

"Go to hell, Ork! It's not me who's got trouble with truth!" Jeena moved closer to speak in a voice heard by only her, Orchid and Alythia. "Does your soon-to-be hubby know who you came running to for cash after Daddy cut you off? Now are we still in the mood to discuss the truth about how you earned that loan money, Ork?"

"Why are we still friends?" Orchid sneered.

Jeena was equally livid. "That's a question I ask myself daily."

"Well, maybe we shouldn't trouble ourselves with the question anymore."

"Fine by me!"

"Guys—" Alythia tried to make a stab at maintaining order but it was hopeless.

Any attempts at peacemaking could scarcely be heard once Zeke recovered and felt up to defending the blow to his ego. He barreled away from the table, intent on going after Jeena. It took the combined efforts of his friends to turn him from that course of action.

"Let him go!" Jeena refused to retreat and beckoned Zeke forward. "Let the bum-coward go!"

Zeke howled his rage, threatening to break the hold

his friends had on his arms and midriff. Through the melee, Gage and Alythia found each other's eyes. They shook their heads in regret and then focused on separating their friends.

Jeena was bolting through the restaurant with Alythia at her heels. "I don't want to hear it, Aly! Not this time. I'm takin' the first flight the hell out of here."

"I'd ask you to book me a ticket, too, if I didn't have this last meeting with Clive."

Jeena's steps slowed. She smiled and turned back to Aly. "Least one of us got somethin' out of this trip."

"Honey, don't worry about Ork." Alythia gave Jeena's upper arms a squeeze. "She's got a lot on her mind with the wedding and all."

"Aly girl, I don't plan on worrying about Orchid Benjamin ever again. I've had enough of this freak show we call a friendship." Jeena made a show of wiping her hands and then gave Aly's cheek a soft pat. "When you start being honest with yourself, you'll realize you've had enough, too."

"We've been through worse."

"Hmph." Jeena leaned her head back and inhaled deeply. "You know our band of misfits would've busted up a long time ago if it hadn't been for you always being the peacemaker."

Aly hugged herself. "I'm no peacemaker."

"You are, and so much so that I bet you haven't even gotten to have much fun with Gage because of all this mess."

"I didn't come here for that."

"Oh, come off it, girl. I've seen him, remember?"

Aly gave a teasing smile. "I don't think he's so impressed with me. I wasn't even inducted into the mile-high club."

"Consider yourself lucky. Look at where membership got the rest of us."

Aly's playful smile began to wane. "Mur says he's a playa—the 'hit 'em and quit 'em' kind."

"And it's most likely true," Jeena solemnly conceded. "What man wouldn't use a face and body like he has to enjoy women and often? But I doubt Mur was looking out for you when she said it. She's just upset because she never had the chance to go after him herself."

"And what about you?" Aly smoothed a tuft of Jeena's clipped hair behind her ear. "You were going after him, too, wanted him to become a client."

"No, Aly, not that, never that!" Jeena laughed. "I want space in that new high-rise of his." Her amusement doused suddenly. "It's gonna be next to impossible getting him to take me seriously now, with him thinking I'd be running a brothel out of it."

Aly led Jeena to a less trafficked area of the lobby. "So what *are* your plans for it?"

"A career placement office." Jeena looked to Aly as though expecting her to laugh and nodded appreciatively when she didn't. "I, um…I want to get some of my…escorts out of the business. So many of them wind up doing certain things out of sheer desperation and what they perceive as failure in the real world. A place like this could help." She nodded then, more deliberately. "They wouldn't feel self-conscious that the folks in my office would be looking down on them for *any* reason."

"It's a great idea, Jeen." Aly squeezed her arm.

"Yeah…it would've been, but I can forget it now that

Gage's good buddy is probably back there putting the last nail in my coffin."

"Well, don't forget…you, um, probably had just a teeny bit to do with that. Don't give up, okay?" Alythia urged once they'd stopped laughing.

"I won't…." Jeena considered, working kinks out of her neck. "Gage isn't the only one who makes the decisions anyway. There's a long list of stuffed shirts that get to chime in and choose the best bid."

"Bid?" Aly's bright eyes narrowed. "For renting office space?"

"Not just any office space. *Prime* real estate in the heart of downtown."

"You're sure?" Aly felt her breath grow labored. "Sure it belongs to Gage?"

"No, and that's the thing. He's keeping his name out of the forefront."

"Then how do you—"

"I come across a lot of info in my line of work. Gage Vincent may make all his money being the *top* dog, but he doesn't make it by being the *only* dog. He's very good at placing people right where he wants them."

"But you're sure he's the lead in all this?"

"Well, nothing's for sure." Jeena leaned against the wall. "Unfortunately, none of my clients are members of his inner circle regarding the thing, so I decided to take a stab at talking to Gage directly." She studied her manicure and shrugged. "Once Orchid and Jay announced their engagement, I figured…one mutual friend looking out for another mutual friend and all that jazz…."

"Right…" Aly dropped down onto the arm of a nearby chair, her thoughts on the building she herself was hoping to secure lodgings inside.

"Right." Jeena's smile was sour yet easy. "I'm gonna go and book that flight." She tugged Aly into a hug. "Thanks, sweetie."

Alythia watched Jeena until she had disappeared into a small crowd gathered in the elevator bay.

"Margarita sampler, ma'am?"

Alythia tuned in to a smiling young woman who was garbed in a metallic blue bikini with a stark white wrap tied asymmetrically over the bottom. On her palms, she balanced a round tray of margarita shots.

Aly took one of the shots and downed it. "Forget the samples and lead me to the nearest pitcher," she said.

Aly's midmorning meeting with Clive Weeks was two parts laughter and light chatter and one part business. She'd all but camped out at the seaside bar that the helpful waitress with the tray of margaritas had guided her to. When she'd asked Clive if he would mind moving the meeting there, he'd been all too pleased by the location change.

Another pitcher of margaritas later, the two had shaken hands on the deal. Clive had even spoken to his lawyer about the preliminary paperwork to set things in motion. When Clive and Aly had parted ways, she maintained her comfy spot on the cushiony peach sofa that occupied one corner of the terrace. After several long moments of people and view watching, she called Marianne to share news of the Anegada boutique and then breached the subject she'd really called to discuss.

"Well, info about who the decision makers are is being closely guarded but…" Marianne's sigh came over her end of the line "…rumor is that Vincent is the 'top dog' just like Jeena said."

"Rumor? Do you think that's all it is?"

"So far? Well, yeah...but a person wouldn't have to do much homework to put something like that together. It's no secret that he's leasing several office spaces in that building. It stands to reason that he'd go about acquiring the rest and just own the building outright. Everybody knows the man is as smart as he is patient. It's one of the things that makes him so successful."

Aly felt a sharp chill and began to curse the shorts she'd donned that morning. "Is there any way to make sure, Mari?"

"Well, there's always a way. I've heard some of our competitors for the new space have already...reached out, sending bribes to some of the top folks."

"Money?"

"Money, sex, promises for sex." Marianne ticked off the list.

"Great." Aly feathered fingers across her brow.

"You all right, hon?"

Aly smiled and shook her head. "I'm good, but I'd feel a lot better if you could find out who we're really looking to go into business with."

Feeling depleted and defeated following her chat with Marianne, Alythia decided that an escape to the beach was in order. She certainly couldn't get into any trouble there. At least, that was what she hoped when she made her way to a surprisingly quiet strip a ways down from the beachfront bar.

Armed with one of the bar's fruity drinks and a tote bag of top picks from her reading list, Alythia set out for some hopefully uneventful time to herself. Inspired by the margarita-promoting waitress from earlier that day, Aly had slipped into her most daring two-piece for her quiet escape. Still, she kept the lavender bikini hidden beneath a cover-up until she'd reached a more private stretch of beach.

"Hiding?"

"Is it that obvious?" Alythia pulled off her floppy straw hat and looked up at Gage, who stood just a few feet away.

"Just a little." He took a couple of small steps closer to her, shuffling the fine sand beneath his black sandals as he moved. "Not a very good spot, you know?"

She smiled, staring out over the serene and utterly striking blue waters. "I really didn't expect it to be completely foolproof."

A teasing wince narrowed his liquid brown stare. "Ouch."

Alythia winced, as well. "Gage—"

"Would you come with me?"

"I— Come…where?"

"A better hiding place."

Alythia gave a little shrug, following Gage's eyes faltering to the valley between her breasts, which were emphasized by the cut of her bikini top. "This one looks pretty good to me."

"You'll disagree with that soon enough."

"You sound sure of that." She visored a hand to her brow to study him more accurately.

"I've got every reason to."

"So? Where is this oasis?" When he simply looked toward the water, Alythia frowned his way for a second before she followed the direction of his gaze. She hadn't noticed the sailboat before and wondered if he had orchestrated the navigation to coincide with his response.

"A jet and a boat, Mr. Vincent. I'm impressed." Aly appeared anything but as she returned her attention to the book she'd been reading.

"I'll keep that in mind when I buy a sailboat." He nodded toward the sea. "That one belongs to Clive." He circled her slowly, retrieving her cover-up from where she'd tossed it over her tote bag. "Come with me. You'll be able to read a lot more out there than over here."

"Oh?" She closed her book. "Because we'll be all alone out there and uninterrupted?"

"There's that." He smiled, sparking the deep single dimple as he rubbed her cover-up between his fingers. "Aside from the crew, we'll be on our own but I was referring to the sun." He squinted toward the gorgeous skies above. "You wouldn't want to risk damaging that skin." His expression was blatantly appraising as his eyes trailed her body.

Alythia couldn't deny his point. She had brought a folding seat but hadn't thought to bring an umbrella. Gage then offered his hand. Aly regarded him only a few more seconds before she accepted his hospitality. Gathering her belongings, she stood. Gage relieved her of her things, helped her into her cover-up and escorted her in the direction of the pier.

"Incredible." Despite her hesitation, Aly couldn't fake nonchalance and act as though the view from the bow of the boat wasn't extraordinary.

"Thanks," she said in reference to both the refill on her mojito and the hour of solitude she'd enjoyed aboard the boat.

Gage gave her a mock toast with his own glass. "Thanks for coming along." He sipped of his mojito and then turned his back on the view to study her instead. "I wasn't sure where we stood after this morning."

"Do you mind if we don't...?" Aly set down her drink and returned to the two lounge chairs covered by a massive umbrella.

"Not a problem." Gage swallowed back half of his mojito and joined Aly.

"Clive's really created something special here, hasn't he?" Aly drew her legs up to her chest and regarded the expanse of blue sea and sky as far as she could see.

"Yeah...he's, um...he's got a habit of spotting that kind of thing."

Alythia looked over her shoulder, intending to ply Gage with an agreeable look. The raw hunger she saw in his eyes froze her instead. When he moved to close the distance between them, she shook her head.

"Gage—" Surprise had rendered her speechless, incapable of finishing her statement. He'd taken her by the waist and placed her in a straddle across his lap, relieving her of her cover-up as he did. He settled her beautifully and Aly could feel herself melting when he was nudging the middle of her bikini bottom with the obvious erection beneath his denim shorts. He fondled one cheek while his other hand disappeared into her hair, drawing her into his kiss.

Aly could hear herself moaning even before their tongues engaged. Her nails rasped across the silken whiskers darkening his gorgeous face as her full lips suckled his tongue. She withdrew from the kiss, biting her lip on a moan when his thumb drifted to her thighs and he began a stunning assault on the nub of sheer sensation above her femininity. She shuddered, overwhelmed by wave after wave of delight as he worked the nub with greater intensity.

He laid her across the two chairs, slowly relieving her of the bikini top with long tugs of the ties that secured the garment. She was barely halfway out of the top when his face was buried between the pert, dewy globes.

For a time, he nuzzled his face in her cleavage, sighing her name as he did so. Alythia arched sharply when he helped himself to a ravenous suckling of her firming nipples. Then, incredibly, she was being treated to another marvelous caress when his fingers grazed the petals of her womanhood. Just barely did he venture inside her walls. Alythia hungered for him. She desperately circled her hips on his slight caress.

"Gage…"

She could say nothing further, but apparently the sigh of his name was enough to cool Gage's hormones.

"You're right," he said, pressing a last kiss to the valley between her heaving breasts. Withdrawing his fingers, he drew her top back into place and smiled down. "This isn't the place."

"No." She shook her head. "No, Gage, I didn't mean—"

He silenced her with a soft kiss. "We should head back anyway. The crew is discreet but we shouldn't push it."

"Gage?" She pushed herself up on the lounge when he left her.

Chapter 9

As flavorful tropical drinks with charming umbrellas had kept Aly in a calm frame of mind for much of the day, she figured, why tinker with what was working? She took a late lunch in her suite, refusing to acknowledge the voice that cried "coward" in her mind.

She'd told Clive that she'd be leaving early and the man insisted on treating her to dinner before she vanished. A phone call to Jeena proved to be the bright spot when the woman shared that she wouldn't be leaving until 11:00 a.m. the next day.

Alythia talked her friend into getting dolled up and meeting for drinks before her dinner with Clive. Jeena was in so long as drinks were involved. Aly was glad Jeena hadn't asked why she wasn't trying to spend the evening with Gage. Though Aly still needed confirmation on whether Gage was connected to that building.

But didn't she have that already? And why did it matter? She hadn't done anything wrong. It wasn't as if she'd been trying to seduce him into accepting her bid.

No. She *hadn't* been, but she hadn't had all the facts, either. What would it mean for her to have them and not tell him? Especially if their relationship became more…physical? She wished herself luck with that and refused to think of what had happened between them earlier on the boat. Besides, if the man was as smart as he seemed, then he'd simply write her off as another wild woman, given what he'd seen over the two and a half days they'd known each other.

Then was not the time to think of that, though, Aly decided. Not with another fruity drink calling her name. Still, she checked the clockface visible beneath the bracelets adorning her wrists.

"We hear you're leaving us, miss," a bartender noted when Alythia had claimed a spot at the L-shaped glass bar in the restaurant where she was to meet Clive.

"Word travels fast." Aly didn't hide the surprise from her face.

"Friends of Mr. Weeks's get our highest attention, of course."

"Of course." Aly smiled.

"On the house." The man presented a glass of wine.

Smile widening, Aly raised the glass in toast. "Thank you." She sipped, relishing the cool and subtly fruity taste of the blend against her tongue before she swallowed. She turned on the stool and observed the area and was energized by all the bodies moving to the affecting rhythms produced by the band that had come in from St. Croix to perform that evening. She had tried to encourage Jeena to stay a while longer and enjoy more of the band, perhaps do a little dancing, but Jeena was obviously in no mood to try her luck with another member of the opposite sex. Alythia celebrated her friend's decision, her smile waning when Dane Spears came into her line of sight.

"Don't go, please." Dane raised his hands, seeing Alythia preparing to scoot from the barstool. "I just want to apologize."

"You don't owe one. Not to me."

Dane's lips thinned as he accepted her meaning. "I'm still sorry that things got so out of hand." He shrugged, sending a quick ripple through the snug crimson crew shirt he wore. "Once it all started to go off track, nobody knew how to get it right again."

"Dane—" Aly sighed impatiently and then deigned to give him a quick glare "—just because we have mutual friends about to marry doesn't mean we're obligated to be friends." Again she made a move to leave.

"Please." Dane moved before her. "I really do feel bad about all this." He dropped a hand to her shoulder, left bare by the flirty swing dress she sported.

Aly gave a pointed look toward his hand, which he promptly removed. "It's in the past." She slipped off the barstool, leaving him no choice but to back away. "The resort's a big place with more people coming in every day. I'm sure we'll all make new friends soon enough."

Dane nodded, his gaze appraising. "I see why G's so attached to you."

Alythia smiled, resisting the urge to roll her eyes.

Dane moved closer. "Things might've been nicer had I met you first."

"Ahh…Dane…I don't know." Her smile becoming more genuine, Alythia retrieved her drink from the bar.

"Slapping and punching necks really isn't my speed. I like to aim for places a bit more memorable." With that said, she threw a sultrier element into her stare and let her gaze drift below Dane's waist. She waited until his expression confirmed that she was understood and then left him standing alone at the bar.

Despite Alythia's underlying threat, Dane had apparently not taken full benefit of the hint. He looked ready to follow but instead ventured in the opposite direction.

Gage was relieved to see Dane walking away from the bar area, since his friends were the last people he wanted to see. He was too busy hoping his scheme with Clive, albeit contrived, would work. He'd played a hunch that Alythia would want to catch the first flight back to Charlotte following another disastrous exchange between their friends.

Once Clive had confirmed that, the two put their heads together and had come up with the goodbye dinner to celebrate the beginning of their new business alliance. What Alythia didn't know was that Gage would be her dinner partner instead of Clive. Gage could only hope that evening would fare better than all the rest.

When he arrived at the restaurant and set eyes on his intended date, Gage could only chuckle over his new stream of rotten luck. Alythia had taken a place on one of the four long rust-colored sofas that had been situated to form cozy seating in the clearing that separated the restaurant's bar and dining areas.

Of course, the area being located in virtually the middle of the place made it impossible to miss anyone seated there—especially any *woman* seated there alone and most especially when she looked like Alythia Duffy.

Apparently the man cozied up next to her had decided to stake a claim instead of merely observing.

"Having your usual, Mr. V?" a bartender inquired when Gage propped an elbow on one of the high-backed chairs. The man was already placing Gage's favorite brew on the counter.

"How long's Miss Duffy been here?" Gage asked, still watching Alythia across the room.

"About fifteen minutes, sir. She was talking with Mr. Spears a little earlier."

"Hell," Gage grumbled too low for the barkeep to hear. "Is he still around?"

"I saw him not long ago. I'm sure I can track him down for you, sir."

"Don't bother." Gage threw back a swig of the beer, dropped several bills to the bar and stood.

Alythia laughed over conversation from the man seated a bit too close to her. That laughter curbed when she saw him straighten and appear less amused as he stared up over her head. She turned, following the line of the man's gaze, looking back and up.

"Gage?" She didn't mask her surprise at finding him next to the sofa. "What—"

"Clive asked me to join you guys for dinner."

"Oh…" She blinked and then waved toward the man seated at her right. "Roger Harrison, Gage Vincent." She waited for the men to shake hands. Her eyes widened a fraction when she noticed Roger wincing when Gage squeezed his hand.

"Nice to meet you." Gage coolly released his hold

on Roger's hand to take Alythia's arm and guide her up from the sofa.

"Uh, Roger, it—it's nice talking to you," Aly threw over her shoulder while she was unceremoniously escorted away.

"We're leaving?" she queried, noticing the restaurant exit in their path. She received no answer and wasn't too surprised. Aly waited until they'd taken an elevator and had ascended a few floors before she fixed Gage with a smug, narrowed look.

"Tsk, tsk, Mr. Vincent. Using business to secure your pleasure. Not very professional," she gibed, studying the twinkle of lights on the panel while the car traveled up.

The words had only just passed her lips when he came to stand before her and blocked everything from her sight.

"Neither is this," he said and filled her mouth with his tongue moments later.

Alythia lost the power to command her legs and simply rested back on the paneled siding of the car. She took Gage with her, curving her fingers lightly about the collar of his shirt, wanting him close while she swayed.

Gage braced a hand on the wall to steady himself, while the other maintained a firm grasp about her neck. His thumb positioned beneath her chin, keeping it propped and perfectly aligned to receive his tongue, which outlined, filled and stroked her mouth. Deft, exploring lunges forced telling moans from her throat.

Aly moaned anew at the sound of the elevator dinging to announce their arrival. The moan was one of disappointment. It gained volume when Gage broke the kiss to rain more along her neck and collarbone.

"Stay…" she begged him, raking her nails through

the sleek cap of dark brown crowning his head and on to the silky whiskers beginning to roughen his strong jaw. She didn't want to leave the confines of the car, truly fearing their moment would end.

Gage returned no reply. Instead, he kissed his way down her frame. In the process, he hit a button on the elevator's control panel, prolonging their exit.

"Gage…" She swallowed, biting her lip and giving in to the strong waves of arousal as he went to his knees before her. "Cameras in the elevator—"

"Not this one," he said, interrupting her gasp.

Powerfully crafted hands roamed her long legs, beautifully shaped and accentuated by a pair of dazzling glasslike sandals. His touch journeyed upward and back toward her thighs in the wake of his mouth. Anticipation ruled Alythia's actions and within seconds she felt a warm rush of moisture collecting on her palms.

Gage's head had disappeared beneath a swath of dress material. The sight of him there sent quivers through her body, forcing her flush into overdrive. Aly felt him there at the crotch of her panties and bit down hard on her bottom lip when she heard his grunt. His nose was nudging the fragrant moistness clinging to her lingerie.

"Gage, I—I'm—" She heard his muffled chuckle and knew he'd correctly guessed that she was about to apologize for her loss of control.

"Will you say you're sorry every time you come apart on me?" Though muffled, his words resonated on the commanding chords of his rich voice.

Alythia couldn't answer and he didn't press, preferring to take her reaction to what he subjected her to as a response. Using the tip of his talented tongue, he traced the stitching along the crotch of her underwear. All the while, he inhaled deeply of her natural fragrance. Aly maintained a desperate hold on his shoulders. The crisp black shirt he wore did nothing to mask their breadth or power. Her fingers flexed into the fabric, fortifying her grip until her hands lost the ability to grasp anything.

Soon her fingers were splayed out along either side of her against the car's paneling. She shouldn't have been concerned about losing her balance. Gage had her secure in his palms, cradling her ample bottom as he intensified his exploration of her body. One hand slipped, gliding around her thigh to allow his thumb a more intimate sampling.

Alythia's lips formed a dual bow when they parted in relish over the touch. She pressed her head against the wall, moving it back and forth out of sheer enjoyment of the curious thumb stroking her femininity outlined against the silky fabric of her lingerie. Then the digit was venturing inside, stroking the slick flesh without the barrier of material.

"Gage—" She'd hoped to choke out more than his name, needing to explain that she was then wholly incapable of controlling her body's reactions. The explanation died on her tongue when his seeking thumb rotated just inside her puckered entrance and then eased in farther.

Gage rose to his full height, keeping his hand and stroking thumb in place. He watched Alythia taking what he gave her, loving the small helpless sounds she shared each time he deepened the stroke or changed its direction. His hypnotic liquid stare never leaving her face, he hit another button on the car's control panel.

Only then did he deprive Aly of his touch to swing her up into his arms.

There were no other guests in sight as they exited the elevator car and arrived in a bedroom.

"Oh." She gave a mild start, blinking in wonder at her surroundings. "My room doesn't do this. . . ." Her voice was small as she studied her surroundings.

"Only two of them do," he explained, carrying her deeper into the room. "The other belongs to Clive in his apartment."

"Clive's very nice to his friends."

"Yeah, he's a peach." Gage reengaged the kiss as the last word silenced on his tongue. He continued a deep exploration of her mouth.

Alythia kissed Gage with an unmasked hunger that gave him the impression that she had no interest in spending their time talking. With a flex of her toes, she angled her foot to maneuver out of the strapless sandals. She arched into his chest when her shoes hit the floor. A smile curved her lips. In moments, Gage swiftly turned Aly so that her back now cushioned the bed that seemed to occupy the entire side of the room.

Their disrobing was frenzied. One quick tug at the row of fastenings below her arm took Aly from her dress to leave her clothed in the sheer panties he had kissed his way through moments earlier. He pulled her hands away when she would have helped him from his clothes. Pressing her wrists to the bed, he gave them a warning press to instruct her to leave them there.

Then he was settling back on his haunches, taking his time to observe her, study her covered by only the scrap of panties. He looked as though he couldn't decide which part of her he wanted to help himself to first.

Again Aly bit down on her lip. Tentatively, she moved to stroke his thigh, hidden but no less potent beneath the dark material of his trousers. She smiled when he permitted the action. Gage took her hand then, lifting it, turning it over to tongue her palm. Aly used her free hand to tug at the tail of his shirt, already conveniently outside his trousers.

Then she was the one taking inventory of what he bared to her view. Aly reached out, intending to stroke his rigid pack but became distracted by the pronounced ridge beneath his zipper.

Wonder filling her eyes, she applied the lightest strokes to the bulge. He let his head slope forward and she grew bolder with her touch. Gage let himself be pleasured for only a moment. He'd wanted her since he'd seen her and having her there threatened to dissolve all that was left of his restraint. He squeezed her hand and left the bed.

Alythia watched him finish disrobing. Her amethyst stare followed every garment that fell, greedily absorbing all that was revealed. She was moving to slip out of her panties when he returned to the bed. Once again Gage caught her hand. He wanted to handle that part himself and did so with relish.

Her quivering returned when he covered her body with his. Immediately, Aly began to luxuriate in the feel of his rich café noir skin creating the most delicious friction against the milky caramel of hers. Still, she moved beneath him with a subtle urgency. Gage resumed raining his famished kisses along her collarbone and then he was cradling her plump, pert breasts for suckling.

Alythia's subtle moves grew even more urgent, renewed moisture pooling in her panties. The incessant nibbling at her firming nipples threw her hormones into a state of frenzy. His perfect teeth subjected the buds to a sensual bruising, his tongue easing in to supply a soothing bath and his wonderfully crafted lips participating in the erotic performance sent Aly gasping and bucking her hips wildly against his.

Gage abandoned the task, his molten chocolate gaze narrowing while an arrogant smirk curved his mouth in response to the state he saw he was leaving her in. He moved lower in the wide bed, giving enthusiastic attention to her belly button until she wriggled uncontrollably and emitted a tiny shriek amid her gasps and moans. He eased the panties down from her hips, dousing each patch of newly exposed skin with a brush from his lips. Once the lacy garment was completely discarded, he settled himself, resting his head on the base of her belly and inhaling as though her scent held some fortifying capability.

Aly raked her nails across the close-cut hair covering his head, feeling him nudge her hand when he moved to outline the Brazilian-waxed triangle above her treasure. Her body arched into a perfect bow when his nose nudged her clit. She trembled wickedly when his lips followed. Gage feasted on her until her hips made a tangle of the turned-down sheets.

Alythia settled into a pool of emotion when his tongue claimed her. The first stroke was deep and branding and she could hear herself panting. The intimate kiss was tireless, robust and provocatively infectious. Gage kept her bottom cradled in his wide palms, lifting her inescapably into the act. His groan carried a ravenous quality as he drank deeply of her.

Soon Alythia could hear sounds of pleading coming from her throat. She wanted all of him and her patience had worn itself out.

Alythia felt a telltale nudging against her pubic bone and she opened her eyes to find Gage setting protection in place. Her hand brushed his in an attempt to offer assistance. The gesture was more erotic than assisting. He shuddered once, incapable of doing more. He rained a long lazy kiss across her clavicle and left Alythia to guide him inside her.

She handled the task with great interest and fabulous delight. The feel of him filling her hand was a treat in itself. She wanted to keep him there almost as much as she wanted him inside her.

That was before she got him inside her. They groaned in sync and seemed to melt deeper into the bed when they were one. Gage wrested out the most helpless sounds that had Aly savoring twin emotions of empowerment and desire. Her triumph over shattering him so was only curbed by his command over her body. His hold was unbreakable at her hips as he filled her, stretched her, rotated and retreated only to replay the move with unfailing eagerness.

Alythia was desperate to wrap her legs about his waist and take him until she passed out from exhaustion and satisfaction. She accepted that she'd have to settle for accomplishing that without the aid of encircling his lean hips between her thighs. Gage kept his hands on her upper thighs, rendering her immobile while he pleasured her as well as himself. His lunges were slow, yet his ability to keep them that way warred with the desire for total surrender inside her.

That desire won and Aly felt her breathing hitch

when he spent himself inside the condom, which was thin enough for her to feel the steady pulse of his release. The sensation made her convulse with pleasure, she was so elated by the rapture threading its way through her. Then she was the one who shattered, giving herself over to the thrill.

Chapter 10

Alythia woke feeling excited and hopeful for the first time since setting out on the grand escape with her friends. She let her eyes drift shut again and snuggled back into Gage. She'd forgotten how many rounds of lovemaking there had been the night before. Afterward he'd drawn her back into him, spooning her into the unrelenting length of muscle and bone that was his body.

Aly had fallen asleep almost instantly. She willed herself back to sleep then, not wanting the day to begin just yet. How she wished the pressures of the day could wait before they intervened. How she hoped to stave off certain revelations, thinking of the confirmation Marianne was sure to have of a certain Charlotte, NC, skyscraper belonging to the man who kept her a willing captive in his arms then.

Aly wiggled against Gage, hoping to at least wake

him. He was dead to the world. Just as well, she thought, hearing the distinctive chimes of her mobile singing a high-pitched melody throughout the rooms of the suite.

Marianne, Aly thought, deciding to let the call go to voice mail. She'd have her answers soon enough. For now, she'd savor a little more time with this man and the dreamscape they'd created together.

Alythia raised her head from the pillow when her phone chimed again. Dread crept through her in response to the sound that time. Moaning softly, she set her head back on the pillow. That wasn't Marianne. This call was coming from a much closer distance and voice mail was most likely not an option.

Besides, she didn't want to risk waking Gage. If this was another act in the great friendship melodrama, then he would hear about it soon enough.

With that, she carefully pulled back the covers that had sheltered their bodies from the cool sea air that had billowed past the wispy curtains during the night. She slipped into the shirt Gage had discarded the night before and made it across the expansive bedroom in time to dig the phone out of the purse she had dropped the night before. She answered just as the third installment of rings began.

"What?"

"Aly, thank God!" Jeena's hysterical voice met the whispered greeting.

"Jeen, not now. I had a really, *really* good night and I was hoping to at least carry it over until lunchtime. Now, unless you're calling me because you need a ride to the air—"

"I decided to take a later flight out."

"Why?" Aly rolled her eyes when she blurted the

query, but she knew the damage was done: her curiosity would not rest until it was sated. "What happened?"

"It's not good."

The reply sent Aly to the arm of the chair she stood closest to. Disbelief stowed away inside her with every syllable she listened to Jeena utter. Later, Aly shut off the phone, holding it to her chest while she bowed her head. She realized she was holding her breath and ordered herself to inhale several times. A small measure of calm was beginning to settle in when she was plucked off the chair.

Gage had gathered her up against him. Kissing her neck, he carried her back to bed, unmindful of her soft urgings for him to wait. He wouldn't and continued his journey. He held her before him and trailed his nose from her collarbone to the sensitive spot behind her ear. His urgency to resume what they'd spent the better part of the evening doing was contagious.

Alythia didn't take much persuading. She let Gage have his way, all the while praying that he'd have his way vigorously. Their interlude was brief but no less sweet than all the others had been.

Gage tumbled her into the bed, only managing to take Alythia halfway out of his shirt, as he was more preoccupied with putting on protection in order to take what he wanted from her. Laughter flooded the room, what with all the kissing amid disrobing and condom applying. He wasn't inside her long before he was coming hard, his touch so overtly possessive that she was following suit moments later. She reveled in the feel of sensuality and freedom she found in his arms.

Afterward, they lay embracing and then Aly treated

her fingers to one final drift across the fabulous carving of his abs and perfect chest.

"I really need to go," she moaned.

"I want to see you later. Here." He murmured the words, eyes closed while he played with her hair.

Alythia didn't answer, instead making a move from the bed. Gage's relaxed pose was merely a veil for the reflexes that launched into action when he felt her attempting to leave him. He put her on her back, securing her to the bed as he covered her.

His features sharpened as his observation of her gained depth. "What is it?"

"Gage—"

"Something's off with you. What?"

She closed her eyes, mentally thumbing through a list of appropriate excuses. "Just some work stuff I need to talk to Clive about since I, um, didn't have the chance to last night." Gage's phone rang then and she valiantly hid her relief. "Is that you?" she asked him.

"It can wait." Gage never looked in the direction of the ring. "It's not just Clive. What else, Alythia?"

"Gage." She pushed herself up and worked to set him off kilter with a sudden and thorough kiss when he would have put her on her back again.

"I really need to go." She spoke the words into his mouth, scratching his rough cheek before breaking the kiss.

Gage reclined against the cushioning that ran the extensive length of the bed's headboard. He watched as she gathered her things from where they had fallen during their heated undressing the night before.

"Should I come and get you later?" He folded his arms over his bare chest. His voice had gone softer, harboring a knowing intensity as though he expected a runaround on the answer.

Alythia's resulting smile held the same knowing intensity. "I'm guessing that later you'll have your hands pretty full."

His phone rang again as if to confirm her suspicion.

"You should get that." She found the bathroom, changed quickly and left him soon after.

"Where is she?"

"Trying to sleep." Jeena's voice sounded as weary as Alythia felt. She took a seat on a swivel chair in the living area of Orchid's suite. "What the hell happened, Jeen?" The details of the earlier phone conversation were still wreaking confusing havoc in her mind.

Jeena groaned, scrubbing her bare face in her palms. "Apparently, the bad vibes finally rolled around to the bride and groom."

"But how?" Alythia spread her hands when she braced her elbows against the turquoise capris she'd changed into after leaving Gage's suite and grabbing a shower in her own room.

"They argued again about all this…damn drama." Jeena reclined in an awkward spread-eagle position on the chair opposite Alythia. "Jayson said he'd considered how long it'd be before she started acting like her friends…blah, blah, blah…."

"So she goes and proves him right?" Aly sounded incredulous, shaking her head when Jeena shrugged. "So how'd it balloon into all the rest?"

Jeena was apparently in no more of a mood to discuss "the rest" than she had been when she'd called Alythia earlier. The look on her face proved it, but she seemed to resolve herself to confess it anyway.

"Myrna caused it to balloon."

"Myrna? But I thought Jayson—"

"Myrna went to make up with Dane."

Aly's groan accompanied her eyes closing.

"And the answer to your question is no, the girl will never learn. She wanted to surprise Dane, had the maids open his room door so she could *wake him up.* He was already…up with Orchid."

"Jesus." Aly clenched her fingers in her hair and gave a tug. "Can this get any messier?"

"Please." Jeena raised her hands as if she were trying to ward off any bad vibes Aly might have unknowingly released with her query. "Don't even ask that. Myrna ran screaming to Jayson and now we're here. Orchid's in the bedroom nursing a bruised cheek from her fiancé."

"So what are *you* gonna do next?" Jeena asked Aly once they'd absorbed a few minutes of silence.

"Clearly there's no reason for any of us to stay. Guess you're not the only one on the way to the airport."

"Wait a minute." Jeena straightened in the chair. "You'd go back to Charlotte now? What about Gage?"

"You said it yourself." Aly's voice had taken on progressively more weariness. "The bad vibes finally rolled around to the bride and groom. Won't be long before they roll around to me and Gage."

"I don't believe that, Aly."

"I slept with him." Alythia spread her hands as though nothing more needed to be said. "I slept with him and I've known him all of what? Two days?"

"And the problem? It was consensual, right?"

Alythia felt the genuine urge to laugh. "Consent? Not hard to get from a woman whose friends have all slept with *his* friends. Just the natural order of things, right?" She bowed her head. "I'm sorry, Jeen…."

"Don't be." Jeena scooted to the edge of the chair. "And Gage isn't his friends. I don't believe he's stupid enough to buy that 'you are who you hang with' crap."

"It's usually a pretty good indicator." Aly smiled at herself. "In spite of what you've always thought, I'm no Goody Two-Shoes. It didn't take much persuasion from Gage." She blinked. "I don't think he had to persuade me much at all. We were pretty much on the same page."

"Of course you were!" Jeena blurted, kicking out a bare foot to emphasize her conviction. "*You* are a dime and Gage… A woman would have to be blind and lacking a shred of emotion not to be affected by what he puts out."

"Do you know why I'm always working?" Aly asked once she'd considered Jeena's words for a time. "Finding a man is…difficult when he has certain assumptions."

"Do you really think Gage has those assumptions?"

"No, I really don't." Aly shrugged. "But sooner or later he will. Just look at what happened between Jay and Ork." Faintly, a voice reminded her that particular love match had been orchestrated.

"Have you ever considered giving the man the benefit of the doubt?" Jeena was asking.

"I did." Aly left the chair and began a slow pace of the room. "This trip has me looking at a lot of things I never bothered to consider before, though. That happily-ever-after Myrna's so desperate to find? I want it, too." She leaned against the frame of the glass doors overlooking the ocean view. "I'm not saying I expect to find it with a man like Gage, but that…that would've been nice." *More than nice,* she admitted quietly.

"This thing between Jay and Ork, compounded with what's already gone down… I don't know if we'd stand a chance."

"And you're too much of a wuss to find out," Jeena accused, looking in Aly's direction.

"Hey, hey? Shouldn't you be in bed?" Clive asked when he found Gage reclining in one of the lounges behind *Alythia's* upcoming boutique later that afternoon.

Gage tried to gain some satisfaction from the breeze drifting over his face and beneath the blue cotton T-shirt that hung outside his jeans.

"She's gone," he said.

"Damn." Clive grimaced and then dropped to the lounge next to Gage. "Sorry our plan didn't work to get you guys a little time alone."

"Oh, it worked." Gage grinned self-indulgently. "It worked very well, and thank you very much. Problem is that reality intervened, as it usually does."

"So what happened?"

Gage made quick work of explaining the latest upset. "So instead of a wedding, we may all wind up having seats to a trial. Orchid says she's bringing Jay up on assault charges."

"That *is* a mess." Clive stroked his dimpled chin and then frowned. "What does that have to do with you and Alythia, though?"

"Not a damn thing." Gage's full, robust laughter came through. "But we keep getting caught up in it just the same."

"So you're just gonna hang out here for the rest of the trip?"

"Why not? Already got a great view for it."

"So you're just gonna let it go?"

"Maybe I should, man. . . ." Gage mopped a hand across his face and scratched the smattering of whiskers that threw his face into further shadow. "Everything that's happened… It's been nothin' but a mess."

"And is that what you think of when you think of you and her together? A mess?" Clive received no answer and seemed to take it as a good sign. "Are you gonna let her go?"

"Hell, no, I'm not."

The fierce response spoken abruptly and without hesitation brought a satisfied smile to Clive's face. "So what are you waiting on?"

"I don't know *how* to go after her." Gage shook his head when he heard the hearty laughter coming from Clive's direction. He didn't begrudge the reaction.

"Since when do *you* have confusion about going after the opposite sex?" Clive teased.

"Never wanted to try playing for keeps before." Gage's reply was simply spoken.

Clive sobered. "You really feel that way about her or is it just that you're not ready for her to leave your bed yet?"

"I *never* want her to leave my bed." Gage gave Clive a level gaze. "But that's about sex. I still don't know what else it is about her that I can't shake. The sex was…" He closed his eyes, obviously working to locate the proper descriptive word or phrase.

Clive smirked, wind whipping light hair about his tanned face. "I got it."

"But there's more and I—I mean it when I say I don't know *how* to go after her."

"Well maybe it's not something you can plot or strategize over like a business deal." Clive stood. "Maybe it's one of those things you're just gonna have to trust your gut on."

"Hell, Clive—" Gage worked the heels of his hands into his eyes "—that's what got us all into this mess."

"Sounds like you need to decide whether you're gonna sit here until the perfect plan materializes before the woman you want distances herself physically *and* emotionally." Clive dropped a playful slap to Gage's cheek, then his shoulder and then turned to leave.

Gage studied the vibrant view with bland interest for a time before he dug out his mobile.

"All is well, boss," Webb confirmed when he answered after two rings.

"Glad to hear it." Gage settled down deeper on the lounge, holding the phone at his ear using the crook of his shoulder. "That's not why I'm calling. I need you to help me find someone."

Chapter 11

Alythia decided to focus on work. It was the one thing that she hadn't screwed up. She had decided not to return to North Carolina with everyone else. Despite their misunderstandings, Jeena and Orchid went back to Charlotte together, Orchid on the warpath with Jayson Muns in her sight. Myrna had suddenly discovered she had a photo shoot that had taken her off to parts unknown. Word was that the guys had all returned together.

Aly could only imagine how heated *that* onboard conversation had become. No, she was in no hurry to return home. Instead, she decided to pay another visit to Aspen and her boutique there. There was nothing that required her immediate attention, other than inventory, which her staff could handle as well as or better than she could.

Nevertheless, Alythia needed the escape. As cowardly as the move might have been, she needed the time to herself. She needed the stillness, the peace of mind the place provided.

That peace was one of her main reasons for selecting the town for the new boutique. There were few African-American-owned businesses there, which made her store, Alythia, something of a novelty and provided her with a delightful profit. Not to mention a getaway.

The girls knew she had opened the Aspen boutique but not that she'd secured digs there, as well. The condo commanded a hefty portion of her earnings, but it was an investment that had proved worthwhile. The condominium was in the same building as her store and served as a home to those who visited Aspen frequently throughout the year. Aly didn't know if her workload would require such extensive travel, but she hoped that it would.

While the building's first floor was home to such establishments as bookstores, eateries, boutiques and salons, the upper floors were dedicated to high-end condominiums. All areas provided splendid views of rolling hills of white that were often dotted by tracks of skis and snowboards, which trekked across the fresh powder on and off throughout the day and much of the night.

The place was the epitome of serenity whether it was teeming with snow seekers or was bereft of bodies, with only the waves of snowy hillsides and distant white-capped mountains. The place had repaid her in more ways than the obvious. Her contentment. That satisfying peace of mind was at its highest whenever she spent time there, and never had she been so in need of solace.

Aly took another sip of the steamy white jasmine tea

before setting the mug on a stone end table that flanked a massive sofa, which lent a glorious vantage point for enjoying her view or the TV, whichever held her fancy. She snuggled into the thick fleece blanket that was usually thrown across the back of the sofa and nuzzled her head into the arm of the chair while she enjoyed the late-afternoon scenery.

The forecast had called for a fast-moving early-season storm that the meteorologists weren't anticipating would be much trouble. Still, fresh powder was always cause for celebration, and Alythia only wanted to hunker down and enjoy the show.

With the exception of the shallow lamplight filtering in from the short hallway leading to her bedroom, the condo was dim. That would change as the moon rose. Aly felt her eyelids grow weightier, a testament to her relaxation. She shivered, another bit of proof of her contentedness, yet Aly debated whether to grab a robe to cover the tank sleep dress she'd lounged in for the better part of the afternoon.

She noticed a heavy flake land on one of the sliding glass doors leading out to her wooden balcony. She decided the blanket and hot mug of tea suited her nicely.

She'd been watching the increasing intensity of the snowfall for about twenty minutes when a soft rap fell upon her door. She raised her head from the arm of the sofa, at first thinking she'd misheard. No one ever knocked on her door, not even her neighbors, who were spread out across the four units along the wide U-shaped corridor.

The knock came again and again and Alythia considered the camouflage-print tank gown she sported. Suddenly, the robe sounded like a great idea as she contemplated answering the door. The knock returned and she silently commanded away her silliness. Perhaps the storm was to be a bit more vicious than the forecasters had predicted.

"Coming!" she called out hastily, pushing herself up off the sofa. She grabbed the fleece blanket as an afterthought and tied it in a makeshift sarong about her waist.

As a precaution, she looked through the privacy window and jumped before going rigidly still. She snapped to after a second and then pulled open the door to stare dumbfounded into Gage's devilishly amused eyes.

Aly closed her mouth, which had fallen open upon first glimpse at who stood on the opposite side of the door. Her lips parted again as questions raced through her mind, begging to be asked. She only closed her mouth when those questions refused to leave her tongue.

Gage's smile only gained definition. "Let me help you." He moved closer.

"Gage, what are you doing here?"

He sought to mimic her by making his voice softer and overtly breathy.

The attempt took Aly's mind off her surprise and tapped into her amusement. "I don't sound like that," she insisted.

He was leaning on the doorframe, something seductively male belying his easy expression. "I can recall a few times when you've sounded exactly like that."

Cheeks burning, Alythia bowed her head and silently repeated the question he'd anticipated.

All the while, Gage relaxed against the framing, seemingly delighted in watching her as she tried to get a handle on what was going on.

* * *

He wouldn't deny the fact that he had selfishly cheered the way she'd lived her life. For that lifestyle had kept her available for him. Selfish indeed, he added grimly. It was no way to live, regardless of how he felt it had benefited him. She had brought such a feeling of contentment with her and to him without even knowing it. The least he could do was show her that living didn't mean she was unworthy.

Alythia's verbal skills returned as his thumb smoothed across her jaw. "What are you doing here?" The words tumbled out.

"You left me without saying goodbye." He set his head at a stern tilt. "I tend to take stuff like that personally."

"Gage, I'm sorry, it—"

"Tsk, tsk. Although this would be the time for apologies, I'm afraid you've worn out your welcome with all those *sorrys.* You'll have to come up with another, *better* way to get your regrets across." In case she was confused, he let his chocolaty stare travel the length of her body.

"I can't."

"Why not?" His query held a simplicity, as if he honestly had no clue about any of the drama that had befallen them over the past four days.

"I…" She licked her lips. "Are you alone?"

"Very alone." He exaggerated his disappointment with a forlorn shrug. "Sent my friends back on the plane, took another one here."

Aly smiled, seeking to make light of the moment. "You trust them not to talk your pilots into carrying them off on another adventure?"

Gage left the doorframe and Aly straightened, as well. She tilted back her head in order to maintain eye contact when he looked down at her.

"I don't give a damn where they go as long as they don't wind up here."

"I can't sleep with you," Aly virtually moaned when he cleared the door and pushed it shut.

"Can't or won't?" He rested against the closed door.

"Does it matter?" she countered.

Shrugging more casually then, Gage pulled off the hat he wore. "Really it doesn't," he said while tossing the knit cap back and forth. "Either way poses a challenge, but it's nothing I can't handle."

"Gage—"

He snagged her wrist, drew her flush against him, and the rest of her comment collapsed. She shivered instead, a fact she could have attributed to her fleece blanket tumbling to the floor or the cool leather of the black bomber jacket he'd yet to remove. Her bare skin reacted to the chill that penetrated the clingy fabric of her gown.

His mouth moved along the slim line of her neck while his hands charted a similar course along the curvaceous plane of her body. Every part of her reacted, her nipples already contracting against the leather, her sex aching for his attention. Alythia squeezed her eyes shut.

"Gage…" Her hands found their way inside his jacket to rest over a team emblem emblazoned across the sweatshirt beneath. "Wait…"

"Forget it." He let the words merge into the kiss he sought to punish her with.

Aly then lost any ability to stand, her strength abandoning her even as she labored to twist and arch herself against him while heightening the fire of her kiss. It was no matter as Gage balanced her bottom in his hands and perfectly aligned her sex with his. The fiery intensity of their kiss eventually had its strength-stealing effects on Gage.

Keeping her sealed against his tall, unyielding frame, he leaned against the door. Soft, intermittent groans resonated from his throat as he squeezed her almost unbearably close as if seeking to feel her through the barrier of his clothes.

Gage acknowledged Alythia's resistance. He ended their kiss in midthrust of his tongue and pressed his mouth to her ear. "Are you trying to tell me to stop? Alythia?" He tapped her bottom to encourage her answer.

She gave an obedient shake of her head and sent a slew of blue-black waves into her face. "Only to wait..." she managed.

His gaze was easy, sympathetic and without a shred of mercy. "Afraid I can't do that."

When he kissed her then, Aly accepted her fate. Melting, turning into a pliant mound of sensation beneath his hands, she worked at taking him out of his jacket. She didn't make much headway, preoccupied as she was by his kiss. She accomplished her task while he crossed the room, cradling her high against him. Aly was able to push the jacket from his shoulders just as he settled in the armchair that sat catercornered to the sofa.

Gage had her straddle his lap, which sent the hem of her gown rising to the crease of her thighs. The wispy panties she wore beneath the garment sent a growling obscenity from someplace deep in his throat. Kissing resumed, tongues battling fiercely as they moved feverishly, desperate to be closer. Aly whimpered, shifting her thighs when his fingertips brushed the hem of her panties' crotch.

She whimpered yet again when he withheld in giving her the caress she wanted. She dropped a playful slap across his dark, lovely face, having spied his lopsided grin. Gage, in return, brushed his fingers a little closer to the center of the garment's dampening middle.

Shameless, she raked a thumbnail across the shadow of whiskers that blessed his face with a fully dangerous and sexy appeal.

She gasped into his skillful mouth, emitting a tiny grunt. At last he ignored the barrier of material separating his fingers from her core. Desire had completely drugged her by then, and she was unable to even return the ravenous thrusts of his tongue against hers. Her mouth was a weak, circular O, suitable only to grant escape to the countless signs of satisfaction he coaxed. The slow dips and rotations of his middle finger set her femininity on a continuous moisture cycle. Greedily, Alythia rode the exploring finger, her lashes fluttering uncontrollably as she hungered for the release she knew his touch would provide.

"No…Gage, please…don't…"

He'd intentionally stopped the love he was making to her, observing her with a wry smile in place. "Are you done with wanting me to wait?"

"Yes…please, yes…" she moaned in tandem with wriggling her hips, urging his fingers into movement.

Gage braced off the back of the chair, then drew the sweatshirt up and over his head with one hand without removing the other from its naughty position. Alythia spasmed vigorously when her fingers grazed the sleek, toned wall of his chest even as her hips resumed the sensual rhythm they performed above his waist.

Gage took the time to release her hips and relieve her of the gown. The task was barely done and he was nourishing himself at her breast as though she had the power to curb his famished state. He'd removed a condom from the back pocket of his jeans and was pressing the packet into her palm. He left her to handle the necessary chore, preferring to share his attentions between her chest and her intimate folds, which were slick with the moisture her passion had conjured.

She was quivering terribly. Gage kept one breast captive in a secure yet gentle hold and subjected its nipple to infrequent rounds of suckling and insistent brushes from his thumb.

Alythia applied the protective sheath perfectly once she'd unfastened his button fly to free a stunning erection.

Gage muttered something in the neighborhood of impatience. Abandoning her breasts, he suddenly dropped his hands to her hips, lifted her and filled her with the thick proof of his virility. She had no trouble allowing him to direct her moves and chanted his name in a thankful litany.

Gage rested his head back against the chair, studying her as he worked her body to his gratification. For a time, Aly held her hands over his where they handled her hips. Then she was smoothing them over her tummy and across her rib cage. Briefly, she cupped her breasts, making him groan while bringing more potency to his already fortifying thrusts.

Once Aly moved on to thread all ten fingers through her hair, Gage indulged in more nourishment, suckling her nipples, still budded and glistening from his earlier attention. Aly wrenched out a sound fueled by pleasure and pain when his grasp on her hips took on a viselike intensity. She dropped her hands across his once more and was satisfied that they would maintain the delicious rhythm they had perfected.

Gage surrendered then, unable to uphold any promises he'd foolishly made to put his hormones on the back burner and devote himself primarily to her fulfillment. Burrowing his head into her chest, he realized that he had lived up to his promise. He could feel her climaxing, shuddering in unison with him as they submitted to waves of pleasure that rolled them in a seductive storm.

"Why'd you leave without saying goodbye to me?" Gage kissed the top of Alythia's head.

They had moved from the large armchair to the sofa, where they shared the blanket and took in the sight of the steadier snowfall. The condo was moonlit and quiet but for the minute tapping of the snowflakes against the glass doors leading out to the balcony.

"Didn't I just make up for leaving?" she asked.

He dropped another kiss to her head, gathering her impossibly close. "You definitely made up for it."

Alythia discovered she had been wrong. She'd only *thought* she'd known true contentment lounging there alone on her sofa. But *this* was it and if it wasn't, it was certainly a damn sight closer than she'd been a few hours ago. She didn't want anything to infringe on that and curved into Gage as she tried to will away the conversation.

"Why'd you go, Alythia?"

"You know how it is," she huffed. "Work to do..."

"Right, business worries *can* make you forget everything."

Regret forced Aly to close her eyes. She didn't want him to think that her work was enough to make her forget him. "Coming here was all I could do to forget everything that went on back there, Gage."

"That's got nothing to do with us, Alythia." His arms about her tightened in sync with the hardening of his voice.

"I can't understand how you can feel that way." She clenched a fist to the center of his chest and held it there. "These are people we'll have to see all the time."

"Not necessarily."

"Are you suggesting we dump our friends?" Her tone was playful.

"Not at all, but it'd be hard to get tugged into crap if we aren't around."

Aly braced herself on an elbow and gaped down at him. "Are you talking about not going back?"

"Yeah..." He shrugged as though the plan were perfectly logical.

Alythia couldn't believe what she was hearing and that fact was amplified as she studied him with a look of amused disbelief. Gage graced her with a roguish wink and tucked her back between his arm and chest.

"Look at that snow," he marveled, and put another kiss to the top of her head.

Chapter 12

"You live here?" Aly figured more words would fail her as she stood just inside the grand corner condo.

The place occupied the opposite end of her floor. There were only two of the L-shaped units, one at either end of the hall. Alythia had considered herself blessed to have acquired the spot she had and often wondered about the kind of people who could afford digs on such a scale and rarely use them.

Gage kept his place leaning on the condo's open door, arms folded over a lightweight burgundy hoodie. He seemed more interested in watching her observe his home than in the place itself.

Aly was drawn to the wall of glass that filled the far right and rear wall of the living room. The scene before her eyes was stunning and provided an almost panoramic view that was impossibly more spectacular than her own.

"How long have you lived here?"

"Let's see..." Gage focused on something in the distance. "Since yesterday." He smiled when she turned on him with an exasperated look. "I had to be sure I'd have somewhere to stay if you decided not to let me into your place last night."

Alythia was on the verge of laughter. "And I guess all the hotels in Aspen were full?"

"Anegada spoiled me." He shrugged. "I'm used to being close to where you are now, I guess."

"All in the span of a few days." She shook her head. "This is a pretty penny to drop on a place you'll never use."

He eased his hands into the pockets of his navy carpenter's pants and frowned over her prediction. "Why do you think I won't use it?"

"Do you have business here?"

"Sure do." He shut the door, rested back against it. "I was at work all night last night."

"Be serious." Alythia fought against smiling and failed.

"I am."

Her smile wavered. "Don't tell me you bought this place for me?"

"Would that scare you?"

The quiet seriousness of his voice held Alythia speechless for a moment. She didn't know what to make of the steady gaze or easy stance next to the door, with which he beckoned her.

"You don't know me, Gage."

"I'm trying to fix that."

"Why?"

"Why not?"

Aroused, exasperated, angry at herself for not trusting that *he* was so right for her, she rolled her eyes and turned back to observe her understatedly plush surroundings.

Gage dropped his easy expression. In its place emerged uncertainty. For the thousandth time since he'd taken off after her, he asked himself what the hell he thought he was doing. He wasn't unaware of his manner with women. Truth be told, his reputation wasn't much better than that of his closest friends, but such things only elevated a man's appeal, didn't they?

Unfair or not, women always fared far worse in the blows dealt to their reputations. It was an unfailing truth, whether the blows were earned or inherited. He'd toyed with reconsidering the Aspen trip, telling himself that he was in for an uphill battle.

Regardless of its awesomeness, he knew that she'd regretted sleeping with him in Anegada. That regret had probably carried over to what had happened between them the night before, as well.

And what about himself? He considered. Did he now imagine himself in love with her because of the mind-blowing sex they'd enjoyed? No…that wasn't why he was there. Of that he was certain. The final hours of the Anegada trip were prime examples of hell in a handbasket. Such a beautiful environment tainted by such ugliness. Yet all he could think of while keeping the offending parties separated was how badly he craved the contentment Alythia's presence provided him. She'd been an anchor in a storm and he had fallen in love with her.

There was a knock at the door. Alythia watched as Gage answered. He admitted a small man dressed in dark trousers with a white shirt and a bow tie. The man brought with him a square table set for two and carrying silver platters with coffee and juice carafes.

The server smiled in Alythia's direction as he pulled the covers from the platters to reveal steaming dishes of fluffy scrambled eggs with pancakes, bacon and fruit.

"So, then, your brother-in-law is the epitome of the perfect man?" Gage asked.

She and Gage were halfway through their filling breakfast. They had discussed Gage's upbringing as an only child and being without cousins, as his parents were only children, as well. Alythia sat riveted by stories of family vacations to Spain and Africa—places she could scarcely imagine as a child. When it was her turn to share, she couldn't help but feel a little self-conscious about her humdrum upbringing. Gage, however, seemed completely absorbed in her stories. Encouraged, Alythia felt more engaged as her talk moved to her older sister's true-love tale.

"She wouldn't agree that Owen's the perfect man but… Well, the girl's always been a little silly." Aly joined in laughing with Gage at her sister's expense.

"He does stay busy, though." Alythia relaxed in her chair and sipped at her almond coffee. "Life of a lawyer, I guess."

"Wait a minute." Gage's eyes narrowed suspiciously. "Is your bother-in-law Owen Hays? The attorney?"

"That's him." Alythia beamed.

"I've seen your sister." He regarded Aly with heightened appraisal. "I'm thinking her husband is *very* devoted to her." He placed a finger alongside his temple. "Your parents shared an awesome gene pool with their girls."

"Thank you." She nodded, gracefully accepting the compliment. "But it's not just good genes that caught Owen's eye. Angela did everything right."

"How so?"

Feeling rejuvenated by the fabulous breakfast and the wintry view, Aly didn't mind talking. "She was just a great example. No one *told* her to be. I guess she felt like she had to be for me, the baby. There weren't many shining examples where we're from. . . ." She placed her mug on the table and propped her chin on the back of her hand.

"Making sacrifices and walking good paths…they aren't things people just do because others need or expect it. There has to be a real good deep-down reason that gives them the ability to see it all through."

As she confided to him, her amethyst stare alight with love and admiration for her sister, she imagined that Gage must have been wondering how much of that "real good deep-down" *she* had.

"Angie already had four years under her belt as a prosecutor—a damn good one—before she met Owen. She'd worked hard enough to call her own shots, but working that hard doesn't leave much time to develop relationships." Aly shrugged her brows. "Good thing for her, too—helped her live up to that lofty goal of saving herself for marriage."

"You think that's why Owen was interested?" Gage leaned closer, resting both elbows on the table.

"Isn't that what all men want?" Alythia averted her eyes. "To be the first and the last?"

"Some men only care about being the last." An animal intensity sharpened his features. "You only care about that when you've found the right one."

Aly wouldn't let herself fall under the spell that his liquid gaze was wholly capable of weaving. "It was obvious to Owen that Angela was the right one." Her intention had been to keep the conversation on funny family stories, but she found herself discarding the decision.

"How'd you find me, Gage? Why?"

"I put my already overworked assistant to work on it, got my results fast," he told her at last.

Aly nodded, following the invisible design her fingers traced on the tablecloth. "Are you used to getting your results quickly?"

"In some things."

"Business?"

"Always."

"Women?"

"Frequently."

"You forgot one," he said when it seemed she was done with her questions. "Things that matter," he supplied.

Aly regarded him curiously. "Doesn't your business matter?"

"Things that last, then."

"What's your track record there? With things that last?"

"Not sure," he responded, but he looked uncertain. "I never went after anything I truly cared about lasting."

"Your business—"

"Business isn't even in the same hemisphere as this, Alythia."

She ducked her head, trying to soothe her uncertainties about the words she was about to utter. "Why'd you come to find me, Gage? You and I enjoyed Anegada for the most part. There would've been no harm in letting it end there. Considering…"

"You're right." Absently, he stirred at the honey butter that had been left behind following their breakfast. "I guess a big part of that enjoyment is what brought me out here. A big part, but not even half of it."

"How long can you stay?" Suddenly she wasn't altogether sure that she wanted to know the other part of what brought Gage Vincent to her doorstep.

"I'm the boss." He reclined in his chair again. "I can stay for as long as I want."

"And what of your overworked assistant?" Her smile was playfully judgmental.

"It'll be good for him to be in charge for a little longer. Besides, I've got him at work on closing a pretty big deal. I shouldn't get back too soon and have the poor guy thinking the boss is micromanaging."

Alythia laughed, though she was all too aware of the "deal" Gage's assistant was most likely trying to close.

"Thank you for this." She cast an appreciative look around the room. "I, um…I really do need to check on things at the boutique."

He nodded. "Dinner later? We'll go out." He chuckled, correctly reading the smile she returned. "We'll be around lots of low drama, I promise."

"Gosh…not even a lovers' spat?"

"*Especially* not a lovers' spat."

"It's a date!" Aly threw back her head to laugh again.

She caught the sheer heat flooding Gage's eyes as he only watched her.

"I should go." She pushed out of her seat. "This was really nice."

Alythia stood while Gage continued to recline in his chair. She was passing him when he snagged her wrist and tugged her down into a kiss that grew wet and needy in a second. Aly was moaning weakly and entwining her tongue around his in a lazy tangle before she bit his lip softly and repeated the erotic action. She was in his lap a moment later.

Willpower was nonexistent where Gage was concerned, and she could accept that. In his arms, she could imagine that they could be more. It didn't matter that reality screamed they could be nothing more than a fling.

Gage patted her hip, broke the kiss to drop one behind her ear. "I'll see you later," he whispered.

It was no small feat for Aly to draw herself away, but she managed. She made a dash for the door before she said to hell with business and uncertainty and returned to take what she wanted from him.

Outside his door, she rested back to slow her breathing and was summoned from her haze by the chiming of her phone. Marianne. Alythia changed her mind about answering. Casting a lingering look across her shoulder at Gage's door, she turned and sprinted down the hallway toward her own.

Charlotte, NC

"Great," Marianne Young whispered when her call went to voice mail. She considered hanging up and then decided to give her client the news Mari guessed Alythia had been dreading.

"Aly, it's Mari. Looks like Jeena was right. Gage Vincent *is* the silent power hovering over the new downtown space. Call me. We should discuss how you want to handle it. Talk to you soon."

Marianne ended the call only to have the phone ring less than a minute later. "Aly?" she greeted without checking the faceplate.

"Webster Reese," a deep voice countered.

"Oh! I—I'm sorry." Marianne collapsed back into her desk chair.

"I'm the one who should apologize, Ms. Young."

"Oh?"

Webb chuckled at her bewildered tone. "I didn't mean to upset you the other day when I called for information on your client Alythia Duffy."

"Oh…Mr. Reese." Marianne remembered then. "It's okay—"

"No, it's not, and I apologize a lot better in person."

"Mr.—Mr. Reese, are you…asking me out?" Mari leaned forward in her chair, threading fingers through her reddish-brown bangs. "That's really not necessary and it probably wouldn't be a good idea anyway."

"Oh?" Webb let his bewilderment show.

Mari cringed. "We're, um…we're kind of caught up in a business deal."

"Business?" Webb's bewilderment showed no signs of waning.

"My client's trying to secure retail space in a building your boss owns. We've submitted a bid and everything."

"Yuck. I take it our bosses don't know any of this."

"Just told mine via voice mail."

"Ouch." Webb followed up with a grunt. "I think I'll just stay a little too busy to inform my boss."

Marianne cringed again. "He won't take it well, I guess?"

"I can't say, Ms. Young, but something tells me that *I* don't want to be the one to tell him."

"Dammit..." Alythia had just replayed Marianne's message in hopes of hearing a different version and had not gotten her wish.

Perhaps she *was* making a mountain out of a molehill. Maybe it wouldn't rattle Gage in the least to discover that the woman he was seeing wanted space in a prime piece of real estate that he owned. Maybe he wouldn't think that she'd been sleeping with him to better her chances at securing it.

Maybe he wouldn't think that—if she hadn't slept with him two days after meeting him.

"Stop, Aly." She tried to focus on getting ready for dinner. The comb stilled in her hand and she studied it through the mirror without really seeing it. Then she was hurling the wide-toothed instrument across the room and holding her head in her hands when it hit the wall.

Chapter 13

The Soup Niche lived up to its name as a popular locale for the most savory soups and stews in the area. While its menu downplayed the obvious, the Niche held equal appeal for the high-end jet-setters and college-aged X Gamers who frequented the area. It was a place that made a person feel right at home and it was exactly what Alythia needed that night.

She and Gage had opted for jeans and bulky sweatshirts instead of more casual-chic attire, both of which were in fine form at the Niche. Between drinks, appetizers and the main course, Aly had taken off her gray hiking boots and tucked her legs beneath her on the oversize gold armchair she occupied at their table for two.

"Is this okay?"

Aly shook her head when he grinned. "You know it

is." She looked around at the dining room, fire lit courtesy of the wild flames licking the wide hearths that occupied various corners of the cozily designed room. "I haven't had the chance to come here before. I definitely won't forget it."

"Neither will I." Gage gave a pointed look toward a few high-enders who had decided on a more upscale style of dress to enjoy their soup dinner in.

"They're only being respectful of the food." Aly inhaled the intermingling of aromas.

"Never thought of it that way." He shrugged while slathering a roll with an obscene amount of butter. "I'd rather pay my respects to the food by eating it."

"Agreed." Aly raised her spoon in a mock toast and then followed suit when Gage dug into a deep bowl of hearty beef stew.

They were completing their second bowl of stew from their personal soup tureen set in the center of the table when the server arrived to replace their empty beer pitcher with a fresh full one.

Gage settled back to study his date while the waiter supplied their refills. His cocoa stare maintained a knowing frequency as he watched Alythia, who had grown increasingly quiet as the food disappeared. Once the waiter had finished with the refills, Gage reached for his chilled mug and helped himself to a healthy swig.

"Gage? I need to tell you something."

He smiled. "Okay."

"I got a call from Charlotte."

Gage's mug hit the table with a thud that sent the beer sloshing up over the mouth of the glass. The liquid coated his hand.

"Calm down." Aly reached over to dab a napkin at his wet skin. "It's not about our friends—it's about business."

Gage took the napkin and handled the task of drying his hand. His movements were virtually mechanical, his gaze curiously expectant.

"The call was from my business manager. She's been working to help me secure a spot in the downtown area." Aly pushed her bowl aside and then laced her fingers on the table. "Word is it's a building that *you* own."

His expression revealed nothing. "How do you know it's mine?"

"I didn't…at first, but my manager's very good at her job. When your assistant called trying to help you find me…well, it wasn't too hard to connect the dots."

"How long have you known this?" Gage maintained his unreadable expression.

"I swear I only found out this afternoon." Aly brought her clasped hands to her chest. "Marianne left a message but I—I didn't listen to it right away."

"Alythia." He measured the nervous excitement in her eyes. "Honey, it's your turn to calm down."

"But I never intended to deceive you with this."

He reached over to pull one of her hands from her chest. "Alythia, stop. It's all right."

"It is?" She blinked.

"Exactly what did you expect me to say or do?" He looked toward the hand clutching the front of her emerald-green sweatshirt. "Did you think I'd call you names and leave on the first flight back to Charlotte?"

"Something like that." She pressed her lips together

and then shook her head. "Aren't you at least a *little* pissed that we…have this thing between us?"

"It seems like we always have things between us. Honestly, I'd rather it be about business than our friends."

"Agreed," she sighed, though her expression and the weakness of her voice said otherwise.

Gage fidgeted with the stem of the once-frosted mug. "People say I'm good at what I do because I'm patient."

"I may've heard that somewhere." She smiled.

"I don't know how that could be totally true when I'm possessive as hell." His gaze was level and unwavering toward her. "I say all that to get you to understand that I don't plan on walking away from this or roaring at you for thinking you had deceived me. If that's what you were banking on, you probably shouldn't have told me you'd discovered that news in the first place."

She gave him an appraising nod. "So there *is* a way to rile your temper. I was starting to wonder."

"You have no idea." His smirk was equal parts amusement and ferocity.

Aly gave in to her laughter then. "These have been the strangest days of my life. I didn't have any intentions of falling in love when I went to Anegada, only to build my stores and have a little fun if time permitted. Then not only do two of my friends get caught up in unbelievable drama in the span of a few hours, but another goes from being adored by her fiancé to being hit by him." She brought her elbows to the table and cupped her hands around her face. "How'd I get so damned lucky?"

Alythia's playfully exasperated tone went unnoticed by Gage, who'd heard little else following her mention of falling in love. He wondered whether she meant it or if she'd simply been using it to describe how close they were becoming.

Her grin weakened. "Things are moving very fast."

"Too fast for you?" he asked.

"I don't know." She laughed. "Not much compares to what's been going on. I think it scares me a little."

"Do *I* scare you?"

"If you were any other man…perhaps."

His gaze faltered to the tablecloth. "Why do you suppose that is?"

"It could have a lot to do with your money and who you are."

"But no?" His tone was hopeful, as if he sensed there was more she wanted to add. "What?" he pressed when she shook her head.

"Discussing this might put us in forbidden territory," she warned.

"I can take it."

"All right. It has to do with your friends."

"Forget I asked."

She laughed softly. "You really care a lot about them."

"And I don't know if that's an asset or a flaw."

"It's admirable." She laughed again when he snorted.

Gage slumped back in his chair and worked his fingers over the cap of sleek brown covering his head. "The last few days have been like straws breaking my back and it's weird because I never cared before." His lone dimpled smile was one of surprise.

"Issues like this creep up often anytime we get together. Somebody says the wrong thing to a woman, somebody's seen with a woman and called out by *an-*

other woman, who thought she was the only one.... Our screwups are infinite." He patted a hand to his chest. "I'm including my own screwups in there, Alythia."

"And here we are." Again she scanned the golden-lit dining room. "We've known each other all of four days and you really believe you can stay here in Aspen and turn your back on your life in Carolina."

"Do you remember what I said about being patient?" He watched her give a slow nod. "There's a lot going through my head about us right now. One thing I do know is that I want to know you and that's gonna take time, given my own...reputation. It'll probably take a lot of time."

The server returned to clear away some of their dishes. Gage and Alythia waited patiently, silently absorbing all that had been said during the course of their meal.

"We've already skipped ahead several steps," Gage continued once the waiter had moved on. "Guess that doesn't go a long way in proving my rep isn't well deserved."

"Hmph. And *I* guess that can go double for me."

"Why?" He inclined his head. "Why should it go double for you?"

"Please don't try and pretend you don't know." She grinned broadly. "It always goes double for women. Sex, business—the standards are always double."

"So would you have a problem if we scrapped the standards?"

Aly stretched languidly in her chair. "I'd *love* to scrap the standards."

"Think we can?" His rich, chocolaty stare narrowed.

"Sure." Her demeanor was cool yet a tad cynical.

"As long as we stay in our own private corner here in Aspen like you've suggested."

"But that's not reality, is it?" Gage sighed as though he were reluctantly turning himself toward that very mode of thinking.

"We'll have to face it sooner or later, you know? I'd rather face it before things between us get too…complex."

Gage kept his thoughts silent, admitting that things between them were already "too complex" as far as he was concerned. He knew if she were to ask that they end things right there, he'd do everything in his power to persuade her to change her mind.

"Will you come back to Charlotte with me?" he asked.

"There're still some things I need to check in on at the shop, but I could—"

"No, Alythia…I'm asking if you'll come back *with* me."

Understanding pooled in her extraordinary eyes. "With you. *With* you, with you? Like…we're a couple?"

A teasing wince softened his features adorably. "I promise it won't be as bad as you're making it sound."

"Are we gonna be met by a slew of reporters and paparazzi?"

His laughter drew attention and that was no surprise. The sound was hearty, genuine and oftentimes quite contagious.

"I promise I don't merit that kind of confusion."

Aly still appeared doubtful. "I don't know…. I do my best not to draw attention."

"And I'm happy about that but you're too damn beautiful to stay in the shadows and too damn beautiful to venture out there alone." He tugged the sleeve of her shirt. "I've got faith in you and if all this goes to hell, we always have Aspen."

"Or Anegada." Aly reached for her mug and raised it in toast.

Gage laughed again and reciprocated her gesture. "That'll make Clive a happy man," he predicted.

After dinner Gage and Alythia strolled the village, which was a forest of white following the previous day's storm and the light dusting from earlier that day. Alythia kept a tight grip on the arm Gage offered, and not so much out of a need for steadiness, she silently admitted as they navigated the wintry streets.

It was the sheer pleasure of being close. The warmth and security radiating from his tall, lean frame heightened her need at every level. She smoothed her hands over his biceps. The unyielding hardness of it was in no way diminished by the heavy jacket or sweatshirt worn beneath.

Alythia gave a quick laugh when she realized they had crossed the block where her boutique was located. "I didn't know we'd already walked so far. That's my shop there." She pointed toward a storefront boasting a snow-dusted gold canopy and French double doors.

"Take me for a tour?" Gage asked, smiling when she tugged his arm and led them across the lightly trafficked street.

Aly made quick work of unlocking the door and deactivating the alarms. Leaving the blinds closed, she hit the panel for the recessed lighting along the polished hardwood floors and drop ceiling of carved maple wood. The scant illumination added an effective gold dousing to the boutique's main level.

"It's very simple." She smiled contentedly and added a flourishing wave. "I'm still getting a feel for the place."

"Simple is good." Gage strolled the area, taking in the coziness created by mock Queen Anne chairs and love seats. He appeared drawn to the rows of clothing, paying specific attention to the array of frilly garments.

"Why don't you wear this stuff?" His gaze was on the lingerie he fingered.

"I wear it all the time." Clasping her hands at her back, she slowly approached the lingerie section. "You've only known me a week, remember. Not much time to display my entire wardrobe," she joked.

He nodded, eyes still fixed on the delicates. "What's upstairs?" he asked.

"Office and fitting room." She looked toward a spiraling brass staircase.

"Give me a private showing?"

"Ha! You've been getting those all week."

"Not like this." He waved a few of the pieces he'd taken a great liking to.

"I beg to differ," she still argued.

Gage continued to wave his preferences. "But the customer is always right, right?"

"Are you in the market for lingerie, Mr. Vincent?"

"I'm in the market for lingerie with you in it."

"A showing, then?"

"A showing."

Alythia accepted the pieces he offered and then led the way up the wide oak stairs secured by the brown framework. The stairway opened up into an elegant yet comfortably furnished fitting area. With the press of another button, lighting was activated from stout black lamps that occupied the middles of glass tables next to deep butter suede armchairs along the rear wall of the room.

"The boutique doesn't make a habit of modeling, sir," she teasingly informed him, "not even for customers such as yourself."

He caught her elbow and pulled her to him when she would have moved past. "What kind of customer am I?"

"Persuasive…and a little intense."

He wrinkled his nose and Aly felt her heart flip over the guileless affect the gesture cast across his gorgeous features.

"That makes me sound scary."

"Not the vibe I get at all." She moved closer with every word he uttered. Their lips were but a breath apart when she pulled away.

"Over here are our dressing rooms." Her manner was breezy as she waved her hands to direct his attention. "Seating areas are here, as well as our coffee-and-Danish nook. Though they're closed right now due to the time." Her smile was playfully apologetic.

"What's there?" He looked toward a small hallway just beyond the fitting rooms.

"My office suite." She motioned to the garments he'd selected. "Do you have a preference?"

"Definitely."

She feigned distaste at his one-track mind even though he had every part of her body set on tingle. "Please choose, sir." She gave the lingerie another shake.

He did so obediently, cocking his head to the left to

indicate his choice. Alythia turned for the rooms. She didn't get far. He had her flush against him the instant she was within reach. He was crushing her mouth beneath his tongue, thrusting, exploring, branding.

Alythia moaned without shame, hungrily engaging in the sultry duel. One hand hung limp at her side, the garments she grasped threatening a descent to the floor as the hold weakened. With her free hand she massaged his nape, her glossy nails just grazing the soft hair tapering there.

"Hey?" She managed to draw back, sliding her finger to outline the alluring curve of his mouth. "You wanted a showing, didn't you?" She easily sensed his reluctance in releasing her and left him with a saucy wink before sauntering to one of the fitting rooms.

Needing something, anything, to keep his mind off of her naked and less than twenty feet away, Gage took his own personal tour of the area. He thought of how very much the space reflected Alythia's personality—airy yet with a warm tug that enhanced the contentment he was coming to cherish about her. It was a place that enveloped its guests in a cocoon of welcome.

"Those chairs are to die for!" Aly called out from the dressing room. "They'll put you to sleep if you're not careful!" She was hanging the strap of her bra to one of the room's satin padded hooks when his arms snaked about her waist. Her legs went to water, his hands smothering her breasts as his mouth brushed her ear.

"Guess I'll have to find something to keep me up, then."

"I…don't allow this sort of thing in here, Mr. Vincent." Her voice was a breathy whisper. She let her head rest back against his shoulder.

"What sort of thing?" He plied her with examples, his thumbs flicking her nipples until the buds protruded. As he fondled her steadily, his unoccupied hand drifted down the lithe, lovely line of her body. Briefly, he fingered her naval, smiling when she wriggled insistently.

Aly bowed her head, biting her lip while a flurry of sensation engulfed her. Weakly, her hands covered his at her breasts, and she nuzzled her back against his chest, luxuriating in his strength.

Gage suckled her earlobe, his fingers skirting the lacy waistband of the charcoal-gray panties she wore. "Open your eyes, Alythia."

His command was soft, effectively coaxing her cooperation. She watched as his fingers disappeared inside the wispy material at her hips, nudging them lower the deeper his hand journeyed. Her lashes fluttered.

"Don't you do it." His command was firm that time. The hand at her breast flexed, giving her a tiny jerk to encourage her to oblige.

In the dressing room mirror, she watched as the panties she wore were pulled to her upper thighs, leaving her most private asset bared to his gaze. Gage smoothed the back of his hand across the bare triangle of flesh above her femininity. Dually attentive, he launched a slow nibbling of her shoulder.

"Don't do it..." he ordered, more playfully that time when he saw her lashes fluttering as he gnawed her satiny skin.

Alythia was desperate to shimmy out of the panties and turn to face him. Gage denied that with another flex around the breast he molested. She was left no choice but to stand and witness the play of emotion across her face when his thumb stroked the bud of hypersensitive flesh at the apex of her thighs.

An orgasm-promising spasm rippled through her, helped along by his constant manipulation of her nipples, which seemed to cry out for attention, given their erectness.

Alythia watched her mouth slacken beneath the weight of desire as he intensified the caress to her clit while thrusting his middle finger high, deep inside and then rotating and giving her leave to enjoy the treat, wildly uninhibited.

She murmured his name, turning her head while feverishly brushing the panties down her legs and off of her ankles. She was panting, her mouth desperately seeking his. Unmindful of his instructions against turning, she did just that and without ever breaking the kiss they shared.

Moments later Gage had her in his arms and was carrying her from the fitting area and down the short corridor that led to her office. Inside, there was no need for light. Mutual desire guided their fingertips. She began to undress him. Gage offered his assistance only when she took too long with the button fly of his jeans.

She led him to the sofa, her intention to straddle him and greedily put him inside her. Gage's intentions differed. The second he felt the sofa, he put Alythia on her back beneath him. She could hear the belt buckle at his jeans clink as the denims were roused. Gage made quick work of checking his pockets for the condoms he'd pushed inside them earlier that night.

Alythia was glad he hadn't requested her assistance,

for she didn't think she had the strength to perform the task of securing their protection. Those concerns happily vanished when she felt him spreading her, filling her to the hilt with him. Instantly, her hips lifted into a gentle writhe, stirring sensation for them both.

Then came the familiar sounds of moisture squelching produced by their coupling. Gage kept one of Alythia's thighs pressed to the wide sofa. He set the other high, opening her to a deeper plundering with his thick erection. Ego-soothing arrogance rested beneath possession as he took pleasure in the sighs and cries he forced past her mouth.

Gage emitted his own sighs of abandon. His handsome dark face was sheltered in the crook of her neck, where muffled groans of satisfaction were buried. Without warning, he pulled Aly to her desk, where he positioned her and took her from behind.

The darkened room was brought to life by their mingled gasps and groans of delight. Gage dragged wet kisses between Alythia's shoulder blades, marking the line of her spine with his tongue. He covered her breasts in his hands, pulling her back against him while his thrusts claimed a lovely savagery. Alythia could scarcely catch her breath, but words of complaint had fled her vocabulary. What remained of their evening passed in a lusty blur.

Chapter 14

"Well, what's this?" Alythia murmured, crossing her bare legs and resting an elbow on her knee in order to lift her mobile to a more comfortable viewing level.

Gage shook his head and grinned, not bothering to turn when he heard her across the bedroom. They had finally gotten around to christening his condo. "Let me guess," he called from where he stood preparing two coffees. "Our destination calls?"

"It's a text. Orchid wants to see me."

"About the wedding?"

Aly was stunned. "Do you still think there's gonna be one?"

"It'd be somethin' to see." His torso shook when he chuckled.

"Well, I guess I really should touch base with everybody." Aly returned her attention to the phone. "I only told Jeena I need to get away but I didn't tell her where I was going."

Gage crossed to the bed and handed her one of the steaming mugs of coffee he'd poured from the portable coffeemaker in the bedroom alcove. "They don't know you have a boutique here?"

"Oh, they do." Aly tightened her grip on the mug and straightened the pillows at her back. "But not that I have a condo here or that I've even thought about moving here."

"Have you really considered that?" He joined her on the bed. "You could be that far away from your sister? Your only family?"

"I think Angie would be happy about it." Aly warmed her hands around the mug. "All the sacrifices she made to keep me on the straight and boring path and still I become best friends with the very influences she tried to steer me clear of." She grimaced then, sending wavy swirls into her face when she bowed her head.

"That's not fair." She sipped the perfectly sweetened and creamed coffee. "I don't know what motivated Orchid or even Myrna but I do know Jeena didn't set out to become what she is."

"But we can't all run boutiques, can we?" Gage reclined on his side of the bed with his arms folded over his bare chest.

"We both dreamed of being businesswomen, since we were kids." Her expression softened with memory. "For me it was the clothes and the attitude, hmph, and then I realized that it *was* just about clothes for me. It went deeper for Jeena, though." Aly lowered her mug and set it on the night table.

"She always said she wanted to make things better

for people. Though she didn't mean in a sexual way," Aly tacked on ruefully. "She didn't have a hard-nosed sister to push her the way I did. Right out of high school she went to work for a telemarketing firm."

Aly laughed suddenly. "Jeena *really* loved it. I've never met anyone who *really* loved telemarketing but she did. She really was great at it because she honestly believed in what she was doing." Easing down on the gargantuan sleigh bed, Aly relaxed on the pillows.

"She started researching and trying to learn all she could about starting her own firm, but things... They just veered off track."

"How?" Gage took her hand and began to toy with her fingers.

"One of the supervisors asked Jeena to set him up with one of the floor operators. Jeena said he felt comfortable enough to ask her because she'd been talking his ear off about all that telemarketing research she'd been doing." She smiled when Gage tickled her palm.

"Turned out...telemarketing wasn't the operator's only job and she point-blank told Jeen that it was gonna cost the man."

"Let me guess—he paid?"

"Passed the funds right through Jeena and the rumored madam was born."

Gage could only shake his head in wonder.

"We have our faults, but I love those wenches." Her mouth began to tremble. "I only wonder if we're good for each other anymore. All we do lately is fight."

"I can relate to that." Gage set his head deep in the pillows and stared up at the ceiling. "A wise man once said the best way to stay friends is to stay away from each other."

"So sad." Still, Alythia burst into laughter.

"But true," Gage added when his laughter had subsided.

"And sometimes necessary."

"Yeah…"

Gage continued to stare up at the ceiling without really seeing it.

"Do you think you'll have to have that kind of conversation with any of your friends?"

"Maybe one." He mopped his hands over his face and groaned. "Maybe all…"

"Maybe we all should've thought twice about that trip."

A grim smile curved Gage's mouth. "Would've been helpful if Jay and Orchid thought twice before letting their families push them into a phony marriage. I don't think they were ready for a relationship, let alone a marriage."

"And what about us?" Alythia hesitated. "Do you think *we're* ready?"

"Well, we definitely didn't have the time to find out in Anegada."

There was no laughter and Gage squeezed Aly's hand, giving a tug to encourage her closer. "In Anegada I was very much infatuated with you," he said when she was tucked into him.

"And here?"

"Coming to Aspen was about satisfying my possessive streak." He felt her sharp inhale, knowing the confession had stirred her. He cupped her chin, squeezing until she met his warm stare.

"Wanting to *stay* in Aspen is my patient streak kicking in and telling me you're a woman to wait on for however long it takes."

"That could take a long time. Lots could happen in all that time." She squeezed the hand still holding hers. "Given our brief history, chances are high that a lot *will* happen."

"I believe we can survive it." He kissed the back of her hand.

"You're putting a lot of trust in the fates."

"I'm putting a lot of trust in us."

He kissed her then, sweetly at first. Aly changed all that with the sigh she gave while arching into him.

"Nervous?"

"Probably not as much as I should be." Aly sighed as she studied a spectacular view from her seat on Gage's jet a few days later.

"We're going home." He pulled her up from the seat. "What could possibly go wrong?"

Alythia dissolved into laughter. "You're a funny guy."

"Funny but sexy. Makes all the difference."

She melted. "Yes, it does. . . ." His words had turned her boneless. Any lingering pangs of nervousness evaporated when he jerked her into a throaty kiss. Gage brought her onto the long seat on the other side of the bar and positioned her in a straddle on his lap.

Aly wanted to feel his skin beneath her fingertips and was all too anxious to relieve him of the shirt he wore loose at the collar and hanging outside his olive-green trousers. She had time only to unbutton his shirt and splay her hands wide across the sleek plane of his chest before he turned the tables and put her beneath him on the luxurious surface of the seat.

"Take off your shirt," she murmured against his jaw, taking delight in the smooth, flawless surface though she silently admitted to missing the display of whiskers he'd sported since the Caribbean. She felt him go still against her and then his head fell to her chest.

"Gage?" She waited and then kissed his temple. "What? What's wrong?"

"I won't do this here, not here of all places."

Aly barely needed a second to understand his point and realize that she agreed. "Guess this jet does have a few too many memories."

Gage lifted his head and propped her chin on his fist. "I can promise you we'll definitely make memories of our own, but not just yet."

Her bright eyes sparkled. "You've got me curious." She curled her fingers into his collar and studied their surroundings. "You think our memories can top the ones already in circulation?"

"Lady, you have no idea." Gage gnawed her neck until she begged him to be merciful.

The day was sunny and bright if just a tad nippy when Alythia and Gage deplaned in Charlotte late that afternoon. Gage nudged her when he heard the sigh she expelled over the scene that greeted them. No reporters or paparazzi, only airport personnel and two town cars waiting on the tarmac.

"Told you I wasn't *that* important."

"Mmm…probably the calm before the storm."

They cleared the mobile staircase and Gage escorted her to one of the two town cars.

"Hey, Rich."

"Mr. V." A tall, broadly built man greeted Gage with a vigorous handshake. "Everything's in the trunk. We're all set."

"Sounds good. Take Ms. Duffy anywhere she needs to go."

"Gage, no," Aly whispered, turning to pat his cheek. "I don't need all this. I drove my car out here, remember?"

"I had your car sent back. It's waiting with a full tank in your driveway."

"This is great service."

He dipped his head. "We only aim to please." He took advantage of the closeness to inhale her subtle perfume. "Thanks, Rich," he said without looking in his driver's direction. "I'll call you, all right?" he told Alythia once Rich was settling in behind the driver's seat.

Aly was frowning, her fingertips gaining more purchase as they clutched Gage's shirt. "You're not coming with me?"

"I'm guessing you've got a lot to do." He outlined her mouth with his thumb.

It was true, but just then Aly was thinking only of how very much she'd like to go anywhere they could make love.

Gage kissed her cheek subtly, following the gesture with a pat to her hip. "Go handle your business. I'll handle mine."

"When will you call me?" She couldn't help it. She didn't want them to part ways.

He smiled, brushed another kiss across her cheek. "Not very long. Promise."

They shared another spontaneously heated kiss

and then Gage was bundling her into the town car and knocking on the hood to send the driver on his way.

"Miss Orchid will be down soon. May I get you anything else, Miss Aly?"

Alythia smiled and held the teacup closer to her chest. "No, thanks, Sienna, the tea is fine," she told the Benjamins' housekeeper. Alythia was a bit relieved to wait a little longer to chat with her friend. Like her work, the discussion was another in a long line of activities that would keep her mind off Gage.

It'd been a week and she hadn't heard from him. At first Alythia criticized herself for being surprised by that. After all, they had known each other for only a brief span of time. Was she still so naive as to believe he'd truly fallen as deeply as she wanted to think? Was she so naive to believe that he had fallen as deeply as she had?

Then another possibility occurred to her. Maybe he didn't believe she had fallen as deeply as *he* had. Perhaps this was his attempt at giving her the time to decide whether she was ready to accept what he was offering.

Truth be told, Alythia admitted she hadn't really given Gage much reason to believe that she was ready. She guessed he was leaving it to her to decide and she smiled into her teacup. Now she only needed to manage a tea party with Orchid and hope the discussion wouldn't wage too much war on her nerves.

"Alythia, girl!"

Aly noted she wouldn't get that wish if Orchid's high-pitched, gasping tone could be taken as any sort of sign.

Orchid arrived in the sunroom with a flourish. She

was all smiles and drew Alythia into a hug with kisses to spare.

"Oh, honey, it's so good to see you. How are you really?" Orchid gasped anew, her heavy perfume wafting just as powerfully as the flowing sleeves and hem of her white chiffon lounge dress.

"How are *you?*" Alythia probed carefully, studying Orchid with a narrowed and suspicious stare. "How are you doing, Ork?"

"Oh…" Orchid waved a hand. "I may be named after a flower, but I'm sturdy as a weed."

The comparison had Alythia laughing in seconds. Arm in arm, they took a few steps to take seats on a white sofa in the middle of the airy sunroom. The chair was adorned with lavender throw pillows.

"I *am* sorry for the way things turned out, Aly." Orchid had topped off Alythia's brew before she prepared a cup of the fragrant tea for herself. "I hate myself for wasting everybody's time with that damned trip."

"Oh, girl." Aly reached out to squeeze Orchid's hand. "Your heart was in the right place. You only wanted to share your happiness."

Orchid gave an unladylike snort and set the teapot back in its place atop a glazed burgundy ceramic warmer. "Aly, the marriage was a sham," she at last admitted, leaning over to draw her hair back through her fingers. "A business deal between our families." She laughed then. "I still can't believe Jayson and I were dumb enough to agree to something so antiquated. Hmph." She massaged her temples. "I guess that proves we really are too idiotic to sustain a marriage."

Aly put her teacup back on the table. "You shouldn't be so hard on yourself. You and Jay were already under a lot of stress trying to pull this off and that didn't ease up with all the other stuff goin' on between everybody else."

Orchid sucked her teeth and rolled her eyes in an obvious display of disregard for their other girlfriends. "I should've expected them to pull that bullshit."

"Ork…they didn't *pull it* on their own, you know?"

Orchid offered up another snort. "If they had behaved like ladies, the guys never would've pulled any of that stuff with them."

"Orchid…" Aly shook her head in wonder that the woman could be so obtuse. "Myrna and Jeena were damned in their eyes before they ever met Dane and Zeke. To hell with what anyone says—*reputations* are the real first impressions, whether they have merit or not."

Again Orchid rolled her eyes and then just as easily set a regretful look in place. "I only hate that you and Gage got caught up in all this and didn't have a chance to get to know each other. There were sparks flying there, right?"

"Ork—"

"Did you have time to see if there were *any* flames kickin' there?"

"We had *some* time together," Aly conceded.

Orchid looked ready to explode beneath her expectancy. "And?"

Alythia shrugged. "We're taking it slowly."

Orchid looked satisfied. "The rest of us could've learned a lot from you guys."

"Not really." Aly folded her arms across her tummy and leaned forward. "Gage and I…we moved fast, too, and I still don't know how much hell there will be to pay because of it."

"You guys looked happy, though."

Alythia couldn't deny that. "Gage Vincent is a man a woman can fall in love with very easily."

"I'm happy for you, Aly. For real." For all her good cheer however, Orchid's easy expression faded into something tight. "Makes me regret what I'm about to tell you."

Bracing herself, Alythia wondered if she was about to experience a little of the hell she'd just spoken of.

"Gage may have already told you, but I'll go on and confirm…I'm suing Jayson."

"For what?" Alythia blurted.

Orchid made a quick waving motion toward her cheek. "Have you already forgotten what happened, Aly?" She looked offended. "The fool actually had the nerve to hit me."

"And that was wrong." Alythia ventured forward carefully. "Wrong, just like the wrong you did in sleeping with one of his best friends when you were supposed to be there celebrating getting married."

Orchid came down a bit from her self-righteousness. "I regret that." Her stare faltered then.

"How in the world did it happen, Orchid? Why?" Aly turned to face her friend more fully. "Whether the marriage was a sham or not, things at least had to be going well in the bedroom. You guys were pretty…demonstrative. Or…am I mistaken?"

A sudden and uncharacteristic look of total honesty claimed Orchid Benjamin's fair-skinned face. "Sex has always been my escape, Aly." She sighed. "Pouting and wanting to get back at Mommy and Daddy for not having that chocolate waterfall at your seventeenth birthday party? Have some sex and all will be well." She shared the insight as though she were a television announcer promoting some grand new product.

"Dammit… Such an idiot." Again Orchid drew her fingers through her hair. "I guess that's what that night with Dane was about. Part of it, anyway. Some of it was me just wanting to show Myrna that she'd picked another toad and that she still hadn't found her happily-ever-after Prince Charming."

Aly leaned over to top off her tea again. "And the other part?" she asked.

"Jayson." Losing interest in maintaining perfect posture, Orchid slumped on her side of the sofa. "We had a fight about my 'friends.' That little show between Jeena and Zeke on the terrace during our group breakfast and then there was something that happened with Myrna and Dane at one of the clubs—it all pulled quite an audience. Jayson said that Clive called a little get-together with them. He told them some of the other guests had voiced concern that he allowed that sort of…element into his resort."

Alythia held the teapot but didn't pour. She was suddenly frozen to her spot. "Gage didn't say anything."

"Chances are he wouldn't." Orchid smiled sourly. "Most of the unfavorable remarks Clive's staff had received were about the women who had been causing such a ruckus."

Aly put the pot back on the warmer. She'd suddenly lost her taste for more tea.

"That's what we argued about." Orchid sat a little straighter on the sofa. "Then our *chat* led him to revealing that his family was having second thoughts about him getting tied up with someone like me. All this was even before the trip. Before we even announced the engagement. They want the Benjamin-family respect and society status but not a— How was it that he put it?" Orchid inclined her head at a thoughtful angle. "Oh, yeah, they wanted the society status but not a whoring fiancée-turned-wifey."

"Sweetie..." Aly scooted close to squeeze Orchid's hand. "I'm sorry."

"It's no big." Orchid shrugged. "I slapped him, or rather it was the big-ass bag I was carrying that delivered the blow." She smirked. "It bruised that ego of his, all right, and I guess he wanted to show me that he wasn't goin' down like Zeke. Had to hit me to show he wasn't a punk."

"Ork, do you really think suing him is the answer? Can't you just let it rest? Jay's gonna have enough on his plate dealing with the blow Dane gave him by sleeping with you."

"Hmph, Dane." Orchid's eyes narrowed a fraction. "Do you know he didn't even try to stop it? It was like he had no idea that I was about to marry his best friend. I was just another woman to bed. He was just as much the slut in all this as I was."

"Maybe that's the takeaway here." Aly leaned over and smoothed a lock of hair behind Orchid's multi-diamond-studded ear. "You're better than all this, hon. You always have been. No one *all* bad would befriend a poor nobody from the wrong side of town like me."

Orchid's eyes suddenly flashed with defiance. "You're the best person I know, Alythia Duffy." She sniffed a little as though a sob was on the horizon.

"You've helped me through some times no money can fix," she said.

Alythia cupped her cheek and smiled. "This time *you're* the only one who can fix it. Sex has been the easy way out for you. Maybe it's time for a more complex plan."

Finally, Orchid nodded. The move was slow but determined. "I'll do the heavy lifting but will you still be there for me to lean on from time to time?"

"Hmph." Aly shook her head. "Where else do you think I'd be?" She tugged her friend into a hug.

Chapter 15

In spite of the vastness of Vincent Industries and Development, Gage had created his successful enterprise using funds from a small loan he'd secured from his parents. He had refused any additional help from them and had used the money to acquire a modest five-story brick building far away from the sleek downtown high-rises and other businesses. Yet Gage had remained humble and true to his roots. He'd continued to conduct business from the simple office space that his impressive array of business associates and aspiring business associates knew to be his headquarters.

Gage hadn't remained completely averse to vanity, however. The building's top floor had been reserved as his private office, complete with a small living, dining and gaming area. The primary office space was state-of-the-art and expansive, providing the man in charge with whatever he needed to tend to his every interest.

Just then, the man in charge was mixing work and play as he took part in an overseas conference call while trying to reach the next level on the newest military-themed video game in his collection.

"I like that, Oscar. An in-person meeting sounds good," Gage agreed, all the while wincing in response to the maneuver he was attempting to complete on screen.

"Yes!" He celebrated the outcome of the risky gaming move. "We'll make it happen soon!" Gage drew the call to a close, the luster with which he completed the conversation having more to do with his satisfaction over his gaming performance than with the upcoming meeting with his associates in the U.K.

He removed the phone's headset and was gearing up for a reentry when a knock landed on his door. The exciting game was totally forgotten.

"They told me to come on up." Alythia took a tentative step just past the doorway, her uncertainty evident. "Is this a bad time?"

Slowly, Gage left the leather lounge chair where he'd taken the call. "Your timing's never bad."

"You said you'd call."

"I know." Gage maintained his spot by the chair. "Then I thought it might be better if you took the wheel on that."

She nodded. "That's what I figured."

"So what's the verdict?"

"I'm scared." Her response was simple and she accompanied it by slapping her hands to her thighs in a show of surrender. "Those feelings aren't going to go anywhere anytime soon. But I'm not ready to let all that win."

Obvious relief softening his attractive, dark face, Gage began his journey toward her. "Can I take you out now? Show everyone you're mine?"

"That sounds rather possessive, Mr. Vincent."

"You're damn right it is, Ms. Duffy." He spanned her waist, squeezing her hips. He moved on then to skim her bare skin beneath the petal-pink drop-tail blouse she wore.

"I don't know if we can be trusted out and about on Charlotte's city streets on our own, though. We may need chaperones." She sighed.

His mouth was at her neck. "What have you got in mind?" he murmured, the words holding an absent quality, as he was far more interested in ravaging the satiny flesh behind her ear.

"Dinner and maybe…some dancing…." She waited for the last to capture his attention and smiled when he raised his head to watch her expectantly. "Angela and Owen have a date night at least once a month. They'd like to share this one with us."

"I like it." He gave a singular nod and then the brilliant chocolate tone of his gaze grew heated. "I can't promise to be on my best behavior, though, even with two chaperones."

He kissed her and Aly delighted in the lazy nudging of his tongue against hers.

"What?" Gage read the weariness in her eyes when he pulled back.

Alythia pressed her lips together to gather her resolve. "I know about the meeting Clive called with you and the guys after that thing with Zeke and Jeena."

"Hell." Gage growled the curse and moved away.

"Did you think I couldn't handle knowing?" Aly followed him deeper into the office.

"It was pretty stupid." He leaned against his desk. "We were all at fault with it."

"But *we* were the unsavory element." There was no accusation in her tone.

Gage reached for her hands. "Clive's soft heart is gonna get him in some real trouble one day. He knew the sort of drama he was letting himself in for when I called and told him about Jay getting married and us wanting to take a group trip to the resort. But he's never been able to say no to a friend."

Alythia shook her head. "Well, that makes two of us since I just told Orchid I'd be her support system while she works on remodeling her character."

Gage kissed the back of her hand just as laughter burst out between them.

"Sorry for interrupting the cash flow."

Angela Hays's vibrant hazel eyes sparkled with satisfaction. She raised her wineglass to toast her little sister. "No apologies necessary, Aly-cat. In Owen's case an interrupted work flow signals free time to take his sexy wife on that Paris trip she's been hinting at."

"And the hints haven't been all that subtle." Owen Hays clinked his glass to Gage's as the two newfound friends shared a laugh.

"But that was one case I didn't mind walking away from." Owen sobered and smoothed a hand over his shaved head. "Wouldn't be good for anyone involved to follow up on it." He sent his sister-in-law an encouraging smile. "How'd you leave things with her, Aly?"

Alythia hid her hands in the bell sleeves of her emerald wrap dress. She had just told her dinner partners that Orchid might be of a mind to rethink her plans to sue her ex-fiancé. "I tried to get her to see what was right, tried to remind her that despite what anyone thinks, she *did* have a sense of right and wrong."

"Hey, now!" Owen rubbed his hands together. "That's enough to bring back my appetite."

"Oh, Lord…" Angela rolled her eyes. "Whose appetite were you using to devour that slab of flesh over there?" she said, eyeing the remaining half of the massive rib eye that Owen had ordered.

"This can wait till I take a break." Owen stood and offered a hand to his wife. "Dance with me, girl."

Angela rolled her eyes again but giggled like a small girl and didn't hesitate to accept her husband's request.

"Despite what *anyone* thinks, she did have a sense of right and wrong." Gage replayed Alythia's words when they were alone at the table. "Was that a dig at anybody in particular?"

"No." Aly pushed aside her dessert fork and rested her arms on the table. "But I do think it's fair to wonder when our feelings about our friends will get the better of us."

"Well—" Gage was pushing back from the table then too "—until we reach that point, I'll take you for a dance. Owen had the right idea."

Aly winked. "Told you he was quite a man." She took the hand Gage offered.

The music was sensuous but it kept a tempo not quite suited for the snug hold Gage kept her in.

"Your possessive streak is showing again, Mr. Vincent."

"Good. I guess that means I've achieved my goal." His hand firmed at the small of her back and he drew her into a kiss that grew deeper with each second that passed.

Aly was first to regain consciousness of their surroundings. She tugged at his tie until he freed her mouth.

"So what's showing your possessive streak supposed to achieve?"

"It's supposed to remind me that it's past time for me to get you out of here and into someplace with more privacy."

"We haven't even had dessert yet, you know?" She bit her lip on a smile.

"Well, well, Ms. Duffy." He began to gnaw at her neck. "You're so very right about that," he muttered.

Alythia took a detour toward the ladies' room when she and Gage left the dance floor. She was touching up her lipstick when a familiar voice caught her ear.

"Well…well, they say the quiet ones are usually the freakiest."

"Mur!" Aly called, whirling from the mirror and happy to find her friend standing just inside the bathroom.

"I see one of us came back with a man." The remark could have been considered playful were it not for the distinct look of reproach in Myrna's alluring eyes.

"Mur…don't." Aly raised a hand wearily. "Can't we just put all that petty stuff that happened in Anegada behind us?"

"That's sweet." Myrna folded her arms across the

square bodice of the black baby-doll dress that flattered her long legs. "And it's easier for some than others."

"Honey, Dane—Dane wasn't worth it. Orchid said that he had no qualms about sleeping with her and that he didn't think twice about what she had going on with Jayson."

"Oh, please! Like she cared!" Myrna stalked about on the open-toed stilettos she wore. "The only thing she probably gave him time to tell her was where his bed was."

"Myrna, stop." Alythia slashed the air with a wave of her hand when she ventured forward. "We've been friends too damn long. Too much is invested in us for you to let some snake like Dane Spears ruin it."

"Oh, Dane didn't *ruin* us, Aly. Our weird friendship has been circling the bowl for years." She gave Alythia a judgmental once-over. "You don't even want to associate with us, always using business as an excuse to get out of spending time with us." She suddenly smiled. "But then again, I guess it was all worth it. I hear congrats are in order."

Aly frowned. "What are you talking about?"

"I guess all that private time you want everyone to think you weren't giving to one of the most powerful men in town paid off. Seems you're one of the lucky bastards about to grab digs in that swanky new downtown high-rise of his."

Alythia stilled noticeably. "How do you know that?"

Myrna slowly threw up her hands. "Aly, please… you're not the only one with powerful friends, or bed partners, I guess I should say…." She regarded Aly more closely then. "Whoa…you didn't know you were in, did you? How interesting. I wonder why that is? Why hasn't that cutie of yours told you what I'm sure you've been waiting to hear for months?"

Myrna paced the outer area of the powder room, tapping a finger to her chin and presenting herself as a study in concentration. "Maybe he knows you were just screwing him for the building. Though that's no hardship, as gorgeous as he is. Guess he just wants to…milk you a little longer before he gives you the good news and your walking papers."

Alythia blinked, assessing the new information.

Myrna's apologetic look was belied by a triumphant smile. "Forgive me, Aly. I'm not trying to hurt you, girl." She shrugged and headed for the door. "You were a good friend, but you should be prepared for little run-ins like this, especially if you plan on holding to the claim that you would've gotten that space if you *hadn't* upped the ante on your bid." She winked and pulled open the powder room door. "Enjoy your dinner. Owen and Angela look great."

Then she was gone. Aly returned to studying her mirrored reflection.

The couples said their good-nights shortly after dessert. Alythia had enjoyed the entire evening in spite of her "toilet talk" with Myrna. Part of her mourned the loss of such an old friendship. Though it *was* indeed a lost friendship. She could accept that. Myrna was angry over a lot more than her, and it would take a very long time for her to come back around.

Still, another part of her was wickedly peeved, but at Myrna or herself Alythia couldn't be completely certain.

She was so absorbed in her thoughts, in fact, that

she didn't realize they were parked outside her complex until Gage was at the passenger side of his truck and freeing her from the seat belt.

She blinked and was suddenly all smiles. "What a great night, huh?" She took the hand he offered and stepped out of the car.

"Owen and Angela are so much fun to hang out with. Thanks for coming with me. . . ." Alythia rambled on so much that she didn't take much notice of Gage's extreme silence.

They headed into her downtown apartment building and covered the ten-flight elevator ride to her floor.

"Can I get you anything?" Aly offered once they were inside the apartment and she had tossed aside her things en route to the kitchen.

"You can tell me what Myrna wanted."

Alythia stopped short, turning and frowning a bit when she discovered that he hadn't left the foyer. Gage was still resting back on the front door, hands hidden in the deep pockets of his trousers. Alythia retraced her steps, her expression screaming a question she couldn't form the words to ask.

Gage read it easily enough and shrugged. "I saw her at the restaurant, figured she'd find a way to get time alone with you."

"She came to congratulate me." Aly smiled dourly at the question coming to his handsome face and continued. "Seems I've been accepted into the new downtown space." She ducked her head, fiddling with the edge of one of the wrist-hugging sleeves of her wrap dress. "Were you going to tell me, Gage?" She kept her head down.

"No." His answer was simply stated and he took her

by the wrist before she could move away from him. "And I'm leaning toward us having a 'do not discuss' clause in all matters having to do with our businesses."

"A 'do not discuss' clause." Aly ignored her desire to smile. "I don't think I've ever heard of one of those before."

"Good, 'cause I just came up with it." He raised a broad shoulder, letting it slide up along the door where he still reclined. "I'm known for being innovative like that."

"Well, it's definitely that." She didn't resist leaning in when he tugged.

Gage made no effort to relinquish his stance against the door. He had a strong hold on her wrist, and his hand at her neck cradled her there with a gentleness. His kiss was a subtle cross between commanding and cajoling. Soon Aly's fingers were entwined about the fabric of his jacket lapels, tiny moans escaping her as she took what he gave and reciprocated with her own brand of passion.

With a pat to her cheek, Gage withdrew from the kiss but remained near. He studied her face, searching her bright eyes with a measuring fire. "You aren't gonna do something crazy like refuse to take the space, are you?" He rested his head back against the door. "I'll break my own rule this time and tell you that I left all of the decision making to my assistant and the rest of the team. Until you told me, I had no idea you were even connected to the bid pool."

"Thank you. And no, I'm not going to back out of accepting the space." She shook her head when he gave her a mock look of surprise. "I've wanted a more upscale location for a long time and that was before I even knew you or knew that you were connected to it all."

"So we're okay?" He pulled her closer into him.

Alythia curved her hands about his tie. "We're okay."

His sigh held a melodramatic flavor. "I'm sorry, but I'm gonna need more than your word on that, Ms. Duffy."

"More? What more do I have to give?" She played innocent with relish.

The liquid-chocolate intensity of his stare harbored a more molten quality when it traveled the length of her. "You ask the best questions." His lips closed on her earlobe, where he barely suckled.

The move was hypnotic and so much so that Alythia didn't even realize he'd located the ties and fastenings of her wrap dress until she felt the rush of cool air against her bare skin. The front of the chic dress hung open to reveal the lacy emerald-colored bra-and-panties ensemble she wore underneath.

Gage's branding touch spanned her waist, curving around to provide a cradle to her bottom as he lifted her off her feet. Aly didn't care where he took her so long as he didn't let her go. She let her nose trail the line of his jaw and the side of his neck adorned by the cologne he wore.

She was jolted suddenly by the cool wood beneath her bare bottom. The sensation roused a gasp from her lips. She realized he'd somehow removed her panties on the way to the high message table in the foyer where he'd placed her.

Aly needed but a moment to acclimate herself to her new position. She let Gage brush the dress from her shoulders while she worked to relieve him of his own clothing. As usual, he was more intent on having her naked first. He gave playful slaps to her hands when they got in the way of him achieving that. Alythia, however, was too determined to have him as bare as he wanted her. When he slapped at her hand, she retaliated with a slap to his and fixed him with a bold, saucy smile when he chuckled his surprise.

Eventually they met on common ground, both gloriously nude and hungry for the sensual friction their bodies provided when they made contact. Gage braced suddenly weakened hands on the message desk. His long legs had gone rubbery beneath Alythia's attention. She was hungrily suckling his earlobe and emitting soft feminine sounds of desire that stirred his arousal and ego as deliciously as her thumbs stroked his nipples.

When she let her mouth cascade over the rippling dark-coffee pecs of his stunning chest, he rested his forehead to the crook of her shoulder. He shuddered when she began a merciless assault on his nipples with her lips and tongue, while her hand closed over his sex and began working him with erotic fervor.

"You're killin' me. . . ." he moaned.

Aly smiled and brushed her thumb across the tip of his erection. "I don't think so," she mused.

"Alythia...please..."

She shivered, wanting very much to extend that particular plan of foreplay, loving the power of driving such a man out of his mind. Still, she was just as much a slave to her own needs and wanted him inside her just as much as he wanted to be there.

Gage had already taken a condom from a well-stocked jacket pocket before Alythia had unceremoniously tugged the garment from his shoulders and let it fall to the floor. Now the item lay on the message desk and Aly fumbled feverishly for it.

He had hardly given her time to fully secure their protection when once again his hands were cupping her bottom. Focus unwavering, he positioned her as deftly as Aly guided him toward her core. Gasps and groans colored the foyer simultaneously. The volume of the fevered sounds heightened with every vigorous thrust from Gage or wicked twist of the hips from Alythia. The table added its own groans to the melee, creaking in protest of them enjoying one another so freely, inhibitions be damned.

Gage finally took Aly off the table and held her to the wall, without ever breaking his connection to her. To ensure that, Aly locked her legs at his lean waist, her sensation cresting at the feel of him stretching her intimate walls and the delight of her bare nipples grazing his.

Their moves had carried them to the doorway of the living room. Aly cursed the relentless press of the framework into her back but she wasn't about to complain. It was of little importance; Gage had already grown tired of that venue and was depositing Alythia on the back of her sofa moments later. Still they were intimately connected and Aly luxuriated in both the soothing cushions beneath her bottom and his exploration of her body. He held her thighs apart, preventing her from locking her legs about his waist. Instead, he wanted to penetrate, to mark her as deeply as he could.

There was nothing Gage needed to prove to himself. She was his. Yet he wanted to leave no doubts of that in her mind. That night was to be about him giving her his all. The thought had a shattering effect and he was then releasing himself inside the condom's thin sheet far more quickly than he had intended. He gnawed her cheek and shoulder, patting her bottom and loving the feel of her continuous clutch and release of his shaft.

"Alythia?" He felt himself refueling for another round and the need for additional protection was in order.

"Mmm…?"

"Where's my jacket?"

"What?" Gage probed when he heard the short laugh Alythia gave in to her coffee the next morning in her small kitchen.

"You're not an easy man to figure out." She smiled.

"In what way?" He looked playfully insulted. "I thought I laid myself pretty bare last night."

"I'll say." She sipped of her coffee and then cradled the mug between her hands. "One day you're commanding the head of a table on board a lavish jet and the next you're here having bacon and eggs in my little kitchen."

"And they're damn good eggs, too." Brows raised, he was already leaning over the table to help himself to more of the fluffy scramble. He took note of her expression and suddenly feigned uncertainty.

"Should I be down on your cooking or complaining over the cramped dining space?"

"No…and thanks for being so considerate. I can definitely do without the colorful commentary about my residence."

"Good, because I really want us to have dinner here tonight." Gage cleaned his plate of the second helping of eggs. "Since you took care of breakfast, I'll handle dinner."

"You? Cook?"

Gage shook his head. "I said I'd *handle* dinner—never said I'd cook it."

"That's too bad." Alythia set her amethyst gaze to appraising his torso, hidden by a partially buttoned shirt. "Nothing sexier than a man who cooks."

"Does Owen cook?"

Aly laughed. "That's one of the few things he prefers to leave to Angela. He only visits the kitchen to eat."

"I see. In that case, I'll put cooking lessons on the list ASAP."

"No need." Aly propped her bare feet on the unoccupied chair at the small round table they shared. "There *are* other places to be talented besides the kitchen, you know?"

"Hmm… You may be right." Gage tapped his chin, finished off the rest of his juice, wiped his mouth and hands, and then stood.

Alythia accepted the hand he offered and the kiss that followed.

"Walk me out?" He made the request as his sensuous exploration of her mouth continued.

Eventually, cooler heads prevailed over hormones. Arm in arm, Gage and Alythia made their way to the front door.

"I'll see you for dinner." He patted the bare hint of cheek visible at the hem of the sleep T-shirt she still wore and indulged in another quick plundering of her mouth. Then he left.

Aly watched him go, waving him on down the hall when he pivoted to return to her door. As he disappeared down the hall, Aly thought about how used to this she could become.

"Head out of the clouds, Aly. . . ." she whispered, and headed back to the kitchen to clean up from breakfast. The kettle continued to simmer on the stove, sending its sounds of steaming water into the air. Additionally, there was the dull drone of the television newscaster delivering the morning forecast and traffic conditions.

Alythia only barely paid attention to the voices as she wiped down the table and loaded the dishwasher. Soon, though, she was riveted to the television screen, having done a double take when she saw footage of Orchid leaving some arts event she'd attended earlier in the year. Beneath the footage, a caption read Local Heiress Sues Former Fiancé.

Slowly, Alythia settled in one of the dining table chairs and mourned her friend's decision. She set her forehead against her palm when the newscaster added that prominent Charlotte attorney Owen Hays would be arguing Ms. Benjamin's case.

Alythia was massaging her temples when the doorbell rang. She wondered if it was at all possible to fake not being at home. But the fact that it may have been Gage was enough to get her out of the chair. While she would've loved to forget everything and fall into his arms for the rest of the day and night, she knew that probably wouldn't happen for a while. Aly cursed the fact that she and Gage were once again on the cusp of another friendship melodrama.

At the door, Aly gave in to a significant measure of relief. Marianne, not Gage, stood on the other side of the door.

"Mari, hey—"

Marianne moved fast past her before Alythia could give her a proper greeting. Mari kept hold of Aly's upper arms while pushing her into the foyer.

"We may have a problem," she said.

Chapter 16

News of *Benjamin v. Muns* had reached Gage by the time he'd arrived at his office building. He'd stopped off at his condo for a change of clothes, regretting that he hadn't checked the news before leaving. His staff, however, had wasted no time informing him of the brewing storm or the fact that he already had guests waiting in his office.

Gage didn't need to ask. Since he'd just left Alythia, there were only three other people his staff was under clear orders to grant immediate access.

At the elevator he hesitated. He very much wanted to return to his truck and heavily contemplated going back to Alythia's. Foregoing his wants, he moved onward and before he knew it, he was seated behind his desk. There he looked out over the stony faces of his friends as they recovered from the shock he'd just given them.

"What the hell do you mean you won't back Jay on this, G?" Dane was first to recover from his surprise.

"I don't think I was unclear." Gage's expression harbored a stoniness surpassed only by the grimness of his voice. Without waiting on another reply from Dane, he turned his next words to Jayson Muns.

"We go way back, Jay."

"All the way back," Jayson confirmed with a brief nod.

Gage returned the gesture. "I'll help you however I can while you deal with this thing but I stand by what I just said. I draw the line at sitting up in a courtroom with you as part of this wall of support Dane's talkin' about."

"G, that's bull—" Dane began.

"And how the hell are *you* offering support to Jay when you're responsible for all this?" Gage interjected.

"Aw, Gage, please! How long we had each other's backs? Jay knew I was just lookin' out for him."

"Lookin' out?" Gage felt as though he was on the verge of laughter.

"I meant to show him what that wench was really like." Dane planted a fist to the center of his chest as though giving credence to his plan. "She didn't need much coaxing, hardly any. What the hell kind of wife would she have made for our boy?"

"How'd you get him to buy that crap?" Gage's tone was incredulous, his eyes narrowed with blatant disbelief.

Dane's lips curled on the beginnings of a snarl. "I didn't have to get him to *buy* a damn thing. He already knew it was true. Everybody in town knows what Orchid Benjamin is behind all that money and family respect."

"Jay—" Gage turned back to Jayson, having silently acknowledged that Dane Spears was blind to everything except his own self-importance and opinion "—you *did* hit the woman. Don't forget that. What D's suggesting makes it look like we all approve."

"And that would be wrong, G," Dane chimed in before Jay could summon a reply. "It would be wrong if it wasn't for the fact that Jay was protecting himself."

Gage did laugh then. "You're not suggesting that he claim this was all self-defense?"

"G? She *did* hit me first. That's the truth of it," Jay said matter-of-factly. "She hit me and I—I reacted. Granted, not in the best way, but after what happened with Zeke and Jeena, I wasn't taking a chance with the woman's violent streak."

"That's gonna be your statement for the press, Jay?" Gage set his elbow on the arm of the desk chair and massaged the bridge of his nose. "Please don't tell me you're bringing that into evidence." He shook his head when there was no response from Jayson. "If you are," he continued, "you should know that Alythia's brother-in-law is no slouch in the courtroom." He fixed Jay with unmasked sympathy.

"You better hope Owen Hays doesn't present witnesses from that little spat. Even though Jeena was at fault, Hays will find all the other folks who were there and saw the three of us trying to hold Zeke down from going after her. They'll try to make it look like we're a bunch of woman beaters if we sit there and back you in this. I want to support you, man, but that sort of comparison doesn't sit well with me." Gage let his thoughts rest on Alythia.

"That's it, isn't it?" Dane was apparently thinking of Aly, as well. "You don't want to stick by a friend you've known since forever, because you don't want to upset your latest piece of candy?"

"D—"

"And a delicious piece she is." Dane barreled ahead over Gage. "Not that I've had the pleasure of sampling—"

"Dane, man, easy," Zeke said, having seen the murderous narrowing of Gage's eyes and the clench of his fists.

Dane, however, had found a line to tug. "It's cool, Zeke, it's cool. Gage here just needs to ask himself if he really, *really* thinks *Alythia* is any better than the rest of her friends, who are skanks."

Gage stood, crashing his chair into the credenza that spanned the length of his desk. Zeke and Jayson came to their feet, as well, ready to separate their friends if the meeting turned physical.

"Gage!"

Webb Reese burst into the office then. Desperation had overridden all sense of decorum as he interrupted the goings-on between the four tense men in the room.

"Was she worth it, man?" Dane roared, waving a hand toward Webb.

"Webb?" Gage didn't miss the guilt flash on his assistant's face.

"Is that how Ms. Duffy got her new downtown digs, Webb?" Dane was smug and shrugged at Gage. "Guess your right-hand man is gonna try keeping it all quiet a little longer. Trust me, man, no one's gonna hear a peep out of me." He turned to Webb. "At least be honest with your boss. You know he's been good to you. Tell him how Alythia Duffy's right hand girl gave up the panties to close the deal."

Webb shook his head wildly and spread his hands. "Gage, I swear, it wasn't like that."

"I swear it wasn't like that." Marianne spread her hands in a supplicating fashion across the nook counter.

Alythia squeezed Marianne's hands and gave them a tug. "*I* believe you, but you know it won't be hard for someone to make it look like you slept with Webb to give me a leg up on the bid…pun intended." She smiled sympathetically when Mari put her forehead on the counter.

"But I didn't even sleep with him," Mari moaned. "We didn't even go out together."

"I— Huh?" Aly tapped her fingers to her brow.

"I never even talked to Webb Reese before the day Gage asked him to call and help him find you. Sounds like Gage didn't have any way to contact you."

"No." Aly picked at the microscopic balls of lint that clung to the worn sweatpants she'd thrown on when Marianne arrived. "The trip to Anegada wasn't about matchmaking." She smirked. "At least, we were all stupid enough to believe it wasn't. We were going to celebrate our friends' wedding. Anyway, no numbers or emails were exchanged."

"Well, I told him I couldn't help. I didn't even know the guy. No way was I giving contact info on one of my clients." Marianne finally helped herself to the piping-hot herbal tea Aly had served her.

"So he—Webb—tells me that one of the sales associates at the boutique suggested he give me a call. I think he even got your cell number and shared it with Gage, but I guess you didn't answer."

"And then he showed up on my doorstep in Aspen."

Marianne cringed. "Sorry."

"Don't be." Alythia didn't try to hide her contentment and hugged herself. "It was the best time of my life."

"I'm glad." Marianne bent her head to shield her face with tousles of her reddish hair. "Even so, I told Webb that I couldn't just give your info to someone I didn't know and then he dropped Gage's name and I…" She sent Aly a resigned look.

"I really am so sorry about this, Aly. Hmph, an apology is why Webb called." Marianne tugged at the tassels of her white sweatshirt. "He said he was sorry for upsetting me when he called. I told him it was fine but he said he wanted to take me out and make it up but I didn't think it was a good idea." She burst into quick laughter.

"So of course I run into him at Rooney's." She cited a cigar bar that was popular with the business crowd after hours.

"We were both there." Marianne put her head in her hands. "He was there with someone I knew and they introduced us. Afterward we stayed a little longer, had a few drinks…"

"Nice…" Aly reached over to help herself to Marianne's tea.

"Aly, I promise it didn't go any further than that. We talked about our jobs, but the conversation *never* brushed up against our clients or our clients' business. I know I'm probably making a mountain out of my molehill of a dating life." She brought her elbow to the counter and propped her chin on her fist. "I just thought you should know."

"I appreciate it." Aly massaged her nape. "It's amazing how many molehills have brushed up against me and Gage's relationship in the short time we've known each other."

"So…we're good?" Mari cringed again.

Aly squeezed her hands and nodded. "We're good. You're fine."

Marianne's expression harbored a trace of uncertainty. "And what are *you* gonna do?"

Aly made her way around the breakfast nook. "Guess it's time to face another round of music. I can only hope this is the last movement."

"Something tells me I've really come at a bad time." Alythia stood in the doorway of Gage's office and observed what looked to be a war zone.

His expression gave away nothing when he stood from the heap of books and picture frames. "What makes you say that?"

"Just a lucky guess." She hooked the strap of her purse over the office doorknob and tentatively ventured deeper inside the room. "Have you seen the news?" she asked.

"You're referring to the trial of the decade?" Gage tossed a scant glance toward the wreckage on the floor and grinned. "Yeah, I heard. I heard a lot today."

"Did it have anything to do with the tornado that swept your office?"

Gage tossed the picture frame he carried back to the mess on the floor. "Dane wants to get a support group together for Jay. Wants all of us to rally together and sit in his corner at the hearing."

Alythia couldn't help it. She laughed.

Gage's sour expression showed signs of improvement and he smiled.

"Are you serious?"

Gage shrugged. "Sadly, yes." He kicked at some of the wreckage.

"Men are strange." Aly shook her head and brushed off a bit of debris from one of the chairs before the desk and took a seat there. "So quick you are to forgive the betrayals of your boyhood friends."

Gage took his turn at bursting into laughter then. "You're very mistaken, Ms. Duffy, so let me school you. Men like that are few and far between." He laughed again, but the humor fueling it had curbed considerably. "I'm starting to think that my old friend Jay doesn't have as much going on upstairs as he used to."

The duo indulged in more laughter. Unfortunately, the good vibes spent themselves far too soon.

"So is that what led to this recent redecoration of your office?" Aly scanned the room again.

Sighing, Gage took a seat on the corner of his desk and seemed to be weighing his response. "The 'redecoration' happened after my assistant, Webb Reese, came to tell me about his date with your business manager—Marianne?"

Aly only nodded as more of the pieces began to fall in place.

"Somehow Dane knew about it already. He got vocal over it. Things got ugly."

"Gage." Aly scooted to the edge of her chair, his explanation motivating her into a vocal spree of her own.

"Whatever Dane said, it—it wasn't like that. Marianne says she and Webb, it was all just by chance—"

"Alythia—"

"They met at a cigar bar. They didn't even *meet* there, just happened to be there at the same time and—"

"Alythia, stop."

The underlying thickness of his voice caught her attention and she obeyed. Her heart sank as she acknowledged that he'd finally had enough.

"Guess you're sick of this, huh?" Nervously, she fingered the pleats of her skirt.

Gage massaged his forehead. "You have no idea how much…and I think it'll all get worse before it gets any better."

"Yeah…" She bowed her head, unable to look at him. She raised it quickly, however, at his next words.

"I think I'm falling in love with you, Alythia Duffy, and I'm sick of just *thinking* it—I'm ready to know it."

Aly expelled the breath she hadn't realized she'd been holding. "I think I'm falling in love with you, too. But our…attempts at getting to the *knowing* stage haven't been too successful, have they?"

Gage left the desk and pulled Alythia to her feet. "Say that again." He cupped her face, brushing at both her cheeks with his thumbs.

She smiled, not at all confused by his command. "I think I'm falling in love with you, too."

His kiss was quick yet deep and probing in its brevity. Afterward he held his forehead to hers.

"I can't accept what Jay did but as a friend I can't turn my back on him. Can you understand that?"

She nodded. "If you can understand that I'll need to

be a friend to Orchid or Jeena if Zeke decides to come after *her.*"

Weak albeit easy laughter hummed between them then.

"One trial at a time, all right?" Gage pleaded.

"We're a couple of saps, you know?"

"And still our friends depend on us…." Gage murmured, skimming his lips along her temple.

"That's because they all know we won't turn our backs on them."

Gage returned to the desk and took a seat, keeping Alythia standing before him. "Too many years, too many memories, I guess." He planted a kiss to the centers of her palms.

"You think we can handle what's coming?" Aly linked her arms about his neck.

"I trust us." He drew her down, nuzzling her ear. "I think we could use some rejuvenation time before we head back into the storm, though."

"Just what did you have in mind?" She leaned back as far as he would let her.

"I was thinking about this little place called Anegada." Gage sighed and tugged Alythia back into the sweetest kiss.

* * * * *

THE ARGENTINIAN'S DEMAND

CATHY WILLIAMS

CHAPTER ONE

EMILY EDISON STARED resolutely ahead of her as the elevator purred upwards to the twentieth floor, disgorging employees along the way. It was the morning rush at Piccadilly Circus, in the towering glass building where she worked in the heart of London. She rarely experienced this because she rarely came to work later than eight in the morning, but today…

Slim fingers tightened on the neat leather satchel at her side. Inside the bag her letter of resignation felt like an incendiary device, waiting to explode the minute it was released from its fragile containment. When she tried to imagine how her boss would take this she felt slightly sick.

Leandro Perez was not going to be happy. When she had begun working for him over a year and a half ago he had already been through countless secretaries, the most successful of whom had barely lasted a fortnight. Change, in this instance, was *not* going to be as good as a rest…

'They take one look at him,' his long-suffering and fairly elderly PA had told her, two days after her arrival at the company, 'and something unfortunate happens to their brains. But you, thank God, seem to be made of sterner stuff. When I told Leandro that I would stay until I found a successful replacement I had no idea I would still be here after six and a half months…'

Emily had taken to the job like a duck to water. Theoretically, at the age of twenty-seven, she was still young enough to be susceptible to having her brains scrambled by a man who could turn heads from several blocks away, but he did nothing for her. His outrageous good-looks left her cold. The deep, rich velvet of his voice with that ever so slight sexy Argentinian accent did not put her off her stride. When he strode round her desk to look over her shoulder at something on her computer her nervous system remained perfectly stable and functioning. She was, as had been predicted by his previous PA, made of far sterner stuff.

But right now, riding the elevator by herself, because the last employee had scuttled through the doors somewhere around floor ten, she felt queasy with nerves even though she asked herself…at the end of the day, what could he do? Throw her through the window? Condemn her to immediate exile somewhere on the other side of the world? Threaten to lock her up and throw away the key?

No. The most he could do would be to get very, very annoyed—and annoyed he most certainly would be…especially considering that only a fortnight ago he had given her a glowing appraisal and a correspondingly glowing pay rise, for which she had been immensely grateful.

She inhaled deeply as the lift doors opened and she emerged onto the opulent directors' floor of the wildly successful electronics company her boss owned and ran with ruthless efficiency.

It was just one of his wildly successful companies. They ranged from publications to telecommunications and he had recently, for a little light relief, begun a programme of investment into boutique hotels in far-flung places. Such was the vastness of his wealth that he could weather any sluggish profits he made from that venture—although, if the first three hotels were anything to go by, he would yet again discover that he had the Midas touch.

She would miss all this, she thought, looking around at the busy department. Plants and artfully arranged smoked glass partitions maintained a certain amount of privacy for the various secretaries who helped keep the machinery ticking over. Several waved at her.

She would miss the occasional lunch with them in the office canteen. She would miss the stunning surroundings of a building which was a tourist attraction in its own right. She would miss the adrenaline-fuelled pace of her work, its diversity, and all her responsibilities—which had increased a hundredfold since she had started.

And would she miss Leandro?

For a few seconds she paused and frowned towards the thickly carpeted corridor that led to his massive office suite.

Her heart picked up pace. She might not have drooled over him, the way some of the other girls did, but she was not completely immune to his impact. She was in full possession of twenty-twenty vision and she would have had to be blind not to be aware of just how sinfully sexy the man was. The fact that he represented everything she despised didn't detract from that unassailable truth.

And, yes, she confessed to herself, she would most certainly miss working with him. He was nothing if not a challenging employer—indeed, the most brilliant, energetic, vibrant and demanding man she had ever worked for.

Before she could get carried away on that tangent, she refocused her mind, pursed her lips and smoothed her skirt with shaky hands. As always, she was dressed like the ultimate professional. Charcoal-grey pencil skirt, sheer flesh-coloured tights, black court shoes, a crisp white blouse and the matching charcoal-grey jacket that completed the suit. All this despite the fact that it was June and the weather was heating up with every passing day. Her pale blonde hair was neatly coiled in a bun of sorts, out of harm's way.

She strode confidently towards Leandro's office, pausing en route to dump her satchel and her briefcase on her desk, which was in her own private outer office, before knocking on the interconnecting door.

Behind the door, Leandro glanced up from his computer and then pushed himself away from the desk. This was a first. His secretary was late, and he was disconcerted to find that he had wasted far too much time wondering what was keeping her. The fact of the matter was it wasn't even nine yet. Her working day was not due to begin for…another ten minutes.

'You're late,' was the first thing he said as soon as she had entered his office.

On cue, his midnight-black eyes swept over her, taking in the prim suit, the even primmer blouse, the severely restrained blonde hair. She was as cool as an ice maiden. Very little ruffled her feathers, and when she looked at him she did so without the slightest flicker of interest. There were times, in fact, when he almost suspected that she might not even like him very much—although he invariably put that down to the workings of his imagination.

Women liked him. That, he conceded without a trace of vanity, was a given. He assumed that it was due to a combination of the way he looked and the reserves he had in his bank account. Money and a halfway decent appearance were almost always a guarantee of lively interest from the opposite sex.

'Technically,' Emily told him calmly, 'I'm not even due in for another eight minutes.'

She looked at her boss, seeing him in a different light now that she knew she would soon be on the way out. She would hand him her letter of resignation just before she left for the day, and thus spare herself the full force of his anger.

He really was, she thought with a detached eye, a thing of great beauty. Black hair was swept back from a face of chiselled perfection. He had lashes most women would have killed for. And there was a lazy, shrewd, perceptive depth to his dark eyes that could, she knew, be at once disturbing and exciting. There had been instances when she had caught him looking at her with a mixture of mild curiosity and lazy masculine appreciation, and for all her toughened resistance she had been able to see just what it was about him that had women drooling.

He was tall—at least four inches taller than her, and she wasn't petite at five foot eleven—and even in a suit, it required very little imagination to guess at the muscular physique underneath.

Oh, yes, he had the full package—and it drove women nuts. She knew because she had full access to his private life. She chose gifts for his women—five and counting over the past year and a half. She ordered elaborate bouquets of flowers when, sadly, their time was up and he was ready to move on to a new model. She fielded his women's calls and, on one memorable occasion, had had to handle a personal appearance at the company.

He invariably dated obviously sexy women. Curvaceous, dark-haired beauties with big breasts and come-hither eyes. The sort of women who always commanded far more male interest than any skinny supermodel ever could.

Involvement in his personal life was *not* something she was going to miss, and it reminded her of why, despite the stunning good looks, the agile brain, the sharp acumen, and those flashes of wit that could bring a grin to the most poker-faced of spinster aunts, she still didn't like the man.

Leandro frowned but decided to let it go, even though

her cool response had carried just a hint of rebellion behind it.

'And might I expect this to become a habit?' he enquired with raised eyebrows. He pushed himself away from his desk and relaxed back in his chair with his hands folded behind his head. 'If it does, then some advance warning would be appreciated. Although…' he allowed a few seconds of silence '…considering the amount you're paid, you might find my tolerance of your clock-watching a little limited.'

'I won't be clock-watching. I never do. Shall I bring you a refill for your coffee? And if you let me know what you want done about the due diligence on the Reynolds deal I can get started…'

For the rest of the day, however, Emily *did* watch the clock—something she never had in the past—and with each passing minute her nerves became a little more stretched.

Was she doing the right thing? It was a big step. Handing in her notice would signal an end to her substantial salary, but what choice did she have?

At a little before five-thirty, with her resignation letter burning a hole in her bag, she debated her options. Of course she had options. Who didn't? But when you got right down to it all her options aside from the one she was going to take now led to the same dead end.

She cleared her desk with the feeling that she was looking at it for the last time. He would certainly ask her to leave immediately. For starters, she was privy to confidential information. Would she have to sign some sort of disclaimer? It sounded like the sort of thing that might happen in a B-rated movie, but who knew? When it came to business, Leandro was not a man to take any chances.

He glanced up briefly as she entered the office, took in

the very obvious fact that she was dressed to go and pointedly looked at his watch.

'It's five-twenty-five…' Emily forestalled any sarcasm '…and I'm afraid I have some…stuff to do this evening…'

She normally worked until after six—sometimes far later if there was a lot to get through.

'I've completed all those emails you needed to be sent to the lawyers in Hong Kong and forwarded them to you for checking. You'll find them in your inbox…' She hovered, reached into her bag and withdrew her resignation letter. 'There's just one more thing…'

Leandro picked up the uneven tenor in her voice and stiffened. He looked at her narrowly and indicated the chair facing his desk. 'Sit.'

'I'd rather not. As I said, I'm in a bit of a rush…'

'What's going on?'

It was more of a demand than a question. Today was proving to be full of surprises—at least as far as his secretary was concerned. Kicking off with her late arrival at work, she had spent the day in a state of mild distraction, jumping when he happened to come up behind her so that he could review something on her computer, working with the ferocious absorption of someone intent on pretending that there was no one else in the office, and barely able to meet his eye when addressed.

All of those minute changes were so under the radar that he knew they would have passed unnoticed by anyone other than himself, but his antenna was sharp when it came to detecting nuances—especially nuances in a woman with whom he had spent the past eighteen months working in close quarters. She was his secretary, but he had, in actual fact, spent a hell of a lot more time with her than he ever had with any of the women he had taken to his bed.

So…what was going on?

Leandro was intrigued, and what startled him was the acknowledgement that he had actually been intrigued by her for a long time. Intrigued by her aloofness, her detachment, her almost pathological desire for privacy. Intrigued because she was the only woman he had ever met who barely reacted to his presence.

She did her work with the highest level of efficiency, and even when they had worked late on several occasions, and he had ordered in a takeout to keep them going, she had politely refused to be drawn into any form of personal conversation, preferring to keep everything on a professional footing. Chinese food, chopsticks and no downtime. Instead intelligent discussion of whatever deal they had been working on, with her notes spread next to her on the desk.

'What do you mean?'

'I mean, Emily, that you've been acting strangely all day…'

'Have I? I've managed to complete all the tasks you've set me.'

She sat, simply because he kept staring at her and remaining on her feet felt oddly uncomfortable. She had planned on handing him her letter of resignation and leaving perhaps before he could even open it. It now looked as though that option would be removed from her.

Now that she was on her way out—now that she knew she would never clap eyes on him again—she was oddly aware of his potent masculinity. It was almost as though she had now given herself permission to look at him—*really look at him*—without the barrier of her inherent scorn for the type of man he was standing in the way, acting as blinkers.

Something dark and forbidden raced through her, making the hairs on the back of her neck stand on end. Those dark eyes were so…so brooding…so intense…

She looked down quickly, angry with herself and wondering where that sudden powerful awareness had come from. Surreptitiously she extracted the letter from the satchel and licked her lips.

'You're not a performing seal.' Leandro relaxed back into the leather chair and looked at her. 'There's more to your job than simply completing the tasks set. Granted, you're not the most open book in the world, but something's definitely off with you today. You've been acting like a cat on a hot tin roof and I want to know why. It's impossible to work if the atmosphere in the office isn't right.'

He picked up his fountain pen—an expensive present from his mother, who firmly believed that letters were still written and technology and computers were simply a passing phase. He twirled it idly between his fingers and Emily watched, guiltily mesmerised by the movement of his long fingers.

'Perhaps,' she said in a stilted voice, 'this might go some way to explaining my behaviour. Not that I've noticed anything amiss. I've done my job as efficiently today as I always have done.'

Performing seal? Was that how he saw her? As someone who came in, did what she was expected to do to the very highest standard, but lacked in all personality? Dull? Boring? An automaton? She had kept her distance and had kept her opinions to herself. Since when had that been a crime? Her mouth tightened and she swallowed back an intense temptation to tell him just what she thought of him.

Leandro looked at the white envelope in her hand and then looked at her.

'And that is…?'

'Take it. Read it. We can discuss it in the morning.'

She made to rise and was told to sit back down.

'If a discussion is warranted, then we'll have the discussion right here and right now.'

He reached for the envelope, slit it open and read the brief letter several times.

Emily schooled her features into a mask of polite detachment, but she had to unclench her hands and her heart was racing—beating so fast that she felt it might burst through her ribcage.

'What the hell is this?'

He tossed the letter across the desk in her direction and Emily snatched it before it could flutter to the ground. She smoothed it on her lap, staring at the jumble of words. Granted, it was a very brief letter of resignation. It said that she had enjoyed her time working with him but felt that the time had come for her to move in another direction. It could not have been more dry or unemotional.

'You know what it is. It's self-explanatory. It's my letter of resignation.'

'You've had fun and now it's time to move on…am I reading it correctly?'

'That's what it says.'

'Sorry. Not buying it.'

Leandro was shocked. He hadn't seen this coming and he was furious at what he saw as inadequate advance warning. Furthermore, *he* was the one who generally decided when one of his employees was ready to be shown the door. He had had enough experience of simpering young girls batting their eyelashes and getting into an annoying flap every time he looked at them and asked them to do something simple.

'If I remember correctly, you had a substantial pay rise recently, which you very happily accepted, and you informed me at the time that you were perfectly satisfied with the working conditions here.'

'Yes. I…I…hadn't thought about resigning at that point in time.'

'And yet less than a month later you have? Did you have a sudden revelation? I'm curious. Or have you been looking for a replacement job all along and just biding your time until the right one came your way?'

The thought of another endless series of airheads was not a pleasant one. Emily Edison had been the perfect secretary. Intelligent, unflappable, always willing to go beyond the call of duty. He was used to her. The thought of getting in to work and not having her there at hand was inconceivable.

Had he taken advantage of her? Of her quiet efficiency? Her willingness always to go the extra mile? He rejected any such notion before it had had time to take root. He *paid* for her to be willing to go beyond the call of duty. He was pretty sure that she would be hard pressed to find another job as secretary in the heart of London where the pay equalled what she got.

'Well?' he prompted. 'Has someone made you an offer you can't refuse? Because if that's the case, consider whatever offer you were tempted by doubled.'

'You would *do* that?'

Her mouth fell open. Performing seal she might very well be, but he valued her, and although she knew that through a process of intelligent deduction, it was gratifying to hear it put so starkly into words.

'We work well together,' Leandro said bluntly. 'And I expect that I am sometimes not the easiest man in the world to work for…'

Expecting a standard negative response to that statement, he was disconcerted when it failed to be delivered.

'Is that it?' he asked, leaning forward with frowning intensity. 'Have you got a gripe against *me*...?'

He couldn't quite conceal the incredulity in his voice

and Emily, for the first time, looked at him with cynical directness. Of course never in a million years would Leandro Perez *ever* think that *any* woman wouldn't be one hundred per cent happy to be in his presence. She might have bucked the trend by *not* being one in that long line of women who swooned the second those dark, intense eyes settled on them, but even so he would *still* assume that he had an effect on her because that was just the sort of man he was.

A player. Someone so inherently aware of his massive pulling power that it would be just inconceivable that it might not work on *some* women.

'I haven't got a gripe against *you,*' Emily said slowly.

She felt a thrill of recklessness, because right now, at this very moment in time, she was permitted to speak her mind. By tomorrow afternoon she would have cleared her desk and would have disappeared from here for good, with no need for references from him—although she knew instinctively that they would be very good, because he was, for all his faults, scrupulously fair.

Leandro tilted his head to one side and kept his eyes firmly fixed on her face. Her colour was up. Was she *blushing?* He hadn't associated her with such a girlish reaction. She was always so self-possessed…and yet…

His dark eyes drifted down to her mouth. She had full, soft lips, and even if they had registered somewhere in his subconscious before now he certainly felt as though he was seeing them for the first time. Perhaps she had shed that ice-cold image, because there were cracks in it now, through which he wanted to pry, find out what lay underneath.

Emily sensed the shift in his attention—from boss trying to uncover the reasons for her sudden unexpected resignation to boss looking at her with *masculine interest.*

Her skin tingled. She felt as though she was in the grip of an acute attack of pins and needles.

'No?' Leandro drawled. 'Because your expression is telling a different story.'

Emily, so accustomed to being the dutiful impeccable secretary in his presence—the secretary who never allowed her personal feelings to tip over into the work arena—stiffened.

'If you must know, I've never enjoyed having to do your dirty work for you.'

'Come again?'

She couldn't quite believe that she had just said what she had. The blood rushed to her head and she knew that she was as red as a beetroot. Gone was the frozen, aloof façade she had kept up for the past year and a half.

She looked at him with defiance and took a deep, steadying breath. 'Presents for those women you no longer had any use for…goodbye gifts you couldn't even be bothered to choose…arranging opera tickets and theatre tickets…booking expensive restaurants for women I knew I would be sending those goodbye gifts to in a few weeks' time…That should never have been part of my secretarial duties…'

'I don't believe I'm hearing this.'

'That's because you're not accustomed to anyone telling you anything you don't want to hear.'

Leandro released a long, sharp breath and sat back to look at her. Her face was alive with genuine, sincere emotion. She was leaning forward in the chair, and of their own accord his eyes drifted down to the prissy top.

He wondered what she looked like underneath it—wondered what it would feel like to make love to his icy secretary who was now in the act of revealing the sort of passion that could make any red-blooded man burn. He wondered what that hair would be like let loose. Hell, he didn't even know how long her hair *was*! His intense curiosity extinguished any anger he might have felt at what she had just said. At any rate, it was certainly true that he wasn't accustomed to being criticised.

'So you didn't like your involvement in my personal life?' he murmured.

'Maybe Marjorie was accustomed to doing stuff like that, but I feel you should have established whether *I* would mind...'

'I guess if you felt so strongly about it you should have said something earlier...'

Emily blushed, because he was absolutely right. And why hadn't she? Because she had needed the money and she had been keen not to put a foot wrong.

'There's nothing more annoying than a martyr who puts up with the unacceptable and only says her piece when she's handed in her resignation...which brings me back to the *why...*'

'Well, like I said, I feel it's time to move on... I realise you will probably want me to leave immediately, so I thought I could just pack my things up and be done in a day...'

'Leave immediately? What gives you that idea?'

'What do you mean?' Emily asked in some consternation. 'Of *course* you want me to leave immediately. You don't see the point of employees hanging around once they've handed in their notice. I remember quite clearly you saying that they need to be removed from sensitive information, and also that their demotivation can spread like a virus...'

In actual fact she had only known of a couple of instances of employees handing in their notice. Pregnancy and emigration being the reasons. Mostly people stayed with the company because the pay was second to none—as were the working conditions.

'Marjorie stayed on for quite a while before she finally left…that seems to fly in the face of your *sensitive information* theory…'

'Yes, but…'

She looked at his raised eyebrows, the slight tilt of his head, and for a second she wondered whether he was just toying with her.

'My responsibilities have been far greater.' She stumbled over her words as she contemplated the prospect of working out her notice having told him in no uncertain terms what she thought of certain aspects of her job…

'True,' Leandro agreed.

He allowed the silence to thicken and deepen. *Immediate departure? Why?*

'And you're telling me this because…?'

'Why would you want me around if you think I'm an annoying martyr?'

Emily took a different approach, but Leandro Perez was not a man who could be browbeaten, and even as she tried a different ruse she felt the sinking sensation of knowing that her departure would not be going quite according to schedule. She had been short-sighted, had dropped her mask, and now she would be stuck for at least another month with their boss-secretary relationship not on the safe footing on which it had always rested.

'You have a month's notice to work out,' Leandro informed her flatly. 'You've lost your mind if you imagine that you're going to leave me in the lurch with a string of unsuitable candidates turning my working life upside down.'

And he was honest enough to admit to himself that it rankled…the fact that she had been happy to jump ship without a backward glance when she must have known that he depended on her! What the hell had ever happened to *a sense of responsibility*?

He offered her an expression of thoughtful contemplation and politely waited for her to try and find a few more pointless excuses.

Emily envisaged one long month of interviewing prospective candidates for a guy who would almost certainly reject all of her choices. She had handed in her notice and he wasn't going to make life easy for her. And now that she had been foolish enough to actually tell him what she thought about his antics involving the opposite sex…

No, life was not going to be a walk in the park at all over the next four weeks.

'But of course you *do* have a point,' he mused, resuming the light tapping of his fountain pen on his desk. 'You *have* assumed far greater responsibilities than Marjorie ever did. She always maintained that she was hanging on to new technology by the skin of her teeth whilst knowing very well that there was no way I would ever get rid of her because of her length of service. She worked for my father in Argentina. Did you know that?'

'She didn't mention it.'

'She was over there on holiday after university and looking for temporary work so that she could improve her Spanish. She applied for an office job at my father's company and he liked her. Said she had spirit. He employed her on the spot, and as things turned out she fell in love with a local guy, married him and remained working for my father until eventually she and her husband moved over here years ago so that she could be close to her family.

'Two of her daughters married English guys and now live here as well. When she moved she came as a package deal to me, but in truth her heart was never in the upward climb. She did a damn good job, but you…' He relaxed back and folded his hands behind his head. 'You're quick…you're professional…you never need to be told anything twice…'

Emily accepted the flattery with as composed a demeanour as she could muster and reminded herself that it came with the massive downside of being asked to work out her notice. But the pleasure of being complimented so elaborately brought colour to her cheeks.

'Which is why I can't afford to lose you immediately, and also why you were rewarded with so much responsibility…so much confidential information on clients… For all I know—' he sat forward suddenly, taking her by surprise '—you could be moving on to one of my competitors… Who knows? You're a closed book, Emily…'

'Moving on to one of our competitors…?'

Leandro raised his eyebrows at that unconscious slip of the tongue, but he didn't relax his posture, and nor did he come even close to cracking a smile.

'Are you being *serious,* Leandro?'

Somehow she had managed to avoid using his name for the majority of her time working with him and it felt strange on her tongue. She was catapulted back to that odd sensation she'd had earlier, when she had suddenly and inexplicably become *aware* of him—aware of his startling sexuality, aware of the dragging power of his personality when work was not the issue at hand.

'I'm always serious when it comes to work.' Leandro, still leaning forward with his elbows splayed on the desk, was looking at her very carefully. 'As you might have gathered by now, I'm not a man who takes chances when it comes to my companies…'

'I get that—but I would *never* disclose anything confidential to anyone!'

'Better safe than sorry, though, wouldn't you say…?'

Would she even miss him?, he thought, enraged with himself for even thinking it.

'I'll get in touch with the agency first thing in the morning.'

Distractedly she thought that a person could get lost in those dark eyes of his, which were resting on her with lazy, brooding speculation, and then she mentally slapped herself on the wrist for letting her imagination get the better of her.

Not only was it foolish but it was entirely inappropriate, given the current circumstances.

'No need just yet…'

Whoever said that a good head for business precluded a talent for creative thinking?

'I have a project that's coming to an end on a small island in the Caribbean. Finishing touches to one of my hotels before the grand opening in six weeks' time. I need to be there personally to sign off on the details…'

Not strictly true, but it would certainly serve his purpose at this juncture. No way she was going to just up sticks and disappear into the sunset without a backward glance. Furthermore, she intrigued him—and now, with this peculiar letter of resignation, she was intriguing him even more.

'That's not a problem. I'm more than capable of covering in your absence, and of course I will communicate daily on email. I can even begin sifting through prospective replacements so when you return you only have to interview the handful I've selected…'

'Not precisely what I had in mind. I *do* have to keep an eye on you—as you have so aptly brought to my attention… So here are my thoughts: you and I will travel to my hotel and test-drive it, so to speak. Make sure the nuts and bolts are all in place, the paperwork is spotless, the teams are ready for when the place opens… And, of course, out there you will be removed from any temptation to get in touch with anyone who might be interested in buying sensitive information and it will give me time to get my people to firewall anything that could be stolen… What do you think? No, scratch that. Just get your passport, pack a suitcase and book two first class tickets for us to leave first thing in the morning. Much more fun than sifting through potential candidates for a job, wouldn't you agree?'

Emily blanched. 'What sort of timescale are we talking about?' she asked faintly.

There seemed little point in taking issue with his implication that she might be a common thief. His suspicious nature had helped get him where he was today, and it was as ingrained in his personality as an icy wasteland was in hers.

'Well, you *do* have to give me a month's notice… I imagine a fortnight should suffice when it comes to overseeing the final touches of the hotel…'

'*Two weeks?*'

'You sound shocked. I know you have a passport, so where's the problem?'

'I'm sorry, but I'm not going to be able to do that.'

'And that would be because…?'

'Because I have certain commitments.'

'And would these "commitments" be related to that letter of resignation you produced an hour ago?'

'Yes.'

Emily drew a deep breath and looked away. She could feel curiosity emanating from him in waves. Leandro Perez had a brilliant and enquiring mind. Was he about to let her go without trying to delve into the precise reasons for her resignation? How naive she had been to imagine that that might have been the case.

'I'm all ears—because I'm still paying your salary and asking nothing that breaches the bounds of your duty.'

'I realise that. It's just that…that…'

'That what?'

'I'll be leaving London. I'm getting married…'

CHAPTER TWO

FOR A FEW seconds Leandro wondered whether he had heard correctly. *Getting married*? It was as ludicrous as if she had suddenly announced that she was resigning so that she could fulfil a lifelong ambition to climb backwards up Mount Everest. No, it was even more ludicrous—because never, not once, not for a passing moment, had she intimated that she had any kind of social life. She might very well have kept her personal life to herself, but there wasn't a woman on the face of the earth who could resist letting slip something as big as *that*.

Furthermore, where was the diamond rock she should be wearing on her finger?

'I'm not buying it,' he said.

'I beg your pardon?'

'You heard me, Emily. I'm not buying it.'

'How…how *dare* you?'

A tidal wave of pure red rushed through her head. The cool, aloof persona—the one that was her constant companion—vanished under the force of her anger. Anger that he had the nerve to think she was lying. Anger at the implied insult that she was just so dull, so boring, that it was inconceivable anyone might want to marry her. Anger that he just couldn't believe she wasn't one of those simpering girls who would not have been able to resist the compulsion to blab to her boss about a fiancé in the wings.

The sheer arrogance of the man was unbelievable. But why did that come as any great surprise? Hadn't she witnessed first-hand just how arrogant he was in his dealings with women? Hadn't she seen for herself how he treated them? Like playthings to be picked up and then dumped the second their novelty value wore off.

Memories of the past and her own experiences of someone with that same lethal power to destroy hurtled towards her like a rocket with deadly cargo, and she deflected its impact with a little less than her usual practised ease.

'How dare I what?'

'How dare you presume to know anything about me?' Emily bristled. 'Just because I haven't mentioned my private life, it does not give you the right to assume that nothing goes on in it!'

'I'm curious as to the whereabouts of this fiancé of yours when we have spent hours working until all hours of the night—which, incidentally, wasn't that long ago. In fact… if my memory serves me right…three weeks ago we had a run of several Chinese takeout nights when that Dutch deal was on the verge of completion. I can't imagine any testosterone-fuelled young man wanting his woman cooped up with her boss into the early hours of the morning… Or maybe those late lie-ins I gave you made up for the inconvenience…?'

He appeared to give this some thought and then shook his head slowly, his dark eyes fixed on her face all the time as his curiosity bloomed into a driving, unstoppable need to *know more.*

'No…' he drawled. 'You've never had any problem with unsocial hours. That would have featured on the menu had this fiancé been on the scene. So…how long has it been going on?'

'That's none of your business,' Emily said through stiff lips.

'I'm making it my business,' he responded coolly, 'in light of the fact that it appears to be influencing your ability to do your job.'

'It's not influencing *anything*…'

'You've already informed me that you have a problem accompanying me to the Caribbean to oversee the end of this project. I'd term that as *influencing your ability to do your job...* Look, Emily…' He sighed and raked his fingers through his dark hair. 'We've been working together for almost two years. We've had an excellent working partnership—aside, of course, from your simmering resentment about the way I conduct my love-life…'

And where, he wondered, had *that* come from? Poor experiences in the past with some guy who broke her heart?

'Is it just so damned inconceivable that I might have a passing interest in something as groundbreaking as your engagement? Forget the fact that you're going to leave me in the lurch…'

'I have no intention of leaving you in the lurch. I shall make sure I find a suitable replacement.'

He noticed the way she had clumsily tried to evade his question. Fascinating.

'Leaving that aside for the moment, how long have you been going out with this mystery man? What's his name, anyway?'

'Are these questions still in line with the fact that you're *not buying* what I've told you?'

'I'm mystified by the lack of an engagement ring on your finger,' Leandro said mildly. 'Perhaps you took it off this morning when you were washing the dishes, but I feel certain I would have remembered seeing it before…'

'I'm not a great believer in engagement rings,' Emily mumbled uncomfortably.

'And yet there must be romance and passion there if you don't feel comfortable travelling with me for a fortnight to wrap this hotel business up…'

He had never seen her like this before. Her hectic colour brought a liveliness to her face that was captivating. She looked like a different woman. Still beautiful, but animated now, no longer with that impassive mask designed to keep the world at arm's length.

He had never been into blondes, but interest was kicking in. He wondered whether that was because the lines between their professional relationship and the personal were beginning to blur. Hell, what an inappropriate reaction! The woman had just announced that she was about to tie the knot with some guy and here he was, assessing her in ways he had never done before and allowing his imagination to break its leash and take up residence in entirely unacceptable fantasies that involved him getting down and personal with this new, intriguing creature squirming in front of him.

'His name is Oliver,' Emily admitted reluctantly, steering the conversation away from all talk about romance and passion.

The mere notion of those foreign emotions was enough to make her lips curl with cynicism. Romance? Passion? Why not throw love into the mix while he was about it?

Leandro detected the shadow that crossed her face, the way her full lips tightened fractionally. He had never really known what was going on in his secretary's head and he wondered idly whether she knew just how much of a challenging gauntlet she was throwing down in her evasiveness.

For someone like him—someone to whom women had always been prepared to bare their souls, whatever his response, indeed, who would have been prepared to do anything to net his interest—her obvious reluctance to divulge even the most innocuous of facts about her situation was a compelling reason for him to keep pushing.

Thinking about his varied and changeable love-life made him distractedly recall that fleeting, gone-in-a-heartbeat expression that had crossed her face at the mention of romance and…what else was it he had said…? *Passion.*

Was this mysterious fiancé less an object of passion than a…a last resort guy? Underneath that controlled exterior, was she just plain scared of ending up on the shelf? Or maybe some experience of someone who hurt her had left her wary of romance? Was that it?

The questions raced through his head and he didn't bother to fight his curiosity in chasing answers.

A fortnight in the Caribbean, aside from allowing him to be personally on hand to make sure the project was launched smoothly, promised to be an interesting experience.

'Oliver… Oliver what…?'

'You wouldn't have heard of him.'

'The expression *pulling teeth* springs to mind…'

'Camp,' Emily said through gritted teeth. 'His name is Oliver Camp.'

'And Oliver Camp would object to your accompanying me on a business trip, would he?'

'I'll come.'

Arrangements might have to be put back a few weeks, but in the long run that would make little difference. They were both keen to tie the knot and get the whole thing over and done with, but sometimes Fate threw a spanner in the works, and in this instance the spanner came in the form of a very large, very muscular and hellishly dynamic guy who effectively had her in his pocket.

At any rate, arguing with him would, in the end, be counter-productive. She had never known him to give anything up without a fight—and a winning fight at that.

'Wonderful news! So glad you've come round to the idea…'

He glanced at his watch and stood up, and Emily reluctantly found herself surreptitiously following the economical fluid movement of his long body. She seemed to have stored up remembered images of him, so that she felt almost familiar with the sight of his strong forearms sprinkled with dark hair, the way he unrolled the sleeves of his white shirt, the length of his fingers…

It alarmed her, and she looked away hurriedly and followed suit, standing up as well.

'I trust you'll make all the necessary arrangements first thing in the morning?' He strolled towards the door and slipped on his jacket.

'Are you leaving work already?' Emily directed the question to his broad back and he looked at her over his shoulder.

'So it would appear.'

He *never* left work before seven. Even when his diary was free of all meetings or conference calls, as she knew it was now.

'How come?' she found herself asking, and instantly regretted her impulsive question.

What on earth was wrong with her? Had some crazy recklessness been unleashed inside her? Was it all downhill from here on in? She had another month of his company! Was she going to work that month trying to put a brake on whatever nonsense her mouth decided to come out with? All her reserve seemed to be unravelling.

'Come again?' His dark eyes roved over her flushed face and he raised his eyebrows.

'I apologise. Of course it's none of my business when you decide to leave the office. I just thought… I wondered… You usually take the opportunity to consolidate stuff after normal working hours when the phones aren't ringing quite so much…'

Leandro turned fully to face her and leant indolently against the wall. 'You're flustered.'

Was that designed to make her feel even more hot and bothered? If so, it worked. She could feel heat tingling in her cheeks. 'I'm not at all flustered,' she lied. 'I'm merely… merely…'

'Demonstrating a perfectly natural human curiosity as to an alteration in my usual routine?'

'It's…'

'Absolutely none of your business.' Leandro shrewdly nailed what she had been about to say again—that the time he chose to walk out of his office was not a matter she was entitled to question. 'However, as you appear to be in such a rush to leave…for whatever "stuff" you claim you have to do…' He invited a response to this prompt and was unsurprised when none was forthcoming. He shrugged. 'I thought I'd call it a day. At any rate, there are things I need to do if I'm to be out of the country for a couple of weeks…'

Emily lowered her eyes. He was currently without a woman. She had dispatched the last hapless member of his harem several weeks previously. The poor woman had not had a very long run, although in fairness her brief appearance in his life had certainly been an expensive one, and she had left the better for several expensive items of jewellery and a red moped which she'd claimed matched her preferred choice of nail colour and was essential for getting around London.

So was there another waiting in the wings? She felt the familiar antipathy towards his life choices rise up into her throat like bile. She knew she shouldn't. People lived their lives the way they chose to live them, and she should be indifferent and non-judgemental, and yet…

Leandro continued to look at her. He felt as though he were seeing her in 3D for the very first time. At least partially in 3D. Certainly he realised that her pose was very familiar to him, although it had always been one to which he had paid next to no attention. Whenever he had casually asked her to buy a parting gift for a woman she had always lowered her eyes in very much the same way as she was doing now. Her mouth would purse and she would comply with whatever he asked without complaint, but, yes… in the light of what she had told him about her views on his love-life…

Disapproval was stamped on her face. It was running through her head that he was leaving early because he had a hot date with a woman. Leandro decided that he would give her all the freedom she wanted to imagine what she clearly considered the worst interpretation.

'Right. I'll see you in the morning, Emily. And…' He paused, just in case she thought that she might disappear without a backward glance and leave him high and dry. 'Don't even consider doing a vanishing act, because if you do I'll pursue you to the ends of the earth and take you to court for breach of contract. I've been an exemplary employer and I expect exemplary service in return—even if it's only for the duration of a month. Understood?'

'I wouldn't dream of vanishing.' But there would be some loose ends to tie up before she went away with him.

On her way back to the tiny bedsit she rented in South London, she contemplated those loose ends and was frustrated to discover that her mind wasn't completely on the task at hand.

In fact her wayward thoughts insisted on disappearing around corners, streaking off down blind alleys and generally refusing to be tied down. After that conversation with Leandro, which was *not* one she had predicted, she found that she couldn't quite get the man out of her head.

She unlocked her front door and realised that she didn't quite know where the commute had gone, because she had been so busy playing over that encounter in her head.

Now, looking around her ridiculously small bedsit, she grounded her thoughts by reminding herself that once this matter had been sorted, once this marriage was out of the way, she would no longer have to live in a place that was, frankly, a dump. The paint on the walls was peeling, there were signs of rising damp, and the heating system was so rudimentary that it was preferable to leave it off in winter and just make do with portable heaters.

She wondered what Leandro would think if he were ever to stray accidentally into this part of the world and into her cramped living quarters.

He would be horrified. On the salary she was paid she should have been able to afford somewhere more than halfway decent in a good part of London. But after her money was spent there was precious little left for life's small indulgences, such as passably comfortable living quarters…

She got on the phone to Oliver before she could begin to wind down, and he picked up on the second ring.

There would be a slight delay in their plans, she told him, and sighed wearily. She perched on the chair in the hall. It was so uncomfortable that she felt her landlord must have redirected it to the house when it had been on its way to the skip to be disposed of, because that was all it was good for.

In her head, she pictured Oliver. The same height as her,

fair hair, blue eyes—hardly changed at all from the boy of fifteen she had once dated for the laughably short period of three months, before exam fever had consumed her and before he and his family had sold their mansion and disappeared off to America. They had kept in touch sporadically, but even that had faded after his parents had died in an accident ten years previously.

'What sort of delay?'

She explained. Two weeks away, and then she would be back and they could progress. She knew that it was a delay barely worth writing home about, but she was desperate to get this whole thing wrapped up—although she made sure to keep that desperation out of her voice.

She spent the rest of the evening in a state of mild panic. Two weeks abroad with Leandro. Two weeks in the sun. Sunshine was synonymous with holidays, with relaxing, and yet she would be on tenterhooks the whole time, guarding herself against…

Against what…?

As she continued to tie up her loose ends—loose ends that *needed* to be securely tied up before she left—her mind continued to play with that suddenly persistent question.

Guarding against *what...*?

Unbidden, thoughts of Leandro floated past her walls of resistance, lodged themselves in her head. Thoughts of how he looked, the way he had stared at her with those dark, semi-slumbrous eyes, the soft, silky angle of his questions, the way their conversation had dipped into murky uncharted territory…

There had been no mention of what sort of clothes she should take. She vaguely knew the layout of the resort—knew that it comprised individual cabanas on the beach: sweet little one and two-bedroom huts that looked as though they had been there for time immemorial but which in fact were equipped to the highest possible standard and had only been standing for six months tops.

They formed a charming cluster in front of the main hotel, which itself was small and likewise very organically designed. There was a pool which mimicked a waterfall, plunging into a quirkily laid out lake, but each of the cabanas came with its own plunge pool anyway.

It was the height of luxury and, like it or not, she was not going to be able to pull off her usual uniform of starchy suits and sensible court shoes.

Swimsuits, shorts, sundresses. The sort of clothes she didn't possess. And she had neither the time nor the inclination to go out on a shopping spree.

The prospect of facing him the following morning was not a pleasant one, and she made sure to arrive, yet again, shortly before nine. If he interpreted that as some sort of restrained rebellion then so be it.

In fact she arrived to find a message on her desk telling her that he would be out for the day. Judging from the list of instructions for her, it seemed that he had hit the office even earlier than he normally did.

And the number one instruction was for her to sort out flights to the island. As if she were in any danger of forgetting it!

By five Emily was drained, and she was getting ready to leave when the phone rang and she was accosted by the dark timbre of his disembodied voice down the line.

How had she spent so long never being affected by that? How was it that his voice had never made her toes curl the way it was doing now?

In the act of putting on her jacket, she literally had to sit down and control her breathing as he demanded a debrief on the various things he had asked her to do. Had she sent those emails to the Hong Kong subsidiary of the electronics plant he was taking over…? Had she seen the response from the Briggs lawyers…? The Glasgow arm of his telecommunications outfit needed confirmation of price bands for new contracts and—could she make sure to hard copy all the relevant data by the morning…? And, last but not least, had she booked their flights.

Leandro relaxed back in his chauffeur-driven car. He had spent the day in a buoyant mood. He had one more company under his belt after some hard bargaining, and the following day…

Underneath his annoyance and frank bewilderment at Emily's decision to resign, his shock at the reason she had given and the uncomfortable sense of betrayal at her short notice and lack of forewarning, there was a tug of intense satisfaction at the prospect of them travelling to the Caribbean.

He had spent a lot of the day thinking of her. He had played over in his mind the conversation they had had, the changing expressions on her face. She had been…*shifty.* She had answered his questions when pushed, but he had been left with the feeling that her answers only skimmed the surface.

The fact that satisfying his curiosity would ultimately have no bearing on her departure was an irrelevance as far as Leandro was concerned. He got a kick just thinking about travelling down an unpredictable path for once when it came to the opposite sex.

Was he becoming jaded? It was a question he had never asked himself. He was thirty-two years old, in his prime, and he enjoyed a wide-ranging and satisfying love-life. Or so he had always imagined. Now he wondered whether it was quite as satisfying as he'd thought if he could find himself so taken over by the pleasurable novelty of discovering this untapped side of his secretary.

The last woman he had dated had faded from the scene three weeks previously and here he was, becoming *fixated* by this new vision of Emily Edison—an Emily Edison who was suddenly so much more than the sum total of her parts.

Hell, he had been *fantasising* about her! Wasn't that a little bizarre?

Had he reached a stage where novelty was so compelling? He had nothing against marriage, per se. He assumed he would marry eventually. Someone suitable. Someone from an equally wealthy background. He had had a narrow and salutary escape years ago, from a woman who had played the hard to get game to perfection. She had teased him for just the right length of time, convinced him of her shyness and her indifference to his money… Her real agenda had been uncovered only because he had happened to overhear a conversation she'd had on the phone to her mother…

So, sure, he would marry in due course—someone he knew was not after his money. His sisters were all married, after all, and his parents had had a long and satisfying marriage. He could enjoy the freedom of a bachelor life for as long as he wanted. But how satisfying, *exactly,* had that been of late?

He frowned and thought of the women who had cluttered his life over the years. Beautiful, sexy, compliant, always willing to fall in with whatever he wanted. On paper, it sounded good enough, but the reality of it was slightly different. His boredom threshold was narrowing with each passing relationship. The thrill of the chase had vanished a long time ago.

'The earliest flight I could get was for the day after tomorrow,' Emily said now with staccato crispness.

She wondered where he was now. Back at his apartment? In a restaurant waiting for some hot date? She didn't want to waste time taking any mental detours in search of such details.

'Time?'

She told him. Just vocalising the details of their flights brought home to her the reality of the trip.

'Take tomorrow off,' he said wryly. 'I expect you'll have all sorts of…*things* to do before we go…'

'That's fine.' Emily adopted her best businesslike voice. 'I'm sure there will be things that need completing on the work front before—'

'Emily,' he interrupted decisively, 'I'll be in before seven tomorrow morning. I'll make sure whatever needs doing gets done.'

'But won't you want me to take care of the work transfer? Get Ruth on board to field the correspondence…?'

'We're not travelling to the outer ends of the Amazonian rainforest,' he informed her. 'There will be an internet connection. The bulk of the correspondence will be dealt with by us. You can see it as work as usual bar a change of scenery.'

'Oh, good,' Emily breathed.

Instantly Leandro had to fight down a spurt of annoyance.

'Which doesn't mean,' he added, 'that I'm expecting you to pack your starchy suits and high-heeled shoes…'

'I *do* realise that that wouldn't be appropriate,' Emily snapped.

'The swimming pool will be up and functioning…'

Emily pretended not to hear that. 'Will you want me to meet you at the airport?'

'I'll send my driver for you. Or I can swing by your place and get you en route…'

'That won't be necessary!'

She shuddered at the thought of Leandro Perez seeing where she lived. If he were curious about her now, then he would certainly be collapsing under the weight of questions should he ever step foot in her house and see her sparse, substandard surroundings.

'And it won't be necessary for you to send your driver for me, Leandro. If you don't trust the public transport system, then I'm happy to get a taxi and charge it to the company.'

'Fine.' He banked down his irritation.

A fortnight in the Caribbean… Sure, there would be work to be done, but still…sun, sea and sand.

A driver to fetch her and her enthusiasm was nil. But then…

His mind swung back to the mystery fiancé about whom he knew nothing.

'So, what did…I forget his name…have to say about your trip abroad with the boss?' Leandro asked, smoothly diverting the conversation to a destination which spiked his curiosity. 'All hunky-dory with the time you're going to be spending with me?'

'Why shouldn't he be?'

Emily tried and failed to imagine the situation Leandro was hinting at…a jealous lover laying down ground rules, maybe phoning every hour on the hour just to make sure that nothing untoward was going on… And then she went hot at realising where her mind was heading.

She could virtually hear the sound of him shrugging nonchalantly down the end of the line.

How had they managed to travel to this place where their conversations led away from work onto treacherous quicksand? Where her grip was so uncertain? Even removed from his presence, in the sanctuary of her own office, she could feel herself burning as her blood thickened and her mouth dried up.

Her breasts felt suddenly heavy, her nipples tingly and sensitive, and a rush of pure shame flooded her. Whatever this door was that had opened up a crack between them, she was determined to shove herself against it as hard as she could until it was closed again.

'Well, if you're absolutely sure that you won't need me at work tomorrow…'

Leandro gritted his teeth as she once again skirted around the conversation he found he was keen to have. The eager, obliging and annoyingly forthcoming women he was used to had faded completely in their attractiveness. He marvelled that he had not become irritated with them before. Compared to Emily's sparing, guarded, tightly controlled boundaries, they now seemed utterly lacking in any sense of challenge.

And a good challenge had always been something he enjoyed getting his teeth into.

'Absolutely… Go out and have some retail therapy…'

'I don't do retail therapy,' Emily responded automatically.

'*All* women do retail therapy.'

'All the women *you* know do retail therapy. At any rate, I shall take the time to pack and…and…'

'And…?'

'There are a couple of things that I shall need to do before I leave… It's a long time to be out of the country…'

'A fortnight?'

Emily sighed. Leandro Perez was persistent. If he wanted to acquire something he acquired it—whatever obstacles got thrown in his way. It was just the way he was built. He had once told her in passing, over a meal delivered to his office courtesy of one of the top restaurants in

London because they had needed food after twelve hours of solid work on a thorny deal, that persistence was a gene he had inherited from his father.

'He taught me,' Leandro had said drily, 'that if you want something you have to go for it, and that the things you most want seldom drop into your lap like ripe fruit falling from a tree…'

Emily had inwardly sniggered. That being the case, he had clearly never really wanted any of the women he had dated, because one of the most stunningly predictable traits they had in common was their ability to fall like ripe fruit from a tree straight into his lap.

She had said with her customary politeness that sometimes you just had to give up on certain things because that was the wiser option, and had then immediately clammed up when he had tried to draw her into an explanation of what she had meant.

'Yes. A fortnight.'

'You took two weeks off last year in a stretch…' he reminded her.

'But I didn't leave the country.'

He had assumed she had. Of course when he had shown interest she had shrugged her shoulders and thrown him a something and nothing reply.

'Where did you go?' he asked curiously. 'I recall you took a fortnight off in October…not a brilliant time of year to relax in this country—not if you're looking for anything other than wall-to-wall rain and wind…'

'Last October the weather was beautiful.'

She tensed as he unwittingly came close to a subject she definitely had no intention of talking about. He might have dragged Oliver's name out of her, but that had been unavoidable. She should have had the foresight to know that her resignation would prompt his curiosity. Beyond that, however… No, there were no more roads she would be lured down.

'Was it?'

'Yes, it was. You must be keen to get off the phone, Leandro. Are you at home?'

'Not currently.'

Emily wondered where he was and assumed the obvious. Her voice was correspondingly cool when she said, after a brief hesitation, 'I'll make sure not to disturb you for the remainder of the evening, even if I need to ask you anything.'

'And why would that be?'

'I'm assuming that you're on one of your dates.'

She could have kicked herself. Yet again her tongue had run away from her and she needed to rescue this unruly twist in the conversation—one that had been prompted by *her*!

She wondered if the stress of everything happening in her life at the moment had weakened her defences. Whether, combined with that, the sudden, unexpected shift in her normal working relations with Leandro had further thrown her off course.

Kicking herself every time she slipped up wasn't going to help matters.

'In which case,' she added briskly, 'I wouldn't dream of interrupting.' She emitted a forced chuckle at this point, if only to demonstrate to him how fatuous she actually found their conversation. 'I do know that you don't like to be disturbed when you're with one of your…your…'

'My…? Don't forget you've made yourself crystal-clear on what you think of my…my… Now, how *would* you describe them…?'

'I never said anything about the sort of women you go out with,' Emily muttered. 'I only told you that I don't like running errands involving them on your behalf. I've only met a couple of them and they both seemed very…very…nice…'

'Damned with faint praise.'

'Oh, this is ridiculous!' Emily burst out angrily. 'I don't want to be having this conversation with you. If you're out with someone then I'll make sure you're not disturbed. If you need to get in touch with me tomorrow for some reason then you have my mobile number. I shall make sure I check it at regular intervals just in case.'

Leandro, who had no time for any show of histrionics in women, relaxed and half closed his eyes. This was the most rattled he had ever heard her. In fact over the past twenty-four hours she had blossomed into a real three-dimensional person, and he was enjoying the conversation—passing histrionics and all.

'And you'll be in London should I need to call on you to come in for some reason? Highly unlikely but, as you pointed out, a fortnight with both of us out of the office is unheard of…'

'No,' Emily said shortly. 'I probably won't be in London if I have a day off. Would you like me to come in to work after all?'

'No…'

Leandro found his mind wandering off course as his imagination, previously rusty, kicked into gear. A day off having mind-blowing sex with the mystery fiancé?

'I think I'll cope. You go off and do…whatever it is you have planned. Excluding, of course, that terminally boring retail therapy which you're not into. I'll see you at the airport. Bring your computer, Emily. And don't forget…pack for the weather…'

CHAPTER THREE

EMILY ARRIVED AT the airport with time to kill. She had had a sleepless night. Various random scenarios of what lay ahead of her for the next two weeks had ensured a disturbed sleep and now, with the bustle of people around her pulling cases, peering around for check-in desks, browsing in the shops and buying stacks of magazines and confectionery, she anxiously glanced around for Leandro.

He had instructed her on where to meet him. Whilst every other check-in desk was fronted by long queues, the first-class check-in for their flight was calm and empty. She could see people glancing at her with envy and kept her eyes firmly pinned in front of her.

She had packed economically and sparingly and kept her wardrobe as neutral as possible for a fortnight in the sun. Nothing flowery or girlish. Nothing to suggest that she was there for any other reason aside from business. Her single one-piece swimsuit was black. She had no intention of frolicking in a pool in a bikini. Or even stepping foot in one if she could help it.

Leandro's dark, deep voice behind her made her jump; she swung round to find him far too close to her for her liking, and automatically took a step back.

'I hope you haven't been waiting too long.' His voice was amused as he gave her the once-over.

Her fair hair was neatly in place, pulled back from her face and twisted into her style of choice, which was a bun designed to demonstrate that its wearer was anything but frivolous. She had traded in the more severe grey suit in favour of something a little less formal but still, in the end, a suit. Cream jacket with sleeves to the elbow, navy blue tee shirt underneath, cream skirt and a pair of flat shoes. Her entire outfit shrieked *business*, and if he hadn't had a tantalising glimpse behind the stern façade, he could have been forgiven for thinking that the woman looking up at him was completely devoid of personality.

But, oh, she wasn't. Never had been. Even though she had tried her hardest to camouflage that fact. And now…

'Can't stand airport waiting…'

He held out his hand for her passport and Emily stood back while he handled the check-in. Did he notice how the young girl behind the desk had gone bright red and was stumbling over her little speech about the first-class lounge and where they could find it? Or, as a practised charmer who worked his way through glamorous women the way a gourmand worked his way through a Michelin-starred meal, was he casually immune to the attention he commanded from the opposite sex?

Her lips thinned and she turned away.

'Which is why,' he continued, striding off as she fell in step with him, 'I tend to get to airports as late as possible. Tell me how your day was yesterday? What did you do?'

'I…I…had a few things to put into place…'

Leandro looked down at her. In flats she reached slightly above his shoulder and it made a change from the women he dated, who were all much shorter than he was.

'You've brought your computer, I take it?'

Emily exhaled a sigh of relief that he wasn't going to pin her down into trying to avoid yet another inroad into her private life. 'Of course I did.' She launched into a discussion on some of the deals he was currently working on and ignored his patent lack of animated response. 'Did anything urgent crop up yesterday?' she asked, if only to ensure their conversation remained on neutral ground.

He turned to look at her.

'Are you really interested?'

They had both stopped and the crowds parted around them. For a second her breath caught painfully in her throat and, having made a concerted effort not to look at him—*really* look at him—she now discovered that she couldn't peel her eyes away.

Next to him, she knew she looked stiff, awkwardly dressed in her lightweight suit which was hardly suitable for long-haul travel but which felt so much safer than a pair of comfortable trousers and a casual tee shirt. He looked cool, sophisticated, expensive. He was wearing a pair of black jeans and a polo shirt with a discreet logo on the front. No jacket. Loafers. His pull-along case was a small black leather affair, with no glaringly obvious outward evidence of having cost a lot, but it was easy to tell at a glance that it did.

Her mouth went dry as he continued to stare at her with those dark, dark eyes which had never before seemed to impact on her senses the way they were doing now.

'Of course I am. Why wouldn't I be? I've been working on some of those…um…deals for weeks…months…'

Leandro broke the connection and began walking again towards Immigration, where they were waved through, and directly to the first-class lounge, where once again they were treated to the very highest levels of respect and fawning.

She would have said that money talked, but she knew that he would have commanded the same attention if he had been broke. There was just something about the man that seemed to make people automatically obey.

'And yet you won't be seeing the conclusion of most of them. So why bother to feign interest?'

'Just because I'll be…leaving…it doesn't mean that I'm not one hundred per cent committed to doing my utmost to…to…make sure the work gets done on them.' She found herself sitting on a plush sofa and a waiter appeared from thin air to take orders for drinks or food—presumably whatever they wanted.

Leandro shrugged. 'In that case why don't you call up the Edinburgh file on your computer and we can go through it.'

He gave her the most polite of looks and Emily struggled to manufacture a smile in return.

He was bored. He obviously thought that mentally she had already defected, and he could barely summon up an interest in discussing work with her. It made sense. The only reason she was tagging along on this jaunt was because he wanted to keep an eye on her and make sure she didn't get up to Heaven knew what. Treason? The illegal sale of company secrets to 'the other side'? Didn't he know her *at all* after nearly two years of working with her?

No. He didn't. He didn't know a thing about her. And, if she could spring an engagement on him, a fiancé lurking in the wings, then he must wonder what other surprises she might have in store?

With less than her usual aplomb she dutifully brought up the file and was keenly aware of him shifting his big body towards her so that they could browse through the information together.

She went through all the motions. After a lifetime of holding her emotions in check there was no tremor to her voice, nothing at all to betray her crazy jumpiness. She could feel his eyes moving from the screen to her profile and wanted to scream at him at least to do her the favour of fully concentrating—because if he didn't then her nerves would fray just a little more at the edges.

'Have you any idea how hot it will be when we land at the airport?' he asked, when she had finished a long-winded spiel on the various obstacles that had been put in the way of the deal completion, and Emily grimaced.

'I didn't think we were discussing the weather,' she said, which teetered precariously on the edge of being lippy—not that it mattered, considering she was practically no longer his employee and in no need of a reference.

'Is the rest of your wardrobe along the lines of what you're wearing now?'

Emily edged away from him and snapped shut her computer, turning to return it neatly to the smart case she had brought with her.

Why did she feel like a fool?

For no reason she was suddenly overwhelmed by an image of herself as a woman in her twenties, buttoned up and careful, always on her guard. She could barely remember a time when she hadn't been that way. The last boyfriend she had had—a brief six-month fling four years previously—had been an unmitigated disaster. Her inexperience had been agonising and her inherently suspicious nature had gradually seeped into the relationship, suffocating it, until they'd parted company amidst a welter of embarrassing platitudes about keeping in touch and remaining friends. They never had.

Then she thought of the women Leandro dated: sexy, full-on women, who weren't cocooned in a veritable fortress of self-protective defence mechanisms that would have rivalled any Victorian maiden's chastity belt.

What must he think of her?

She told herself that it hardly mattered, and yet her tight mouth, silenced on everything that was in the slightest bit personal, now seemed ludicrous and childish.

Emily drove aside that disturbing vision of herself and cleared her throat.

'I…I naturally want to dress in a suitably…er…'

'Restrained manner for an eight-hour flight to the Caribbean?'

'I wouldn't have felt comfortable in jeans and a tee shirt,' she said flatly.

A tide of colour washed up her face and she had to bite back the nervous temptation to jump into a qualifying speech when he remained looking at her in silence.

'And you feel comfortable in a starchy linen suit?'

'It's practical.'

'If you say so.'

He pulled out his top-of-the-range sleek tablet and flicked it on.

Emily interpreted that as a signal that their conversation was over. She had brought her book with her, a lightweight crime thriller, but would he launch into a sarcastic aside about her choice of reading matter if she fished it out of her handbag? So instead she extracted some material she had printed off the last day she had been at work—background reading on the holiday compound to which they were headed—and buried herself in it.

Leandro, working his way through a series of emails from his family to which he owed replies, glanced across to where her lowered head and stiff body language were visible signs of her armour.

What *was* it about this woman? And why was he suddenly so obsessed with finding out what made her tick? He wasn't taking her to the Caribbean to remove her from possible secret-sharing with competitors. She would never do any such thing and he knew that. No. He was taking her with him because…he wanted time with her. Time in which he could indulge his sudden curiosity. Or maybe it irked him that she could just walk out on him when he needed her? Since when did women walk out on him? Even though it might be on a professional basis…

One thing was for sure: it was going to be a hellishly long flight if they both maintained the tight-lipped silence she seemed to want.

Attuned to her on a level that was frankly irritating, he boarded the plane, settled into his seat—a comfortable recliner that could convert into a full bed at the press of a button—and he noted with some amusement that even when all the lights had been switched off and they could do as they pleased she remained upright, reading a book which she had ferreted out of her bag.

He reclined his seat, switched off the little reading light, debated whether to rescue her from her obvious discomfort by introducing a little light work-related banter and then decided against it.

How, Emily thought crossly, could the man just *fall asleep*? On a plane?

He was way too long for his seat, even when it was fully down, converted into a bed. She stole a sidelong glance at his averted profile. There was something vulnerable about a person when he was asleep. The lines that gave his face definition were smoothed out into peaceful tranquillity and she found herself mesmerised by the way he looked.

He was no longer the hard-edged boss who'd so recently been threatening her with the force of his personality and the animal magnetism of his physical presence. There was a boyish handsomeness to his face that made something inside her squirm.

She returned to her book, but found herself glancing

across again and again to him, her eyes lingering on his face, then drifting down the length of his body to the broadness of his chest, the strength in his hands which were lightly clasped on his stomach, the muscular length of his legs…

She gulped and looked away quickly, her heart thumping inside her, as she took in the obvious bulge of his crotch.

What on earth was happening to her?

If she had been really and truly engaged, anticipating marriage to the man of her dreams, then she knew that her thoughts would not be striking off at a tangent now—that she would be able to look at Leandro and not feel this unaccustomed rush of forbidden attraction. But she *wasn't* really and truly engaged, was she?

Abruptly she turned away and thought about Oliver—the guy her boss thought she was crazy about…the guy who should have been jealous and possessive of her. What a joke. Yes, she would be marrying him, but her reasons were all cynically practical.

She needed the money and he would be her passport to that.

She must have drifted into a sleep of sorts, and to feel herself being shaken awake was so disorientating that she gave a little yelp of alarm and jerked forward. It took her a few seconds to register where she was. Not in her bed but on the plane, her seat still fully upright. Her heart was going like a jackhammer inside her and she could taste the remnants of her dream as it was chased away by Leandro's hand on her shoulder, shaking her.

Her immediate instinct to pull away fought against the lethargy of being abruptly awakened and she stared at him.

'What are you doing?' She had left her linen jacket on and it had rucked up. Through the stiff fabric his hand was warm and heavy, burning a direct path to her shoulder. It acted like an anchor, weighing her down so that she felt she couldn't move.

'What the hell were you dreaming about?'

'What?'

His face was so close to hers that she could feel his warm breath fanning her cheek. His hair was tousled and he looked achingly, sinfully sexy, all rumpled and bedroom-eyed.

'Dreaming,' Leandro repeated, his hand moving from her shoulder to absently caress her neck and jawline. 'You were dreaming, Emily.'

'I woke you up. I'm sorry.'

She could scarcely breathe. She was hyper-conscious of his hand on her face. She was certain that he barely realised what he was doing, but *she* was all too aware of it, and yet she found that she couldn't budge an inch, couldn't retreat to the safety of her own side of the seat.

'Don't worry about me,' he cut in impatiently.

His eyes roved over her flushed face and lighted on her parted mouth. Immediately and without warning he felt the pain of sudden arousal. Her cheeks were pink, her hair was struggling free of its constraints and appeared to be longer than he had imagined, and her wide blue eyes were hazy with the remnants of confusion. She looked every bit the young girl she was—the girl she tried so hard to conceal beneath an icy, untouchable veneer.

A wayward thought insinuated itself into his head. She looked *sexy*. Sexy and, with those parted lips, eminently kissable.

'What were you dreaming about?'

'Nothing.' Emily drew back and he removed his hand from her shoulder. She felt its absence in a way that disturbed her, but she kept her gaze as steady as she could on his face.

Yes, she had been dreaming, and the dream came back to her now in jagged bits and pieces. Oliver. Actually marrying him. What that would entail. A nasty dream of dark shadows and fear. And wrapped up inside the dream had been Leandro—although now, awake, she couldn't remember what exactly he had been doing there.

'Quite an extreme reaction for a dream about nothing.'

'Did I…mention anyone…?'

Leandro stared down into her blue eyes and wondered what accounted for that wary look.

'No,' he admitted. 'But you yelped as though you were scared.'

'I've never been a quiet sleeper,' Emily said truthfully, if only to explain herself.

'No?'

She hesitated and threw him a reluctant smile which he found unreasonably captivating—perhaps because it was such a rare occurrence.

'I went through a period of sleepwalking when I was… younger…when I was in my early teens. Ever since then I've been a jumpy sleeper.'

Leandro imagined her as a young teenager and immediately wanted to know more about her, wanted her to open up to him before she released the shutters and returned to hide behind them.

'That must have driven your siblings mad,' he murmured encouragingly.

'I don't have any siblings. I'm an only child.' No big secret there, and yet it felt like a confidence of huge proportions.

'So this marriage must be a big deal for your parents…?'

'I…'

Leandro continued to lock her with his dark eyes, making retreat from the conversation difficult.

'It's just me and my mum.' Emily's mouth tightened. As soul-baring went, this was as far as it was going to go—she was amazed that she had actually got to this point in the first place.

Leandro waited and then into the deepening silence said lightly, 'Peace and quiet…'

'What do you mean?'

'I mean, as an only boy with four sisters, peace and quiet was never something I could bank on from one day to the next.'

'Four sisters…?' Emily grinned and stole a glance at him. When he raised his eyebrows and smiled at her she felt her pulse quicken and her skin prickle. Aeroplane chatter, she thought a little nervously. No harm done.

'Four sisters—and they all liked experimenting with their make-up on me…'

Emily burst out laughing and Leandro thought that she didn't do nearly enough of that. He wondered whether her fiancé brought out that side of her—the side that would spontaneously laugh, would make her shed the look of someone carrying the weight of the world on her shoulders… And he felt a spurt of irritation towards the man…

'I don't believe you!'

'Believe it.' He grinned with wry amusement. 'Clearly I was only four or five at the time, but I still bear the scars.'

'And you didn't develop a taste for wearing make-up in later life?'

Leandro burst out laughing. 'So far I can happily avoid cosmetic counters…'

'Then the scars can't have been so ingrained.'

Their eyes tangled as they both shared the same moment of relaxed banter and for a few seconds Emily's heart seemed to skip a beat—several beats. Her mouth went dry and there was a strange roaring in her ears.

'Have you...? Have you...?'

'Have I what?'

'Have you...got any idea as to whether there are any last-minute things that might need doing at the hotel when we arrive...?'

She barely recognised the breathlessness in her voice, but at least she had managed to drag the conversation back down to Planet Earth—although when he lowered his eyes and moved fractionally further back she felt herself missing that moment of warmth that had suddenly and unexpectedly ignited between them.

Leandro wondered if she might just scrabble in her multi-purpose handbag and extract her laptop computer so that she could hide behind it.

'I've appointed some good people to oversee all the building work. Everything should be in pristine condition when we arrive. Bar cutting a ribbon, the place should be up and running and ready for its first happy holidaymakers to arrive.'

'Its first extremely wealthy holidaymakers...'

'Are you telling me that you disapprove of people who have sufficient money enjoying expensive holidays abroad?'

'Not at all.'

But bitterness had found its way into her voice. There had been a time, when she was growing up, when she had been on those sorts of holidays. She could barely remember them—she had made great strides in blanking those memories out of her head—but right now they crept back in. Those holidays as a child, when she and her parents had gone to expensive hotels in expensive destinations.

'No, of course I don't,' she said in a more normal voice. 'After all, if your hotel is fully booked then it provides countless jobs for the locals, and I know from reading the literature that it's all going to be eco-friendly. The food will be locally sourced…everything's been cleverly done to cause as little disturbance as possible to the natural environment…'

'You're beginning to sound like a tour guide,' Leandro said drily.

He realised that he would miss this about her—her ability to absorb the bigger picture of any deal he undertook, to transform it into much more than a money-making exercise.

What was she thinking…handing in that letter of resignation?

He raked his fingers through his hair in frustration and shifted in his seat. However much he paid, there was a limit to how much space was available on an aircraft, and right now he wanted to walk about, flex his muscles—do something highly physical to counterbalance the restlessness inside him at the thought of her dumping him.

No, he amended mentally, she wasn't *dumping him*. She was moving on to greener pastures.

It was a notion that didn't make him feel any better. Greener pastures with some guy she could barely bring herself to mention! Was there something wrong with the man? He felt there probably was or she would have pulled out a wallet full of photos by now, however tight-lipped she was by nature.

'Perhaps that might be my next job,' Emily quipped without thinking.

'So you *will* be getting another job after you're hitched to this man of yours…?'

He wondered where the time had gone. They would be landing in under an hour and he felt as though he could have carried on talking to her for another eight.

'Possibly,' Emily murmured vaguely. 'Gosh. Is that the

time? I must go to the ladies'…freshen up… I can't believe the time's gone so quickly! Literally *flown past…*!'

Leandro scowled and watched as she slipped out of the seat. Keen eyes followed her hands as she smoothed the prissy shirt and readjusted the equally prissy jacket. She was as slender as a reed and he wondered if she worked out.

He turned to gaze out of the window, down at the bank of clouds. He was finding it hard to get his mind off the woman. Usually on long-haul flights he could devote his time to work. Huge amounts could be achieved with the luxury of not being interrupted. He glanced down at his laptop and realised that he had barely skimmed the surface of what he had optimistically intended to do.

He was in the act of snapping shut the laptop when he looked up and saw her returning from the bathroom.

For a few seconds, he was deprived of the power of coherent thought. She had brushed back her hair and done away with the sensible bun. Instead she had swept it into a low ponytail which hung over one shoulder like a gold, silky rope. Her hair was long. Much longer than he had imagined. She had also done away with the jacket, and her clinging tee shirt, while still the height of modesty, was sufficiently tight to show off the shape of her high, small breasts.

Emily didn't want to look at him as she walked back to her seat. She felt conspicuous and she wasn't entirely sure why, because her outfit was hardly revealing.

'Your turn.' She addressed the armrest. 'It's now or never.'

Leandro was grappling to find something to say. For the first time in his life he was lost for words as he mumbled something before sliding past her.

The plane landed and the passengers were disgorged into an early evening which was still sticky and warm.

'We need an interconnecting flight to the island,' he said to her. 'I have a private island hopper on standby.'

He fought an insane urge to release her hair *just to see what it looked like loose.* It joined the host of other inappropriate thoughts that had recently afflicted him and he cursed himself yet again for looking at a woman who was taken by someone else. There were plenty of fish in the sea, he had always thought, for him not to be bothered with trying to catch one that belonged to someone else.

But he wasn't *trying to catch her,* he reasoned firmly to himself as they cleared their bags and were ushered to the adjoining strip where their plane awaited them. He was simply trying to work her out—and if he happened, in passing, to notice how crazily attractive she was, then who could blame him? He was a one hundred per cent red-blooded male after all!

She moved with a calm, unhurried grace that didn't try to draw attention to itself. In the closed confines of an office it was something he had never really noticed before, but it was evident now, when she was surrounded by open space.

He was aware of her asking questions about their flight to the island and joking nervously about the reliability of such a small plane, which looked barely big enough to hold a handful of people, and he was aware that he was responding in a perfectly natural manner. All the time his rebellious mind was on a rollercoaster ride.

What would she look like without those clothes on? With that long vanilla-blonde hair spread across a pillow and that half-smile of hers inviting him to take her? Her body would be smooth and supple and pale, her breasts small and shapely, with rosebud nipples… He wondered what they would taste like. The thought of filling his mouth with one of them brought him back down to earth with an agonising bump just as they boarded the light plane.

'I've never travelled like this before.'

Leandro looked at her. Already, outside, darkness had descended abruptly, and the violet colours that had streaked the sky had faded into deep velvet blackness. As the little plane taxied down the runway and took off like a small, buzzing mosquito they could have been anywhere in the world. Anywhere hot. The temperature was in the eighties and Emily's face was shiny with perspiration.

'In a small, dangerous object hardly bigger than a washing machine and with the engine of an underpowered lawnmower?'

'Please don't say that.'

Leandro laughed with genuine amusement. 'Don't worry. This plane wouldn't dare drop out of the sky with *me* on board.'

Emily relaxed. His voice was light and teasing and she felt some of her nerves about the short flight begin to ebb away. 'I had no idea you had such power over inanimate objects,' she returned in similar vein, because it distracted her from a worst-case scenario that involved them all plummeting to the ground in a disarray of twisted metal.

'Reassuring, wouldn't you agree? I know the pilot personally. He's excellent.'

'Have you ever been in something as small as this before?'

'I can go one step better. I've flown something not dissimilar…'

'You haven't?' She found she was totally absorbed by what he was saying. His lazy, teasing gaze held her spellbound.

'When I was sixteen.'

'I don't believe you.'

Leandro chuckled and threw her a superior look that was strangely boyish. 'Flew over my father's ranch in a light aircraft which he kept securely housed out of reach of curious juvenile hands—or so he fondly imagined.'

'You *stole* your father's plane?' She grappled with the twin notions of living on a ranch which housed its own personal light aeroplane and Leandro as a teenager, breaking and entering to get his hands on it.

On the back burner were all her fears about being on such a tiny plane, about having to spend a fortnight in his company, about what lay ahead of her beyond that…

'I hijacked it for an hour and a half…'

'Your parents must have been worried to death. How dangerous!' But hadn't she always known that he had that devil-may-care side to him? It was part of what made him such a formidable opponent in the business arena.

'Not dangerous,' Leandro murmured in a low drawl that sent shivers rippling up and down her spine, 'just challenging. And if I know anything about myself it's that I can never back away from a challenge…'

Why did she feel that the remark went beyond the remembered thrill of flying solo at the age of sixteen? Why did she feel such a shiver of fierce, dark *excitement*? It terrified her, and not for the first time since she had confessed to her engagement to Oliver she wished desperately that the man she was committed to marrying was more than just a means to a very necessary end. More than ever she wished that she could hold on to him as a barrier against the effect Leandro seemed to be having on her.

'But surely even if you'd flown with someone before you would have been scared…?' Her heart was thumping inside her and every nerve-ending in her body felt primed, on red-hot alert.

'Of course I wasn't scared,' Leandro said with a casual shrug and the same half-smile that made her feel so unsteady. 'I was a teenager. Since when do teenagers feel fear? And besides,' he admitted, 'I'd had a few flying lessons with one of the ranch hands. I only felt afraid when I landed the plane and spotted my parents waiting for me.'

He threw back his head and laughed.

God, it was heady having her attention focused so completely on him. It made him feel like the teenager he no longer was. He was quite accustomed to having women hanging on to his every word, but *this* woman…

'What did they say?'

'Grounded for life.' He grinned. 'Of course it was impossible for them to stick to that threat. Grounded for three days and then a course of flying lessons, so that if I ever felt inclined to take the plane up again they would at least know I would be able to fully handle the controls…a win-win situation, as it turned out…' He smiled fondly at the memory. 'We're going to be landing in a few minutes…'

Emily hadn't even noticed that the plane had been dipping lower, but now she broke free of his gaze to peer down into velvety darkness. She could just about make out twinkling of lights as they looped down. They hadn't removed their seat belts and she clutched the arm of her chair until her knuckles were white. Anyone would have imagined that she had never flown before, and of course she had. Many times when she had been younger. But never in something as tiny as this.

They bumped to a shuddering stop and then they were out in the warm Caribbean night, with the sounds of tropical insects all around them. It was a little disorientating. The island was small and there was none of the usual chaos of a proper airport.

She didn't resist when he cupped her elbow with his hand to guide her towards the little terminal, which was empty except for a few employees. Behind them their bags were being brought on a trolley. The sound of the soft, lilting accents around her was as foreign as the sounds of the insects and the fragrant warmth of the night.

This might be a horrendous work-related trip during which she would be closeted with a man who got to her whether she admitted it to herself or not, but she still felt the stirrings of excitement at being out of London, on exotically foreign soil.

Without looking at him, she reached to undo the ponytail and shook her hair free, before scooping it all up once again in a fluid gesture, back into a ponytail—a high one.

Against the darkness surrounding them and the smooth, deep mahogany skin of the airport workers who had surrounded them, and were laughing and chatting as they wheeled their bags through, her paleness was intensely eye-catching. He would go as far as to say *erotic.*

And from nowhere sprang the disturbing thought that this was not merely a challenge…this was danger.

CHAPTER FOUR

THE WOMAN WAS ENGAGED!

Over the next two days that was the only thing that acted as a brake on an imagination that was now firing on all cylinders. That brief moment of companionship on the island hopper—when she had let her guard down, when he had felt as though he was seeing yet another tantalising glimpse of the woman she really was under the mask—had disappeared.

Frustratingly, she had retreated behind her professional façade, and he had had no time to try and work his way beneath it because much of the time they were in the company of other people.

On the island he was nothing short of a minor celebrity. The locals loved him. He had been single-handedly responsible for creating a huge number of jobs. He paid very well. He had sent several of them on courses abroad. Everyone was looking forward to a boom in tourism, thanks to his innovative hotel. His influence had trickled its way into all sectors of the economy.

As soon as they'd arrived they'd been told the great news by the manager in charge of the project that a television crew from one of the major channels in America would be coming for a few days, to cover the opening of the hotel and analyse what it meant for the economy.

Emily felt as though she had entered a strange new world where she had suddenly been elevated to celebrity status purely because everyone seemed to think that she came as part of a package deal with Leandro.

They'd been wined and dined by the great and the good on the island. The local paper had snapped pictures of them. And in the ensuing hectic whirlwind of social activity she had thankfully been able to shakily put her working hat back on and keep it firmly in place.

Her swimsuit had remained at the back of a drawer, and if she had attended dinners and luncheons in attire that was a little over-formal for the surroundings, then at least she felt comfortable in her clothes, and she had firmly resisted the pleas of several of the local businessmen's wives to go shopping for more 'Caribbean-style stuff'. By which she had deduced they meant sarongs, flip-flops, transparent floaty dresses and other bits and pieces which she knew would have made her feel even more vulnerable than she already did.

Now, tonight, for the first time since they had arrived on the island, they would be dining alone in the hotel restaurant, sampling the standard of the cuisine. A selection of taster plates would be brought for them, along with suitable wines.

'Perhaps you and Antoine should do that on your own?' she had suggested the night before. 'I mean, he *is* the head chef. Wouldn't it be more appropriate if you had him there with you?'

'He'll be behind the scenes,' Leandro had pointed out, in a tone of voice that had suggested he knew very well that she was trying to avoid his company. 'Do you suggest he cooks, then quickly changes out of his chef clothes and scampers over to my table so that he can pretend that he's tasting his own food for the first time?'

Emily looked at her reflection in the mirror and felt a

shiver of nervous tension ripple through her. She had been given one of the luxury cabanas which sat nestled amidst palm trees and cleverly landscaped lawns that were bursting with colour. She had been told to evaluate it in as detached a manner as possible and get back to him with any suggestions for improvement.

There were none. The cabana was the last word in luxury, from the cool bamboo furniture to the sophisticated adjoining wet room. There was also a thoughtfully positioned full-length mirror, to accommodate women who wanted to make sure that they looked perfect when they stepped foot outside the cabana, and it was this mirror which now reflected back to her an image that was stunningly different from the one she had spent the past year and a half cultivating.

The sun had given her skin a pale gold hue and brought out a sprinkling of freckles across the bridge of her nose. Against the tan her eyes appeared bluer, her lashes thicker and her hair lighter.

Instead of the habitual bun, which she had continued to wear even out here, she had decided to leave her hair loose, and it fell over her shoulders and halfway down her back in a display of wild abandon. The heat and humidity had done something to it—brought out curls and waves she'd never known she had.

Returned to the wardrobe were her neat ensembles. She had brought out one of her two less formal dresses—a turquoise wraparound that showed off lots of leg and bare arms. It was nothing anyone could possibly consider *daring*, and yet as she did a half-twirl in front of the mirror she *felt* daring.

Leandro, having a drink in the bar, was only aware of Emily's entrance because the little group of men he was chatting to all fell silent. Drink in hand, he turned around slowly and for a few seconds his mind went completely blank. He took a fortifying gulp of rum and water and forced himself to smile and move towards her, murmuring a few words to the guys around him by way of taking his leave.

'The television crew will be arriving tomorrow,' he said, dragging his eyes away from her with difficulty. 'Lots of promotional shots which will benefit us and benefit the community here at large.'

Emily smiled politely. He hadn't said a word about how she looked, and although she hadn't dressed for him it would have only been courteous to pay her some sort of compliment, wouldn't it?

'That's brilliant!'

'And, if you look to your left, you'll see that they've specifically laid a table for us. It's a demo of how all the tables will be laid when the place is full. I've told my people here that there must be no shortage of attention to detail. Feel free to comment on the job they've done…'

'Of course.'

She was so conscious of him next to her that she felt faint. Something about being there, seeing him in different surroundings…

She might be at great pains to stick to formalities, but he was not. His clothes were cool and casual. No suit, no tie, no restrictive jacket. Now he was in a pair of light-coloured Bermuda shorts, a black polo shirt and loafers without socks. And a couple of days in the blazing sun had lent his complexion an even more burnished hue.

Could the man look any sexier? She had to feebly remind herself that this was just the sort of package that gave him a sense of entitlement to women—the sort of casual sense of entitlement that repelled her.

'But I'm sure it'll all be perfect—just as the room is perfect.'

'That's the difference between a good hotel and a really great one. A great one takes nothing for granted and never gets complacent.'

Had he been complacent about *her*? Was that why she had handed in her resignation? However little need there might be for her to hold down a job, surely an intelligent woman like her would still want the distraction of work that provided a challenge? Unless, of course…

'Are you pregnant?' he asked abruptly as they sat at the table opposite one another.

It took a few seconds for the softly worded question to sink in. Emily had been absently admiring the surroundings. The eating area was fashioned along the lines of an enormous gazebo. It was covered, so that diners would be protected from the elements, but open at the sides so that there was an unimpeded view of the sea, now just a dark body of water lapping gently along the shore. Bird-feeders had been strategically placed on the outside so that during the day there were always birds dipping down to feed and filling the air with their chorus. It was idyllic.

'I beg your pardon?'

'It never occurred to me, but it makes sense. The rushed marriage, the resignation letter… Are you pregnant? Because if you are then I have no problem keeping the job open for you until you feel fit to return to work…'

He pushed his chair back and angled it to one side, so that he could cross his legs while he kept his eyes firmly pinned to her face. In the mellow pool of light her face was soft and flushed…

There was an expression on it that he couldn't put his finger on until she said, with biting cynicism, 'I'm anything *but* pregnant. Kids?' She laughed and took a long gulp of the wine that had been brought over to them. 'That will *never* be on my agenda.'

As hooks went, this one was irresistible. Leandro had never experienced such intense curiosity about a woman. On every level he wanted to know more, even though he recognised the weakness behind the pull on his senses.

'I thought it was the dream of most women to have children...' he murmured encouragingly. 'Diamond rock on the finger, walk up the aisle, the pitter-patter of tiny feet...'

'Not me.' Emily took another energy-boosting sip of wine and realised that her glass was empty. It was quickly refilled. Part of the excellent service.

'And does the lucky guy in your life know that?'

'What lucky guy in my life?' She was momentarily bewildered. 'Oh. Oliver.' She shrugged. 'Absolutely.'

'You seem very young to have made such a momentous decision...or perhaps your fiancé is behind it? Is he divorced? Maybe with a family of his own already? Sometimes middle-aged men with grown children don't want to add to the tally when they decide to marry someone much younger than them...'

Emily recognised fishing when she heard it, and although she should have terminated the meandering conversation the wine had dulled her senses. She wasn't accustomed to alcohol. She could feel herself wavering on the brink of saying more than she would ever have dreamt of saying had she been her usual careful, alert self.

It was so strange, being here with him. In the warm, shadowy night he was no longer her boss, no longer the man she privately scorned, no longer someone in whom she should never confide. The boundaries between them were blurred, and his deep, lazy voice was oddly enticing.

'I didn't think we were here to talk about me,' she said, in a voice that lacked its usual firm conviction.

Leandro sipped his wine and allowed the conversation to drop as they consulted their menus. He chatted briefly about the offerings for dinner. Her soft hair fell in waves around her face and he was mesmerised as she tucked a few strands behind her ear and chewed her lip thoughtfully at the menu.

Perhaps there should be more fish, she thought aloud. After all, they *were* in the Caribbean, and wouldn't guests expect more than just a couple of fishy options?

'I take it you like fish…?'

'Love it. Especially as I don't often cook it at home.'

Leandro wondered what her home was like. A reflection of her complex personality? Sharp modern designs? Abstract reproductions hanging on the walls?

'I don't often cook,' he said by way of an amused rejoinder, and Emily tilted her head to one side and looked at him.

'You know what? That doesn't surprise me.'

'No? And why is that?'

'Because men like you don't.'

Leandro stilled. He looked at her narrowly and she met his eyes without blinking.

'Men like me?' he said coolly. 'Are we going to revisit the tired topic of the way you think I use women?'

He sat back as their starters were set in front of them and plates neatly adjusted to the perfect position. Their glasses were refilled but then they were left alone, which was good. Her attention had drifted down to her starter, but Leandro thought that if she figured she could now change the conversation and start talking about the table service, or some such other bland topic, then she would have to think again.

'You have lots of money,' she mumbled, picking at her starter and then digging in with more enthusiasm because it was delicious—a cool salad of leaves and fresh mango with spicy prawns piled on top. 'Why would you cook for yourself when you can pay someone else to do it for you?'

'Because I may actually *like* cooking but lack the time to put into it.'

'Do you?'

'Do I what?'

'Really like cooking but just don't have the time to do it…?'

'Not exactly…' Leandro shot her a sexy grin that made her breath catch in her throat and brought a reluctant smile to her lips. 'I *have* produced the occasional successful omelette, but I'm no expert in the kitchen. Well…' He shrugged his broad shoulders in a gesture that was typically *his*. 'Growing up with a horde of sisters *does* have its advantages…'

'Aside from plying you with make-up when you were young, they spoiled you? Is that what you're saying?'

She thought wistfully of when she was a kid, always wishing for a sibling… Now, more than ever, it would have been nice to have someone with whom she could share all her worries. Her destiny would still not have been the big happy family scenario, but at least she wouldn't have been on her own coping with all her problems.

'An only boy…' He tilted his head and looked at her with a half-smile. 'What can you expect?'

He was momentarily distracted by the removal of plates and kept his curiosity at bay as she chatted about the food, made all the right noises about its quality. He refilled her glass and called for another bottle of wine to be brought to them. Only when their main courses were set in front of them did he return to the subject that had been on his mind.

'So,' he drawled, 'you were telling me about the fiancé with the family…'

Emily blinked. 'I have no idea what you're talking about.'

'You don't want kids because he already has a few of his own…?'

'Of course he doesn't have any kids!' She wondered how it was that her wineglass seemed to be permanently full. When she tried to marshal her thoughts they swirled away, just out of reach. She tried to grasp hold of an image of Oliver. 'He's the same age as me!'

'So neither of you is interested in prolonging the family line…'

'Do *you* intend to have kids? Get married? Settle down?'

She couldn't picture it. No, he was the sort of guy who would never settle down, and if he ever did then he would carry on leading the bachelor life. There were men like that. Handsome, charming, wealthy men, who just took what they wanted and didn't care about the people they hurt in the process.

Maudlin tears of self-pity tried to push their way to her eyes and she looked down hurriedly at her plate. Mysteriously, she had managed to finish most of the food that had been put in front of her, although she couldn't remember taking a single mouthful.

'Of course.'

Leandro pushed his plate to one side and sat forward. It was dark in the restaurant, with only the light from hanging lanterns and from the moon illuminating the tables. But he thought her voice sounded suspiciously unsteady, and the way she was staring down at her plate…

'Are you…'

'I'm fine,' she said abruptly. 'I don't usually have this much to drink. You were telling me about your plans to have a wife and children… I apologise. It's none of my business.'

Her head felt thick and cloudy. The sounds of the insects were clearer at night, and along with the warm, slight breeze and the magical, lazy lapping of the sea on the sandy beach they acted as a soporific drug, lulling her into puzzling territory. Part of her knew that they should not be talking like this, shouldn't be breaking down the barriers between them, but it just felt inevitable at that moment.

'I should tell you that I think the meal was wonderful…' She fought to drag the conversation back into familiar terrain. 'How did you manage to get hold of Antoine? He's a real find…'

'You're changing the subject.'

'Because this is about work, Leandro. This isn't a…a holiday… This isn't about two people getting to know one another. I'm here because I had no choice and…and…' She felt woozy. 'I think I'd like some coffee…'

'Of course.'

He ordered them both coffee before seamlessly continuing the conversation.

'And why shouldn't we make an attempt to get to know one another? Believe me, I'm the last person in the world to ever condone working relationships straying beyond sensible, acceptable boundaries, but making harmless small talk over a meal doesn't constitute that. So you have a fiancé. Why the secrecy? Do you think that by talking about him you're somehow going to cross enemy lines? You can't say that you'll be jeopardising your job or your references because you've handed in your resignation…'

He raked his fingers through his hair and wished she would stop looking at him with those huge, blue, dreamy eyes. She'd had a little too much to drink and the effect of the alcohol had been to soften her expression. She was leaning towards him, elbow on the table, chin propped in the cup of her hand. The blue dress—some sort of complicated wraparound affair—looked as though it was hanging onto its shape by the skin of its teeth. A couple of tugs and it would unwrap itself and drop to the ground in a pool of slippery fabric. His fingers itched to do just that—tug her free of it.

Her damned fiancé would have had a heart attack—*several* heart attacks—if he had been able to decipher the thoughts Leandro was having about his beloved girlfriend.

'And, to answer your question about my intention to have a family of my own one day...'

He was irritated to find himself spurred into speech. It definitely wasn't his usual style. And certainly not on a subject he had always been at great pains to avoid discussing with the opposite sex. Experience had taught him that leading questions about his long-term plans when it came to commitment usually ended badly.

But her attention was rapt, short-circuiting his common sense.

'Yes?'

Leandro shook his head and stared out for a few seconds at the open water. The beach was semi-lit and the black surface of the sea was streaked silver from the light. In accordance with his strict instructions, staff were keeping themselves at a distance.

'When the time is right and I meet the right woman,' he said gruffly, 'I won't hesitate to tie the knot.'

'Meet the right woman...?' Emily emitted a low, mirthless laugh. 'I never took you for the romantic sort...'

'No, I know exactly the sort you took me for. You made that crystal-clear.'

'Are you angry with me for telling you what I thought?'

'Surprised. Too surprised to be angry. And yet you never stopped to consider that I might have been one hundred per cent transparent in my dealings with women...'

'What do you mean?' Emily shot him a perplexed frown.

This dangerous conversation was thrilling. Every muscle and tendon in her body felt stretched to breaking point. She didn't want to carry on talking about this, delving into areas that should have been kept separate, and yet she just couldn't seem to resist. She was literally holding her breath and hanging on to his every word.

'I never led any of them on.'

He fixed his dark eyes on her face and thought he might have liked to let them linger there—but staring had its limits, and since when was he the kind of guy who *stared*?

'I never made promises I didn't feel I could keep. They knew what they were getting into from day one and I treated them like queens.'

'And yet none of them was your special soulmate…'

'You've got to kiss a lot of frogs… Is that what you did, Emily? Before you chanced upon Mr Right?'

'I haven't been on a worldwide search for a soulmate.'

Leandro looked at her, head inclined. Someone hovered, waiting to ask them how their meals had been, and he waved them aside without taking his eyes off her face. 'Does that mean that your fiancé has fitted the bill before you've even had a chance to explore all possible options?' he asked softly.

'I suppose you could say so,' Emily muttered.

She wiped her mouth and sat back, shakily aware of how close she had come to baring her soul to him.

'And now, if you don't mind, I'm a little tired.' She backed that up with a delicate forced yawn. 'So I think I'll retire to bed. Perhaps you could tell me what our plans are for tomorrow? Meetings? I know the TV crew are coming, so I expect you'll want to do…er…stuff in preparation…'

'What sort of stuff?'

'I don't know!' Emily snapped. 'Stuff. Make sure the

photos are taken from the right angles! I don't know anything about how the media circus works in a case like this!'

'Hardly a media circus. Some poor sod has landed the job of reporting on a fairly frivolous development on a tropical island. It's not going to make headlines across the world. And, in answer to your question, I'll let my PR team handle it. It'll be their first big tourist push and it'll be interesting to see how they cope. So tomorrow...why don't you take a little time out? We can have a look around the island.'

'Time—time out?' Emily stammered.

'It's the weekend. Even I am not such a slave-driver that I would insist you work weekends...'

He summoned Antoine and whilst he chatted with him, complimenting him on the meal and asking detailed questions about various culinary options for picky tourists, Emily took time out to digest what he had said. A day of sightseeing. Just the two of them? He certainly hadn't hinted at a convenient entourage of any kind.

Her mind was in a mild state of panic as she rose to her feet, to find that the effects of a little too much wine were far more pronounced now that she wasn't sitting down.

With difficulty, she took small, concentrated steps alongside him as they made their way out of the restaurant to their respective cabins, and as luck would have it a sudden attack of dizziness in combination with a lack of familiarity with her surroundings worked in perfect unison to send her flying over a dip in the ground.

She had a few panicked seconds during which she attempted to steady herself, and then she was on the soft ground, blood gushing from her foot where it had scraped against a protruding stone.

She didn't know which was worse. The stinging of her foot or the humiliation of being helped to her feet by Leandro and then, even more embarrassingly, finding herself swept up into his arms and carried to her cabana like a sack of potatoes.

'Don't struggle.' He anticipated the protest she was about to make. 'How the hell did *that* happen? No, don't bother. You've had too much to drink.'

She might be tall but she was light. Her slender arms looped around his neck, and the soft feel of her body pressed against his made him grit his teeth together, because his body was again responding in ways that disregarded the constraints imposed by his head.

'I'm fine to walk,' Emily muttered half-heartedly.

'Your foot is pouring blood.'

'That's an exaggeration.'

'I'll sort it out.'

'Surely there must be a first aid…um…person on site?'

'Not in place yet…'

Was that strictly true? Leandro was pretty sure that he could get all the medical help required at the snap of a finger—but, hell…what was the point for a little cut on a foot? Nothing he couldn't handle. He'd never been queasy when it came to blood. In fact, he had once debated whether to go down the medical route but had decided against it. He positively *liked* a bit of blood!

'Many staff will fall into place once the hotel is fully operational. At the moment only essential members of the team are here…'

They had reached her cabana, which was unlocked, and he nudged the door open. For a few seconds the space was disorientating in its darkness, then he found the light switch and somehow managed to turn on the overhead light without putting her down.

The cabana was split into a large bedroom with an en-suite bathroom, an outer room which functioned as a sitting room, with comfortable chairs, a table, a television and a bamboo desk on which, he noted, she had placed her computer, and a compact kitchen area with basic facilities for making tea and coffee. There was also a fridge, which was restocked daily with water and soft drinks, and above the fridge a range of small, exquisitely hand-carved cupboards.

In one of the cupboards was a comprehensive first aid kit and Leandro deposited her gently on a sofa in the sitting area, with orders to stay seated, while he fetched it. He also got a bowl of water from the kitchen and a face towel from the bathroom. En route, he noticed the bed—the indentation of her head on the pillow, the shoes casually kicked off and lying on the ground, the clothes over the back of the chair. She might give the impression of being Miss Prim and Proper, but the air of charming disorder in the room told a different story. He spotted, in passing, a bra hooked over the cupboard handle and half smiled—because that, if anything, was the sort of undergarment he associated with her. Plain, white, simple…

'Okay…'

'Honestly, Leandro, this is totally unnecessary. I can handle a little cut.'

'You're lucky you didn't twist your ankle. I'll have to make sure that the routes back to the cabanas are more adequately lit.'

'You mean for those foolhardy guests who have too much to drink?'

Her voice sounded unnaturally high, but then how could it not when he was kneeling like a supplicant at her feet, gently removing her sandal so that he could soak her injured foot in the warm water in the small basin he had managed to find in the kitchen? The feel of his hands on her skin made her tremble. Who would have imagined that such big hands could be so soft and caressing? What would it be like to have them caress her everywhere? To have them trace the contours of her naked body…every indentation?

She had to suppress a shameless urge to groan aloud just at the thought of it.

How had she ended up in this place? Engaged to a man for reasons no one should be, and stupidly drawn to another when she knew the attraction was not only futile but also sliced through every notion she had ever had about men who played around? Men who didn't know the meaning of the word commitment? Men who ruined other people's lives…?

But he never led them on…he never made promises he couldn't deliver…

His words came back to her in a contradictory rush and she blocked her mind off to them.

'Haven't you ever been…foolhardy?' he asked softly. 'Had a little too much to drink? Said a few things…done a few things…that you semi-regretted in the morning?'

He looked straight at her before she had time to avert her eyes and she reddened.

'Not that I can recall,' she muttered uncomfortably.

Leandro sat back on his haunches with her foot still in his hand. 'Really?'

Emily tugged her leg and he returned his attention to sorting out the cut on her foot. It was a simple matter of cleaning the wound and applying a bandage. In fact, it barely needed a bandage at all, but he was taking his time. She had, he noticed, remarkably slim ankles and beautifully shaped feet, her toenails neat and short.

'I've always been a very careful person. I'm not sure I'll be able to go on a sightseeing tour with you tomorrow, Leandro. Not with my…damaged foot… Walking will probably be difficult…'

'Always?'

'Sorry?' Emily was temporarily confused.

'You said that you've *always* been a careful person…'

He sat back and inspected his handiwork with a critically appreciative eye. Neatly bandaged, neatly cleaned.

He levered himself up and before she could protest he was sitting on the sofa next to her, depressing it with his weight, far too close to her for his liking.

'Aren't you a bit too young to be careful *all the time*?'

'I'm just not inclined to take risks,' Emily returned defensively.

And was her engagement part of that pattern of not taking risks? Leandro wondered. Had she decided on a safe bet? Someone who didn't set her world alight because having her world set alight would be taking a risk, and she didn't do risk-taking? Was that why she was so tight-lipped when it came to discussing the one thing in her life that she should have been shouting from the rooftops?

He remembered that feeling he had had—that feeling that she was *aware* of him, aware of him as a man…

In his head, strands of information were rearranging themselves, reconfiguring into bite-sized pieces he could deal with,—bite-sized pieces that made perfect sense as soon as he began thinking laterally, as he was now doing.

She didn't love the guy she was engaged to. When she spoke about him it was with reticence and a certain amount of caution. Maybe she liked the man, but more likely she simply saw him as a rescue package because she feared entering her thirties without a partner and he was a safe bet—someone from her childhood who had resurfaced. He didn't challenge her, but neither did he repel her. The poor guy was probably besotted with her. She had cool, eye-catching killer looks. Doubtless he fancied himself in love and she was going along for the ride because something was better than nothing.

The thought that she might be attracted to *him* appealed to a part of Leandro that was instinctive and primal and intensely satisfying.

'I don't think your foot should come between you and a relaxing day exploring the island,' he murmured, with a slow, lazy smile that she found vaguely disconcerting. 'I've cleaned all the blood, and I'm pleased to tell you that it's a surface cut only. In fact barely in need of a bandage. But, as a careful person, you'll appreciate that it's better to be safe than sorry…'

'There's nothing wrong with being careful.' Emily felt drawn to justify herself. 'You apply that to all your work dealings…'

'Ah, but that's where it ends.'

'Is it? I thought you were very careful not to get too involved in your personal relationships,' she answered with asperity, and then flushed—because what was the point in trying to resurrect barriers only to trample them underfoot the second she was drawn into a non-work-related conversation with him?

'*Touché*—although I'm not sure your comparison is valid.'

'What time do you anticipate we will be leaving in the morning for this sightseeing tour?' Emily couldn't meet his eyes. She could still feel the sensation of his hands on her foot and her body was still tingling from thoughts that had no place in her head. 'If I'm up to it.'

'You'll be up to it.' Leandro stood up, returned the basin to the small kitchen and then strolled to the window to gaze briefly out into the darkness before turning to face her. 'I'll get Antoine to prepare a picnic for us…'

'Is that really necessary? We could always return here to the hotel…'

'We'll be out for the day, Emily,' Leandro said gently.

'Back late afternoon. It may be a small island, but there's no rush, is there? And…' He paused and allowed his eyes a leisurely roam. 'Avoid the starchy clothing. Swimsuit, towel, sunblock…you won't need any more than that…'

CHAPTER FIVE

EMILY COULDN'T REMEMBER the last time she had been on holiday. Any holiday of any kind, barring the good old and bitterly remembered days when she had still been caught up in the illusion of happy family life. When her parents had taken her abroad on expensive holidays to expensive destinations. Those didn't count. And for the better part of her adult life...well, there had been no opportunity, no money, no time...and hardly any inclination when she thought about it.

Now, as she stood in front of the mirror and contemplated the girl staring back at her, she was disturbed to find that she felt in a holiday mood. The warmth, the salty smell of the sea, the uninterrupted sound of waves lapping against a shoreline, the lack of crowds which imposed an atmosphere of serenity and intimacy...

Sometimes it was hard to drag herself back to the reality of the situation. That she was here because of work—because she had handed in her notice—because he didn't trust her not to fly to his competitors and divulge state secrets. Or maybe simply because it was within his power to make her stay and complete her full notice, so he would.

And as soon as she began thinking that she likewise remembered *why* she had handed in her notice. Because her life was about to change. Because she was going to get married. To Oliver. For reasons which were complex and cynical and somehow made her feel immeasurably sad. But when she felt herself spiralling down that road she always managed to yank herself away from the brink.

Except now—right now, right here—with the windows to the cabana flung open on a view of lush, breathtaking, Technicolor beauty, she could feel dissatisfaction creep up on her. Dissatisfaction and melancholy at where her life was going. She would never experience this again—this feeling of simmering excitement because she was looking forward to a day out. With a guy who…

She turned away abruptly from the full-length mirror and flung her towel, her sunblock, a tee shirt and a pair of shorts, her book and her hat into the colourful canvas beach bag she had been tempted into buying from the hotel shop.

Her foot was completely fine and she had removed the bandage and replaced it with a strip of plaster. It felt odd to leave her laptop behind, charging on the desk in the little sitting room. She had so far managed to tote it along everywhere with her, like a solid, tangible shield against personal contact with Leandro. Fat lot of good it had done her.

Here she was with her hair swinging down her back in a plait, dressed in shorts and a tee shirt like a teenager, with her sensible swimsuit underneath and a simmering sense of excitement when she should have been feeling apprehensive and resentful at spending the day in his company.

She had eaten breakfast in her bedroom and spotted Leandro as soon as she entered the reception area of the hotel. Everyone was gearing up for the big photo shoot. There was a general air of excitement. The casual clothing of the staff which had been in evidence previously had been jettisoned in favour of uniforms: crisp white and mint-green. Amidst all this Leandro cut a commanding figure, surrounded by some of his employees who were hanging onto his every word.

Her heart skipped a beat as she stood at the side and looked at him. After all this time working for him, spending hours upon hours in his company, she marvelled that she could have kidded herself into believing that he had absolutely no effect on her—that she was immune to his looks. It would seem not. Images of him had obviously been stored in her memory bank, and now there was no need to be near him to know the way his eyes crinkled when he smiled, the curve of his sexy mouth, the imperious set of his features.

She took a deep breath and walked confidently towards him as the little cluster of dark-skinned, smiling people greeted her and broke away, scurrying off in different directions.

'They're thrilled with all of this, aren't they?' Emily asked politely.

She had to stop herself from staring at him. He was wearing a pale blue polo shirt and khaki shorts that showed off the length and strength of his muscular legs, liberally sprinkled with dark hair.

'Wouldn't you be?' Leandro looked down at her—at the impossibly fair hair, the long, slender legs, the sexy, boyish physique. She looked incredibly young without the suit, without make-up, without the severe hairstyle.

'I guess so.' Emily laughed, eyes carefully averted, shielded with one hand against the blinding glare of the camera flashes. 'How long will they be here?'

'Wrapped up in a day. We should miss the thick of it. Unless, of course, you'd like to be photographed for the spread?'

'Absolutely not!'

'Why not?' Leandro drawled. 'Are you camera-shy? No need, you know. I imagine you're incredibly photogenic...'

Emily reddened and wondered whether this was a flirtatious remark—then immediately chided herself for being over-imaginative. This was just how he was. Innately charming. It was why women found him so irresistible. It was why…

The natural conclusion of this train of thinking should have been her being led down a well-trodden and familiar path. Innately charming, irresistible—hence womaniser and general player whose modus operandi involved breaking hearts.

However, she lost the thought before she could follow it through. She was too busy playing with the idea that he found her photogenic.

She tripped along behind him towards a buggy which was only slightly bigger than a motorised golf cart and handed him her bag, which he tossed into the back seat, where it joined a massive picnic basket and a cooler containing, she assumed, an assortment of cold drinks.

'Do you know how to drive this thing?' She hesitated as he held the door open for her.

'If I can fly a plane then I can certainly drive this little motorised tin can. Besides, there's no traffic to speak of around here, and you have my word that I will protect you as though my life depended on it.'

Emily felt another quiver of *something*—something that made her feel hot and flustered and a little bit scared.

'I hope you've brought your sunblock?' He glanced across at her as he swung himself into the driver's seat and reversed the buggy at alarming speed, sending up a little flurry of gravel. 'You look like you burn easily.'

'I'll be fine, thank you.'

'You're already a little sunburned on the bridge of your nose.'

Emily automatically rubbed her finger along her nose and kept her eyes firmly fixed ahead of her.

'So, tell me what you think of the hotel—how you're enjoying your stay here…'

Having tuned in to those barely visible reactions she had whenever she was in his presence—reactions which he now concluded had always been there, cleverly hidden underneath a polished professional exterior, Leandro now found that they were all he could notice. The way she blushed whenever he surprised her with a remark that was non-work-related, even the most innocuous. The way she looked away, nostrils slightly flared, at the faintest whiff of a *double entendre.*

She fancied him—and where did that leave her so-called fiancé? His curiosity had been aroused and, like an itch, he was determined to scratch it, determined to get to the bottom of the enigma. And playing at the back of his mind was the tantalising notion that if she fancied him—and he was certainly having trouble stamping down his suddenly hectic libido—then where might that lead?

If she figured she was in love with this guy she had jacked her job in for, then wouldn't he be doing her a favour in showing her that that was certainly not the case? Wouldn't he be sparing her a lifetime of unhappiness and regret by demonstrating the unavoidable truth that if she was attracted to other men, specifically *him,* then hitching her wagon to some guy out of desperation was not a solution?

'It's the most beautiful place I've ever been to in my entire life,' Emily answered truthfully. 'The scenery is amazing. So unspoiled. I wonder if the island will remain that way once it's discovered.'

'The minister for tourism here—or for such tourism as exists at the moment—seems to be a very discerning guy.'

Leandro was still caught up in his thoughts, still acutely aware of her sitting so close to him that the smallest shift in his body weight would bring their thighs together.

'He appreciates how important it is to keep the flavour of this island. It's a fine line. Over-development would kill the tourist industry faster than civil war, and he gets that.'

'You're very lucky that you were the first to stamp your mark here…'

'I prefer to think of it as being astute rather than lucky.'

He slid his eyes along to her and inhaled sharply. She was trying and failing in an attempt to keep her hair from flying all over the place as they sped along the small empty road parallel to the sandy strip of coastline. On one side acres of coconut trees meandered towards the town and the outlying suburban areas. On the other more coconut trees separated the road from the beach, and the striking blue of the water could be glimpsed through their slender spiralling trunks. The sky was a perfectly cloudless milky blue. Sea breezes kept the temperature just right, preventing the tropical heat from becoming unbearable. He had chosen the spot for this hotel very carefully.

'Were you always like this?'

'Like what?' Leandro asked, raising his eyebrows in a question.

'Astute when it comes to business?'

'You mean was I doing deals at the age of ten? No. But I inherited the hard-working gene from my father and grew up with the belief that an expensive education was not a right but a privilege—one to be appreciated and used well. And what about you, Emily? Was it always your ambition to be a personal assistant?'

'You say that as though it's something to be…ashamed of.' She turned to him and glared.

'Far from it. Behind every successful businessman

there's always a personal assistant, making sure that all the nuts and bolts are taken care of.'

'I wanted to be a vet,' Emily admitted, because somehow, despite his qualification, he had still managed to make her job sound *pedestrian.* And there was a part of her that wanted him to know that she had once fancied herself as destined for all sorts of things—grand things.

'A vet…' Leandro murmured, and saw her give a curt nod from the corner of his eye. 'That's a far cry from being someone's personal assistant…'

'Yes, it is.'

'Demands high grades…'

'Do you think I wasn't clever enough to get them?'

'Far be it from me to think any such thing. You forget—I've worked with you for nearly two years. I know how clever you are.'

'Now, why does that sound so patronising?' But she laughed and gave up the unequal fight between the wind and her hair. 'I can smell the sea. It's amazing.'

'Look through there—through that clump of trees. Do you see a path? Well, that's where we're going.'

'How on earth do you know about this place?'

'The hotel manager is a fount of information and was only too happy to steer us in the direction of the best beaches.'

He swerved off the road and brought the buggy to a bumpy stop just where the Tarmac gave way to rich soil and the dense, lush foliage that was so much a feature of the tiny island. With the engine killed, the sound of the sea reached her, and she held her face upturned to the sun, enjoying the bliss of the warmth on her skin.

Okay, so it might not be a holiday, but for the first time in as long as she could remember she felt removed from the low-level stress that accompanied her everywhere.

They walked through the roughly hewn path, down a gentle incline and through a bank of coconut trees, emerging onto a strip of sand that was fine, white and powdery. The beach stretched in a half-moon crescent and the sea was as calm as a lake and a piercing turquoise.

Emily stared out, squinting against the sun. She felt free—free from all concerns and worries. She felt like a young woman without a care in the world, and she marvelled that she could have forgotten what that felt like. This was a taste of normality and she savoured it, knowing that its visit would be fleeting.

When she turned around it was to find that Leandro had flung a massive beach rug on the sand and had stripped off to his swimming trunks. The sight of him, bare-chested, was even more breathtaking than the scenery she had been gaping at moments before.

Goodness, had she been fantasising about this all the time she had been working for him? Underneath the blistering scorn and her composed demeanour, had she fooled herself into imagining a detachment that had never been there?

He certainly lived up to any fantasy a girl could have. His shoulders were broad and muscled, his stomach washboard-flat, and the sprinkling of dark hair on his chest was aggressively, challengingly masculine.

She found that she was having trouble breathing, and in a desperate attempt to conceal her shameful reaction reached into the bag over her shoulder and whipped out her sunglasses, which she stuck firmly on the bridge of her nose.

'I take it you're not going to spend the day in shorts and a tee shirt?'

His own clothes had been dumped on the rug, along with the shoes which he had kicked off. Even his feet, she noted distractedly, were unfairly sexy. How was that even possible?

'I'm not a strong swimmer.'

'Don't worry. I'm here. I won't let you be swept away by any treacherous undertows…'

'You're certainly a man of many talents,' Emily bantered uneasily. 'You can fly planes, drive off-road cars and now cross-channel swimming…'

'The cross-channel bit might be taking the talented streak a little far…'

Alert now to her body language, Leandro was feeling the pull of attraction tucked away behind her nervous laughter and light-hearted remarks—and, hell, it had him firing on all cylinders. He folded his arms and tilted his head to one side, his body language redolent of a man waiting. Waiting for her to strip off…

No big deal. Her swimsuit was as daring as a nun's habit. A black one-piece. Yet she was still burning with self-consciousness as she pulled the tee shirt over her head and eased her shorts off, folding both neatly and depositing them on the rug without once glancing in his direction.

'I didn't realise we would be staying in one spot,' she muttered. 'I thought you mentioned exploring the island.'

'And we'll be doing just that.' Leandro began walking towards the water. 'But the drive was just so hot that I thought we could kick off the day with a little swim to cool down. Coming?' He threw the word over his shoulder.

She watched, hesitating, as he waded into the sea and then, when he was quite a long way out, pushed off and began to swim vigorously, until he was just a small speck on the horizon.

Safely far away.

Only then did she venture in. A quick, harmless paddle…

But the water was shallow, and very clear, and amazingly warm. Unable to resist the temptation of actually doing a little proper swimming, she eventually took the plunge. She hadn't been in a public swimming pool, let alone the sea, for as long as she could remember, and although she was an okay swimmer, it was comfortingly reassuring being able to feel the sand under her feet. She flipped over, ducked under the surface, emerged and lay on her back, eyes closed against the glare, arms outstretched as the water lapped around her still body.

She wasn't aware of Leandro slicing through the water towards her until she felt his arms, his body, and in a state of surprised panic she spluttered back to reality, half ducking under before breaking the surface, arms flailing, because the comforting bank of sand was no longer within reaching distance of her toes. And the more she flailed—partly out of surprise at discovering that she had drifted away from the shore, and partly because Leandro's wet proximity was throwing her into a state of mental chaos—the tighter he circled his arms around her.

'Hey! I've got you!'

'And you can let me go! Right now!' She tried to pummel his chest, but that was near impossible given the situation.

'Clasp your arms around my neck, Emily, and we can swim back to shore. You drifted.'

'I'm perfectly…capable…of swimming back unaided!'

She gave one final liberating push and began striking back towards the beach, her swimming jerky and frantic.

She waded out angrily. He was right behind her. There was no need for her to turn around to ascertain that fact. What the heck did he think he was playing at?

'I don't appreciate being…being…' When she finally spun round she was safely wrapped up in her towel and breathing so fast that she felt on the verge of hyperventilation.

'Being…?' Leandro drawled silkily.

He took his time sitting down, reaching for his shades,

then stretching himself out on the rug with his legs lightly crossed—the very picture of a man utterly at ease, oblivious to her spluttering anger.

Emily looked at him. She was overreacting. She knew it. She had told him that she wasn't a strong swimmer and she had managed to float her way out of her depth… He had probably fancied himself as lifeguard, saving a damsel about to find herself in distress.

'I'm sorry if you thought I was…in trouble,' she said ungraciously, before quickly remembering that she was still his employee, he was still her boss—even if it didn't feel like that out here, far removed from their daily routine. 'And I appreciate that you thought you needed to save me. I *can* actually swim, Leandro. I just can't enter competitions.'

She wished she could see his eyes, get a handle on how he was reacting, but his dark sunglasses hid everything.

'Why don't you lie down and recover?'

He patted the space next to him without glancing in her direction and Emily looked at his hand with the suspicion of someone eyeing up a deadly snake.

'But don't forget to apply sunblock. I can do without it because I'm dark, but…'

'You don't want the liability of a secretary who can't perform her duties because she has to take to her bed with sunburn?'

Leandro lifted his shades and looked at her evenly. 'For the past year and a half I've wondered what was going through your head. I now realise that you were wrapped up imagining the very worst about me. If you don't want to protect yourself from the sun, then by all means don't.' He replaced his sunglasses and folded his arms on his chest.

She had been dismissed. Along with her churlishness, her childishness, her petty heated responses.

'Have you been to *all* of the beaches on the island?'

She lay down and resumed their conversation in a placatory voice.

Without having to look at him, with only the sky above her to witness her nervous jumpiness, Emily felt a little more at ease.

'I…I suppose you must have had to do a great deal of background checks before you decided to invest your money in this venture…'

'Why did you decide to choose secretarial work over becoming a vet if your grades were good…?'

'I beg your pardon?'

'I visited the island once, shortly before you joined me. I made sure everything and everyone was in place and then I delegated—so, no, I *don't* know every beach on the island. That's your question answered. Now answer mine. Why sit in front of a computer when you could be in the great outdoors, tending to sick animals?'

Leandro didn't need to look at her. He could *sense* her confusion, her unwillingness to run with this conversation. Behind the dark shades his eyes were closed as he allowed the silence to develop between them.

'And don't…' he rolled onto his side and propped himself up on one elbow so that he was now looking at her profile, taking in the way her nostril quivered and her tongue slipped out to moisten her lips '…even *think* of changing the subject…'

Emily kept perfectly still but she could feel his eyes on her. He wasn't going to give up. Perhaps he was bored—perhaps that was what lay behind this curiosity which had never been in evidence before.

His normal weekend in London would have been packed with fun and probably spent in the company of his latest woman. Maybe trawling through overpriced jewellers so that he could let the lucky lady choose something involving diamonds followed by lunch somewhere cool and hip, an afternoon romping in the sack and then something cultured…a night at the opera. The lucky lady might not get to grips with it, but she would certainly appreciate the glamour of the event…

Instead here he was, stuck in Paradise with *her*. His curiosity had been piqued by her resignation, by her tight-lipped responses when questioned, and with nothing better to do on a Saturday, with the sun beating down and none of the usual distractions, the devil was beginning to work on idle hands.

Those semi-flirtatious remarks…the lazy drift of his eyes towards her…standing there the way he had so that he could watch her peel her tee shirt off and strip down to her swimsuit…the relentless way he insisted on dragging their conversation away from the polite and into the murky waters of the personal…

She was leaving his employ. There was no longer any particular need to cultivate distance between them. That worked both ways. Maybe, in the absence of anything better to do, he wanted to have some fun with her.

'I have no idea why you would be interested in my…my past life choices, Leandro!' Emily laughed lightly.

'Call me crazy, but some of us are like that. Interested in other peoples' past life choices…' Not strictly true, of course. He had never been over-curious about any of his girlfriends' past life choices. Perhaps that was because they had always insisted on telling him all about them…

'It was too expensive,' Emily said bluntly.

'Too *expensive*?'

'That's right.' Suddenly restless, she sat up and wrapped her arms around her legs.

Leandro sat up as well, so that they were both now staring out at the glittering sea.

'You probably don't know what it feels like to have to reconsider your options because there's just not enough money in the bank. But some of us do.' And yet, she thought bitterly, it need not have been that way. She should have been able to fulfil her dreams. But instead she had had to resort to a Plan B she had never considered while growing up.

'Your family could not have helped you realise your ambitions...?'

'I will not discuss my family.' She glanced across to him with a cool, unreadable expression.

He was locked out. It was as if the shutters had dropped, sealing off all points of entry. Why wouldn't she discuss her family? What was so taboo about that? But then, what was so taboo about discussing her engagement? Clearly quite a lot.

'Well, then,' he drawled with lazy insistence, 'why don't we discuss your boyfriend?'

He turned to face her and removed his shades. Then he reached forward and removed hers. Just like that. Before she had time to take preventative measures. Before she could pull back from feeling the touch of his fingers on her face.

'I thought we'd covered that topic already.' She began raising her hand to her face, to brush away the feel of his fingers, then thought better of it and lowered it to her side. Instead she stood up and put on her tee shirt before strolling down to the shoreline, just far enough for the warm water to lap over her feet before ebbing away.

Everything about this situation screamed danger, and yet she felt so...so *alive.*

Antennae she hadn't even known she possessed warned her that he was behind her without her having to turn around.

'Have we?' Leandro murmured.

He was standing slightly behind her, the warm breeze whipping her hair against him, and his fingers itched to reach out and yank that little blue elastic band out of her hair so that he could appreciate it loose and unencumbered.

'Spoken much to him since we've been here?'

'I don't think that's any of your business,' Emily blustered.

'Missed him much?'

'How dare you ask questions like that?' She spun round to look at him and immediately regretted it because she was now only inches away from him. The broad, naked width of his powerful chest confronted her like an implacable wall. 'And…and…*can't you put on a tee shirt?*'

'Why? Does it bother you seeing me like this?'

'Of course it doesn't!'

'So why would I want to put anything on? It's hot.'

'We should be thinking of carrying on with this tour,' Emily said agitatedly. 'We'll never cover the island at this rate.'

'The island is the size of a postage stamp. Trust me. We can stay here for another hour and still cover it twice over before dark. The reason I ask whether you're pining for your one true love is because I don't think you are.'

'I beg your pardon?'

'You heard me, Emily. You haven't mentioned the man once since we've been here.'

'I'm an extremely private person. You know that.'

'So private that when Nigel Sabga, the hotel manager, asked you whether you were married you told him that you didn't believe in marriage?'

'You were *eavesdropping* on our conversation?' It had been a question asked in passing and answered truthfully and without thought. But then, she hadn't realised that Leandro had been lurking behind a wall somewhere, earwigging.

'You probably didn't see me. I was sampling some of the wines behind a screen in the dining area.'

He stared at her until she felt hot colour crawl into her cheeks.

'So… Peculiar remark, wouldn't you say? For someone about to tie the knot with the love of their life? But then, I don't imagine he *is* the love of your life.'

'You don't know what you're talking about, and you have no right to…to…'

'Of course I have no right!' Leandro shrugged his shoulders with eloquent nonchalance. 'But you're soon to be my ex-employee. All bets are off when it comes to walking carefully round one another. Why are you marrying the guy if you don't believe in marriage? Are you scared of ending up on your own? You shouldn't be. You're not old enough to have such fears…'

'Of course I'm not scared of ending up on my own,' Emily retorted scornfully. 'Why should I be?'

'Who knows how you feel on the subject?' He paused, dark eyes still fixed on her flushed face. 'After all, you're marrying a guy you clearly don't love, for reasons best known to you, and from what I can see it's not a marriage driven by that other all-important criteria either…'

'I have no idea what you're talking about, Leandro.' Caution and common sense told her to do something—anything rather than stay where she was, like a fly trapped in a spider's web—but her head was refusing to take orders. 'What *"all-important criteria"* are you talking about?'

For a few seconds she really was puzzled, but realisation dripped in and she went bright red. Sex. That was what he had been talking about. What else?

She tried to activate the appropriate response of disgust

at a man whose mind could only travel down one track, but it seemed that in the space of only a few days he was no longer the one-dimensional figure she had pegged him to be.

She jumped to her feet and began walking restlessly towards the sea, before branching off to explore the rest of the beach and give herself time to harness her chaotic thoughts.

When she sneaked a look over her shoulder it was to find that Leandro had lain back down on the beach rug, hands folded behind his head, sunglasses firmly back in place. The very picture of relaxation.

Emily tightened her lips and continued to walk away from him. If the beach had been longer she would have disappeared and left him to his own devices for as long as she possibly could, but after ten minutes she was forced to stroll back towards him. He had not moved a muscle. Had he even noticed that she had walked away?

'What are you trying to say?' She addressed his prone figure and he lifted his sunglasses to squint up at her.

'Come again?'

Gone was the cool, controlled woman who had performed her duties without once revealing the slightest hint of what went on behind the polite facade. Bit by bit he had witnessed that façade being eroded at the edges, turning her from a statue into a living, breathing woman—a woman with depth and passion and the sort of complexities that could keep a man riveted for a lifetime.

'That remark you made… You know nothing of my relationship with Oliver!'

'I don't have to,' Leandro responded wryly.

He replaced his shades, concealing his eyes, and infuriatingly looked as though he might be on the point of nodding off to sleep in the tropical sun.

'And what does *that* mean?' Irritated, she poked him in his side with her toe.

He caught her foot before she could pull it away.

'I really would avoid doing that,' he drawled, removing the sunglasses to lodge them on the top of his head.

'Or else what?'

Leandro dealt her a slashing smile and kept hold of her foot. 'If you start touching me you might find that I start touching you back...'

Emily's heart slowed and heat suffused her face. She had never been so conscious of her body before—even though he wasn't looking at it, even though his eyes were firmly fixed on her face, even though his expression, despite the innuendo behind his words, was deceptively amused.

'And that's what I'm talking about...' he continued, with silky-smooth intent.

Emily stared at him in silence. She didn't want him to carry on. She really didn't want to hear what he had to say on a subject she had no desire to talk about. But she felt like a rabbit, frozen in the headlights while a car moved inexorably at full speed towards it.

'Ah, I see you get where I'm coming from...'

He sat up and his hand snaked to her wrist, tugging her down beside him so that she half fell onto the rug before shuffling into a sitting position whilst glaring impotently at him.

'The cat is out of the bag, Emily. You're no longer the personal assistant hiding behind a bland exterior with a non-existent private life.'

She was so close to him that he could see the flicker in her eyes...could almost *smell* the scent of an awareness she was desperate to conceal.

'You're engaged to be married to a man for whom you have feelings of...what? Exactly? Certainly not love and—let's be honest, here—definitely not physical attraction. And do you know how I've come to that conclusion?'

He ran his thumb along the side of her cheek in a gesture that was shockingly intimate and she pulled away sharply.

'Point proved. I've come to that conclusion, my dear personal assistant, because you're attracted to *me*...'

CHAPTER SIX

EMILY WAS NOT looking forward to the evening that lay ahead of her, terrifying in its uncertainty, filled with the dreadful potential to do damage in places she least wanted.

'Because...my dear personal assistant...you're attracted to me...'

She recalled Leandro's absolute amused certainty as he had spoken those words, the way his dark eyes had held hers for just a second before roving indolently over her, touching every part of her body until she felt as though she was going to go up in flames.

Of course she had denied any such thing vigorously. She had schooled her features into a mask of disdain. She had reminded him that she had been his secretary for nearly two years, so how, she had asked pointedly, had he only now reached such a ridiculous conclusion? She had informed him coolly that the hot weather must have gone to his head.

Then she had taken refuge in the sea, putting her limited swimming skills to the test and striking out until she'd realised that if she didn't swim back to shore he would probably do something insane, like try and rescue her yet again.

The thought of those strong arms around her had almost made her lose her stride.

He had pulled back the curtain and revealed the monster. The sexual attraction she had been feeling—the one she had tried desperately to conceal—had been exposed and held up for inspection, and even though he had politely allowed the matter to drop she knew that his conclusions had not changed.

They might just as well not have bothered with the trip round the island. She had barely been able to notice a thing. The delicious lunch, eaten in the charming miniature botanical gardens, surrounded by wildly colourful flowers and the sound of birds and insects, had been wasted on her. She had brought her phone with her, thinking that she would capture some of the sights, but in fact she hadn't taken a single picture.

She had been too busy thinking about what he had said and feverishly agonising about the myriad ways he could make the rest of her stay uncomfortable.

She now longed for the safety of those London office walls. She wished that she had avoided this wretched overseas situation by fabricating some kind of clever excuse.

Failing that…

She looked at her reflection and saw, despite the tumultuous churning in her head, the image of a relaxed young woman nothing at all like the expressionless personal assistant who had made a virtue out of being impassive, remote and professional.

She had caught the sun. Despite frequent applications of sunblock her skin was lightly tanned and satin-smooth. Her already fair hair was dazzlingly blonde, lightened by the sun. Forced into summer clothes, her body seemed more exposed than she could ever remember noticing.

She should have been getting a tan for the guy waiting for her back home, but instead she was caught up fighting emotions that had no place in her life, and being apprehensive that somehow those emotions, which she could barely quantify, would take on a life of their own and start demanding attention she couldn't afford to give them.

She would have to return to the topic, like it or not, and dispatch it with a version of the truth—just enough to ensure that things returned to normal. Or as normal as was possible while they were trapped here on Paradise.

She left it as late as possible to join Leandro for dinner. The photo shoot had taken place and she knew that he had been booked for a personal interview and a series of pictures to accompany the article. The last thing she wanted was to be involved and have her picture taken. The entire crew would be staying the night on the hotel compound, sampling the rooms, but an offshore boat had been laid on for them so that they could enjoy dinner out at sea.

Emily thought that they must have fought to get the dream job of a lifetime on this photography stint.

Running nearly an hour late, she found him nursing a drink at the bar, and she faltered before taking a deep breath and walking confidently towards him.

'Am I supposed to consider this fashionably late?' Leandro enquired when she was standing next to him.

She still couldn't quite get used to not seeing him in a suit. Every time she laid eyes on his bare brown arms, his muscular legs, that glimpse of chest visible behind the casual shirt with the top buttons undone, she felt the force of impact anew.

No different now. He was, thankfully, in a pair of long, cool khaki trousers and a dull blue polo shirt, loafers without socks.

'I fell asleep and didn't wake up in time,' Emily lied.

'You've caught the sun.' He beckoned across a waiter and ordered a bottle of wine. 'I thought we could try somewhere different tonight. One of the restaurants in the town.'

'I'd rather stay here,' Emily interjected quickly, because the thought of yet more unchaperoned time with him was the last thing she wanted. 'I'm feeling a little too tired for going out again…'

'Despite the long sleep?'

He marvelled that away from the grey London skies and the impersonal office setting she could have undergone such a dramatic change. The severe hairstyles had all but been abandoned. Instead of her habitual bun she had braided her long vanilla-blonde hair into a loose plait which was draped over one shoulder and tied at the end with a scruffy red elastic band. Devoid of all but the most basic make-up, and wearing no jewellery whatsoever, she still managed to look classier and more tempting than any of the heavily adorned women he was accustomed to dating.

Her dress was a silky flowered shift which exposed as little as possible and yet still managed to get his imagination going.

And that was without thinking back to how she had looked in that unadventurous swimsuit! All long limbs and ballet dancer grace…

He felt the push of an erection and forced it away with difficulty.

'The sun tires me out,' Emily told him vaguely. 'I think I'd spend half my time in bed if I lived over here.'

'Interesting thought.'

Their eyes tangled briefly and she looked away, flushing. There she went again, she thought with annoyance, rising to a bait she wasn't even sure he had consciously planted. Proving to him that what he had said about the whole *attraction thing* was true. An indifferent woman didn't blush whenever there was the slightest bit of innuendo behind a remark!

If she had been with her previous boss, a fatherly type in

his sixties, she would not be trying to fight down the colour invading her cheeks and staring at the bartender with the desperation of a drowning swimmer searching for a life belt in open water.

'How did the photo shoot go?'

'You missed the post-shoot excitement,' Leandro said drily. 'Drinks on the house nearly put paid to their boat trip out to sea. I asked the skipper to make sure the crew kept an eagle eye on the lot of them. *Man overboard!* is not what I want to hear drifting across the water while we're in the middle of our meal.'

Emily smiled reluctantly and cradled the wine in her hand. She allowed herself to be amused by his rendition of the photographer who had tried to get him into various artificial poses, and the journalist covering the feature, who had stumbled over her words and asked him the same question several times.

By the time their starters had been brought to them—casual hors d'oeuvres, because neither of them had the appetite for anything more substantial—they had moved on to a more serious conversation about the effect the article would have on business and then to the wider topic of the effects of tourism in small, undiscovered places.

Even talking shop, she was aware of him in ways she had never been before—or had never *thought* she had been before.

Almost without her being aware of it, her eyes took in the smallest changes in his expression, the movement of his hands as he lifted the wineglass to his mouth, the way he had of leaning back in the chair, half smiling, head tilted to one side, listening to her when she said something…

Leandro was beginning to find the work chat tiresome. So many other areas of conversation were up for grabs.

'There's something I feel I ought to tell you,' Emily

began uncomfortably when the wooden board with their starters had been cleared away and there was a lull in the conversation.

'I'm all ears.' Leandro sat forward and looked at her with dark intent. 'Of course if it involves an animated discussion of world events, then I might find my attention drifting…'

'It's always interesting to talk about what's happening in the world,' Emily said. She looked to find, with some surprise, that she had finished her glass of wine and, following the direction of her eyes, Leandro leaned across to pour her a refill.

'I shouldn't,' she murmured, acquiescing.

'Because you might trip again? I might enjoy coming to the rescue… I did last time…'

There was no mistaking the flirtatious innuendo even though his face was perfectly serious, as was his voice.

'I'm not the sort of woman who has time for knights in shining armour,' Emily told him crisply, but she couldn't meet his eyes and instead chose to focus on the attractive displays of hibiscus flowers that dotted the bar counter. 'And *I* happen to find world events fascinating. I guess, from what you're saying, it's not the sort of thing you like talking about with the opposite sex!'

'I can't say I have known many of them who would have had the remotest clue as to what was happening outside their immediate range of vision.' Leandro raised his eyebrows with wry amusement. 'So what you're telling me is that the boyfriend isn't your knight in shining armour?'

'I understand why you're curious about my…my situation…' Emily mumbled. 'I know you think that I should be more…excited…about the whole getting married thing…'

'Ah…' Leandro settled back and waited for her to continue. 'It all seems a bit sudden,' he prompted as the silence lengthened.

Out of the corner of his eye he could see their food being brought over to them with all the smiling enthusiasm he had taken note of over the past few days. It couldn't be happening at a worse time. He didn't want her to retreat behind any more banalities about the state of the world.

Restlessly he waited as platters of food were placed in front of them. Fresh fish, plantain, plates of local sweet potatoes, yam and aubergine.

'You were saying…?' He resumed the conversation when the waiter had faded away. He was keenly aware of her deliberate attempt to avoid catching his eye. Curiosity ripped through him—not a mild stirring of interest, but a sharp, biting feeling that raced through his veins like a shot of pure adrenaline.

'Oliver and I go back a long way…' She cleared her throat, focusing on how she could placate his inquisitiveness with just enough of an explanation. 'I mean, he's been abroad working, but when he returned we picked things up…'

'Picked what up? Hot sex?'

'We don't *all* see sex as an answer to everything.'

'I'm curious as to why you're with the man.'

'It's something of an arrangement,' Emily told him, without inflection in her voice. 'Something that suits us both. We get along fine with one another…'

'You're marrying for convenience because you *"get along"*? There must be more to it than that.'

'I'm not into romance,' she said with a trace of bitterness in her voice. 'I'm into…security…'

'Explain.'

'There *are* no more explanations, Leandro,' she told him pleadingly. 'I'm your secretary. I don't have to answer these questions, but I'm doing it because I know you're curious and I know what you're like. You won't give up and we're stuck here…'

She concentrated on the food on her plate and felt his eyes on her, burning a hole straight to the deepest part of her where her thoughts were hidden.

'So what do we do about this situation?' Leandro drawled, closing his knife and fork on yet another fantastic meal.

'Well, I will, of course, carry on working for you until my notice is up. I'll try and source my replacement before I leave, obviously, but if I can't find anyone you're satisfied with, then I'm going to leave anyway.'

'I wouldn't have it any other way!' He spread wide his arms in a gesture of magnanimous generosity. 'Let's go for a walk on the beach.'

'I beg your pardon?'

'It's an exquisite night. Do you hear the insects just above the sound of the water lapping on the shore?' He allowed her a few seconds to appreciate the imagery. He hadn't been aware that he had such a poetic streak to his personality.

'A—a walk?' Emily stammered.

'Or a dip in the sea. There's something special about swimming at night.'

'I definitely won't be doing *that*!' Emily said, horrified at the idea.

'That's fine. We'll settle for just the walk, in that case…'

She wondered how she had managed to be railroaded into this when, fifteen minutes later, she was standing on the beach with him. There was a slight breeze, but nothing to deflect the warmth of the night. The sky was clear, with the stars out, and the sea was just a silvery body of water.

Leandro had rolled up his trouser legs and kicked off his

shoes, which were lying somewhere by the little outcrop of rocks leading up to the hotel gardens.

'You'll need to take those sandals off,' he suggested, turning around to look at her, a tall, dark, shadowy looming mass of pure muscle and undefined, exciting threat. 'There's nothing worse than sand in your shoes. Very uncomfortable.'

Reluctantly Emily slipped off the sandals and dangled them in one hand. Leandro reached out, removed them from her loose grasp and tossed them in the general direction of where his own shoes were.

'Don't worry, they'll be fine. Enjoy the sensation of sand between your toes.'

The hotel beach was long and unspoiled. As the hotel compound was left behind them the broad strip of sand, banked on one side by the dark water and on the other by an equally dark mass of tightly packed coconut trees, assumed a strangely intimate air.

Jittery, Emily lurched into an awkward, stilted conversation about something trivial she had read about online that was happening back in England. A dreary story concerning two celebrities and an on-screen feud that had ended in fisticuffs. After Leandro's amused remarks about his girlfriends taking no interest in world affairs she had felt suddenly dreary and dull and pedestrian in her interest in what was happening on the big stage, although trying to raise a laugh about a ridiculous piece of showbiz gossip hardly seemed an improvement now.

She petered out into awkward silence and only realised that he had stopped walking when she glanced sideways to find no one next to her.

Bemused, she turned around and looked at him. He was standing perfectly still, arms folded. In the darkness there was no way that she could decipher the expression on his face.

'So...' he drawled.

'So?' She felt a little shiver ripple through her body, and of their own accord her disobedient legs jerked into action and headed slowly in his direction, until she was standing right in front of him, staring up into his dangerously sexy face.

'What are we going to do about our...little situation...?'

'What situation are you talking about?'

'You know exactly what I'm talking about, my dear secretary.' A light gust blew some strands of hair across her face and he brushed them back and then kept his hand where it was, by her ear, which he proceeded to caress idly.

Emily had never experienced anything quite so erotic in her life before.

She had been in two relationships—if they could be called relationships—in all her twenty-seven years.

The first when she was nineteen, with a boy she had convinced herself she fancied because he fancied her, and his enthusiastic pursuit had broken down her natural caution. But the spark had been missing and it had eventually fizzled out into a nondescript friendship which, in turn, had disappeared in the mists of time. She had no idea what had happened to him.

The second, four years later, had been a similar disaster, she knew at least in part driven by her guilty knowledge that she was young and couldn't live the rest of her life in nun-like celibacy. A little tipsy, she had gone back to his place. Yet again there had been no spark, and they had returned to the point from which they had started. Just friends.

And since then...nothing.

Except, she considered with painful awareness, life had

not been quite a desert of cobwebs gathering on her sexuality, had it? Because she had to admit grudgingly that beneath the contempt she had strenuously told herself she felt for her wretched boss there had been something else. Something that had put a spring in her step every morning when she had set off for work—something that had made her never resent it when she had been asked to work ridiculously long hours…when she had been cooped up with him as he nailed down one of his legendary deals…

And now here she was. She could feel herself staring up at him for an inappropriately long time, barely breathing, drawn irresistibly like a moth to a flame.

'Do I?' she croaked, defending herself with what little was left in her armoury. She was so hotly aware of that absent-minded caress on her ear that she felt she might faint.

'Of course you do,' Leandro asserted, in the voice of someone stating the obvious.

He dropped his hand and began walking, so that she fell in step with him. He could feel her presence beside him, nervous, quivering, and yet she was driven to remain even if a part of her might be telling her to flee back to the safety of the hotel.

'You're getting married for reasons that escape me,' Leandro murmured. 'You're not attracted to the man and you don't love him… Okay, security might be an appealing part of the deal, but I honestly can't think that it would constitute reason enough…'

'I never said that I didn't love—'

'Of course you did.'

'Stop pretending that you know what's going on in my head!'

'An *arrangement*. Isn't that what you called it?'

Emily heard the hard edge in his voice and cringed. Put like that, it sounded…sordid. At best. And yet he didn't know the half of it. But it wasn't his business! None of it was!

'There's nothing wrong with an arranged marriage,' she muttered impotently. 'It happens. Some people might say that the most successful marriages are the ones that are made for sensible, practical reasons.'

'And you're one of those people…?'

'You're a practical man. You can see where I'm coming from!' There was a desperate, pleading tone to her voice that made her cringe inwardly.

How had she got to this point? Girls should have dreams, shouldn't they? She never had. Not as far as she could remember. Or maybe her dreams were so far in the past that she could scarcely remember the sensation of having them, of ever having dreamt of the walk up the aisle, the blushing bride dressed in white, bursting with happiness and anticipation.

'I'm practical, Emily, but when it comes to the institution of marriage I still believe in it. I would no sooner dream of arranging a marriage for myself because it suited me for practical reasons than I would consider freefalling off the side of a building without a harness. Of course…' He thought of his one failed gold-digger mistake. 'I would be sensible when it came to choosing a woman… I would pay particular attention to the fact that people from similar backgrounds tend to forge lasting relationships. But within those parameters…well…a marriage without love and good sex as a foundation is a marriage without a point.'

'Well, we can't all be the same, can we?' Emily muttered, breaking their intense eye connection to spin away and begin walking shakily towards the far end of the beach.

The further they walked away from the hotel, the darker the beach and their surroundings became. The strip of sand narrowed towards the end, tailing off into an outcrop of dramatic rocks of different shapes and sizes—some towering upwards, others flat and squat—and between them the sea surged and fell back in a repeated motion, sending up flicks of spray as it did so.

Emily turned away from the dark mass of menacing rock to find that Leandro was right there, a few paces behind her, just as menacing.

With a sigh of pure frustration she headed towards the trees and sat down on a fallen trunk that lay on the beach like the body of a long, slender, inert snake.

She drew her legs up and folded her arms around them, resting her chin on her knees and staring sightlessly out to the ocean as he sat heavily next to her.

'I believe in marriage because I had the example of my parents,' Leandro said slowly. 'So, whilst I might fool around with women, like I say, they always know the score. And when the time comes for me to marry my head might play a part, but I intend to do it for all the right reasons. So tell me, Emily, how is it that you have no such illusions that it's possible for two people to marry because they actually believe in love…?'

Emily didn't say anything. If anyone had told her two months ago…two *weeks* ago for that matter…that she would be sitting on a beach having a conversation with her boss that defied all rules of propriety, she would have laughed in disbelief.

'It occurs to me that I don't know a damn thing about your background…' Leandro broke his own rule of allowing silence to propel a conversation. He raked his fingers through his hair.

'Why would you?' Emily finally volunteered. 'Updating you on my background was never part of my job description.'

'And you were always so damned efficient when it came

to sticking strictly to the job description and never putting a foot out of line… So here's what I'm thinking: you don't believe in marriage and you don't believe in the fairytale concept of falling in love because of something that happened to you in the past. Either a disastrous relationship with some guy or else your family background…something there… Tell me if I'm heading in the right direction with either of those theories…'

'I don't have to tell you anything,' Emily protested weakly.

'But there's where you're wrong. Because you've just been thrown a curve ball in your neatly arranged plans for your neatly arranged marriage to this mystery guy who does nothing for you but apparently fits the bill because he's *convenient*.'

Emily turned to stare at him. His eyes glittered in the darkness. She could *sense* the dangerous intent inside him even though his body language was relaxed and casual, his arms resting loosely on his knees.

'What curve ball?'

'Why, us, of course. You and me and the sizzling flare of attraction we feel for one another. And don't bother trying to deny it, Emily. Maybe it was there lurking all along and it took this…'

He looked around him and she knew that he was not only referring to the lush tropical setting but to the fact that they were so far removed from the comfort blanket of surroundings with which they had always been familiar and which had always imposed strict guidelines to their interaction.

He returned his dark gaze to her mesmerised face. '…to bring it out into the open. But there you go. It's out in the open. Maybe I would have forced it back into the box if I had believed for one second that you were truly in love with your fiancé, but you're not, and that explains why you're drawn to me just as I'm drawn to you… What you have might be convenient, but it's no protection when it comes to the pull of raw, physical sexual chemistry, is it…?'

Raw...physical...sexual...chemistry... Just those four words, verbalising what had been going on between them underneath the surface, sent a slow, rolling tidal wave of intense excitement coursing through her body. Suddenly breathing was difficult, and she was vibrantly aware of every part of her body, from her tingling nipples to the dampness between her legs, wetting her underwear, making her want to shift and squirm.

'My father…' She rushed desperately into speech, terrified that her body was going to let her down and vaguely aware that she had never felt anything like this for any man in her life before. Although she knew she could never, ever *like* Leandro, despite what he had said about his fair treatment of women, she still didn't want to go there. Or rather she knew, just *knew,* that she shouldn't.

'Your father…?' Leandro was so focused on what his own body was doing and the heat between them that it took him a few seconds to latch on to this surprising turn in the conversation.

'When I was fourteen I found out that he had been unfaithful to my mother…' Her voice hitched. This was a story she had never related to anyone before. She felt as if she was buying time, sharing this confidence, *putting off the inevitable...*

She firmly clamped her brain shut on that alarming thought.

'I'm sorry. That must have been tough on you. Fourteen is an impressionable age.'

'Some of us were flying planes solo and others were… yes…dealing with other things…' She smiled wryly.

His gentle tone of voice had disarmed her, but then

hadn't he been full of surprises since they had got here? Hadn't she reluctantly been forced to see him in a different light? No longer the authoritarian boss but a man who could be thoughtful in his dealings with the locals, shrewd with their concerns, ambitious on their behalf?

The way he had left his guy in charge of the entire photo shoot, allowing the man to take on the responsibility, while he, Leandro, disappeared tactfully for the day… Even though it was, in the end, an important event that could have a significant impact on the hotel either way.

'If it had been a normal case of infidelity things might have been different.' Emily shrugged. She had thought to have boxed the past up and sealed it away, but now it felt as though it had been lying very close to the surface indeed, controlling her behaviour and taking charge of her actions without her even realising.

Leandro listened, his head tilted to one side. He had never encouraged too many confidences in the women he dated. He had always seen that as a step through a door he did not wish to open—a door that would remain firmly shut until the right woman came along—a step towards giving them ideas that weren't justified. But this one woman had hardly been an open book over the past two years, and the fact that she was opening up now did something to him—roused him in a way he couldn't quite put a finger on.

'I mean, loads of kids grow up with warring parents, and so when a divorce happens they're braced for it. My parents never fought. They were a model couple. My father was always attentive, so when it happened it was like a bolt of thunder on a clear summer day. It was just after Christmas—beginning of January. My mother had the crazy idea to do some spring cleaning. Dad was away and she thought she'd have a go at his office.'

She banked down a stupid rush of tears at the memory.

'I remember she was singing along to something on the radio and then there was silence…and silence… When I finally clocked that and popped in she was curled up on the floor, whimpering. There were photos all around her. Photos of a young Thai girl. With Dad and with a toddler. To cut a long story short, it turned out that the perfect husband and the perfect dad had been having an affair with this girl he'd met in a bar in Bangkok. For over five years. While my mum had been keeping the house in order and looking after me, patiently waiting for him to return from his so-called working trips abroad, he had been leading a double life. In an instant everything I'd relied on was blown apart.'

Her lips thinned into a line of bitterness.

'It all came out in the wash, of course. He confessed to everything. Not only had the woman had his child, but at the time all of this was exposed she was seven months pregnant with their second. In a heartbeat my father went from being a man I loved and respected to a stranger who was repellent and disgusting.'

'That's…awful…' Indeed Leandro could barely get his head round the enormity of such betrayal and how it must have affected an impressionable teenager.

Emily looked at him and relaxed, because what she saw on his face was genuine concern and sympathy and it felt as if those were two things she had never had before when it came to her past, because the story had never been told.

'Is she still alive…?'

'Yes.' Emily glanced down, because that was where the story ended as far as Leandro was concerned.

'And along the way you came to the conclusion that relationships with men were not to be relied upon…?'

'We all have learning curves,' she said with a shrug. 'Mine just came a little earlier and a little harder than most.'

'So you're going to settle with a guy who makes you feel

safe because if you don't give anything to him then you can't get hurt.' When she didn't say anything, he continued, changing tactic, 'And can I ask where your father is now?'

'Don't know, don't care.' One hundred per cent true.

'Marry this guy,' Leandro said slowly, 'and you build a prison for yourself.'

'I don't care what you think.'

'You've forgotten what it is to trust because of past experience...and you've got it into your head that I'm just the sort of unreliable player who uses women merely because I have a healthy sex life...'

Emily's eyes dropped to his beautiful mouth and her thoughts became muddled and uncertain. She was only aware of the sexy curve of his lips, the beauty of his face, the leashed masculine power of his body.

'Like I said, I might have fun with women but I don't conform to being the kind of man who could ever do what your father did. The thought of it repulses me on every level. I think you're making a mistake, marrying this guy of yours for the wrong reasons, but in the meantime, before you settle down to a life of predictable mediocrity, why don't you take a little time out to live a little, to let your passion rule your head...?'

Emily was vaguely thinking that he had barely skirted round the real reason she was marrying Oliver. If only he knew the steps she had been prepared to take—because, yes, if you didn't give anything to a man, then how could you end up getting hurt?

'I would never touch another man's woman,' he murmured, reaching to stroke her cheek, 'but then again...'

His mouth met hers and he was temporarily lost, drowning in the most amazing sensation of having his kiss returned, tentatively at first, then with more of that passion he had sensed lurking below the surface.

He broke apart, breathing heavily. 'You're no man's woman, are you...?'

CHAPTER SEVEN

'PLEASE...' EMILY PULLED away but her stubborn feet would not let her flee. She remained where she was, staring up at him, trembling like a leaf in a gale, tightly hugging herself in an attempt to impose some order on her runaway thoughts.

'Please...what...?' Leandro enquired softly. 'Please take me right here...? Right now...?'

'No' She took a couple of steps back, trying hard to free herself from the stranglehold of his presence.

'But you want me to...' He closed the small gap she had created. 'And I understand why. You're marrying someone you shouldn't be marrying for reasons that shouldn't exist... You might think you're choosing the safe option but, like it or not, you're attracted to me and you want to explore that. Don't you?'

'Of course I don't!' She spun away, headed down to the water's edge and felt the sea curl around her feet then ebb away. She could feel him approaching her, darkly and dangerously persistent.

She *could* sleep with him. Oliver wouldn't mind. In fact he would probably applaud it. She could snatch this experience and see what it felt like to have sex with a man she was violently attracted to. It would be a first.

She stiffened when she felt his hands firmly on her shoulders.

Her thoughts were all over the place. Love was an illusion—something she could never believe in and would never fall for—but lust…

She was only finding out now that that was as real as the ocean spreading out in front of her and as full of terrifying unknowns…

The feel of his mouth against her neck sent a violent shudder through her, because she had not been expecting that. With a will of its own her body curved back against his and she heard the sound of her own soft sigh.

'You want this,' Leandro murmured.

He marvelled that he could keep his voice steady, because his libido was running rampant, doing all sorts of crazy things to his breathing.

'And so do I. But I don't want guilty histrionics afterwards… This is just us…you and me…doing what our bodies are telling us to do before you prance up the aisle with Mr Convenient…'

'I know what you must think of me…' Emily muttered as she slowly turned to face him.

There was so little space between their bodies that she could feel the heat emanating from him. She placed the palm of her hand on his chest and stared up at him. Every nerve, muscle, tendon was straining towards him in anticipation.

'It doesn't matter what I think of you…'

'It does to me!'

'Why?' Leandro bent his head and kissed her slowly, tenderly, prising her mouth open with his tongue and then taking his time to taste her. He could *feel* her hesitancy just as he could *feel* her helpless craving for them to take what had flared up between them through to its logical conclusion.

What *did* he think of her? Did it matter? Sure, she had worked for him for nearly two years, and during that time, when he thought about it, they had developed a curiously close bond, but she would be on her way in the blink of an eye and he wouldn't see her again.

All that mattered was the here and now, and satisfying this physical craving that seemed to have the power of a tsunami.

So she had been affected by a dubious past, by the example of a father who had betrayed his family…?

Was it his concern?

'I'm not one of those women who sleep around…'

'And I'm not one of those men who use women, despite what you think. So why don't we just agree to keep our opinions of each other to ourselves and to just…enjoy…?'

He hitched up her thin summery dress in one quick, smooth motion and the feel of his hands on her waist, underneath the shimmery fabric, nearly induced a fainting fit.

'What do you think about taking a dip naked…?'

'Are you mad?' Her heart was beating so fast that she couldn't catch her breath properly.

'I shall have to work on that unadventurous streak in you, my dear secretary…'

'Please don't call me that. It reminds me of how crazy this is…it reminds me that you're my boss and I didn't come here to…to…'

'Have wild, passionate sex with me…?'

'Something like that,' Emily muttered.

The liquid pooling between her legs made her fidget and, as if knowing precisely what was going on with her body, he dipped his hand lower, leaving it poised tantalisingly over her lacy underwear, a delicious promise of what she might expect.

'So you won't be fulfilling my fantasies by dressing in your very best work outfit so that I can rip it all off you...?'

The picture he painted was horribly evocative. She had a vivid mental image of herself back in London, in the office, with the door shut as he tore her clothes off before making love to her sprawled across his big desk.

'Never mind.'

Leandro slipped his finger underneath the top of her underwear and lazily stroked her. He delighted in the feel of the downy hair. In fact it was a massive turn-on—and not just because touching her was beginning to make him think that he had been fantasising about it for longer than he cared to admit to himself.

No, that patch of hair was a sexy reminder that *this* was what a woman should feel like, as opposed to the fashionable baby-smoothness he was accustomed to.

He wanted to burrow and nuzzle against her, breathe in and taste the honeyed wetness between her legs, but instinct told him that he couldn't rush things. He didn't want her running away.

She might be marrying for the wrong reasons, might feel nothing but mild affection for her husband-to-be, but somewhere there must still be a conscience telling her that what she was doing was not exactly morally acceptable.

Fortunately that wasn't his problem. He had given her conscience an out clause but he still didn't want her to suddenly decide to take it...not when he was burning up for her, his body raging with need and desire...

He slipped his fingers underneath the lacy briefs and along her crease, seeking out the slippery nub of her clitoris, wanting to play with it until she was begging him to carry on, until her mind was for him and him alone.

Emily gasped. She arched back and gripped his shoulders. They were still fully clothed and there was something wickedly decadent about that—something that made his finger rubbing against her feel shockingly, *wonderfully* intimate.

Leandro curled his free hand into her hair and titled her head back at just the right angle so that he could kiss her senseless, barely giving her the opportunity to surface for air.

'Enjoying yourself?' His voice was a husky murmur and Emily nodded on a groan. 'Do you,' he grunted, against his better judgement, 'feel unfaithful to the man you're about to engage with in joyous wedlock?'

'Please, Leandro…' she panted as he began to rub his finger against her, bringing her to soaring heights before slowing the pace so that she could catch her breath and try and get her brain working.

'*Do* you?'

'No,' Emily whispered. 'I told you… Our relationship… We… It's not physical…'

Not physical yet...

'Shall we go back to the hotel?' he murmured huskily. 'You don't want a midnight swim in the ocean with me, and my practical streak is telling me that making love on the sand might get a little…uncomfortable. When I enjoy you, I want to enjoy you without the distraction of any discomfort…'

Without warning, he swept her off her feet and began walking back in the direction of the hotel.

Emily squealed.

'People will see us, Leandro!'

'Oh, the joy of owning this place. I don't care. I'm sure tongues are already wagging anyway…'

'You haven't said anything, have you?' she asked,

alarmed, and she heard the wicked grin in his voice when he replied.

'I don't have to. Any idiot would have been able to notice the way I've been looking at you for the past few days.'

'*I* haven't.'

'That's because you've been busy trying to keep your eyes off me.'

'I can't imagine what you must think of me,' she muttered against his chest.

She could well imagine. A woman with no moral scruples. A woman who was happy to sleep with her boss while making wedding plans to marry another man. She might have sketched out some of the truth behind her relationship with Oliver—and who knew? Leandro might well have bought it—but she had to admit to herself that he wasn't quite the cad she had always imagined him to be.

She felt that she had deliberately chosen to see the superficial side to him—to see the man who played the field, picking up women and dumping them without a backward glance.

She had never questioned his ethics. Instead she had chosen to equate them with the ethics of her father. She hadn't stopped to consider that Leandro was simply a single red-blooded male who was free to have affairs and to enjoy the single life—unlike her father, who had been married, with a child, and had chosen to fool around in the most despicable fashion behind his wife's back. Where her father had made a career out of deceit and lies, Leandro had promised nothing to the women he had dated.

At heart, he was far more of a romantic than she was, and while that should have absolved her from feeling any guilt she was still overwhelmed by it as he nudged open the door to his cabana and carried her to his bed.

His room was similar to hers, with variations in the

colour scheme and in the local paintings on the wall over the bed. Flowers in her room…birds in his.

She allowed herself a few seconds of distraction, looking around her curiously, registering the clothes neatly folded on a chair—obviously part of room service and tidied by one of the hotel cleaners. She imagined that he was not a man who spent much time keeping his surroundings pristine.

Inevitably, though, her eyes returned to him, to where he was standing at the foot of the bed with one hand on the button of his trousers.

'You were saying…?' Leandro drawled, not making a move towards her.

'What was I saying?'

'I think your conscience was beginning to act up…'

'I didn't think you'd heard.'

'I heard. You want to succumb to a change of mind, Emily? You're free to go. I've always made it a rule never to get into bed with any woman who didn't want to be there.'

'I bet you haven't had anyone who didn't.'

'Are you about to spoil my record? If you are, tell me and I'll get the cold shower running.'

Automatically her eyes skimmed the bulge in his trousers that was vibrant proof of how aroused he was, and all over again her thoughts went into meltdown.

So who cared what he thought of her? They weren't about to embark on a soul-searching relationship, were they? No. They were about to have sex and this might be the only time in her life when she felt this way—out of control, trembling with anticipation for a man. It had never happened before. Who was to say that it would ever happen again?

If he thought she was easy, then so be it. She wasn't and

never had been. The most she could be accused of would be greed. Greed to taste what he had to offer.

Besides, within a couple of weeks she would walk away and never lay eyes on him again. His opinion of her wouldn't matter.

She was guiltily aware of a certain amount of double standards. She had been free to express her negative opinions of *him* and yet she was uncomfortably aware that he was now more than entitled to negative opinions of *her*—and she didn't care for it.

'I'm not having a change of mind,' she denied. 'My feet are sandy.'

'We can have a shower together…'

Leandro dealt her a slashing, sexy smile that made her toes curl.

'And I'm glad you're not having a change of mind…'

'I don't suppose it matters one way or the other, but I'm not…this person…'

Leandro raked his fingers through his hair and looked at her. 'You needn't have this conversation if you don't want to…'

Did he want to become embroiled in her anxieties? Was that what this was about? Absolutely not. And yet, despite what his mind was telling him, he found himself moving towards the bed, sitting on it, facing her. Her legs were crossed and her back was ramrod-straight. Every pore and muscle breathed nervous tension.

'Does my approval matter?' he asked with curiosity.

'Of course not!' Emily scoffed, blushing.

'How you choose to conduct yourself isn't my concern.'

'I realise that, Leandro, but I wouldn't want you to think… I know you've had a high opinion of me work-wise…'

'But we're not talking about work here, are we?' He

gently pushed her back onto the pillows—to hell with the sand on their feet. 'I like the dress, by the way. Have I mentioned that?' He delicately slipped one strap off her shoulder and nibbled the soft skin there.

Emily felt as though a switch had been turned on inside her. The breath caught in her throat. Thinking clearly became an impossible task and she sighed as he continued to lick a delicate trail along her shoulder.

'This dress wasn't made for a bra…'

Her eyelids quivered as he disposed of it, shifting her so that he could unhook it from behind and then allowing her to wriggle free of it whilst keeping the dress intact.

He was mesmerised by the outline of her small breasts pushing against the slippery fabric. Just imagining what they would feel like in his big hands, what they would *taste* like, almost made him groan aloud.

He propped himself up on one elbow and gazed at her averted profile, her face tilted up, her eyes closed and her mouth parted.

'Take your clothes off for me…' he whispered huskily, and Emily turned to look at him.

Desire blazed in her eyes. Part of her couldn't believe she was doing this. Another part revelled in the freedom of being turned on without even having to work at it. She was so wet between her legs that her underwear was uncomfortable. It was shocking and intensely exciting at the same time.

'Don't tell me you're shy…?'

'Of course…er…of course not…' She laughed nervously and sat up so that she could free herself of the dress. His eyes were pinned to her. It was heady, knowing that he was watching—watching as she reached down to grasp the dress so that she could pull it over her head.

Her breasts bobbed, tiny and utterly tantalising, and Leandro couldn't resist. He pinned her to the bed and she gasped as his mouth sought and found one pert nipple, licking and sucking until she was tingling all over, unable to contain her whimpers of pleasure.

She couldn't keep still. Her fingers curled into his dark hair and she wanted his mouth everywhere. He moved from one nipple to the other and she squirmed and panted, took his hand so that she could guide it to the breast he wasn't suckling.

He was still in his clothes! And she was strangely too shy to take charge of undressing him. The hardness of his erection pressing against her was both thrilling and scary. She wanted to touch it but was afraid to. He felt absolutely massive!

He reared up so that he could yank his tee shirt over his head and then, moving to stand at the side of the bed, relieved himself of his trousers and underwear. She found herself sneaking a surreptitious glance at him.

She held her breath and tried not to gape as his nakedness captured every atom of her attention.

Even seeing him in his swimming trunks on the beach, barefoot and bare-chested, had not prepared her for the impact he had on all her senses.

Legs planted squarely on the ground, he watched her with amusement as she stared…and stared…and stared.

When he reached down to touch himself she nearly fainted.

She had tried to splutter out her guilty excuses along the lines of *not being that kind of girl*...but if Leandro had had any doubts on that score they were put to rest now, by her genuine reaction to seeing him standing in front of her in all his naked glory.

She was bright red, and as fast as her hungry eyes skittered away from the sight of him it seemed that they were compelled to return to looking at the very thing that was sending her into such heated confusion. She might have been a teenager in the presence of her very first lover.

'Enjoying the sight?' He grinned wickedly and watched her go an even deeper shade of pink.

'I…I'm not…'

'I get it.' He joined her on the bed and rolled her to face him so that they were looking at each other, their bodies pressed against one another. 'You're not the kind of girl who would have a sordid, short-lived liaison with a man whilst wearing an engagement ring on her finger because she's about to be married to someone else. Admittedly, though, there *is* no engagement ring…'

Because, he thought, love and romance were not part of the package deal. He eased off her underwear and his hand brushed the soft downy hair between her legs. He felt her wetness and gritted his teeth in an attempt to control his wayward libido.

'No,' Emily said breathlessly, 'I'm not.' *And yet she was...*

She moaned softly as he nudged apart her legs to insert his thigh between them, moving it slowly but insistently and sending currents of raging excitement through her.

'My perfect secretary…' he nuzzled her neck and covered one breast with his hand, massaging it while rubbing her stiffened nipple with his thumb '…has revealed complexities I would never have guessed at. Or maybe I would…'

Emily gave up all attempts to have a conversation. There was too much going on with her body. Too many sensations taking over. Everywhere throbbed—from her breasts to the damp patch between her legs, which he was teasing to the point of no return. She eased back and reached down to touch him, to hold him.

'You have to…stop…' she gasped '…doing that…'

'Doing what?' He removed his thigh and instead cupped her with his hand, and this time the rhythmic motion was even more devastating to her senses. 'This?'

'I'll… I won't be able to…hold back…' She could barely manage to speak!

'Good,' Leandro said with silky smoothness, enjoying her open, transparent reaction to what he was doing. In fact delighting in it in a way he couldn't remember having done with any other woman before. 'I'll enjoy watching you unable to hold back…'

He covered her mouth with his and kissed her with drugging intensity. All the time his hand was moving between her legs, and his fingers playing with the sensitised bud of her swollen clitoris was shockingly pleasurable.

She felt abandoned—wild, reckless and utterly liberated. For the first time she was a woman freed of all inhibition, able to enjoy her body and what was being done to it.

What crazy fool had ever suggested that love had to be part of the deal when it came to sex?

Maybe that was where she had gone wrong in the past. Getting to know the guys she had been dating, wishing herself in love, hoping that lust would naturally follow… Somehow it had never crossed her mind that she could just fancy a guy so much that he could drive her crazy with desire.

Least of all would she have figured on the guy in question being Leandro!

There was no embarrassment when she was tipped over the edge and rocked by wave after wave of orgasm. She flung her head back on a deep moan of sheer thrilling pleasure and allowed herself to be carried away.

It didn't matter that he was watching her in this most private of moments.

She arched back, shuddering as she came, and his mouth clamping to her nipple at that very instant was wildly, inconceivably erotic.

She looked at him shyly from under her lashes as her body slowly drifted back to Planet Earth.

With the speed of quicksilver it flashed through her mind that she couldn't have had more dreamily perfect sex in a more dreamily perfect setting.

'You *do* realise I'm not nearly finished with you…?'

'I do realise that,' Emily said gravely, and then, more daringly, 'And I hope you realise that *I* might not be finished with *you*...'

'I like the sound of that.' He sprawled back, inviting her to do whatever she wanted with him.

The man, she thought as she looked at him with openly appreciative eyes, was sexy beyond belief. No wonder women flocked around him like bees to honey.

She straddled him in one easy movement and Leandro delighted in her slimness, in the compact grace of her body, in the smallness of her neat breasts, still wet from where he had been licking them. She had caught the sun, and the bits of her that hadn't been exposed to it were pale and inviting.

He was rapidly coming to the conclusion that there were several things he disliked about the bodies of the women he had dated in the past. Not only the fact that all their body hair had been waxed into non-existence but also that their fullness, their overt voluptuousness, now seemed tacky and overdone. And they all seemed to have had an unhealthy predilection for acquiring all-over tans. He liked those pale lines on her—liked the way the rosiness of her disproportionately big nipples stood out…

He reached up to touch her breasts and she slapped his hands away. 'No,' she said firmly. 'No touching… I want to pleasure you now…'

'I get a ridiculous amount of pleasure from touching…'

Emily laughed. She might have been on some kind of drug, so heady did she feel.

She bent down to kiss him and her long hair fell in a silky canopy around their faces. His lips were hot and hungry and she smiled against his mouth because, strangely, she felt all-powerful. This unbelievably sexy man, *her boss,* was so turned on by her that he could scarcely control himself. His erection was an insistent rod of steel against her. He was so big that she wondered how on earth she would be able to accommodate him. And just thinking about that made her even wetter than she already was.

Her breasts brushed against his chest, setting off a series of chain reactions that were gloriously titillating. She had had no idea that her nipples were that sensitive.

She straightened and then wriggled herself so that she was sitting on his thighs and could hold him in her hand.

'Now it's my turn to watch,' she said.

She pushed her tangled hair away from her face impatiently. Squatting on him, her legs on either side, she made sure that as she stroked him his hardness also rubbed against her. His lazy, drowsy eyes regarded her with amusement.

He was anything but shy. He was a man who was completely comfortable in his own skin, she realised. Indeed, he was a man who was completely comfortable in the person he was.

It was why, she now knew, he could afford the luxury of romance. It was why he believed in marriage. It was why he thought that there was the right person out there for him.

Whereas *she*…

She breathed in deeply and slammed the door shut on the person she was—the person she had never expected to be once upon a time.

Leandro stilled her hand. Had he missed something? For a second he could have sworn that he had lost her, and yet now, as she gazed down at him with a half-smile that would have driven any man crazy, she was as she had been before.

'You...have...to stop...'

'What do you mean?'

'I mean a baby is not something I want...'

Emily nodded, understanding.

Her body was on fire, already missing its closeness to his, as he did what he had to do, fetching a condom from his wallet and putting it on with hands that were, she noticed, not completely steady.

'I don't take chances,' he grunted.

'And I can think of nothing worse,' Emily agreed with heartfelt sincerity.

Leandro was suddenly, fleetingly jealous of the guy she was destined to marry—even if it was to be a marriage of convenience. 'Sex with another guy when you're engaged is one thing...but a baby would be quite a different matter...'

'Catastrophic.' She pulled him towards her. 'Now, stop talking,' she commanded, 'and remember what I said about not being through with you...'

'I remember.' Leandro grinned with wicked pleasure. 'Take charge. I'm completely at your mercy...'

At her sweet, *sweet* mercy.

He loved everything she did to him. He loved the way she lathered him with kisses. He loved the way she teased him with her tongue. He loved the way her hair brushed like silk against his chest when she was down there, sucking and licking and sending him to another planet.

And, boy, he loved her enthusiasm. This wasn't lovemaking as an art form. She wasn't out to impress him with her inventiveness or her clever techniques.

She wanted him, and she wanted to enjoy him, and she wanted him to enjoy her. Simple as that.

When she sat on him and began rocking he could no longer restrain himself. If he didn't control the pace then he knew that the unthinkable would happen. He wouldn't be able to hold off. He would come within seconds, like a horny teenager with no finesse and even less experience.

He rolled her beneath him and took charge, moving into her and thrusting deep, rearing up to watch her face as she responded to every thrust, her legs wrapped around his back.

Still maintaining his rhythm, he bent and covered her mouth with his. His tongue mirrored what his hardness was doing, thrusting and enjoying her slick wetness.

As he moved faster and deeper he rose up, supporting himself with his hands flat on either side of her. He seemed to take in every single little detail of her. The shiny golden softness of her face, the length of her lashes, the little mole just above her right eyebrow, the bleached blondeness of her hair spread across the pillow, the scattering of freckles on her collarbone, the tan lines from where her swimsuit had been…

He came on an explosion of sensation that drove every thought out of his head. From a long way away he heard her cry out with satisfaction and it mirrored his own.

They were damp with perspiration, and as he collapsed on her their bodies seemed to stick together. He hadn't put the air-conditioning on and the overhead fan was inadequate when it came to cooling them down. It crossed his mind that *nothing* would have been adequate at cooling them down. They could have made love on an iceberg in the Arctic and they would still have been as hot as they were now.

'Did the Earth move for you too?' he asked huskily, and Emily nodded with a smile.

That was the understatement of the decade. The Earth had done more than just move! It had swivelled, spun in circles and done several loop-the-loops…

So *this* was what it felt like to be fired up with passion! Now she knew.

'I want to hear you say it,' he breathed, coiling his fingers into her hair and scattering delicate kisses on her mouth until she could feel her body getting fired up all over again.

'I…yes…the Earth moved for me too,' she breathed. 'I mean, I've never…'

'Never what…?'

'I've never…' She traced her finger along his chest, circled his flat brown nipple and watched it tighten at her touch. 'Never felt like that before with a guy…'

'And there have been lots…?'

Since when did he care how many lovers a woman had had before him? Insecure was something he most certainly was *not*, and yet now he wished he hadn't asked the question, because he didn't want to hear that he was just one in a long line of notches on her bedpost.

'No.' She laughed and brushed aside his question, because she didn't want to think about how many women there had been in *his* life. 'I'm not… I've never really fooled around…'

'You should learn from your past—not allow it to influence your present and your future. Your father may have been a monster but he doesn't represent the entire male sex…'

'I don't want to talk about that,' Emily said quickly.

It was a timely reminder of just how vastly different their worlds were. It was easy to simplify situations when you were speaking as a spectator to someone else's world. Not only was she a prisoner of her own learning curve but she also had to remember where she was now—about to be married and with no room for her thoughts to be muddled by a man who had been born with a silver spoon in his mouth.

'Then let's talk about what happens next…'

CHAPTER EIGHT

EMILY SHIELDED HER eyes against the glare of the sun and stared out at a picture postcard scene.

Overhead, the fronds of a palm tree blew lazily in the breeze and provided some welcome shade. If she looked up she would see the blue, cloudless sky, filtered through the branches of the tree. Now, looking outwards, her vista was one of the sea—bold turquoise gradually turning to a darker greeny-blue and then finally to midnight-blue where it was just a sharp line against the sky.

The sand was the consistency of caster sugar and almost the same colour. To her right, the little boat which had brought them here bobbed on the water. And in the distance Leandro was carelessly heading out towards the horizon, cutting a clean line through the calm water. He had no fear of all the things that panicked her when she thought about swimming beyond where she could touch the sea bed. Sharks…giant stingrays…barracuda… Various other unknown but deadly sea creatures waiting to pounce on the unwary swimmer.

He was completely naked. When he emerged from the sea she would feast her eyes on his gloriously masculine body and appreciate every line, every contour, every ripple of muscle. She would watch, fascinated, as he hardened for her. It amazed her just how much she turned him on.

She, likewise, was completely naked on a giant beach towel. They could afford to be here—gloriously naked—because the island was just an isolated dot. Sand, palm trees, flowering wild plants and accessible only by boat. They were the only two people on it, and when they had moored two hours earlier it had taken them under half an hour to walk its entire circumference.

Bliss.

Twenty minutes of walking and then making love in the open air—because *this* was what happened next.

They became lovers.

Just for a moment in time they agreed to give in to the crazy passion that had overwhelmed them. Why not? They were here and they fancied one another.

He hadn't asked her how it was that she could do what she was doing—making love to him with abandon—while counting down the days to her wedding. She hadn't stopped agonising over what his opinion of her would be, but she had acquired a skill for shoving it to the back of her mind. It was a skill she had been called upon to utilise many times over the past four days, during which they had made love like starstruck teenagers.

She had no inhibitions when she was with him. He had taken them all away from her and replaced them with a greedy craving that knew no limits. He didn't have to tell her where to touch him. She just seemed to know.

She watched, smiling, as he began swimming back towards shore, his strokes even and certain, his body becoming more and more defined the closer he got.

Her breath caught in her throat when, after a few minutes, he stood up and raked his fingers through his wet dark hair.

Quite simply put, the man was beyond beautiful, and she never tired of looking at him.

Eyes firmly fixed on her rapt face, even though he couldn't decipher the expression, Leandro lightly held himself and began walking slowly towards her.

He had cooled down after their earlier bout of lovemaking and now he was ready and raring for more. He could feel himself hardening in his hand, and by the time he was standing next to the towel, gazing down at her glorious body, he was rigid.

'Now look at what you've done…' He grinned, and then inhaled sharply as she sat up and took him in her mouth.

His hand behind her head, he stood completely still as she sucked and licked and teased his massive erection until he was groaning aloud and wondering if he should bother to try and control the orgasm that was hurtling towards him.

Never in his life had any woman been able to get him fired up to this extent.

Reluctantly he tugged her away and took a few seconds, trying to regain some kind of control over his body.

'You're a witch.'

He lay down next to her and drew her to him so that they were both on their sides, facing one another, their bodies fused. He nudged open her legs and felt her wetness against his thigh.

He could never have foreseen this. He could never in a million years have predicted that he and his secretary would end up in bed together. But now that they had he couldn't quite understand how it had not happened sooner.

Making love to her felt like the most natural thing in the world.

He kissed her—a long, lazy kiss—taking his time. He moved from her lips to her neck and she arched back as he nibbled the tender skin, targeting just that area by her ear where he knew she loved to be kissed.

The thrust of her breasts proved too tempting, and he

moved downwards to feast on one swollen nipple until she was whimpering and twisting underneath him.

She tasted good and he continued suckling, drawing the nipple into his mouth while he teased the rosebud tip of the other between his fingers.

'You're hot...' Barely shifting, he reached into the cooler they had brought with them, dislodged the lid and fumbled until he had an ice cube in his hand. 'You need cooling down. At least, these tender little nipples of yours do...'

He propped himself on his elbow and rolled the ice cube over the tip of her nipple, then circled it over her breast until she was moaning and giggling at the same time.

'Now, tell me that doesn't feel better...cooler...' He tossed the ice cube aside and continued his ministrations, licking and teasing the stiffened buds and then covering her breasts with kisses, heading south along the flat planes of her stomach.

He dipped his tongue into the indentation of her belly button and smiled as she inhaled sharply.

Her body responded to his each and every touch with exquisite immediacy. He felt as though she was a woman being touched for the first time, and in a way she was. She was inexperienced. Her past two boyfriends had failed to satisfy her. And hearing that had turned him on in ways he could hardly define.

He had made it his mission to do just the opposite—to turn her on to the point where she couldn't keep her hands off him, where she couldn't be in his radius without wanting him.

It was a two-way street, because he couldn't see her without touching her, couldn't keep his hands off her, and couldn't be bothered to try even when they were out in public.

He trailed his tongue lower, taking his time to explore

the satiny smooth skin of her belly, and then he gently parted her legs with his hand, preparing the way for what he would do next. Taste her. Feel her shift restlessly under him. Hear her soft little whimpers of delight.

She tasted of the warmth of the sun, the saltiness of the sea. He burrowed between her legs, licking and exploring every inch of her soft femininity with his tongue. She was damp and slippery and he loved the way she wrapped her legs over him and kept her hands firmly at her sides, fists clenched, every muscle in her body tuned in to what he was doing to her.

It was as if she were concentrating, focusing with her whole body on what was being done to it, with no sensation being taken for granted.

He physically ached from the constraint of not doing what his body was screaming to do—which was to come in her, hard and fast, until he was satisfied.

In the past, however much he'd been turned on by a woman, he had always been able to break things off in the event of an emergency. His mobile phone had always been switched on. The demands of work, even in the throes of passion, had always come first.

With Emily, it was different. He switched off his mobile phone. For hours on end. He was irritated when he got a call that interrupted time spent with her.

He felt her body begin to stiffen as wave upon wave of pleasure washed over her, threatening to take her over the edge.

Reluctantly, he raised himself to kiss her.

'I didn't want you to stop,' she complained, returning his kiss with little fluttery kisses of her own.

'I know. Nor did I. Have I ever told you how delicious you taste down there?'

Emily grinned, her eyes slumberous with a passion waiting to be sated. She wished she could hold this moment for ever—bottle it, perhaps, preserve it in some way so that it could remain intact.

'You may have...'

'I can think of a thousand things I'd like to eat off your body... Not that I imagine I would be able to exert sufficient self-control to do it...'

Emily's mind took flight at that. She watched as he reached across to the pile of clothes next to them, fumbling until he found protection, and all the while she could picture him licking ice cream from her stomach, honey from her nipples, all manner of sweet things from everywhere, until she was driven wild.

She pictured herself doing the same to him.

She was waiting, ready for him as he inserted himself inside her, big and powerful and filling every inch of her.

Her fingers dug into his shoulders as he began to move, thrusting deeper and deeper so that the beach towel was rucked underneath them. Eyes closed, she blindly sought his mouth and found it, and then she lost herself in a never-ending kiss as he continued to bring her faster and faster towards her climax...

When she came, she flung her head back and held her breath, before crying out as her orgasm took over her body, banishing all thought and carrying her away to another place completely.

He was holding her tightly, timing his own climax, holding off before allowing himself to let go, feeling her every reaction and responding to each one with unerring instinct.

They came as one and he groaned and stiffened as he spilled his seed into the condom, wishing with shocking unexpectedness that he could feel her without the protective sheath dulling the sensation.

'I'm hot,' she said sleepily as he disposed of the used

condom and settled down on the towel with his arms around her, their bodies spent.

'Perhaps we should give it a few minutes before we resume activity,' he murmured, grinning. 'I may be superhuman when it comes to making love, but even I have my limits…'

'I didn't mean I was hot *for you*. I meant that I was… *hot*...'

'A man's ego could be crushed…'

He kissed the side of her mouth and then decided to linger a little longer there. And holding her breast would, he decided, feel pretty good too. So small and delightfully soft.

'Let's go for a dip,' he suggested. 'Then lunch. I've had your favourite prepared.'

'You don't know what my favourite is…'

'Of course I do! Sandwiches…brown bread…with ham…all fat cut off…lettuce and tomato, mayonnaise, no mustard. Or chicken salad…no celery… Fried fish is also on the menu…with ketchup and lots of it…'

'How on earth do you know that?'

But she knew how he did. They did a lot of talking, and sometimes about the most inconsequential of things. He had compiled a random set of facts about her just as she had about him.

She felt a stirring of unease blow over her like a cold breeze. She reminded herself that this was just time out—an adventure before she resumed the reality of her life back in England.

'I seem to know a lot about you, my dear secretary. Maybe it's been a process of osmosis over the many months you've worked for me…'

He heaved himself up and extended his hand, inviting her to take it, which she did.

His eyes roamed appreciatively over her naked body as

she stood up, long and slender, with the grace of a ballet dancer. It was a body that should never have been concealed beneath dreary work clothes and prim, unappealing suits.

'I think your pubic hair is going lighter in the sun,' he commented.

Emily grinned and reddened. His fingers were curled into hers and it felt…comfortable.

'I could say the same about you,' she retorted, half running and dragging him along.

'You couldn't.' He spun her round, held her tight and devoured her mouth in a long, leisurely kiss. 'I'm brown and my hair everywhere is dark. Dark enough to defy all attempts by the sun to lighten it. What colour hair does the fiancé have?'

He hadn't meant to ask that. In fact he had decided to avoid all mention of her fiancé. As far as he was concerned, as long as they were out here, the man didn't exist. He had no idea if she spoke to him daily or not at all.

So how was it that the question had slipped out so easily? And, now that it had, how did it make sense that he was eagerly waiting for the answer? When he couldn't care less?

'Fair.' She turned away, not wanting to prolong any conversation on the subject of Oliver.

She had spoken to him a couple of times since they had arrived on the island. Now and again her decision to marry him, for reasons that had made perfect sense before she had become involved with Leandro, jarred on her conscience, no longer seemed quite so clear cut.

She hit the water and dismissed her misgivings by diving in, enjoying the cool against her skin after the heat. She swam out and continued swimming, further than she would normally have done, and only spluttered to a stop when she felt Leandro's arms around her.

'So you don't want to talk about him?' he heard himself say.

They could both still touch the sand but the water was past their waists.

'No, I don't.'

She looked away from him but he caught her face in his hand.

'Why not?'

'Because… You know why, Leandro…'

'Because you don't want to be reminded that I'm your dirty little secret?'

'No!'

'What would you say if I told you that that's how I feel?'

'I wouldn't believe you.' Her heart was beating wildly. 'I mean, we both know that this is just a temporary thing…' And yet why did she wince when she uttered those words which were nothing less than the truth?

Their eyes tangled and he released her. 'Swim back to shore, Emily. I need to head out further.'

'Okay.'

Leandro scowled. She was desperate to get rid of him—desperate to avoid any conversation that might compromise her sense of morality, which was kept conveniently under wraps while she slept with him here but which would, without a shadow of doubt, regain the high ground the second the plane touched down at Heathrow in a matter of a few scant days.

He struck out with the restless feeling that their conversation was not over, and when he finally turned around to head back to the beach, after twenty minutes of vigorous swimming, he had come to the decision that he wasn't going to let it rest.

It irked him further to find that she was in her swimsuit waiting for him, sunglasses in place, hat on, book in hand.

'I thought we could have some lunch now.' Emily licked her lips nervously and laid the book down on the towel next to her.

'Is that why you decided to don the swimsuit?' Leandro reached for his towel, roughly dried himself and then slung the towel loosely round his waist. 'Because you thought that it was time for lunch?'

He sat down, positioning himself neatly in front of the cooler so that she couldn't busy herself taking food out and pouring drinks when they still had a conversation to finish.

'We only have a couple more days left here,' he said.

'I know.' Emily resigned herself to a conversation she wasn't sure she wanted. 'I think we've accomplished everything that we…er…set out to do.'

'I'm surprised you still include yourself in this project when you'll be quitting pretty much as soon as we return to London.'

'I said that I'd stay to effect a hand-over with my replacement and I will.'

Leandro ignored her pedestrian foray into a discussion about work. He wasn't in the mood.

Instead he looked at her in silence for such a long time that she eventually broke eye contact and stared out to sea.

'So, are we going to talk about what's happening between us?'

Leandro's body language mirrored hers, but he was one hundred per cent focused on *her*, even though he, too, was staring out to sea. He could feel her next to him and was alert to every shift in her position. He was aware of her tension, and of her reluctance to be drawn into talking about what he intended to talk about.

Emily shrugged and he fought down a wave of intense

irritation. For some reason he was on the back foot and it annoyed the hell out of him. When it came to women it was not in him to pursue. But this felt like pursuit. He told himself that of course it wasn't. It was the purely understandable reaction of a man facing the demise of a sexual relationship which he knew neither he nor his lover really wanted to end. He wasn't chasing. He was expressing a natural curiosity as to what happened next.

'I don't see the point,' she mumbled at last.

He turned to her, and although he was perfectly still there was a savage intensity to his voice that made her stiffen.

'Can you honestly tell me that you want what we have to end when we return to London?'

'It doesn't matter whether I want it to end or not.'

'I want you to look at me when I'm talking to you.'

Emily reluctantly shifted so that she was facing him.

'And I want to see your eyes.'

He reached across and whipped off her sunglasses so that she immediately felt vulnerable and unprotected.

More than anything else she wished that he would just drop this—wished that they could return to the physicality that was as addictive as a drug. She didn't want to think about whether she wanted this to continue or not when they returned to London because as far as she was concerned there was no option. It would have to end—like it or not. For reasons that were not in her control.

'So talk to me,' he commanded roughly. 'Tell me how it is that you can square this with your conscience—marry another man when you still burn for me.'

'I...'

'Yes?'

'I told you... I'm not romantic like...like all those other women you've gone out with...'

'I get it. You had a bloody awful learning curve when you were young. But don't tell me that you would sacrifice your life on the back of *that*.'

'I wouldn't be sacrificing my life, Leandro.'

'You would be making a foolish choice, and once that choice has been made you will find yourself nailed to it and unable to break free if you should ever want to.'

'There *is* such a thing as divorce...'

'I don't believe I'm hearing this.'

'And I don't believe that we're having this conversation!' Emily cried. 'You should be thankful that I'm not one of those clingy women who wants to latch onto you and never let go! You should be glad that you don't have to deal with mopping up my tears because you want to get rid of me and I won't let you!'

'I should be, shouldn't I...? And yet all I can do is feel pity for a woman who's about to commit herself to a loveless marriage, for reasons best known to her, with the opt out clause of divorce if it proves to be the disaster it undoubtedly will...'

He swivelled round and began offloading the cooler, but his appetite was non-existent.

'I *knew* you would think less of me if we became...became...if we slept together!'

'You're right. I have no admiration for what you're doing.'

'There's a lot you don't know.'

'Then why don't you try telling me?'

Silence thickened between them.

'Oh, I see. None of my business.'

'What do you want from me?'

'Honest answer?' He paused and looked her directly in the eye. 'I want you to have the courage to admit that it would be a mistake to marry a man when you're clearly hot for another one.'

'It's not all about sex.'

'You want me. That's not going to go away when we return to London and you step back into your prim little work suits…'

'That's what this is all about, isn't it?' Agitated, Emily sprang to her feet and spun round to stare down at him. 'You're not ready for this to end because *you* always dictate the terms of your relationships, don't you?'

'That's *not* what this is about!' But Leandro had the grace to flush darkly.

'Of course it is!' She began walking towards the sea but then, as though compelled, she turned back to glare at him, her arms folded, her body rigid with tension.

This was not a place meant for arguing. It was too breathtakingly beautiful. And she didn't want to argue. In fact she didn't even want to think about the fact that Paradise would only be theirs for a few more short days.

'You go out with women and when you tire of them you move on. You're annoyed because you're not ready to move on quite yet!'

'I'm frustrated because I see a woman on the verge of throwing her life away…'

'And, like any decent knight in shining armour, you want to save me from my fate? Is that it? You just want to set me on the right path? You're being one hundred per cent altruistic with no hidden agenda at all…?'

'My agenda is anything but hidden,' Leandro drawled, and the hot intensity of his dark eyes made the blood rush to her face. 'Can you honestly tell me that you want this to end the second we step foot on British soil? Can you honestly tell me that that's even possible?'

'Of course it is. We're just having a… This is just a…a… *dalliance...*'

Leandro looked at her in silence for a long time. Finally he shrugged. 'So be it.'

He began unpacking the picnic hamper, laying things out on the rug which had been provided by the hotel. As always, they had prepared a feast. There was chilled wine, but after a brief hesitation he ignored that and went for the bottled water instead.

'So be it?'

The conversation felt as though it had been killed off ahead of schedule. Was that it? A shrug of the shoulders and onward bound?

'I think it's time we ate, and then we'll head back to the island.'

He tucked into one of the sandwiches and poured himself some water. He wasn't looking at her, but out of the corner of his eye he could see her wary stance, the tense set of her shoulders, the stubborn line of her full mouth.

'Sure.'

'And you can consider your contract with my company terminated as from the second we get back to the UK.'

'What—what are you talking about?' Emily stammered. She sat down on the rug, legs crossed, and stared at the array of food—none of which she felt like eating.

'I'm saying that there will be no need for you to work out the remainder of your notice. You will be free to go as soon as we are off this island. And for the rest of the time that we're here we'll focus exclusively on what we came here to do. Work.'

'And all this just because I won't do as you say?'

When she stared at the sandwiches and fruit laid out in front of her she saw instead a progression of empty, Leandro-less days stretching out as far as the eye could see.

She blinked the disturbing vision away. She was set on a certain course and there was no getting off it. And it would be great not having to work out her notice. Wouldn't it? She would be free to get on with the rest of her life, putting in place the necessary things that had to be done…

'We can… I realise you don't understand why I'm doing what I'm doing, why I'm going ahead with… Well, things are never neatly explained away…' She heard herself fumbling with her words, tripping over excuses she couldn't give him, and she flushed at the cynical twist of his mouth.

'I mean…' She reached out, dry-mouthed, and placed her hand on his.

A world without Leandro felt, right now and right here, like a very bleak and empty world. But she knew that that wouldn't last. She was caught up in a bubble where normal reactions and day-to-day reality were suspended. The second she was back on home ground what she felt would vanish like mist on a summer's day, but for now why couldn't she just reach out and bring him back to her, back to the place where they were as one…?

Whatever he had said, and however disappointed he claimed to be with the choices she was making, surely what they had was so strong that he would not be able to resist the temptation to take this through at least until they left the island? Surely she wasn't alone in wanting that?

'I really don't think so…'

Leandro politely removed her hand and Emily licked her lips and stared at him, mortified at the rejection.

'We're attracted to one another,' she said shakily. 'You said so yourself…'

'We are… But I've come to the conclusion that I'm no longer willing to take what's on offer—not with the baggage involved…'

He had barely tasted what he had eaten. He crumpled the

foil in which the sandwich had been wrapped and tossed it into the open cooler, then looked at her coolly.

'For me, this hasn't run its course. But I have no intention of following it through for a couple more days until you go running back to your cuckolded fiancé...'

It would have been impossible for Emily to have gone any redder.

'So you're giving me an ultimatum? Leave Oliver or else things go back to how they were before we came here...?'

She blinked back tears of hurt and rejection. She should be angry with him for his double standards, for his wanting her to adapt her whole life to suit him when he would not have done likewise for her.

'Throw in my marriage for the sake of a few weeks of fun with you...?'

'Who said anything about it lasting a few weeks? Could be less...could be more...'

'And I'm honestly supposed to sacrifice my future for "could be less...could be more..."?'

'If you could convince me that this future of yours wasn't worth sacrificing then we wouldn't be having this conversation now. In fact I'm presuming that if this future of yours was that meaningful we wouldn't have ended up in bed in the first place...'

He stood up and without the slightest hint of embarrassment flung the towel aside and put on the swimming trunks which he had discarded the minute they had reached the island.

Without looking at him, Emily began clearing away the remains of what they had eaten. Most of it was left and she hoped that the chef wouldn't be upset. The fact was that she couldn't have had another bite if her life had depended on it.

She didn't know what else to say. He had withdrawn

from her, and that was evident in his cool politeness as they packed their things away in silence and the boat went back to the main island, likewise in silence.

Her sporadic attempts at conversation were met with a detachment that chilled her to the bone.

So this was what it felt like, she thought with despair. This was what love felt like. She had fancied herself in complete control of the situation and had thrown herself wholeheartedly into an affair on the assumption that snatching a couple of weeks of undiluted happiness would have no lasting consequences. She wasn't made for falling in love and yet it had ambushed her from behind. Life without Leandro was like staring down the barrel of a gun.

She sat on her hands because she was so tempted to reach out and touch him. When had all her defence mechanisms fallen by the wayside? When had lust turned into love? She couldn't pinpoint a moment in time. She just knew that she would have to grab what was on offer and run with it or else live a life of regret, and she didn't think she had the strength to live with regret. It would not make a happy companion.

The minute they were back at the hotel, after the longest boat ride and Jeep drive in her entire life, he picked up some polite threads of conversation. She thought that it was purely to accommodate the fact that there were other people around them now—people who had cheerfully accepted the relationship between boss and secretary and would have been curious had they witnessed its breakdown first-hand.

But *she* was miserably aware of the change in him. The safety of the future she had planned now seemed as flimsy as a wisp of smoke. So much would have been sorted with this marriage, so many problems solved, and everything would have been fine had she had her heart intact. She would have entered into it as the business proposition both she and Oliver had agreed on.

Now she knew that any such business proposition was just not meant to be, and for a few seconds she was furious with Leandro for throwing everything out of kilter.

He had tossed her a carrot and it wasn't even a very good one. A few weeks—maybe longer, maybe not—of having fun in bed and then he would be off, in search of another playmate.

He promised nothing because he had nothing to give, and whilst she appreciated the honesty she resented the fact that in the end he could wield such power over her. She resented the fact that her ammunition had been so shockingly incomplete. She resented the love that was burning a hole through her.

He turned to her when they were briefly out of earshot of any of the attendant staff. 'Feel free to dine tonight in your room. I have things I need to catch up on and I shall probably be busy for the remainder of the day and this evening.'

He leaned against the wooden railing that skirted the dining area. Heavy bougainvillaea, abloom with bright red and orange flowers, shielded them from the sun and threw his handsome face into shadow. That said, she was still perfectly capable of making out the cold, set line of his jaw and the aloofness in his eyes.

Hesitantly she reached out and placed her hand on his arm. She didn't remove it when he looked at it and then back at her, his expression hard and unforgiving.

'You can look,' he drawled, 'but you have lost the right to touch.'

'No, I haven't.'

She looked him squarely in the face. Her voice was calm and controlled but her heart was beating like a jackhammer and her mouth was dry.

'Come again?' Leandro found that he was holding his breath, watching her face intently, barely able to move a muscle.

'You're right,' she said quietly. 'I can't marry Oliver. Not when this is happening between us. Safety might be appealing, but what we have is too strong to resist. So I'm going to call him as soon as I get to my room and tell him that the marriage is…off…'

CHAPTER NINE

EMILY STRETCHED OUT on the massive king-sized bed and did a slow visual tour of the bedroom.

This was her routine every time she stayed the night at his apartment. Sex, and a great deal of it, then a pleasantly fractured night's sleep during which one or the other might reach out blindly and their bodies would fuse, even though they might both be half asleep, and in the morning while he went downstairs to make them both a cup of coffee before the day began *this*...this visual tour of his bedroom. She was committing it to memory because, although it had been nearly five weeks since they had returned to the UK, she knew that she was living on borrowed time.

Having broken up with Oliver, she had given up on worrying. The problems her marriage to him would have solved were still there, but it was no longer in her to angst over them. The solution she had found had disappeared the day she had phoned her fiancé and told him that the wedding was off.

But what else could she have done? Love had bludgeoned her from behind and she had felt as though her options had been limited. Sleep with Leandro and break off her engagement—take, in other words, what was on offer or else endure a lifetime of bitter regret.

She knew that she was falling deeper and deeper in love

with him. She also knew that it was a feeling that was not reciprocated. She was his plaything. A different sort of plaything from the ones he had dated in the past, but still his plaything. He liked her well enough, and he enjoyed her company, but falling in love was certainly not what he was in the process of doing.

The word *love* never crossed his lips. That was an emotion reserved for the special woman he would eventually find and marry—because, as she had discovered, he really did believe that marriages could work out. You had to be realistic, he had said, and had shrugged with a smile, but love was not an impossible dream. What, he had asked her, would be the point of working, earning money, fulfilling ambitions small or great, if at the end of it you were too cynical, too bitter or too disillusioned to enjoy sharing the rewards with someone else?

Working for him, she would never have guessed it. She had written him off as someone else like her father—just another philandering man who didn't care how he treated women as long as he could get from them what he wanted. Another man who didn't give a damn about his discards.

She had discovered that he was nothing like her father. He occasionally spoke about his exes with affection, and if there had been a higher than average number of girlfriends in the past then, he had laughingly told her, it was because he was extremely cautious about getting too wrapped up with any one woman when he knew, in his heart, that she was not the one for him—not the one with whom he wanted to form a permanent relationship.

In fact, he had assured her, he was the consummate gentleman when it came to the fairer sex.

Emily would have laughed with outright derision at that a few weeks previously, but after digging a little deeper she had discovered that he kept in touch with a surprising number of his exes.

Two he had set up in their own businesses. He was godfather to the children of a few of them, and took his duties as godfather very seriously.

'It's the Latin American way,' he had told her smugly. 'We're big into families… When I eventually settle down I shall expect the lucky lady to agree with me that a nice round number like six is perfect when it comes to children…'

When he spoke like that she could feel something twist painfully inside her.

She assumed that 'the lucky lady' would be from his own country—a sexy, dark-haired beauty who was possibly a family friend and knew the way his world worked. Someone from the same elevated background.

She never asked what this woman would be like or where he might find her. She didn't want to have answers to those questions, and at any rate he would have been surprised had she asked. They were lovers with an understanding. She wasn't looking for anything else and so, like him, could enjoy their relationship without inconveniently wanting more.

And it helped that she no longer worked for him. He had pulled strings, despite her protests, and found her an equally well paid job at a law firm in the City.

The responsibilities were different, but she found that she enjoyed the work, enjoyed the variation in her tasks… enjoyed playing with the idea of possibly becoming a paralegal…

She knew that she should have objected to having him help her get another job. Pulling strings was not something of which she approved. But she needed the money. It was as simple as that. And he had swept aside her concerns by reminding her that she had been a brilliant employee, that Stern, Hodge and Smith should consider themselves lucky to have nabbed her…

All these thoughts were lazily swirling through her mind as she looked at the hand-crafted chest of drawers by the window, the fall of the curtains, the built-in wardrobes fashioned from the same smooth, blond and tan wood as the dressing table.

There was an original Picasso—a small, exquisite sketch—casually hanging over the chest of drawers, and more than anything else that was a constant reminder of how different their worlds were.

She glanced away as she heard the sound of him nearing the room and helplessly watched the door, waiting for him to nudge it open, already anticipating the little thrill of delight that would shoot through her the second she saw him. She hated this weakness in herself, this absolute powerlessness when it came to him, but she accepted it just as she accepted that after a lifetime of being in control, of always remaining on the sidelines, a spectator to any emotion that might suck her under, she was no longer in that position.

'You're up.'

Leandro looked at her with open male satisfaction—looked at the duvet which was making a poor attempt at covering her nakedness, looked at the spread of her blonde hair across the pillow and the way her blue eyes lazily drank him up, as shamelessly appreciative of his nudity as he was of hers.

Emily wound a strand of long hair around her finger and smiled. 'I was up when you left the bedroom.'

'Really?'

'I didn't want you to know because I wanted to see that cute little rear of yours as you walked out of the bedroom.

I didn't want you to be modest and hide it away from me under your dressing gown...'

'Modest? I feel you're thinking of the wrong guy...' He never failed to marvel that she could be like this...soft and sexy and teasing...nothing at all like his dim recollection of how she'd used to be when she worked for him.

He frowned and moved to place her coffee on the table next to the bed. 'You've never told me what the people you work with are like,' he said suddenly.

He eased himself next to her and reached behind to cover her peachy bottom with his hand, so that with very little pressure he could draw her towards him and feel the length of her nakedness pressed against his.

'You've told me,' he continued, nibbling her neck, then the side of her mouth, before drawing back and settling her into the crook of his arm, 'that you get along with them, but what does that mean? It's been a while since I went to see old Hodge. Can't really remember what kind of ship he's running there...'

'It's a tight one, Captain...' She traced his bare chest with her hand. 'Have I told you that I'm interested in maybe doing a bit more than just being a PA? I think I could really do well in law. I enjoy it. I enjoy the precision...'

Leandro grunted. He wasn't that interested in her future career as a hotshot corporate lawyer. 'I was thinking more along the lines of the people you work with. I wouldn't want to have set you up with a job where you're surrounded by bores...'

'Well, you can rest assured that they're all very interesting.'

'*All* of them? Is that possible?'

'It's a great environment, Leandro. I mean, it's different from your office. It's not nearly as big, and there's a much higher concentration of young people of similar educational background...'

It wasn't what Leandro wanted to hear. His scowl deepened. He couldn't quite see when his ridiculously powerful attraction to her was going to end, and if *he* felt that way—if she could hold *his* attention for that length of time—then wasn't it conceivable that other guys would be ogling her? It made perfect sense. And how long would it take her to realise that she could hitch up with someone there? Someone who would tempt her with the offer of a committed relationship...someone who would rival the now ex-fiancé when it came to safety?

Leandro, in a vague way, had always assumed that any love connection for him would come in the form of an Argentinian girl—someone who would understand what was expected of her, someone whose goal in life would be to have his children and run a smooth household...someone whose career would be *him.* And, of course, someone who wasn't after him for his money.

His mother had been the perfect wife to his dad. She had had a handful of children and had been proud to take care of her husband's needs. Was he old-fashioned in thinking that that would be the right sort of woman for him when the time came? As opposed to a career woman who imported nannies to look after her kids and fainted at the thought of staying at home? Or else an empty-headed beauty who would be willing to do whatever he wanted just so long as he kept pouring money into her hands? Someone who would jump ship should the money ever stop?

Emily Edison—secretary extraordinaire, sex bomb extraordinaire and now career woman in the ascendant—didn't fit the bill. So he was a little perplexed as to why the thought of other men looking at her bothered him. He wasn't a possessive man. Such feelings were entirely inappropriate when it came to mistresses.

'Is that a fact?' He straddled her and began lathering attention on her neck, her shoulders, her collarbone. 'And have any of these fun guys of a similar age made a pass at you yet?'

Emily looked at him with muted surprise. 'Are you jealous?'

'I don't do jealousy. I do curiosity.'

'Ah. Right...' She felt a twinge of disappointment but she understood completely. 'I haven't been there long enough to get into any kind of social life.'

'And furthermore you don't *need* a social life as you have me. You're also recovering from a broken engagement...'

Curiosity...irresistible, dangerous, compelling.

Had she *really* broken off with her fiancé? If there had been any doubt then it should have been laid to rest by the amount of time they spent in each other's company. Just like that she had kissed a sweet goodbye to the engagement that had propelled her into handing in her resignation.

But his curiosity had been challenging to shift. Was the guy just biding his time...waiting until what they had blew over?

Somehow the thought of that enraged Leandro, and he looked at her now, his mind playing between the equally unpleasant scenarios of several young men chasing her in her place of work or one young man waiting for her on the sidelines.

There was nothing he could do about an ardent following in her workplace, short of buying the company, sacking the entire lot and replacing them with elderly, happily married men.

A tempting thought, if only it were feasible.

But what of his ex-competition? Cheerfully dispatched

or still hovering in the background, nurturing hopes of a grand reunion? Red roses in his hand and engagement ring still in its box, ready to be whipped out once more at short notice?

He realised that he had wasted more time than he would ever have expected thinking about her ex.

He didn't even know what the guy looked like!

What was to stop him doing just a little background check? Maybe establishing whether the man was still on the scene or not….? Putting his mind to rest that she was his and his alone for the duration of their relationship.

He had never had a chauvinistic bone in his body—was in full agreement that women were entitled to the same rights as their male counterparts in the workplace—but…

He felt primitive with *her.*

It made no sense. He wasn't looking for anything beyond what she had cheerfully told him was on the table. She didn't believe in relationships, in any of the things most women believed in, and so she came to him with no strings attached and no expectations lingering in the background.

And yet, perversely, he was far more intent on reassuring himself that he possessed her utterly than he had ever been with any other woman.

The thought of her trying him on for size because her ex-fiancé didn't quite cut it on the physical front was abhorrent to him.

Worse was the notion that she might leave him and use everything she had experienced as a learning curve with which to re-energise her physical relationship with the ex.

Always presuming that the damned man was still on the scene!

It would take one call and he could put the whole thing into motion. Find out where the ex was…whether he was out of the picture completely…what the man looked like… what precisely he did for a living…

With one number dialled on his mobile he could be in possession of facts which he knew should not concern him and which were, essentially, none of his business.

'Everyone needs a social life, Leandro.'

It took him a few seconds to return to what they had been talking about. 'Come again?'

'*You're* not my social life.'

Emily decided to get that perfectly straight, because falling in love with him was one thing… It would be quite another for him to get any inkling that he was the centre of her universe. Pride would never allow her to give him *that* privilege.

'You're telling me that you have after-work fun with the young lawyers in the company? Drinks in those over-priced, over-stylised pubs that bear no resemblance to what a real pub should look like?'

'I'm too busy finding my feet to have much time for that at the moment,' Emily told him truthfully. 'But I expect I shall in due course. It's a very sociable crowd of young people who work there.'

'And what's happened to…? I forget his name… The ex-fiancé…'

'Oliver.'

'That's it. Is he still on the scene?'

'He's a friend, first and foremost,' Emily said vaguely. 'We keep in touch.'

'Cosy.'

'*You* keep in touch with some of your ex-girlfriends…'

'I don't recall ever having been engaged to any of them.'

'What difference does that make?'

'None of my relationships ever went that far. If and when I ever get to the point where I'm ready to commit and become engaged to a woman, then I sure as hell wouldn't be passing the time of day with her if it didn't work out.'

He leapt out of the bed, grabbing his mobile on the way.

'Where are you going?'

Sudden panic washed over Emily. Always on the alert for signs of boredom setting in, she wondered whether this random conversation about the great big world happening outside their little bubble had reminded him that he was still a single guy—still a guy looking for the right woman. Had talk of broken engagements and near-miss weddings turned him off the thrill of having a mistress? Had it sown the pernicious seed of wanting more than just passing sex?

He had vanished out of the bedroom and she remained frozen where she was. Part of her wanted to rush behind him and demand to know what was going through his head. The other part wanted no such thing—wanted just to stay where she was and hope for the best, hope that things weren't beginning to fall apart between them.

She breathed a long sigh of relief when he returned to the bedroom five minutes later. 'Where did you go?' she asked casually.

'Had to make a phone call.' He chucked the phone onto the stack of discarded clothing on the ground and climbed back into bed with her.

Job done. A single phone call. His man would set everything in motion and have whatever answers he needed before the end of the day.

Leandro didn't like spying, and he certainly would never tell her what he had done because there would be no point, but his good mood had been restored. He had never cared for unresolved issues.

'Now, where were we...?' He dealt her a slashing smile and returned to kissing her, taking up where he had left off and sliding into the soft response of her body as easily and seamlessly as if there had been no awkward conversation between them.

Emily lay back and curled her fingers into his dark, tousled hair. When he touched her she couldn't think, and that was a pretty good place to be.

Her breasts were aching in anticipation of what he was going to do to them, the attention he was going to lavish there. She arched and then sighed as he took one pouting pink nipple into his mouth and began to suckle. He told her often and in great detail how much he loved her breasts, and why. Having spent a lifetime thinking that they were too small, she had learnt to offer them to him, knowing that they turned him on.

In fact the same could be said of her entire body. Was that part of the reason why she had been so susceptible to him? Why she had been unable to stop herself from falling in love with him? Because he had burrowed beneath her fortresses and found the person who had been hiding? The trusting, hopeful girl who had spent so long concealing herself behind a wall of ice?

Fat lot of good it would do her in the end, because he was not available for anything more than a fling, but Emily had learnt to cut short those thoughts when they appeared.

His mouth clamped to her nipple was bliss. He sucked hard, and as he sucked his tongue flicked over the stiffened bud, driving her crazy. She couldn't get enough. She touched the nipple he wasn't attending to, pinching it between her fingers, and he gently pushed her hand away so that he could cup it and play with it himself.

'You can touch yourself down there,' he broke away for a second to say, with a grin that notched up the heat level roaring through her body. 'Keep yourself nice and wet until I get there…'

As if to demonstrate exactly what he meant, he covered

her hand with his and positioned it neatly between her legs, then he slid it into her wetness, pausing only to glance over his shoulder, even more aroused as he watched her play with herself. He could hear the soft, slick sound of her wet fingers and he stifled a groan of pure lust.

He had to press down firmly on his erection to stop himself from being tempted to rush things so that he could hurry towards his own satisfaction.

He let her tease him with her hands and her mouth, but he had to pull back often, because she knew just how to arouse him, just how to tip him over the edge. It was as if she had complete control over his body. And whilst it was bloody marvellous on the one hand, on the other it did require a great deal of self-control and gritting of teeth to stop himself from coming prematurely.

He moved down to lick her stomach, squirming his tongue into the neat indentation of her belly button and enjoying her little whimpers of pleasure. Then he covered her hand with his and eased himself down along her body until he could breathe in the sweet, fragrant aroma of her womanhood.

He parted the shell-like lips and dipped his tongue in—just a quick flick, establishing intent. Then he blew softly, which had her almost completely melting and wriggling, so he stilled her with his hand even though he knew that she would be finding it difficult to keep still.

Her body burned for his. She twisted and he tapped her gently and told her to keep still,

'Or,' he drawled, 'I'll have to introduce a little light bondage… Would you like that?'

The image nearly sent her into meltdown. She nodded and blushed, and then met his eyes with hers and held his stare.

'You're turned on at the thought of it, aren't you, my darling?' Leandro grinned.

If he hadn't been so hot, and so in need of finishing what they had started, he would have hunted down something suitable to take their lovemaking down a slightly different road. But that, he decided, would have to wait. He literally wouldn't be able to hold out for the time it would take to find some strips of cloth…

In fact he could barely hold out long enough after he had licked and teased that swollen bud to equip himself with a condom, but equip himself he did.

Emily felt that her body would combust if he didn't fill her soon. He was so big, so thick, that when he entered her, her entire body was set alive, every nerve-ending satisfied.

But, as usual, he would do nothing until he had ensured protection. Even though she was now on the pill, and even though she had told him more than once that there was no need for him to wear a condom.

Even the pill, he had told her, could fail, and he wasn't going to be taking any chances…

More than anything else this told a story of its own. The guy who wanted a football team of kids would never take chances unless it was with a woman he truly cared about—a woman with whom he could envisage having those children.

Underneath the burning lust, how could he respect someone who had slept with him when she had been engaged to someone else? He had never, ever said anything to give her any reason to believe that contempt laced his feelings towards her, but deep down she harboured that nagging worry.

It was just something else she had conditioned herself to ignore—because what would be the point of analysing it?

She closed her eyes and gasped with pleasure as he

thrust deep into her, and then again, moving strong and hard and banishing her uncomfortable thoughts until sensation took over, spiralling and spilling over into wave upon wave of shuddering orgasm.

Their rhythms matched perfectly. Their bodies were so tuned in to one another that instinct guided them. When they came, they came together.

She felt his big body lose control and, as always, felt the heady sensation of absolute happiness that this man could do this to her and she could do the same for him.

Subsiding back to Planet Earth, Leandro almost missed the sound of his cell phone buzzing from where he had earlier chucked it.

Emily was fond of telling him that he had no respect for his possessions. He treated his expensive clothes as though they'd been bought cheap at a market and were disposable. He had a drawer full of smartphones, most of which had cracked screens. But Leandro found that her gentle nagging did not irritate him in the slightest. On the contrary, he rather enjoyed it—although he wasn't quite sure why.

'Your phone's ringing.'

Emily lay back and stretched and for a few seconds Leandro was driven to watch her, because the movement was so unconsciously graceful.

'I'm busy. I'll get it later.'

'What are you busy doing?'

'I'm busy looking at the woman in my bed.'

Emily blushed and savoured the appreciative gleam in his dark eyes. 'It could be important.'

'Not as important as watching you. Or…' he slid out of the bed, reached down and scooped her up in one easy movement '…as important as having a bath with you. It's fair to say that both those activities take precedence over some work-related issue that can be dealt with later…'

He enjoyed having baths with her. He liked the feel of her body when it was wet and slick with soapsuds. It reminded him of how she had felt in the sea…with his arms around her… Those last few days on the island after she had come to him had been mind-blowing. Occasionally he caught himself wondering whether he shouldn't engineer another spurious work-related trip out there just so that they could repeat the experience…

He had been to numerous breathtaking destinations during his lifetime, but never before had he ever felt the need to revisit any of them.

They took their time in the bath. It was a giant-sized bath, big enough to accommodate him comfortably. He could lie down and she could lie on top of him, her back against his torso, their knees protruding through the bubbles. She could feel him pressing against her, could know exactly how aroused he was, and he in turn could explore every inch of her wet body with his hands, soaping and massaging and generally working them both up to a state of maddening arousal.

His mind drifted back to the suggestion of a holiday with her, back to the island. Or they could go somewhere else. She had been abroad, apparently, as a child—presumably before her father had disappeared—but as an adult she had taken lamentably few holidays. He couldn't quite figure out why that would be when she was so highly paid and could have afforded some pretty good holidays abroad—if not twice a year, then at least once.

He could take her to Paris. Rome. Venice. All three. Or they could go further afield. Mauritius. The Maldives. Some other exotic destination where he could savour her delight and enjoy every new experience with her through fresh eyes. It was an appealing thought.

He would talk to her later, feel out the ground. She was

remarkably independent and he certainly didn't want that to change—certainly didn't want to introduce any element to their relationship other than transitory.

And yet…

They finally emerged from the bath. Standing in front of the mirror, he could watch her reflection—watch as she towelled herself dry, ending up with her hair, which she rough-dried before running her fingers through it, trying to disentangle the knots.

She caught his eye and grinned. 'Your phone's going again.'

Leandro took his time. When he finally made it to his mobile it had stopped ringing and there was a voicemail message to pick up from the guy he had not expected to hear back from so soon. Only hours after instructions had been given. Money certainly bought speed.

In the bathroom, doing something about her hair, Emily was unaware that Leandro had left the bedroom. She dressed, dabbed on some make-up, and when after half an hour he'd failed to reappear she headed down to the kitchen, where he was most likely to be.

His apartment was more of a townhouse than a flat, and spanned three floors of unadulterated luxury. She had become quickly accustomed to the display of wealth and now she bypassed the paintings, the handmade furniture and mirrors, the wood and marble, until she ended up in the kitchen to find him staring out through the French doors with his back to her.

He didn't turn around when she walked up behind him.

'Everything okay?'

Leandro turned slowly to look at her. He had changed into casual clothes and had his hands shoved deep into his pockets. His hair was still damp and was swept back from his face.

'There's a guy who works for me,' Leandro said expres-ionlessly. 'His name's Alberto. I use him when I want sen-itive information unearthed. He's not high-profile in the ompany but he's a key member of my team and he's very ood at what he does.'

'Why are you telling me this?'

'Because I had him do a few background checks on our ex-fiancé…'

'You did *what*…?' Emily made her way to a chair and at heavily.

'Well might you look as white as a ghost.'

'You had no right!'

'You're my woman. I had every right, considering the ircumstances surrounding this relationship of ours, and I an tell that you're just dying to find out what my private nvestigator told me… Or maybe you have an idea… Yes, 'm guessing you do have an idea…'

'I know you're going to jump to all the wrong conclu-ions,' Emily muttered.

'I've heard of marrying for security, Emily, but you eally take the biscuit, don't you?'

His voice was neutral but he could feel pure rage cours-ng through his veins like poison. This was the woman who ad obsessed him to such an extent that he had actually onsidered going on holiday with her! A woman who had ast such a powerful spell that for the first time in his life vork had become a secondary consideration! He had spent o long thinking with the wrong part of his body that the eality of what had been happening under his nose was a itter pill to swallow.

Even worse was the fact that as she sat there, staring up t him with those big cornflower-blue eyes, his body was *till* letting him down!

'I finally understand why you did what you did. Why

you launched yourself into a relationship with me whe there was some sad sack in the background, waiting fo you to show up at the aisle. Because a gay husband doesn' require fidelity, *does* he?'

Emily shook her head mutely.

'You were marrying your gay friend because you fel safe with him. Your father had instilled in you a belief tha you were never to trust a man, but you *could* trust a ma who would never take advantage of you. You could marr someone for affection because it was better than never get ting married. Oh, and of course he came with a hefty ban balance… Maybe you figured that you didn't want to spen the rest of your life working hard but still never really bein able to afford the best. Maybe you thought that a rich gu who could never threaten you on the physical front, wh could never touch you enough to hurt you, was worth th sacrifice…'

Emily, her head lowered, didn't say anything. This wa her big chance to fill in the missing blanks in the pictur he was painting, but what would be the point? This wasn' a committed relationship in which she would fight for him This was a one-sided relationship which was always goin to see her being the mug who got hurt.

And he had got so much right, at any rate…

'So?' Leandro prompted impatiently. 'Have you noth ing to say?'

He raked frustrated fingers through his hair and glow ered at her from a distance. Naturally what they had wa well and truly over, but the thought of her exiting in shroud of silence filled him with impotent rage.

'Shall I continue telling you what I think the ending t this story is?' he thundered, making her jump and forcin her to look at him as he strode towards her and plante himself directly in her line of vision.

'Do I have a choice?'

Leandro turned away. He could *feel* her, and it put him ff his stride. Now was not the time to have any lapses in oncentration.

'I think you figured that you could dump the security nd hang on to me for as long as you could. You know from irst-hand experience how generous I am with my lovers…'

Emily's mouth dropped open and she stared at him in lismay. 'That's crazy,' she said, flabbergasted at his leap-rogging of information to reach the wrong conclusions.

And yet, how could she blame him? Her behaviour had not been straightforward. She had given him half-truths nd the fewest possible details about Oliver she had been ble to get away with. Naturally she had known what he vould think had he discovered that her intended groom vas gay—what *anyone* would think—and so she had con-ealed that small but glaringly important detail. How could he have said anything?

She looked at him helplessly and her blue eyes tangled vith his hostile, cold, dark ones.

'I would never use…'

Wouldn't she? Use someone for money? Hadn't she done ust that with Oliver? And even if it was by mutual agree-nent, did that make the slightest difference?

'I think I should go.' She hovered for the briefest of mo-nents, willing him to beg her to stay. As if he would!

'Is that it?' Leandro heard the edge of what sounded like ury and frustration in his voice and hated the vulnerabil-y that came with it.

'I'm not after your money.'

'Oh, please. I should have seen the warning signs. I once early got sucked in by someone of your kind—someone vho did such a damn good job of pretending that I was al-nost conned into believing the woman wasn't a gold-digger.

To think I was nearly had again. The big blue eyes and th
trembling mouth aren't going to cut it, darling. You can tel
me till you're blue in the face that you weren't with me fo
the money—with sex, I'm sure, a nice bonus on the side–
but face it… You don't deny that you were planning on mar
rying a guy who could never have fulfilled you physicall
because it was *convenient*…because he came with a nice
convenient bank balance…'

'Sometimes we do things that we may not particularl
have mapped out for ourselves when we were young an
idealistic…'

'You're still young!'

'But I dumped the ideals a long time ago!'

If only. She hadn't, had she? No, they had all been wait
ing there for the right guy to come along and turn her worl
upside down… For the right guy to hurt her.

She turned away, trembling. 'I'll go now,' she said stiffl

Surprised, she realised that her hands were balled int
tightly clenched fists and she slowly relaxed them an
flexed her fingers.

'I don't want you to think the worst of me.' The plea wa
wrenched out of her.

'Then why don't you try telling me something to pre
vent that from happening!' Leandro stared at her and the
flung his hands up in a gesture of enraged dismissal. '
thought not! Well, Emily, it was always going to end. An
you know where the door is…'

CHAPTER TEN

LEANDRO HEARD THE doorbell through a haze of too much alcohol. He had always made it a rule never to drink beyond a certain amount. He had been to far too many client events where the champagne had flowed and things had been said and done that were regretted in the cold light of day.

But five minutes after she had walked out of his house the bottle of wine had suddenly become his best friend.

He groggily looked at his watch, registering that it was after midnight and that he was still slumped in the chair in the sitting room where he had been for several hours, bar a couple of essential trips to the bathroom.

He heard the doorbell again, finger-on-buzzer-not-stopping-till-you-get-this style, and swore softly under his breath.

Emily. Who else? For a few seconds he contemplated not getting it, because there was nothing she had to say to him that could possibly alter his opinion of her. Nothing at all.

But he'd spent the past few hours drowning something or other in a bottle and why shouldn't she see it? He'd probably feel a damn sight better if he really offloaded on her! Really told her exactly what he thought about someone who had played him for a fool. He'd thought he could never be had again. He'd been wrong. Wouldn't it feel good to vent that anger and frustration?

He walked in a fairly straight line and yanked open the front door.

Emily, having chewed over the way they had parted company and made the brave decision to return to his house, stared at him in surprise.

'Are you *drunk*?'

His hair looked as though he had run his fingers through it a million times and his shirt was hanging loose over the waistband of his trousers. He was barefoot.

'What are you doing here?'

Was he *posturing? Defensive?* Neither option was cool and he scowled at her, noting in passing that she looked as fresh as a daisy despite the lateness of the hour.

'And how did you get here anyway?' He squinted to see if he could make out a taxi and couldn't.

'Tube and foot.'

'That's bloody crazy,' Leandro growled.

'Not as crazy…' Emily took a deep, fortifying breath and looked at him without blinking. 'Not as crazy as if I were to head back home by tube and foot, because there was a group of drunken teenagers outside the station, but that's what I'll do if you don't let me in.'

It was all bravado. She hoped he couldn't detect the desperate edge to her voice. Of course the outcome of this unexpected visit would change nothing, but she had had no choice but to come. To tell him everything. She didn't want, never mind *expect,* his sympathy, but she had finally come to the conclusion that love wasn't just painful, it also made a shambles of all your good intentions and put you in a place where you just could no longer forge ahead and think straight. You found yourself compelled to do things that went against the grain—compelled to ditch your pride, to become…vulnerable, whatever the consequences.

'You'd better come in, but I should warn you that you're

an uninvited guest and the only reason I'm not shutting the door on you is because I wouldn't send my worst enemy out at this hour, to face the vagaries of public transport.'

Leandro marvelled that he had managed that sentence without slurring his words. He began heading back towards the sitting room and could feel her presence behind him.

The lethargy that had afflicted him seemed to have miraculously disappeared.

'You should drink some black coffee—sober up.'

Leandro swung round to look at her and Emily automatically took a couple of steps back.

'Reason being…?'

'I don't want you falling all over the place when I say what I…I've come to say…'

'Why don't you tell me now and get it over and done with? I'm thinking you've had a chance to rustle up a plausible story, but you can forget it if you imagine that a plausible story can buy you a ticket back to my bed.'

'Do you know something, Leandro? I am mystified as to how I could have done something so stupid as to fall in love with you!'

Leandro stared at her. He didn't need any black coffee. He felt as sober as a judge. And once he'd started staring he found that he couldn't peel his eyes away from her face. She was bright red but she was standing her ground, glaring at him as though she had somehow been forced to utter those words against her will.

'I don't think I heard you correctly.'

'I'm in love with you. Okay?'

Leandro suddenly laughed, leaning against the wall. 'Nice try,' he finally said drily.

The cynicism he should have been feeling was curiously absent. Instead he was filled with a wild satisfaction which he could only put down to having had his ego stroked.

'What do you mean, *"nice try"*?'

'I mean you only jacked the ex in on the back of being able to sustain a relationship with me for as long as it would take to leave with some financial gain and you must be kicking yourself that you never quite managed to reach the point of success…'

In love with him? It was a bloody lie—of course it was. She had economised with the truth to such an extent that he would be a complete fool to believe a word she came out with. He should, he knew, just call her a cab and cut short this pointless conversation before it had time to degenerate into a shouting match. He didn't *do* shouting, or hitting things, but he had a suspicion that she was just the woman to bring that out in him.

Emily continued to glare, then she sidestepped him and headed towards the kitchen, not looking back to see if he was following her, knowing that he was. She was ramrod-straight, her head held high, but her heart was beating a mile a minute and she felt dizzy and sick.

The kitchen was a marvel of up-to-the-minute technology. It had never been her style and she had told him so on numerous occasions, much to his amusement, but she could still admire the stark lines, the clean surfaces and the plethora of high-tech gadgets, none of which looked as though they had ever been used.

There was an advanced and scary-looking coffee-making machine on the counter, sparkling white against the black granite, but she opted for the kettle instead and didn't look at him as she made them both some coffee. Black for him…white with two teaspoons of sugar for herself.

When she did finally turn around it was to see him lounging against the doorframe, watching her with narrow-eyed hostility.

'You should sit.'

'Who the hell do you think you are, Emily? Walking in here after we've parted company and issuing orders?'

'I think I'm a woman who never expected to fall in love with you, or with anyone, and now that I have I find that I can't walk away without…without telling you the whole story…'

'What's there to tell? You were going to marry a gay guy for his money before you decided that I was a better bet. No marriage needed and yet play your cards right, plenty of hot sex, and sooner or later—money…'

'Sit down, Leandro!'

How on earth was she managing to do this? She just knew that she had to lay the whole story on the line for him and then he could do with the information what he liked. Despise her more. Kick her out. Turn her into the butt of his jokes in the years to come. Whatever…

Leandro opened his mouth to protest in automatic dismissal of anyone daring to tell him what to do. Except… hadn't he dumped that all-controlling persona with her?

He shrugged nonchalantly and moved to one of the black leather chairs, turning it away from the chrome and glass table so that he was looking at her.

'Okay.' Emily drew in a deep breath. 'I got engaged to Oliver knowing that he was gay because it suited us both.'

She took a few seconds to get her thoughts into order, to arrange them in a way that made some kind of sense. Hesitantly, she walked across to the table and sat facing him, nursing the mug between her hands.

'You wanted his money,' Leandro said with scathing contempt.

'I wanted his money,' Emily agreed. 'I *needed* his money.'

Her blue eyes were clear and honest when she looked at him, and Leandro did his best to fight the temptation to be sucked into whatever fairytale she was telling even though he knew that what he would hear would be the full truth, no holds barred.

About time. Lord only knew what she was going to come out with. A secret gambling addiction? Debts that had been racked up to the point of no return?

'*Needed*?'

'I told you about my father—about what he had done. What I didn't tell you was that when he took off for Bangkok he took all the money with him. Mum tried to get some kind of settlement but she waited too long, was too dazed by what had happened. During that time he made as much of his money disappear as he could. By the time the lawyers demanded full financial disclosure he was claiming poverty and announcing that he was broke.'

Emily had been young at the time, but she could still remember her mother wondering how on earth they were going to afford to live, to put bread on the table.

'She had to go out to work to make ends meet. We lived in the family home. A mansion. It had been in my mother's family for generations and she refused to get rid of it even though it ate money. In winter whole sections had to be shut off because we couldn't begin to afford to run them.'

'What exactly *did* your mother manage to get from the guy?'

'My father?' Emily sighed. 'A pittance. I had to be pulled from private school, and that was that for holidays. Anyway, all my dreams of a career basically went down the pan because I simply had to go out to work and get a good job—which I did as fast as I could. By then Mum had been ill for a while. Breast cancer. I believe it was brought on by the stress.'

'I'm sorry,' Leandro said gruffly. 'Why didn't you say

something before? And what does this have to do with the gay fiancé?'

He had to return the conversation to a point he could handle.

'I'm getting there,' Emily said quietly. 'My mother has early onset Alzheimer's. It's not serious. But it's going to get worse. Eventually she's going to need proper care, but she still refuses to sell the house and I can't afford to cover the costs on my salary. As it is, most of what I earn goes towards helping her and keeping the wretched house from falling into complete disrepair.'

She ran her fingers through her hair and realised that her hand was trembling.

'I reconnected with Oliver a while ago. He'd been in the States and made a small fortune. He had a proposal for me. He wanted to get his foot back on the ground over here. Property. He had grand schemes for a golf course. Our house sits in a lot of land—most of it wild, wooded. You know… He knows the house well, and the land, and he suggested that if we got married I could sign the house over to him and he would help keep it ticking over. When the time came, in exchange for the house—which he would turn into a high-end country hotel set in its own private golf course—he would give me a sum of money sufficient to give my mother the best possible private care available and to set me up in my own little place. He was willing to bide his time, and figured that he would be able to get in with the small community by being my husband. He didn't think that they would accept him if he came out. It suited me.'

She looked at him defiantly, challenging him to criticise the decision she had taken.

'Everything wrapped up in a neat, sexless package…'

'I couldn't have agreed to it otherwise,' Emily admitted frankly. 'I may not have believed in love or romance, or the value of marriage, but there was no way that I could have had a sexual relationship with someone who was involved with me just as a business deal, so to speak. And then…'

There was no mistaking the sincerity on her face and Leandro could feel a weight beginning to lift from his shoulders. Believing the worst in her had been painful, and now he knew why.

'And then we went to the island and I just couldn't resist *you*...Leandro.' She laughed wryly. 'You were the last man on the planet I would ever have considered a suitable guy, and yet maybe that made my decision to sleep with you easier. You see…I'd never been attracted to anyone the way I was attracted to you. It was like my sensible, practical, cynical self had decided to take a holiday and the new occupants of the house had turned out to be wild, unruly and utterly out of control…'

Leandro was smiling. He wanted to whistle. His soul was soaring.

'It's not funny,' Emily muttered, looking at him with suspicion, because this was *not* in the repertoire of his reactions she had predicted.

'I'm sorry. Carry on. You had just got to the bit where you couldn't resist me…'

Emily cringed inwardly but she got it. She had lied and he had every right to enjoy each morsel of truth leaving her mouth.

'When I decided to break off with Oliver I did it because I knew that I had fallen in love with you, and the thought of getting married because it made sense on a number of practical fronts was just no longer conceivable.' She draped her hair over one shoulder and fiddled with the ends. 'The last thing I was after was any money. I'd already resigned myself to just doing the best I could with what I earned and crossing bridges when I came to them. Because I knew that you and I were never going to last. I knew what you wanted was sex—that you were still looking for the dream girl to provide you with the dream life.'

'Why didn't you tell me the whole truth when you broke off the engagement with your fiancé?' It felt okay for him to nurture magnanimous feelings towards the dearly and now departed ex.

'Because I knew what you'd think. That I had no morals. Who would sacrifice their lives for the sake of money?'

'Except you weren't doing that, really, were you?' Leandro said softly. 'I would have seen someone willing to sacrifice the happiness she didn't think she believed in for the sake of the mother she loved very much. I would have seen a woman willing to accept friendship as a basis for marriage because of altruistic reasons. I would have seen the woman I had fallen in love with.'

It was Emily's turn to stare at him. She wondered whether she had heard right. His expression was soft and intense and open all at the same time, and her mouth went dry because she didn't want to misread anything.

'Have I rendered you speechless?'

'I'm not sure I heard correctly,' she said faintly.

'Then I'll repeat it, because one good confession deserves another, don't you think? I love you. I love you and I didn't even realise it. I wasn't looking for love and I therefore assumed that it wouldn't arrive. God, Emily…' He shook his head and remembered the feelings earlier that had driven him to the bottle. 'When you left today I thought I was going out of my mind. It felt like a part of me had been ripped out, and even then I managed to convince myself that it was because I hadn't taken you for a liar, because I was annoyed, disappointed, angry…'

Emily reached across the table and her hands found his.

They linked fingers. She felt the energy run between them—familiar, exciting and comforting all at the same time.

'You're really telling me that you love me…?'

'You were cynical and didn't believe in love. I was fully committed to the idea, but on my terms and within my control and at a time that slotted in to my schedule. I guess it's fair to say that you weren't the only one to be taken by surprise…'

He stood up, pulling her to her feet and drawing her into him.

'I love you, Emily Edison, and I would like to know if you could take me on—for better or for worse…'

'Are you asking what I think you're asking?'

'Depends… I'm asking you to marry me.'

'You would think that I want your money if I said yes…'

'I would think that you wouldn't have a choice but to let me help you, because that's what people do when they love each other.'

'I…'

'Yes or no?'

Emily smiled. She grinned until her jaw began to ache and she squeezed him tightly, barely daring to breathe in case the moment was broken.

'Yes!'

'You agree to take me on, for better or for worse.'

'For better or for worse…'

'And my worse is that I update that pile of yours so that your mother is happy and comfortable for ever in the place she loves and the place you love too—because I will always love what you love, my darling…'

He drew her apart and brushed some hair away from her forehead.

'I don't know what I would have done if you hadn't shown up here tonight,' he said quietly. 'I would have come to find you, but my pride would have made me take my time, and I shudder with fear to think about what you might have done in the interim. Reconsidered your options about marrying the ex…' He felt sick when he thought about it.

'Never…' She stroked his cheek and kissed the side of his mouth, smiling as she felt the shift inside him as his libido kicked in as effortlessly as hers did. 'You've spoiled me for the rest of the opposite sex…'

'And you'd better keep it that way…'

He held her hand and began leading her out of the kitchen, back up to the bedroom, where he had every intention of sealing their love in bed.

'And I shall keep reminding you on a daily basis how to do that…beginning, my love, with right now…'

* * * * *

LET'S TALK Romance

For exclusive extracts, competitions and special offers, find us online:

facebook.com/millsandboon

@MillsandBoon

@MillsandBoonUK

Get in touch on 01413 063232

For all the latest titles coming soon, visit

millsandboon.co.uk/nextmonth

MILLS & BOON
A ROMANCE FOR EVERY READER

FREE delivery direct to your door

EXCLUSIVE offers every month

SAVE up to 25% on pre-paid subscriptions

SUBSCRIBE AND SAVE

millsandboon.co.uk/Subscribe

WANT EVEN MORE

ROMANCE?

SUBSCRIBE AND SAVE TODAY!

'Mills & Boon books, the perfect way to escape for an hour or so.'

MISS W. DYER

'Excellent service, promptly delivered and very good subscription choices.'

MISS A. PEARSON

'You get fantastic special offers and the chance to get books before they hit the shops.'

MRS V. HALL

Visit millsandboon.co.uk/Subscribe and save on brand new books.

JOIN THE MILLS & BOON BOOKCLUB

- **FREE** delivery direct to your door
- **EXCLUSIVE** offers every month
- **EXCITING** rewards programme

Join today at

Millsandboon.co.uk/Bookclub

MILLS & BOON

THE HEART OF ROMANCE

A ROMANCE FOR EVERY READER

MODERN

Prepare to be swept off your feet by sophisticated, sexy and seductive heroes, in some of the world's most glamourous and roman locations, where power and passion collide.

HISTORICAL

Escape with historical heroes from time gone by. Whether your passio for wicked Regency Rakes, muscled Vikings or rugged Highlanders, a the romance of the past.

MEDICAL

Set your pulse racing with dedicated, delectable doctors in the high-pr sure world of medicine, where emotions run high and passion, comfo love are the best medicine.

True Love

Celebrate true love with tender stories of heartfelt romance, from the rush of falling in love to the joy a new baby can bring, and a focus on emotional heart of a relationship.

Desire

Indulge in secrets and scandal, intense drama and plenty of sizzling h action with powerful and passionate heroes who have it all: wealth, sta good looks...everything but the right woman.

HEROES

Experience all the excitement of a gripping thriller, with an intense ro mance at its heart. Resourceful, true-to-life women and strong, fearles face danger and desire - a killer combination!

To see which titles are coming soon, please visit

millsandboon.co.uk/nextmonth